# THE NIGHT LAND

# THE NIGHT LAND

*by*

## WILLIAM HOPE HODGSON

*introduction by* **ERIK DAVIS**

—

**HiLoBooks**
*powered by* **Cursor**
**Boston, MA** *and* **Brooklyn, NY**
**2013**

Series Foreword © Joshua Glenn 2012-13
Introduction © Erik Davis 2013

This edition of *The Night Land* follows the text
of the 1912 edition published by Eveleigh Nash,
which is in the public domain. In the interest of
reading pleasure, we are publishing chapters two
through eleven (of seventeen) only; Erik Davis's
introduction offers an explanation and recap.
Also, we have excised a few passages from the
remaining chapters in order to arrive at a
manageable length; an unabridged version of
these chapters was serialized by HiLobrow.

Library of Congress Control Number: 2012939660
ISBN: 978-1-935869-60-3

Cover illustration © Michael Lewy 2012
Cover design by Tony Leone, Leone Design

Printed in the United States of America

HiLoBooks
A project of HiLobrow.com, a critical-culture website
founded by Matthew Battles and Joshua Glenn.
Series Editor: Joshua Glenn
For more information, visit HiLobrow.com/HiLoBooks
Follow us on Twitter: @HiLoBooks

HiLoBooks is grateful to Richard Nash for his vision
and publishing acumen.

Powered by Cursor

Distributed by Publishers Group West
10 9 8 7 6 5 4 3 2 1

# HiLoBooks
# RADIUM AGE SCIENCE FICTION

# TABLE *of* CONTENTS

# RADIUM AGE SCIENCE FICTION
*Series Foreword by* **Joshua Glenn**

SEVERAL YEARS AGO, I read Brian Aldiss's *Billion Year Spree*—his "true history of science fiction" from Mary Shelley to the early 1970s. I admire Aldiss tremendously, and I found his account of the genre's development entertaining and informative… but something bothered me, after I'd finished reading the book. Something was missing.

*Billion Year Spree* is terrific on the topic of science fiction from *Frankenstein* through the "scientific romances" of Verne, Poe, and Wells— and also terrific on science fiction's so-called Golden Age, the start of which sf exegetes date to John W. Campbell's 1937 assumption of the editorship of the magazine *Astounding*. However, regarding science fiction published between the beginning of the Golden Age and the end of the Verne-Poe-Wells "scientific romance" era, Aldiss (who rightly laments that Wells's 20th century fiction after, perhaps, 1904's *The Food of the Gods*, fails to recapture "that darkly beautiful quality of imagination, or that instinctive-seeming unity of construction, which lives in his early novels") has very little to say.

Aldiss seems to feel that authors of science fiction after Wells but before the Golden Age weren't very talented. He certainly doesn't think much of the literary skills of Hugo Gernsback, sometimes called the "Father of Science Fiction," who founded *Amazing Stories* in 1926 and coined the phrase "science fiction" while he was at it. He's right: Gernsback's story-telling abilities were as primitive as his ideas were advanced. But does that justify skipping over the 1904-33 era? (By my reckoning, Campbell and his cohort first began to develop their literate, analytical, socially conscious science fiction in reaction to the 1934 advent of the campy *Flash Gordon* comic strip, not to mention Hollywood's "sci-fi" blockbusters that sought to ape the success of 1933's *King Kong*. In other words, sf's Golden Age began before 1937; if I had to pick a year, I'd say 1934.) Is Aldiss's animus against that era due solely to style and quality? I suspect not.

Aldiss's book is hardly alone in sweeping pre-1934 science fiction under the rug. During the so-called Golden Age, which was given that moniker not after the fact, but *at the time*, as a way of signifying the end of science fiction's post-Wells Dark Age, Campbellians took pains to distinguish their own science fiction from everything that had been published in the genre (with the sole exception of 1932's *Brave New World*)

since 1904. In his influential 1958 critique, *New Maps of Hell*, for example, Kingsley Amis noted that mature science fiction first established itself in the mid-1930s, "separating with a slowly increasing decisiveness from [immature] fantasy and space-opera." And in his introduction to a 1974 collection, *Before the Golden Age*, editor Isaac Asimov apologetically notes that although it certainly possessed an exuberant vigor, the pre-Golden Age science fiction he grew up reading "seems, to anyone who has experienced the Campbell Revolution, to be clumsy, primitive, naive."

We should be suspicious of this Cold War-era rhetoric of maturity! I'm reminded of Reinhold Niebuhr's pronunciamento, at a 1952 *Partisan Review* symposium, that the utopianism of the early 20th century ought to be regarded as "an adolescent embarrassment." Perhaps Golden Age science fiction's stars—Asimov, Robert Heinlein, Ray Bradbury, and so forth—were regarded as an improvement on their predecessors because in their stories utopian visions and schemes were treated with cynicism. Liberal and conservative anti-utopians who point out that pre-Cold War utopian narratives often demonstrate a naive and perhaps proto-totalitarian eagerness to force square pegs into round holes via thought control and coercion are not wrong. I wouldn't want to live in one of those utopias. However, I strongly agree with those who argue that the intellectual abandonment of utopianism since the 1930s has sapped our political options, and left us all in the helpless position of passive accomplices.

Sure, some 1904-33 science fiction—Gernsback, Edgar Rice Burroughs, and E.E. "Doc" Smith, for example—is indeed fantastical and primitive (though it's still fun to read today). But many other authors of that period—including Olaf Stapledon, William Hope Hodgson, Karel Čapek, Charlotte Perkins Gilman, and Yevgeny Zamyatin—gave us science fiction that was literate, analytical, socially conscious... and also utopian. Utopian in the sense that whatever their politics, Radium Age authors found in the newly named "science fiction" genre a fitting vehicle to express their faith, or at least their hope, that another world is possible. That worldview may have seemed embarrassingly adolescent from the late 1930s until, say, the fall of the Berlin Wall. But today it's an inspiring vision.

—*Joshua Glenn*
  *Cofounder, HiLobrow.com & HiLoBooks*
  *Boston, 2012*

# HORROR SO WONDROUS
*Introduction by* **Erik Davis**

IF YOU ARE encountering William Hope Hodgson's *The Night Land* for the first time, you may feel a bit like an angler who drags a bizarre and horrible fish out of the deep, something that rings no bells of recognition. A nightmare romance set in the far-flung future and written in a self-consciously antique dialect, *The Night Land* might be a mad poet's prophecy from the eighteenth century or an arch genre workout from the twenty-first. What sort of chimera is this? Is it as archaic as it seems? Is it even edible?

Faced with this literary monster, whose flaws intensify its uncanny lustre, we inevitably grope, we pin-holers, for classifications, for the reassuring schemas of genre, epoch, and style. When Lin Carter reissued Hodgson's book in two paperback volumes as part of Ballantine's remarkable Adult Fantasy series in the 1970s, the work was presented as fantasy: the covers were Boschean nightscapes, and C.S. Lewis was quoted on the very first page, comparing Hodgson's tale to fantasy classics by William Beckford, George MacDonald, E.R. Eddison, J.R.R. Tolkien, and Mervyn Peake. And in a deep spiritual sense, *The Night Land* is a fantasy of this old (modern) school, at once aware of and nostalgically distant from the contemporary world where its readers live. The hero narrator has the innocence, pluck, and skill-set of a knight errant, searching for his insanely idealized love in an ancient landscape filled with gothic monsters, primitive man-things, and apparently supernatural evils. The Narrator's sentimental, quasi-Christian rhetoric of faith and love are also objectively correlated in the story by the mysterious "Sweet Powers of Goodness" that occasionally play the *deus ex machina.* Religious features even mark the topography of the Night Land itself, whose ominous, hunkered-down Watchers recall the Watchers of the *Book of Enoch*, ill angels whose carnal

intercourse with the daughters of men produce the giants, an etiology that is also given by Hodgson.

At the same time, *The Night Land* is demonstrably a work of science fiction, and owes at least as much to H.G. Wells as it does to William Morris, whose founding 1896 fantasy *The Well at the World's End* lent Hodgson the lingo of Lo!s and Maids and *untos*. The story takes place on a future earth whose human inhabitants are utterly dependent on advanced technology and whose bizarre creatures and disturbing environmental conditions are, as with the bleak future landscape that greets the Time Traveler at the close of Wells' novel, presented as naturalistic and evolutionary realities. Untold millions of years in the future, after the sun has bit the dust, planetary life clings to the bottom of an enormous rift in the earth, a Mighty Chasm, a hundred miles deep or so, where volcanic activity provides enough lingering heat and light to support a semblance of existence. Though the Night Land is as fabulous as nightmare, Hodgson's vision of an eternal eclipse is rooted in the inevitable collapse of the stellar heart of our own solar system, an inevitability that even now sends a shockwave of futility echoing back through the gulfs of time. The contemporary nihilist philosopher Ray Brassier, for example, argues that the inexorable fact of cosmic extinction—the inevitable death of the sun, and the ultimate disintegration of all matter in the universe—means that, logically speaking, we are already facing the abysmal and absolute destruction of all life and meaning.

Hodgson's last men and women stare this inevitability in the face, an end game that is as much spiritual as astrophysical. But before that final reckoning, they are protected by the self-enclosing womb of technological civilization. The enormous metallic pyramid known as the Great Redoubt, where the Narrator and hundreds of millions live, is essentially an immense homeostatic urban machine, the first such "arcology" in speculative fiction. As with the vision that inspired, say, the architect Paolo Soleri's Arcosanti experiment in the Sonoran desert, Hodgson's hypercity supports a harmonious and organic neo-medieval social order. However, this utopia is shadowed by an

eerily contemporary sense of natural limits: in this case, the finite power of the waning Earth Current that supports the pyramid and energizes the magician's circle of safety that surrounds the Great Redoubt and keeps the horrors of the night at bay. Crucially, the wane is also on for human knowledge, which, like so many of the life forms found without the pyramid, has atrophied. For all their nobility, the men and women of the mighty pyramid huddle in the belated, benighted shadow of the science whose works, now barely understood, remain their only defense against physical and spiritual extinction.

Here we must lodge Hodgson's weird fish inside another category: the *dying earth*, a subgenre that straddles fantasy and SF and that is arguably inaugurated by *The Night Land*. In contrast to apocalyptic or post-apocalyptic fiction, which turns on a sudden planetary catastrophe, the dying earth instead relies on the immensity of time and the organic demands of entropy to draw humans out of technological civilization, whose corroded remnants clank along in a world increasingly given over to magic, hand-to-hand combat, and social orders of guilds and peasants and lords. Clark Ashton Smith's coruscating *Xothique* stories belong here, as do some great and good-humored Jack Vance fictions, one of which gave this subgenre its name; homage must also be paid to M. John Harrison's uncanny Viriconium stories and to Gene Wolfe's extraordinary *Book of the New Sun*. There were dying earths of a sort before Hodgson—Byron's 1806 poem "Darkness" depicts a bestial world that follows of the death of the sun—but Hodgson was arguably the first to imagine a future decline that also hosts an archaic revival of supernatural spellcraft and the nightmares of the medieval bestiary.

But we should be mindful here, for even the supernatural powers that animate *The Night Land* are framed as knowable objects of science—albeit the (often mocked, and often unfairly so) science of psychical research. Hodgson lived and wrote at a time when the study of the paranormal, especially by the UK's Society for Psychical Research, was carried out by sober if sometimes credulous gentlemen deeply invested in data and

the habits of scientific thought. We must remember, for example, that telepathy was embraced by many in the SPR because it offered a psychological and reductionist explanation for the remarkable insights displayed by Spiritualist mediums, who themselves would reach for more occult or religious explanations. Hodgson tells us explicitly that the psychic powers that undergird his story—and whose greatest practitioners are quite rare within it—were the result of an earlier age's "refinement of the arts of mentality and the results of strange experiments." One psychic phenomenon he depicts even recalls a particularly notable (but inevitably controversial) body of paranormal evidence amassed by the Princeton Engineering Anomalies Research, a now-closed parapsychological lab that discovered small but statistically significant indications that massive group-directed and emotionally-charged thoughts—including global media events—slightly reduce entropy in random number generators. When the millions of the Great Redoubt focus their hearts and minds on a single intention, we are told, things happen, for "to have such great multitudes a-think upon one matter, was to set a disturbance about."

The most startling and original dimension of Hodgson's ancient-future science, however, is its ecology of supernatural evil, one that paves the way for Lovecraft's cosmic horror. Crucially, Hodgson's invisible and preternatural forces, whose ability to destroy the soul is feared far more than death, are given a naturalistic rather than mystical basis. These forces don't want to punish or damn; they want to feed, and their presence on earth is the result of occult science, not religious events. The "Doorways In The Night" that allow the "unmeasurable Outward Powers" to enter the Night Land world are, it is explained, ruptures in the ether, "shatterings" first opened up and exploited by the scientists of old. For a contemporary echo of this Faustian scenario, consider the dark rumors noised abroad about the Large Hadron Collider, which some feared might spawn a black hole that would swallow the earth. Ooops!

Hodgson would later develop *The Night* Land's psychic ecology of invisible forces, soul-eating, and outer circles of darkness

into the explicitly para-scientific cosmology outlined in the later occult detective stories gathered in *Carnacki the Ghost-Finder* (especially "The Hog"). But these yarns cannot beat the disturbing spectral cosmology of *The Night Land* and its hostile frequencies. Perhaps the most unnerving moment in this often unnerving novel occurs in the chapter titled "The Night Land," when the Narrator senses a "queer and improper" sound passing through the night. Hearing a low moaning hum that seems to issue at once from near his head and from some infinite distance, the Narrator recognizes the sound as a Doorway in the Night, an interdimensional fissure whose opening—or shattering—heralds the possible Destruction of his soul. Faced with this possibility, ultimately due to "the foolish and unwise wisdom" of the meddling "olden men of learning," the Narrator prepares to take his suicide capsule. He manages to escape, but feels compelled to tell the tale, for "in truth there was an horror so wondrous and dear about it, that I can forget not." And it is that phrase, "an horror so wondrous," that more than any other captures Hodgson's peculiar and deeply resonant tone of cosmic encounter. Wonder is a primary emotion, the awe of natural magnificence that even the least religious of us feel before an exploding volcano or the immensity of the desert's night sky. But an abysmal and inhuman overtone rides that wonder, at least for those with the ears to listen.

There is another twist to Hodgson's ecology of horror that must move us today, as we face the groans of climate change and other terran catastrophes that are at once uncertain, necessary, and ordained by our own meddling. Hodgson's Outside is not just cosmic but *planetary*. In an essay on the horror of philosophy, Eugene Thacker notes that "horror is about the paradoxical thought of the unthinkable"—a thought that, he argues, presses in upon us from an environment increasingly marked by catastrophe and chaos. Horror is no longer about merely human fears, Thacker says, but about "the limits of the human as it confronts a world that is not just a World, not just the Earth, but also the Planet"—that is, a cosmic rock that is not only indifferent to us but potentially devoid of us as well.

All this bubbled up for me when Hodgson's hero reaches the bottom of the Gorge and hears a "strange and monstrous piping in the night." As a Lovecraft acolyte, I could not help but think on those thin flutes that mindlessly pipe through whatever indeterminable dimensions of spacetime throng the holy throne of Azathoth. But Hodgson's demonic ditty, we come to learn, is a natural thing, piped through a crack in the planet earth.

*

Readers familiar with Hodgson's weird fish will note that this edition leaves over a third of this rather long novel on the cutting room floor, including the lion's share of the second half. Many, including no doubt some grumbling purists, will want to know what manner of gedanken experiment led HiLoBooks to embrace such a radical cut. The simple answer is that, like most commentators, the editors felt that the awesome and transporting powers of Hodgson's uncanny mise-en-scene is undermined by a prose package that, taken as a whole, is awkwardly written, overlong, and mawkish. Though moved by the book's ineffable potency, for example, Lovecraft also called *The Night Land* "seriously marred by painful verboseness, repetitiousness, artificial and nauseously sticky romantic sentimentality, and an attempt at archaic language" that was "grotesque and absurd." Given all this, HiLoBooks felt more people would be exposed to Hodgson's genius through an abridgement. Nor were they the first; Lin Carter also trimmed the original in his edition, and many Hodgson cultists often perform their own manner of cut by strongly recommending to newbies that they skip the opening chapter, which is set in the seventeenth century. Here we learn that the narrator loves his wife Lady Mirdath, aka Mirdath the Beautiful, and that his wife, whom he also refers to, copiously, as My Beautiful One, dies. This opening frame, which is not matched by a closing frame in Hodgson's original, explains the odd prose of the book and the origin of the name Mirdath but also thrusts the reader headfirst into the bubbling and corrosive treacle-stream of sentimentality that was the chief object of this edition's surgery.

As for what befalls the hero and the maid following their entrance into the Gorge, we must be brief. Descending, the Narrator and Naani, who is frequently carried by the former, have a disgusting encounter with the Slug Beast glimpsed on the upward journey. Reaching the end of the passageway, the Maid celebrates by bathing in a pool and is frightened by a serpent. As is his wont, the Narrator picks her up, his gallant-hood checking any consequences that might otherwise have devolved from her nakedness. They enter the Country of the Seas, kiss a lot, fall more and more in love, and have a light brush with a mean bird-thing. Crossing the river, they have a much tougher encounter with the inevitable troop of Humped Men, which leaves them beaten and bruised. They vacation on the little island for a whole chapter, strolling down reincarna-tional memory lane as the Narrator contemplates love and pain and the Perfection of the Beloved; Naani, meanwhile, is never quoted. An encounter with a non-threatening beast on the edge of the shore inspires a short and fascinating meditation on evo-lution. The return through the Night Land is quite abbreviated compared to the Narrator's outward journey, but builds to a resounding climax as a host of horrors besiege the couple dur-ing their final march, when the Narrator carries the spiritually comatose Naani for days on end to make the Great Redoubt. What appears to be a terribly tragic denouement is followed by a happy ending that is clumsy and cloying even for those who saw it coming. Though generally tedious, these chapters defi-nitely have their moments; readers hungry for the whole enchi-lada are encouraged to check out the fourth volume of Night Shade's *Collected Fiction of William Hope Hodgson: The Night Land and Other Romances* or to download one of the more in-expensive copies floating around the net.

## CHAPTER II
### *The Last Redoubt*

SINCE MIRDATH, MY Beautiful One, died and left me lonely in this world, I have suffered an anguish, and an utter and dreadful pain of longing, such as truly no words shall ever tell; for, in truth, I that had all the world through her sweet love and companionship, and knew all the joy and gladness of Life, have known such lonesome misery as doth stun me to think upon.

Yet am I to my pen again; for of late a wondrous hope has grown in me, in that I have, at night in my sleep, waked into the future of this world, and seen strange things and utter marvels, and known once more the gladness of life; for I have learned the promise of the future, and have visited in my dreams those places where in the womb of Time, she and I shall come together, and part, and again come together—breaking asunder most drearily in pain, and again reuniting after strange ages, in a glad and mighty wonder.

And this is the utter strange story of that which I have seen, and which, truly, I must set out, if the task be not too great; so that, in the setting out thereof, I may gain a little ease of the heart; and likewise, mayhap, give ease of hope to some other poor human, that doth suffer, even as I have suffered so dreadful with longing for Mine Own that is dead.

And some shall read and say that this thing was not, and some shall dispute with them; but to them all I say naught, save "Read!" And having read that which I set down, then shall one and all have looked towards Eternity with me—unto its very portals. And so to my telling—

To me, in this last time of my visions, of which I would tell, it was not as if I *dreamed*; but, as it were, that I *waked* there into the dark, *in the future of this world*. And the sun had died; and for me thus newly waked into that Future, to look back upon this, our Present Age, was to look back into dreams that my soul knew to be of reality; but which to those newly-seeing eyes of mine, appeared but as a far vision, strangely hallowed with peacefulness and light.

Always, it seemed to me when I awaked into the Future, into the Ever-lasting Night that lapped this world, that I saw near to me, and girdling me all about, a blurred greyness. And presently this, the greyness, would clear and fade from about me, even as a dusky cloud, and I would look out upon a world of darkness, lit here and there with strange sights. And with my waking into that Future, I waked not to ignorance; but to a full knowledge of those things which lit the Night Land; even as a man wakes from sleep each morning, and knows immediately he wakes, the names and knowl-edge of the Time which has bred him, and in which he lives. And the same while, a knowledge I had, as it were sub-conscious, of this Present—this early life, which now I live so utterly alone.

In my earliest knowledge of *that* place, I was a youth, seventeen years grown, and my memory tells me that when first I waked, or came, as it might be said, to myself, in that Future, I stood in one of the embrasures of the Last Redoubt—that great Pyramid of grey metal which held the last millions of this world from the Powers of the Slayers.

And so full am I of the knowledge of that Place, that scarce can I believe that none here know; and because I have such difficulty, it may be that I speak over familiarly of those things of which I know; and heed not to explain much that it is needful that I should explain to those who must read here, in this our present day. For there, as I stood and looked out, I was less the man of years of *this* age, than the youth of *that*, with the natu-ral knowledge of *that* life which I had gathered by living all my seventeen years of life there; though, until that my first vision, I (of this Age) knew not of that other and Future Existence; yet woke to it so naturally as may a man wake here in his bed to the shining of the morning sun, and know it by name, and the meaning of aught else. And yet, as I stood there in the vast embrasure, I had also a knowledge, or memory, of this present life of ours, deep down within me; but touched with a halo of dreams, and yet with a conscious longing for One, known even there in a half memory as Mirdath.

As I have said, in my earliest memory, I mind that I stood in an embrasure, high up in the side of the Pyramid, and looked outwards

through a queer spy-glass to the North-West. Aye, full of youth and with an adventurous and yet half-fearful heart.

And in my brain was, as I have told, the knowledge that had come to me in all the years of my life in the Redoubt; and yet until that moment, this *Man of this Present Time* had no knowledge of that future existence; and now I stood and had suddenly the knowledge of a life already spent in that strange land, and deeper within me the misty knowings of this our present Age, and, maybe, also of some others.

To the North-West I looked through the queer spy-glass, and saw a landscape that I had looked upon and pored upon through all the years of that life, so that I knew how to name this thing and that thing, and give the very distances of each and every one from the "centrepoint" of the Pyramid, which was that which had neither length nor breadth, and was made of polished metal in the Room of Mathematics, where I went daily to my studies.

To the North-West I looked, and in the wide field of my glass, saw plain the bright glare of the fire from the Red Pit, shine upwards against the underside of the vast chin of the North-West Watcher—The Watching Thing of the North-West. … "That which hath Watched from the Beginning, and until the opening of the Gateway of Eternity" came into my thoughts, as I looked through the glass … the words of Æsworpth, the *Ancient* Poet (though incredibly *future* to this our time). And suddenly they seemed at fault; for I looked deep down into my being, and saw, as dreams are seen, the sunlight and splendour of *this* our Present Age. And I was amazed.

And here I must make it clear to all that, even as I waked from *this* Age, suddenly into *that* life, so must I—*that* youth there in the embrasure—have awakened then to the knowledge of *this* far-back life of ours—seeming to him a vision of the very beginnings of eternity, in the dawn of the world. Oh! I do but dread I make it not sufficient clear that I and he were both *I*—the same soul. He of that far date seeing vaguely the life that *was* (that I do now live in this present Age); and I of this time beholding the life that I yet shall live. How utterly strange!

And yet, I do not know that I speak holy truth to say that I, in that future time, had *no* knowledge of *this* life and Age, before that awakening; for I woke to find that I was one who stood apart from the other youths, in that I had a dim knowledge—visionary, as it were, of the past, which confounded, whilst yet it angered, those who were the men of learning of that age; though of this matter, more anon. But this I do know, that from that time, onwards, my knowledge and assuredness of the Past was tenfold; for this my memory of that life told me.

And so to further my telling. Yet before I pass onwards, one other thing is there of which I shall speak—In the moment in which I waked out of that youthfulness, into the assured awareness of *this* our Age, in that moment the hunger of this my love flew to me across the ages; so that what had been but a memory-dream, grew to the pain of *Reality*, and I knew suddenly that I *lacked*; and from that time onwards, I went, listening, as even now my life is spent.

And now, to go back from my digression, it was, as I have said, I had amazement at perceiving, in memory, the unknowable sunshine and splendour of this age breaking so clear through my hitherto most vague and hazy visions; so that the ignorance of Æsworpth was shouted to me by the things which now I *knew*.

But, presently, I turned from the haze and pain of my dream-memories, once more to the inconceivable mystery of the Night Land, which I viewed through the great embrasure. For on none did it ever come with weariness to look out upon all the hideous mysteries; so that old and young watched, from early years to death, the black monstrosity of the Night Land, which this our last refuge of humanity held at bay.

To the right of the Red Pit there lay a long, sinuous glare, which I knew as the Vale of Red Fire, and beyond that for many dreary miles the blackness of the Night Land; across which came the coldness of the light from the Plain of Blue Fire.

And then, on the very borders of the Unknown Lands, there lay a range of low volcanoes, which lit up, far away in the outer darkness, the Black Hills, where shone the Seven Lights, which neither twinkled nor

moved nor faltered through Eternity; and of which even the great spy-glass could make no understanding; nor had any adventurer from the Pyramid ever come back to tell us aught of them. And here let me say, that down in the Great Library of the Redoubt, were the histories of all those, with their discoveries, who had ventured out into the monstrousness of the Night Land, risking not the life only, but the spirit of life.

And surely it is all so strange and wonderful to set out, that I could almost despair with the contemplation of that which I must achieve; for there is so much to tell, and so few words given to man by which he may make clear that which lies beyond the sight and the present and general knowings of Peoples.

How shall you ever know, as I know in verity, of the greatness and reality and terror of the thing that I would tell plain to all; for we, with our puny span of recorded life must have great histories to tell, but the few bare details we know concerning years that are but a few thousands in all; and I must set out to you in the short pages of this my life there, a sufficiency of the life that had been, and the life that was, both within and without that mighty Pyramid, to make clear to those who may read, the truth of that which I would tell; and the histories of that great Redoubt dealt not with odd thousands of years; but with very millions; aye, away back into what they of that Age conceived to be the early days of the earth, when the sun, maybe, still gloomed dully in the night sky of the world. But of all that went before, nothing, save as myths, and matters to be taken most cautiously, and believed not by men of sanity and proved wisdom.

And I… how shall I make all this clear to you who may read? The thing cannot be; and yet I must tell my history; for to be silent before so much wonder would be to suffer of too full a heart; and I must even ease my spirit by this my struggle to tell to all how it was with me, and how it will be. Aye, even to the memories which were the possession of that far future youth, who was indeed I, of his childhood's days, when his nurse of that Age swung him, and crooned impossible lullabies of this mythical sun which, according to those future fairy-tales, had once passed across the blackness that now lay above the Pyramid.

Such is the monstrous futureness of this which I have seen through the body of that far-off youth.

And so back to my telling. To my right, which was to the North, there stood, very far away, the House of Silence, upon a low hill. And in that House were many lights, and no sound. And so had it been through an uncountable Eternity of Years. Always those steady lights, and no whisper of sound—not even such as our distance-microphones could have discovered. And the danger of this House was accounted the greatest danger of all those Lands.

And round by the House of Silence, wound the Road Where The Silent Ones Walk. And concerning this Road, which passed out of the Unknown Lands, nigh by the Place of the Ab-humans, where was always the green, luminous mist, nothing was known; save that it was held that, of all the works about the Mighty Pyramid, it was, alone, the one that was bred, long ages past, of healthy human toil and labour. And on this point alone, had a thousand books, and more, been writ; and all contrary, and so to no end, as is ever the way in such matters.

And as it was with the Road Where The Silent Ones Walk, so it was with all those other monstrous things … whole libraries had there been made upon this and upon that; and many a thousand million mouldered into the forgotten dust of the earlier world.

I mind me now that presently I stepped upon the central travelling-roadway which spanned the one thousandth plateau of the Great Redoubt. And this lay six miles and thirty fathoms above the Plain of the Night Land, and was somewhat of a great mile or more across. And so, in a few minutes, I was at the South-Eastern wall, and looking out through The Great Embrasure towards the Three Silver-fire Holes, that shone before the Thing That Nods, away down, far in the South-East. Southward of this, but nearer, there rose the vast bulk of the South-East Watcher— The Watching Thing of the South-East. And to the right and to the left of the squat monster burned the Torches; maybe half-a-mile upon each side; yet sufficient light they threw to show the lumbered-forward head of the never-sleeping Brute.

To the East, as I stood there in the quietness of the Sleeping-Time on the One Thousandth Plateau, I heard a far, dreadful sound, down in the lightless East; and, presently, again—a strange, dreadful laughter, deep as a low thunder among the mountains. And because this sound came odd whiles from the Unknown Lands beyond the Valley of The Hounds, we had named that far and never-seen Place "The Country Whence Comes The Great Laughter." And though I had heard the sound, many and oft a time, yet did I never hear it without a most strange thrilling of my heart, and a sense of my littleness, and of the utter terror which had beset the last millions of the world.

Yet, because I had heard the Laughter oft, I paid not over-long attention to my thoughts upon it; and when, in a little it died away into that Eastern Darkness, I turned my spy-glass upon the Giants' Pit, which lay to the South of the Giants' Kilns. And these same Kilns were tended by the giants, and the light of the Kilns was red and fitful, and threw wavering shadows and lights across the mouth of the pit; so that I saw giants crawling up out of the pit; but not properly seen, by reason of the dance of the shadows. And so, because ever there was so much to behold, I looked away, presently, to that which was plainer to be examined.

To the back of the Giants' Pit was a great, black Headland, that stood vast, between the Valley of The Hounds (where lived the monstrous Night Hounds) and the Giants. And the light of the Kilns struck the brow of this black Headland; so that, constantly, I saw things peer over the edge, coming forward a little into the light of the Kilns, and drawing back swiftly into the shadows.

And thus it had been ever, through the uncounted ages; so that the Headland was known as The Headland From Which Strange Things Peer; and thus was it marked in our maps and charts of that grim world.

And so I could go on ever; but that I fear to weary; and yet, whether I do weary, or not, I must tell of this country that I see, even now as I set my thoughts down, so plainly that my memory wanders in a hushed and secret fashion along its starkness, and amid its strange and dread habitants, so that it is but by an effort I realise me that my body is not there in this very

moment that I write. And so to further tellings:

Before me ran the Road Where The Silent Ones Walk; and I searched it, as many a time in my earlier youth had I, with the spy-glass; for my heart was always stirred mightily by the sight of those Silent Ones.

And, presently, alone in all the miles of that night-grey road, I saw one in the field of my glass—a quiet, cloaked figure, moving along, shrouded, and looking neither to right nor left. And thus was it with these beings ever. It was told about in the Redoubt that they would harm no human, if but the human did keep a fair distance from them; but that it were wise never to come close upon one. And this I can well believe.

And so, searching the road with my gaze, I passed beyond this Silent One, and past the place where the road, sweeping vastly to the South-East, was lit a space, strangely, by the light from the Silver-fire Holes. And thus at last to where it swayed to the South of the Dark Palace, and thence Southward still, until it passed round to the Westward, beyond the mountain bulk of the Watching Thing in the South—the hugest monster in all the visible Night Lands. My spy-glass showed it to me with clearness—a living hill of watchfulness, known to us as The Watcher Of The South. It brooded there, squat and tremendous, hunched over the pale radiance of the Glowing Dome.

Much, I know, had been writ concerning this Odd, Vast Watcher; for it had grown out of the blackness of the South Unknown Lands a million years gone; and the steady growing nearness of it had been noted and set out at length by the men they called Monstruwacans; so that it was possible to search in our libraries, and learn of the very coming of this Beast in the olden-time.

And, while I mind me, there were even then, and always, men named Monstruwacans, whose duty it was to take heed of the great Forces, and to watch the Monsters and the Beasts that beset the great Pyramid, and measure and record, and have so full a knowledge of these same that, did one but sway an head in the darkness, the same matter was set down with particularness in the Records.

And, so to tell more about the South Watcher. A million years gone, as

I have told, came it out from the blackness of the South, and grew steadily nearer through twenty thousand years; but so slow that in no one year could a man perceive that it had moved.

Yet it had movement, and had come thus far upon its road to the Redoubt, when the Glowing Dome rose out of the ground before it—growing slowly. And this had stayed the way of the Monster; so that through an eternity it had looked towards the Pyramid across the pale glare of the Dome, and seeming to have no power to advance nearer.

And because of this, much had been writ to prove that there were other forces than evil at work in the Night Lands, about the Last Redoubt. And this I have always thought to be wisely said; and, indeed, there to be no doubt to the matter, for there were many things in the time of which I have knowledge, which seemed to make clear that, even as the Forces of Darkness were loose upon the End of Man; so were there other Forces out to do battle with the Terror; though in ways most strange and unthought of by the human mind. And of this I shall have more to tell anon.

And here, before I go further with my telling, let me set out some of that knowledge which yet remains so clear within my mind and heart. Of the coming of these monstrosities and evil Forces, no man could say much with verity; for the evil of it began before the Histories of the Great Redoubt were shaped; aye, even before the sun had lost all power to light; though, it must not be a thing of certainty, that even at this far time the invisible, black heavens held no warmth for this world; but of this I have no room to tell; and must pass on to that of which I have a more certain knowledge.

The evil must surely have begun in the Days of the Darkening (which I might liken to a story which was believed doubtfully, much as we of this day believe the story of the Creation). A dim record there was of olden sciences (that are yet far off in *our* future) which, disturbing the unmeasurable Outward Powers, had allowed to pass the Barrier of Life some of those Monsters and Ab-human creatures, which are so wondrously cushioned from us at this normal present. And thus there had materialized, and in other cases developed, grotesque and horrible Creatures, which now beset the humans of this world. And where there was no power to take on mate-

rial form, there had been allowed to certain dreadful Forces to have power to affect the life of the human spirit. And this growing very dreadful, and the world full of lawlessness and degeneracy, there had banded together the sound millions, and built the Last Redoubt; there in the twilight of the world (so it seems to us, and yet to them [bred at last to the peace of usage] as it were the Beginning; and this I can make no clearer; and none hath right to expect it; for my task is very great, and beyond the power of human skill).

And when the humans had built the great Pyramid, it had one thousand three hundred and twenty floors; and the thickness of each floor was according to the strength of its need. And the whole height of this pyramid exceeded seven miles, by near a mile, and above it was a tower from which the Watchmen looked (these being called the Monstruwacans). But where the Redoubt was built, I know not; save that I believe in a mighty valley, of which I may tell more in due time.

And when the Pyramid was built, the last millions, who were the Builders thereof, went within, and made themselves a great house and city of this Last Redoubt. And thus began the Second History of this world. And how shall I set it all down in these little pages! For my task, even as I see it, is too great for the power of a single life and a single pen. Yet, to it!

And, later, through hundreds and thousands of years, there grew up in the Outer Lands, beyond those which lay under the guard of the Redoubt, mighty and lost races of terrible creatures, half men and half beast, and evil and dreadful; and these made war upon the Redoubt; but were beaten off from that grim, metal mountain, with a vast slaughter. Yet, must there have been many such attacks, until the electric circle was put about the Pyramid, and lit from the Earth-Current. And the lowest half-mile of the Pyramid was sealed; and so at last there was a peace, and the beginnings of that Eternity of quiet watching for the day when the Earth-Current shall become exhausted.

And, at whiles, through the forgotten centuries, had the Creatures been glutted time and again upon such odd bands of daring ones as had adventured forth to explore through the mystery of the Night Lands; for of

those who went, scarce any did ever return; for there were eyes in all that dark; and Powers and Forces abroad which had all knowledge; or so we must fain believe.

And then, so it would seem, as that Eternal Night lengthened itself upon the world, the power of terror grew and strengthened. And fresh and greater monsters developed and bred out of all space and Outward Dimensions, attracted, even as it might be Infernal sharks, by that lonely and mighty hill of humanity, facing its end—so near to the Eternal, and yet so far deferred in the minds and to the senses of those humans. And thus hath it been ever.

And all this but by the way, and vague and ill told, and set out in despair to make a little clear the beginnings of that State which is so strange to our conceptions, and yet which had become a Condition of Naturalness to Humanity in that stupendous future.

Thus had the giants come, fathered of bestial humans and mothered of monsters. And many and diverse were the creatures which had some human semblance; and intelligence, mechanical and cunning; so that certain of these lesser Brutes had machinery and underground ways, having need to secure to themselves warmth and air, even as healthy humans; only that they were incredibly inured to hardship, as they might be wolves set in comparison with tender children. And surely, do I make this thing clear?

And now to continue my telling concerning the Night Land. The Watcher of the South was, as I have set to make known, a monster differing from those other Watching Things, of which I have spoken, and of which there were in all four. One to the North-West, and one to the South-East, and of these I have told; and the other twain lay brooding, one to the South-West, and the other to the North-East; and thus the four watchers kept ward through the darkness, upon the Pyramid, and moved not, neither gave they out any sound. Yet did we know them to be mountains of living watchfulness and hideous and steadfast intelligence.

And so, in a while, having listened to the sorrowful sound which came ever to us over the Grey Dunes, from the Country of Wailing, which lay to the South, midway between the Redoubt and the Watcher of the South, I

passed upon one of the moving roadways over to the South-Western side of the Pyramid, and looked from a narrow embrasure thence far down into the Deep Valley, which was four miles deep, and in which was the Pit of the Red Smoke.

And the mouth of this Pit was one full mile across, and the smoke of the Pit filled the Valley at times, so that it seemed but as a glowing red circle amid dull thunderous clouds of redness. Yet the red smoke rose never much above the Valley; so that there was clear sight across to the country beyond. And there, along the further edge of that great depth, were the Towers, each, maybe, a mile high, grey and quiet; but with a shimmer upon them.

Beyond these, South and West of them, was the enormous bulk of the South-West Watcher, and from the ground rose what we named the Eye Beam—a single ray of grey light, which came up out of the ground, and lit the right eye of the monster. And because of this light, that eye had been mightily examined through unknown thousands of years; and some held that the eye looked through the light steadfastly at the Pyramid; but others set out that the light blinded it, and was the work of those Other Powers which were abroad to do combat with the Evil Forces. But however this may be, as I stood there in the embrasure, and looked at the thing through the spy-glass, it seemed to my soul that the Brute looked straightly at me, unwinking and steadfast, and fully of a knowledge that I spied upon it. And this is how I felt.

To the North of this, in the direction of the West, I saw The Place Where The Silent Ones Kill; and this was so named, because there, maybe ten thousand years gone, certain humans adventuring from the Pyramid, came off the Road Where The Silent Ones Walk, and into that place, and were immediately destroyed. And this was told by one who escaped; though he died also very quickly, for his heart was frozen. And this I cannot explain; but so it was set out in the Records.

Far away beyond The Place Where The Silent Ones Kill, in the very mouth of the Western Night was the Place of the Ab-humans, where was lost the Road Where The Silent Ones Walk, in a dull green, luminous mist.

And of this place nothing was known; though much it held the thoughts and attentions of our thinkers and imaginers; for some said that there was a Place Of Safety, differing from the Redoubt (as we of this day suppose Heaven to differ from the Earth), and that the Road led thence; but was barred by the Ab-humans. And this I can only set down here; but with no thought to justify or uphold it.

Later, I travelled over to the North-Eastern wall of the Redoubt, and looked thence with my spy-glass at the Watcher of the North-East—the Crowned Watcher it was called, in that within the air above its vast head there hung always a blue, luminous ring, which shed a strange light downwards over the monster—showing a vast, wrinkled brow (upon which an whole library had been writ); but putting to the shadow all the lower face; all save the ear, which came out from the back of the head, and belled towards the Redoubt, and had been said by some observers in the past to have been seen to quiver; but how that might be, I knew not; for no man of our days had seen such a thing.

And beyond the Watching Thing was The Place Where The Silent Ones Are Never, close by the great road; which was bounded upon the far side by The Giant's Sea; and upon the far side of that, was a Road which was always named The Road By The Quiet City; for it passed along that place where burned forever the constant and never-moving lights of a strange city; but no glass had ever shown life there; neither had any light ever ceased to burn.

And beyond that again was the Black Mist. And here, let me say, that the Valley of The Hounds ended towards the Lights of the Quiet City.

And so have I set out something of that land, and of those creatures and circumstances which beset us about, waiting until the Day of Doom, when our Earth-Current should cease, and leave us helpless to the Watchers and the Abundant Terror.

And there I stood, and looked forth composedly, as may one who has been born to know of such matters, and reared in the knowledge of them. And, anon, I would look upward, and see the grey, metalled mountain going up measureless into the gloom of the everlasting night; and from my feet

the sheer downward sweep of the grim, metal walls, six full miles, and more, to the plain below.

And one thing (aye! and I fear me, many) have I missed to set out with particularness:—

There was, as you do know, all around the base of the Pyramid, which was five and one-quarter miles every way, a great circle of light, which was set up by the Earth-Current, and burned within a transparent tube; or had that appearance. And it bounded the Pyramid for a clear mile upon every side, and burned for ever; and none of the monsters had power ever to pass across, because of what we did call The Air Clog that it did make, as an invisible Wall of Safety. And it did give out also a more subtile vibration, that did affect the weak Brain-Elements of the monsters and the Lower Men-Brutes. And some did hold that there went from it a further vibration of a greater subtileness that gave a protecting against the Evil Forces. And some quality it had truly thiswise; for the Evil Powers had no ability to cause harm to any within. Yet were there some dangers against which it might not avail; but these had no cunning to bring harm to any *within* the Great Redoubt who had wisdom to meddle with no dreadfulness. And so were those last millions guarded until the Earth-Current should be used to its end. And this circle is that which I have called the Electric Circle; though with failure to explain. But there it was called only, The Circle.

And thus have I, with great effort, made a little clear that grim land of night, where, presently, my listening heard one calling across the dark. And how that this grew upon me, I will set out forthwith.

# CHAPTER III
## *The Quiet Calling*

Now, OFT HAD I heard tell, not only in that great city which occupied the thousandth floor, but in others of the one thousand, three hundred and twenty cities of the Pyramid, that there was somewhere out in the desolation of the Night Lands a second Place of Refuge, where had gathered, in another part of this dead world, some last millions of the human race, to fight unto the end.

And this story I heard everywhere in my travels through the cities of the Great Redoubt, which travels began when I came upon my seventeenth year, and continued for three years and two hundred and twenty five days, being even then but one day in each city, as was the custom in the training of every child.

And truly it was a great journey, and in it I met with many, whom to know was to love; but whom never could I see again; for life has not space enough; and each must to his duty to the security and well-being of the Redoubt. Yet, for all that I have set down, we travelled much, always; but there were so many millions, and so few years.

And, as I have said, everywhere I went there was the same story of this other Place of Refuge; and in such of the Libraries of those cities as I had time to search, there were great numbers of works upon the existence of this other Refuge; and some, far back in the years, made assertion with confidence that such a Place was in verity; and, indeed, no doubt did there seem in those by-gone ages; but now these very Records were read only by Scholars, who doubted, even whilst they read. And so is it ever.

But of the reality of this Refuge, I had never a sound doubt, from the day of my hearing concerning it from our Master Monstruwacan, who with all his assistants occupied the Tower of Observation in the apex of the Pyramid. And here let me tell that he and I had always an affinity and close friendship one for the other; though he was full grown, and I but a youth; yet so it was; and thus, when I had come to an age of twenty-one years of

life, he opened to me a post within the Tower of Observation; and this was a most wondrous good fortune to me; for in all the vast Redoubt, to be appointed to the Tower of Observation was the most desired; for thereby, even as in these days doth Astronomy, was the natural curiosity of Man eased somewhat, even while thwarted.

Now, let me tell here also, lest it be thought that I was unduly favoured because of my friendship with the Master Monstruwacan, that there was a sound justification for his choice, in that to me had been given that strange gift of hearing, which we called Night-Hearing; though this was but a fanciful name, and meant little. Yet the peculiar gift was rare, and in all the millions of the Pyramid, there was none with the gift to a great degree, saving only myself.

And I, because of this gift, could hear the "invisible vibrations" of the aether; so that, without harking to the calling of our recording instruments, I could take the messages which came continually through the eternal darkness; aye, even better than they. And now, it may be the better understood, how much was to be counted that I had grown to listen for a voice that had not rung in mine ears for an eternity, and yet which sang sweet and clear in my memory-dreams; so that it seemed to me that Mirdath the Beautiful slept within my soul, and whispered to me out of all the ages.

And then, one day, at the fifteenth hour, when began the Sleep-Time, I had been pondering this love of mine that lived with me still; and marvelling that my memory-dreams held the voice of a love that *had been* in so remote an age. And pondering and dreaming thus, as a young man may, I could fancy this aeon-lost One were whispering beauty into my ears, in verity; so clear had my memory grown, and so much had I pondered. And lo! as I stood there, harking and communing with my thoughts, I thrilled suddenly, as if I had been smitten; for out of all the everlasting night a whisper was thrilling and thrilling upon my more subtile hearing.

Through four long years had I listened, since that awakening in the embrasure, when but a youth of seventeen; and now out of the world-darkness and all the eternal years of that lost life, which now I live in this Present Age of ours, was the whisper come; for I knew it upon that instant; and

yet, because I was so taught to wisdom, I answered by no name; but sent the Master-Word through the night—sending it with my brain-elements, as I could, and as all may, much or little, as may be, if they be not clods. And, moreover, I knew that she who called quietly would have the power to hear without instruments, if indeed it were she; and if it were but one of the false callings of the Evil Forces, or more cunning monsters, or as was sometimes thought concerning these callings, the House of Silence, meddling with our souls, then would they have no power to say the Master-Word; for this had been proven through all the Everlasting.

And lo! as I stood, trembling and striving not to be tense, which destroys the receptivity, there came thrilling round and round my spiritual essence the throb of the Master-Word, beating steadily in the night, as doth that marvellous sound. And then, with all that was sweet in my spirit, I called with my brain elements:—"Mirdath! Mirdath! Mirdath!" And at that instant the Master Monstruwacan entered that part of the Tower of Observation, where I stood; and, seeing my face, stood very quiet; for though he had not the power of Night-Hearing, he was wise and thoughtful, and took much account of my gift; more-over, he had but come from the Receiving Instrument, and thought vaguely to have caught the throb of the Master-Word, though too faint to come proper through the Instrument, so that he searched for me, in that I, who had the Hearing, might listen for it, I being, as I have said, gifted in that wise.

And to him I told something of my story and my thoughts and my memories, and of that awakening; and thus up to this present happening, and he hearkened with sympathy and a troubled and wondering heart; for in that age a man might talk sanely upon that which, in this age of ours would be accounted foolishness and maybe the breathings of insanity; for there, by the refinement of arts of mentality and the results of strange experiments and the accomplishment of learning, men were abled to conceive of matters now closed to our conceptions, even as we of this day may haply give a calm ear to talk, that in the days of our fathers would have been surely set to the count of lunacy. And this is very clear.

And all the while that I told my story, I listened with my spirit; but

save for a sense of faint, happy laughter that wrapped about me, I heard naught. And nothing more all that day.

Here let me put down that, because of my memories and half memories, I would time and again dispute with our learned men; they being in doubt as to the verity of that olden story of the Days of Light, and the existence of the Sun; though something of all this was set out, as of *truth*, in our oldest records; but I, remembering, told them many tales that seemed fairy-like to them, and entranced their hearts, even whilst I angered their brains, which refused to take seriously and as verity that which their hearts accepted gladly, even as we receive the wonder of poetry into our souls. But the Master Monstruwacan would listen to aught I had to tell; aye! though I spoke through hours; and so it would be, odd times, that having talked long, drawing my stories from my Memory-Dreams, I would come back again into the present of that Future; and lo! all the Monstruwacans would have left their instruments and observations and recording, and be gathered about me; and the Master so sunken in interest that he not to have discovered them; neither had I noticed, being so full of the things which had been.

But when the Master came back to knowledge of that present, he would rouse and chide, and they, all those lesser ones, would fly swiftly and guiltily to their various works; and yet, so I have thought since, each with a muddled and bewildered and thoughtful air upon him; and hungry they were for more, and ever wondering and setting questions about.

And so it was also with those others—those learned ones who were not of the Tower of Observation, and who disbelieved even whilst they hungered. Listen would they, though I talked from the first hour, which was the "dawn," to the fifteenth hour, which was the beginning of the "night"; for the Sleep-Time was set thus, after other usage and experiment. And, odd whiles, I found that there were among them, men of extraordinary learning who upheld my tellings as tales of verity; and so there was a faction; but, later, there grew more to believe; and whether they believed, or not, all were ready to listen; so that I might have spent my days in talk; only that I had my work to do.

But the Master Monstruwacan believed from the beginning, and was wise always to understand; so that I loved him for this, as for many another dear quality.

And so, as may be conceived, among all those millions I was singled out to be known; for the stories that I told went downward through a thousand cities; and, presently, in the lowest tier of the Underground Fields, an hundred miles deep in the earth below the Redoubt, I found that the very ploughboys knew something concerning my tellings; and gathered about me one time and another when the Master Monstruwacan and I had gone down, regarding some matter that dealt with the Earth-Current and our Instruments.

And of the Underground Fields (though in that age we called them no more than "The Fields") I should set down a little; for they were the mightiest work of this world; so that even the Last Redoubt was but a small thing beside them. An hundred miles deep lay the lowest of the Underground Fields, and was an hundred miles from side to side, every way; and above it there were three hundred and six fields, each one less in area than that beneath; and in this wise they tapered, until the topmost field which lay direct beneath the lowermost floor of the Great Redoubt, was but four miles every way.

And thus it will be seen that these fields, lying one beneath the other, formed a mighty and incredible Pyramid of Country Lands in the deep earth, an hundred miles from the base unto the topmost field.

And the whole was sheathed-in at the sides with the grey metal of which the Redoubt was builded; and each field was pillared, and floored beneath the soil, with this same compound of wonder; and so was it secure, and the monsters could not dig into that mighty garden from without.

And all of that Underground Land was lit, where needed, by the Earth-Current, and that same life-stream fructified the soil, and gave life and blood to the plants and to the trees, and to every bush and natural thing.

And the making of those Fields had taken maybe a million years, and the "dump" thereof had been cast into the "Crack," whence came the Earth-Current, and which had bottom beyond all soundings. And this

Underground Country had its own winds and air-currents; so that, to my memory, it was in no ways connected to the monstrous air-shafts of the Pyramid; but in this I may be mistaken; for it has not been given to me to know all that is to be known concerning that vast Redoubt; nor by any one man could so much knowledge be achieved.

Yet that there were wise and justly promoted winds in that Underground Country, I do know; for healthful and sweet they were, and in the corn-fields there was the sweet rustle of grain, and the glad, silken laughter of poppies, all beneath a warm and happy light. And here, did the millions walk and take excursion, and go orderly or not, even as in these days.

Now there was a Law in the Pyramid, tried and healthful, which held that no male should have freedom to adventure into the Night Land, before the age of twenty-two; *and no female ever.* Yet that, after such age, if a youth desired greatly to make the adventure, he should receive three lectures upon the dangers of which we had knowledge, and a strict account of the mutilatings and horrid deeds done to those who had so adventured. And if, after this had passed over him, he still desired, and if he were accounted healthful and sane; then should he be allowed to make the adventure; and it was accounted honour to the youth who should add to the knowledge of the Pyramid.

But to all such as went forth into the danger of the Night Land, there was set beneath the skin of the inner side of the left forearm, a small capsule, and when the wound had healed, then might the youth make the adventure.

And the wherefore of this, was that the spirit of the youth might be saved, if he were entrapped; for then, upon the honour of his soul, must he bite forth the capsule, and immediately his spirit would have safety in death. And by this shall you know somewhat the grim and horrid danger of the Dark Land.

And this I have set down because later I was to make huge adventure into those Lands; and even at this time, some thought of the same had come to me; for always I went listening for that quiet calling; and twice I sent the Master-Word throbbing solemnly through the everlasting night; yet this I did no more, without certainty; for the Word must not be used lightly.

But often would I say with my brain-elements "Mirdath! Mirdath!"—sending the name out into the darkness; and sometimes would I seem to hear the faint thrilling of the aether around me; as though one answered; but weakly, as it were with a weakened spirit, or by instrument that lacked of its earth-force.

And thus, for a great while there was no certainty; but only a strange anxiousness and no clear answer.

Then, one day as I stood by the instruments in the Tower of Observation, at the thirteenth hour there came the thrilling of beaten aether all about me, as it were that all the void was disturbed. And I made the Sign for Silence; so that the men moved not in all the Tower; but bowed over their breathing-bells, that all disturbance might cease.

And again came the gentle thrilling, and broke out into a clear, low calling in my brain; and the calling was my name—the old-earth name of this day, and not the name of that age. And the name smote me, with a frightenedness of fresh awakening memories. And, immediately, I sent the Master-Word into the night; and all the aether was full of movement. And a silence came; and later a beat afar off in the void of night, which only I in all that great Redoubt could hear, until the heavier vibrations were come. And in a moment there was all about me the throbbing of the Master-Word, beating in the night a sure answer. Yet, before this I knew that Mirdath had called; but now had surety.

And immediately, I said "Mirdath," making use of the instruments; and there came a swift and beautiful answer; for out of the dark there stole an old love-name, that she only had ever used to me.

And, presently, I minded me of the men, and signed to them that they should continue; for the Records must not be broken; and now I had the communication full established.

And by me stood the Master Monstruwacan, quietly as any young Monstruwacan, waiting with slips to make any notes that were needful; and keeping a strict eye upon those others; but not unkindly. And so, for a space of wonder, I had speech with that girl out in the darkness of the world, who had knowledge of my name, and of the old-earth love-name,

and named herself Mirdath.

And much I questioned her, and presently to my sorrow; for it seemed that her name was not truly Mirdath; but Naani; neither had she known my name; but that in the library of that place where she abode, there had been a story of one named by my name, and called by that sweet love-name which she had sent out somewhat ruthless into the night; and the girl's name had been Mirdath; and when first she, Naani had called, there had come back to her a cry of Mirdath, Mirdath; and this had minded her so strangely of that olden story which had stayed in her memory; that she had answered as the maid in that book might have answered.

And thus did it seem that the utter Romance of my Memory-love had vanished, and I stood strangely troubled for sorrow of a love of olden times. Yet, even then I marvelled that any book should have story so much like to mine; not heeding that the history of all love is writ with one pen.

Yet, even then in that hour of my strange, and quaintly foolish pain, there came a thing that set me thrilling; though more afterwards, when I came to think afresh upon it. For the girl who spoke to me through the night made some wonder that my voice were not deeper; yet in quiet fashion, and as one who says a thing, scarce wotting what they say. But even to me then, there came a sudden hope; for in the olden days of this Present Age my voice had been very deep. And I said to her that maybe the man in the book was said to have had a deep tone of speech; but she, seeming puzzled, said nay; and at that I questioned her the more; but only to the trouble of her memory and understanding.

And strange must it seem that we two should talk on so trivial a matter, when there was so much else that we had need to exchange thought upon; for were a man in this present day to have speech with those who may live within that red planet of Mars within the sky, scarce could the wonder of it exceed the wonder of a human voice coming through that night unto the Great Redoubt, out of all that lost darkness. For, indeed, this must have been the breaking of, maybe, a million years of silence.

And already, as I came to know later, was the news passing downward from City to City through all the vast Pyramid; so that the Hour-Slips

were full of the news; and every City eager and excited, and waiting. And I better known in that one moment, than in all my life before. For that previous calling, had been but vaguely put about; and then set to the count of a nature, blown upon over-easily by spirit-winds of the half-memory of dreams. Though it is indeed true, as I have set down before this, that my tales concerning the early days of the world, when the sun was visible, and full of light, had gone down through all the cities, and had much comment and setting forth in the Hour-Slips, and were a cause for speech and argument.

Now concerning the voice of this girl coming to us through the darkness of the world, I will set out that which she had to tell; and this, indeed, but verified the tellings of our most ancient Records, which had so long been treated over lightly: There was, it would seem, somewhere out in the lonesome dark of the Outer Lands, but at what distance none could ever discover, a second Redoubt; that was a three-sided Pyramid, and moderate small; being no more than a mile in height, and scarce three quarters of a mile along the bases.

When this Redoubt was first builded, it had been upon the far shore of a sea, where now was no sea; and it had been raised by those wandering humans who had grown weary of wandering, and weary of the danger of night attacks by the tribes of half-human monsters which began to inhabit the earth even so early as the days when the half-gloom was upon the world. And he that had made the plan upon which it was builded, was one who had seen the Great Redoubt, having lived there in the beginning, but escaped because of a correction set upon him for his spirit of irresponsibility, which had made him to cause disturbance among the orderly ones in the lowest city of the Great Redoubt.

Yet, in time, he too had come to be tamed by the weight of fear of the ever-growing hordes of monsters, and the Forces that were abroad. And so he, being a master-spirit, planned and builded the smaller Redoubt, being aided thereto by four millions, who also were weary of the harass of the monsters; but until then had been wanderers, because of the restlessness of their blood.

And they had chosen that place, because there they had discovered a sign of the Earth-Current in a great valley which led to the shore; for without the Earth-Current no Refuge could have existence. And whilst many builded and guarded, and cared for the Great Camp in which all lived, others worked within a great shaft; and in ten years had made this to a distance of many miles, and therewith they tapt the Earth-Current; but not a great stream; yet a sufficiency, as was believed.

And, presently, after many years, they had builded the Pyramid, and taken up their refuge there, and made them instruments, and ordained Monstruwacans; so that they had speech daily with the Great Pyramid; and thus for many long ages.

And the Earth-Current then to begin to fail; and though they laboured through many thousands of years, they came to no better resource. And so it was they ceased to have communication with the Great Redoubt; for the current had a lack of power to work the instruments; and the recording instruments ceased to be sensible of our messages.

And thereafter came a million years, maybe, of silence; with ever the birthing and marrying and dying of those lonesome humans. And they grew less; and some put this to the lack of the Earth-Current, which dwindled slowly through the centuries of that Eternity.

And once in a thousand years, maybe, one among them would be Sensitive, and abled to hear beyond ordinary; and to these, at times, there would seem to come the thrilling of the aether; so that such an one would go listening; and sometimes seem to catch half messages; and so awaken a great interest in all the Pyramid; and there would be turning up of old Records, and many words and writings, and attempts to send the Master-Word through the night; in which, doubtless sometimes they succeeded; for there was set down in the Records of the Great Redoubt certain occasions on which there had come the call of the Master-Word, which had been arranged and made holy between the two Redoubts in the early days of that second life of this world.

Yet, now for an hundred thousand years, there had been none Sensitive; and in that time the people of the Pyramid had become no more than

ten thousand; and the Earth-Current was weak and powerless to put the joy of life into them; so that they went listlessly, but deemed it not strange, because of so many aeons of usage.

And then, to the wonder of all, the Earth-Current had put forth a new power; so that young people ceased to be old over-soon; and there was happiness and a certain joy in the living; and a strange birthing of children, such as had not been through half a million years.

And then came a new thing. Naani, the daughter of the Master Monstruwacan of that Redoubt had shown to all that she was Sensitive; for she had perceived odd vibrations afloat in the night; and concerning these she told her father; and presently, because their blood moved afresh in their bodies, they had heart to discover the plans of the ancient instruments; for the instruments had long rusted, and been forgotten.

And so they builded them a new instrument to send forth a message; for they had no memory at that time that the brain-elements had power to do thus; though, mayhap, their brain-elements were weakened, through so many ages of starvation of the Earth-Current, and could not have obeyed, even had their masters known all that we of the Great Redoubt knew.

And when the instrument was finished, to Naani was given the right to call first across the dark to discover whether indeed, after that million years of silence, they were yet companied upon this earth, or whether they were in truth lonely—the last poor thousands of the Humans.

And a great and painful excitement came upon the people of the lesser pyramid; for the loneliness of the world pressed upon them; and it was to them as though we in this age called to a star across the abyss of space.

And because of the excitement and pain of the moment, Naani called only vaguely with the instrument into the dark; and lo! in a moment, as it seemed, there came all about her in the night the solemn throb of the Master-Word, beating in the night. And Naani cried out that she was answered, and, as may be thought, many of the people wept, and some prayed, and some were silent; but others beseeched her that she call again and quickly to have further speech with those of their kind.

And Naani spoke the Master-Word into the night, and directly there

came a calling all about her: "Mirdath! Mirdath!" and the strange wonder of it made her silent a moment; but when she would have made reply, the instrument had ceased to work, and she could have no further speech at that time.

This, as may be thought, occasioned much distress; and constant work they had between the instrument and the Earth-Current, to discover the reason for this failing; but could not for a great while. And in that time, oft did Naani hear the call of "Mirdath" thrilling about her; and twice there came the solemn beat of the Master-Word in the night. Yet never had she the power to answer. And all that while, as I learned in time, was she stirred with a quaint ache at heart by the voice that called "Mirdath!" as it might be the Spirit of Love, searching for its mate; for this is how she put it.

And thus it chanced, that the constant thrilling of this name about her, woke her to memory of a book she had read in early years, and but half understood; for it was ancient, and writ in an olden fashion, and it set out the love of a man and a maid, and the maid's name was Mirdath. And so, because she was full of this great awakening of those ages of silence, and the calling of that name, she found the book again, and read it many times, and grew to a sound love of the beauty of that tale.

And, presently, when the instrument was made right, she called into the night the name of that man within the book; and so it came about that I had hoped too much; yet even now was I strangely unsure whether to cease from hoping.

And one other thing there is which I would make clear. Many and oft a time had I heard a thrilling of sweet, faint laughter about me, and the stirring of the aether by words too gentle to come clearly; and these I make no doubt came from Naani, using her brain-elements unwittingly and in ignorance; but very eager to answer my callings; and having no knowledge that, far off across the blackness of the world, they thrilled about me, constantly.

And after Naani had made clear all that I have set out concerning the Lesser Refuge, she told further how that food was not plentiful with them; though, until the reawakening of the Earth-Current, they had gone unknowing of this, being of small appetite, and caring little for aught; but

now wakened, and newly hungry, they savoured a lack of taste in all that they ate; and this we could well conceive, from our reasonings and theory; but happily not from our knowledge.

And we said unto them, that the soil had lost its life, and the crops therefrom were not vital; and a great while it would take for the earth within their pyramid to receive back the life-elements. And we told them certain ways by which they might bring a more speedy life to the soil; and this they were eager to do, being freshly alive after so long a time of half-life.

And then began a fresh matter; though but an old enough trick; for I speak now of the days that followed that re-opening of the talk between the Pyramids. Oft would speech come to us out of the night; and there would be tales of the sore need of the Lesser Redoubt, and callings for help. Yet, when I sent the Master-Word abroad, there would be no answering. And so I feared that the Monsters and Forces of Evil *knew*.

Yet, at times, the Master-Word would answer to us, beating steadily in the night; and when we questioned afresh, we knew that they in the Lesser Redoubt had caught the beat of the Master-Word, and so made reply; though it had not been they who had made the previous talk, which we had sought to test by the Word. And then they would make contradiction of all that had been spoken so cunningly; so that we knew the Monsters and Forces had sought to tempt some from the safety of the Redoubt. Yet, was this no new thing, as I have made to hint; saving that it grew now to a greater persistence, and there was a loathsome cunning in the using of this new knowledge to the making of wicked and false messages by those evil things of the Night Land. And it told to us, as I have made remark, how that those Monsters and Forces had a full awareness of the speech between the Pyramids; yet could they have no power to say the Master-Word; so had we some test left, and a way to sure knowledge of what made talk in the night.

And all that I have told should bring to those of this Age something of the yet unbegotten terror of that; and a quiet and sound thankfulness to God, that we suffer not as humanity shall yet suffer.

But, for all this, let it not be thought that they of that Age accounted

it as suffering; but as no more than the usual of human existence. And by this may we know that we can meet all circumstances, and use ourselves to them and live through them wisely, if we be but prudent and consider means of invention.

And through all the Night Land there was an extraordinary awakening among the Monsters and Forces; so that the instruments made constant note of greater powers at work out there in the darkness; and the Monstruwacans were busied recording, and keeping a very strict watch. And so was there at all that time a sense of difference and awakening, and of wonders about, and to come.

And from The Country Whence Comes The Great Laughter, the Laughter sounded constant … as it were an uncomfortable and heart-shaking voice-thunder rolling thence over the Lands, out from the unknown East. And the Pit of the Red Smoke filled all the Deep Valley with redness, so that the smoke rose above the edge, and hid the bases of the Towers upon the far side.

And the Giants could be seen plentiful around the Kilns to the East; and from the Kilns great belches of fire; though the meaning of it, as of all else, we could not say; but only the cause.

And from the Mountain Of The Voice, which rose to the South-East of the South-East Watcher, and of which I have made no telling hitherto, in this faulty setting-out, I heard for the first time in that life, the calling of the Voice. And though the Records made mention of it; yet not often was it heard. And the calling was shrill, and very peculiar and distressful and horrible; as though a giant-woman, hungering *strangely*, shouted unknown words across the night. And this was how it seemed to me; and many thought this to describe the sound.

And, by all this, may you perceive how that Land was awakened.

## CHAPTER IV

*The Hushing of The Voice*

("Dearest, thine own feet tread the world at night—
Treading, as moon flakes step across a dark
Kissing the very dew to holier light. …
Thy Voice a song past mountains, which to hark
Frightens my soul with an utter lost delight.")

Now, ONE NIGHT, towards the end of the sixteenth hour, as I made ready to sleep, there came all about me the thrilling of the aether, as happened oft in those days; but the thrilling had a strange power in it; and in my soul the voice of Naani sounded plain, all within and about me.

And it came to me suddenly, that it was not Naani that spoke; but Mirdath the Beautiful, from out of all the everlasting night. And I called:— "Mirdath! Mirdath," with my brain-elements, into the night; and lo! the far, faint voice spoke again to my spirit through all the darkness of eternity, saying again those words. Yet, though the voice was the voice of Mirdath the Beautiful, it was also the voice of Naani; and I knew in all my heart that this thing was in verity; and that it had been given to me to be birthed once more into this world in the living-time of that Only One, with whom my spirit and essence hath mated in all ages through the everlasting. And I called with my brain-elements and all my strength to Naani; but there came no answer; neither sign of hearing, though through hours I called.

And thus at last I came to an utter exhaustion; but neither could be quiet, nor sleep. Yet, presently, I slept.

And when I waked, my first memory was of the wondrous thing which had befallen in the sleep-time; for none in all this world could have known those words; save it had been the spirit of Mirdath, my Beautiful One, looking from above my shoulder in that utter-lost time, as I made those words to her, out of an aching and a broken heart. And the voice had been the voice of Mirdath; and the voice of Mirdath had been the voice of Naani.

And what shall any say to this, save that which I had in my heart.

And immediately I called to Naani, once, and again twice; and in a little moment there came all about me the throbbing of the Master-Word, beating solemnly in the night; and I sent the Master-Word to give assurance, and immediately the voice of Naani, a little weak as was it always when she had not the Instrument, but sent the message with her brain-elements.

And I answered her, and questioned her eagerly concerning her sayings of the past time of sleep; but she disclaimed, and made clear to me that she had no knowledge of having spoken; but had slept through all that time of which I made to tell; and, indeed, had dreamed a very strange dream.

And she told the dream to me, and in the dream she had seen a tall, dark man, built very big, and dressed in unfamiliar clothing. And the man had been in a little room, and very sorrowful, and lonesome; and in her dream she had gone nigh to him.

But no more had she memory of. Yet it was a sufficiency, and I, maybe with a mad, strange triumph in my soul, said unto her with my brain-elements that which remained of those words. And my spirit felt them strike upon the spirit of Naani, and awake her memory, as with the violence of a blow. And for a little while she stumbled, dumb before so much newness and certainly. And her spirit then to waken, and she near wept with the fright and the sudden, new wonder of this thing.

And immediately, all about me there came her voice thrilling, and the voice was the voice of Mirdath, and the voice of Naani; and I heard the tears of her spirit make pure and wonderful the bewildered and growing gladness of her far voice. And she asked me, as one who had suddenly opened the Gates of Memory, whether she might be truly Mirdath. And I, utter weak and shaken strangely because of this splendour of fulfilment, could make no instant answer. And she asked again, but using mine old love-name, and with a sureness in her far voice. And still I was so strangely dumb, and the blood to thud peculiar in mine ears; and this to pass; and speech to come swift.

And this way to be that meeting of our spirits, across all the everlasting night.

And you shall have for a memory-picture, how that Naani stood there in the world in that far eternity, and, with her spirit having speech with mine, looked back through the part-opened gates of her memory, into the past of this our life and Age. Yet more than this she saw, and more than was given to me in that Age; for she had memory now and sight of other instances, and of other comings together, which had some confusion and but half-meanings to me. Yet of this our present Age and life, we spoke as of some yesterday; but very hallowed.

Now, as may be conceived, the wonder of this surety which had come into my life stirred me fiercely to its completion; for all my heart and spirit cried out to be with that one who was Mirdath, and now spoke with the voice of Naani.

Yet, how should this be won; for none among all the learned men of that Mighty Pyramid knew the position of the Lesser Redoubt; neither could the Records and Histories of the World give us that knowledge; only that there was a general thought among the Students and the Monstruwacans that it lay between the North-West and the North-East. But no man had any surety; neither could any conceive of the distance from us of that Refuge.

And counting all this, there was yet the incredible danger and peril of the Night Land, and the hunger and desolation of the Outer Lands, which were sometimes named the Unknown Lands.

And I spoke much with Naani concerning this matter of their position; yet neither she nor her father, the Master Monstruwacan of that Refuge, had any knowing either of our position; only that the Builder of the Lesser Redoubt had come out of the Southward World in the Beginning, as they had knowledge of by the Records.

Also, the father of Naani set that ancient Compass to bear; for, as he made explanation to us through the Instrument, so great a power of the Earth-Current must be ours that, perchance it was our force which did affect the pointer from steadfastness. For, indeed, the needle did swing in an arc, as we heard, that held between the North and the South; within the Westward arc; but this it had done ever with them, and so was a very

helpless guide; save that, maybe, as we had thought, the force of the Earth-Current that was with us, had in truth some power to pull the needle towards us. And if this were so of verity, we made a reckoning that set the Lesser Redoubt to the North; and they did likewise, and put us to the South; yet was it all built upon the sand of guess-work; and nothing to adventure the life and soul upon.

Now we, of curiosity; though a million times had it been done in the past ages, set the compass before us, having it from the Great Museum. But, as ever in that age, it did spin if we but stirred the needle, and would stop nowheres with surety, for the flow of the Earth-Current from the "Crack" beneath the Pyramid had a power to affect it away from the North, and to set it wandering. And this may seem very strange to this present Age; yet to that, it was most true to the seeming nature of things; and harder to believe that ever it did once point steadfastly, to prove a guide of sureness, and unfailing.

For, be it known, we knew the positions of the Land by tradition, coming from that ancient time when, in the Half-Gloom they had builded the Pyramid; they having known the use of that ancient compass, and with sight of the Sun had named the Positions; though we of that far future day had forgotten the very beginnings of those Names of Direction; and used them but because our fathers did a million years and more. And likewise we did the same with the names of the day and the night and the weeks and the months and the years; though of the visible markings of these there was nothing but only and always the everlasting night; yet the same seeming very natural to that people.

Now, Naani, having heed to my constant questions, craved with an utter keen hunger that I might come to her; but yet forbade it, in that it were better to live and commune in the spirit, than to risk my soul, and mayhaps die, in the foolishness of trying to find her in all the darkness of the dead world. Yet, no heed had I taken of her commands, had I but known of a surety the *direction* in which she might be discovered; and gained some knowledge of the space between, for this might be named by thousands of miles, or but by hundreds; though a great distance it was surely.

Yet, one other thing there was, that has point in this place; for when I sent my speech out into the night, using my brain-elements, I came to know that, whether I had a knowledge of the North, or no knowledge at the moment, yet did I turn oft with a sure instinction to that Direction. And of this, the Master Monstruwacan took very great note, and had me to experiment many a time and way, and so enclosed about with screens, or with bandages across mine eyes, that I could not, save by that inward Knowing, have any knowledge to point me the way. Yet would I turn Northwards very frequent, by a certain feeling; and seemed unable of speech, if I were turned otherwise by force.

But when we asked Naani whether she had an unusualness in this matter, she could discover none; and we could but take note curiously of that which affected my habits; and which truly I set to the attracting of her spirit; for I had mind that she did be somewheres out that way in the darkness of the world; but yet was this no more than to suppose, as you perceive.

And the Master Monstruwacan wrote a study of this matter of the Northwardness of my turning; and it was set out in the Hour-Slips of the Tower of Observation; and so it came to be copied by the Hour-Slips of the great cities, and made much comment, and much calling up to me through the home instruments; so that with this, and the speech that went about concerning my powers to hear, I was much in talk, and diversely pleased and oft angered by overmuch attention and importunity.

And now, whilst I pondered this matter in all my spirit and being, how that I should some way come to Naani, there befell a very terrible thing. And in this wise must I tell it:—

It was at the seventeenth hour, when all the millions of the Mighty Pyramid slept, that I was with the Master Monstruwacan in the Tower of Observation taking my due turn. And sudden, I heard the thrilling of the aether all about me, and the voice of Naani in my soul, speaking. And I sent the Master-Word into the darkness of the world, and presently, I heard the solemn answer beating steadfastly in the night; and immediately I called to Naani with my brain-elements, to know what thing troubled her in her sleep.

And her voice came into my spirit, weak and far and faint, and so that scarce I could make to hear the words. Yet, in a while I gathered that all the peoples of the Lesser Redoubt were in very deadly trouble; for that the Earth-Current had failed suddenly and mightily; and they had called her from her sleep, that she might listen whether we answered their callings by the Instrument; but, indeed, no calling had come to us.

And they who had been of late so joyful, were now grown old with sorrow in but an hour or two; for they feared that the fresh coming of the Earth-Current had been but the final flicker and outburst before the end. And, even in this short while of our speech, did it seem to me that the voice of Naani grew further off from me; and I felt like to have broken my heart with the trouble of this thing.

And through all that remained of that sleep-time, did I converse with Naani, as might two lovers who shall presently part forever. And when the cities awoke, the news went throughout them, and all our millions were in sorrow and trouble.

And thus was it for, maybe, a little month; and in that time had the voice of Naani grown so weak and far-off that even I that had the Night-Hearing, could scarce make real its meaning. And every word was to me a treasure and a touch upon my soul; and my grief and trouble before this certain parting drove me that I could not eat, neither have rest; and this did the Master Monstruwacan take upon him to chide and correct; for that, if any were to help, how should it be done if I that had the Night-Hearing, and heard even now that the recording Instruments were dumb, came to ill-health.

And because of this, and such wisdom as was mine, I made to eat and order my life that I might have my full powers. Yet was this beyond all my strength; for, presently, I knew that the people of the Lesser Pyramid were threatened by the monsters that beset them; and later I had knowledge from faint, far words whispered in my brain, that there had been a fight with an outside Force that had harmed many in their minds; so that in madness they had opened the gate and had run from the Lesser Pyramid, out into the darkness of the Lands about them; and there had

their physical bodies fallen to the monsters of those Lands; but of their souls who may know?

And this, we set assuredly to the failure of the Earth-Current, which had robbed them of all force and power; so that, in those few weeks all life and joy of living had left them; and neither hunger nor thirst had they, much, nor any great desire to live; but yet a new and mighty fear of death. And this doth seem very strange.

And, as may be thought, all this made the Peoples of the Great Redoubt think newly of the Earth-Current that issued from the "Crack" beneath the Pyramid; and of their latter end; so that much was writ in the Hour-Slips concerning this matter; yet in the main to assure us that we ourselves might each be free from a disturbed heart; though some went foolishly to the other event, and spoke of a speedy danger to us, likewise; as is ever the way. But the truth of our own case lay, maybe, somewhere between.

And all the Hour-Slips were full also of imaginings of the terror of those poor humans out in the darkness of the world, facing that end which must come upon all, even upon our mighty Pyramid; though, as most would believe, so far away in some future eternity, that we have no cause to trouble.

And there were sad poems writ to the peoples of that Lesser Redoubt, and foolish plans set about to rescue them; but none to put them to effect; and no way by which so great a thing might be done; and doth but show how loosely people will speak out of an over-security. Yet to me, there had come a certain knowledge that I must make the adventure, though I achieved naught save mine own end. Yet, it were better to cease quickly, than that I should feel, as now I did feel.

That same night, in the Eighteenth Hour, there was a great disturbance in the aether about the Mighty Pyramid; and I was awakened suddenly by the Master Monstruwacan; that I might use my gift of the Night-Hearing to hearken for the throbbing of the Master-Word, which they had thought to come vaguely through the Instruments; but no one of the Monstruwacans was sensitive enough of soul to account truly whether this was so.

And lo! as I sat up in the bed, there came the sound of the Master-

Word, beating in the night about the Pyramid. And immediately there was a crying in the aether all about me:—"We are coming! We are coming!"

And mine inwards leaped and sickened me a moment, so shaken was I with a sudden belief; for the message seemed some ways to come to me from very near to the Great Redoubt; as that they who sent it were nigh to hand.

And, forthwith, I called the Master-Word into the night; but no answer did there come for a while, and then a faint thrilling of the aether about me, and the weak pulse of the Master-Word in the night, sent by a far voice, strangely distant. And I knew that the voice was the voice of Naani; and I put a question through all the darkness of the dead world, whether she were within the Lesser Redoubt, and safe thus far.

And presently, there came a faint disturbance about me, and a small voice in my soul, speaking weakly and out of an infinite distance; and I knew that far away through the night Naani spoke feebly, with her brain-elements; and that she abode within the Lesser Pyramid; but that she too had heard that strange pulse of the Master-Word in the night, and that message:—"We are coming! We are coming!" And vastly had this thing disturbed her, waking her within her sleep; so that she knew not what to think; save that we were devising some method to come to them. But this I removed from doubt, saying that she must not build on vain hoping; for I would not have her doubly tortured by the vanity of such believing. And, thereafter, having said such things as I might, though few they were, to comfort her, I bade her, gently, to sleep; and turned therewith to the Master Monstruwacan, who waited in quiet patience; and had no knowledge of that which I had heard and sent; for his hearing was but the normal; though his brain and heart were such as made me to love him.

And I told the Master Monstruwacan many things as I put my clothing about me; how that there had indeed been the calling of the Master-Word; but not by any of that Lesser Redoubt; but that, to my belief, it had come from nigh about the Great Pyramid. Moreover, it was sent by no instrument; as I wotted that he did guess; but, as it seemed to me, by the brain-elements of many, calling in unison.

And all this did I set out to the Master Monstruwacan; and with something uncertain of fear and trouble in my heart; yet with a blind expectation; as, indeed, who would not. Though, no longer was I shaken by that first thought of Her nearness.

And I said to the Master Monstruwacan that we should go to the Tower of Observation, and search the Night Lands with the great spy-glass.

And we did this, and lo! presently, we saw a great number of men pass over the Electric Circle that went about the Pyramid; yet they came not *to* us; but went outwards towards the blackness and the strange fires and hideous mysteries of the Night Land. And we ceased from spying, and looked swiftly at one another, and knew in our hearts that some had left the Mighty Pyramid in the Sleep-Time.

Then the Master Monstruwacan sent word to the Master Watchman that his wardership had been outraged, and that people left the great Pyramid in the Sleep-Time; for this was against the Law; and none ever went out into the Night Land, save the Full Watch were posted to the Great Door; and at a due time, when all were wakeful; for the Opening Of The Door was made known to all the Millions of the Great Redoubt; so that all might be aware; and know that no foolishness was done without their wotting.

Moreover, ere any had power to leave the Pyramid, they must pass The Examination, and Be Prepared; and some of this have I set out already. And so stern was the framing of the Law, that there were yet the metal pegs upon the inner side of the Great Gate, where had been stretched the skin of one who disobeyed; and was flayed and his hide set there to be a warning in the Early Days. Yet the tradition was remembered; for, as I might say it, we lived very close about the place; and Memory had no room whereby she might escape.

Now the Master Watchman, when he heard that which the Master Monstruwacan had to tell, went hastily with some of the Central Watch from the Watch-Dome, to the Great Gate; and he found the men of the Sleep-Time Watch, with the Warder of the Gate, all bound, and stopt in the mouth, so that none could make outcry.

And he freed them, and learned that nigh five hundred young men,

from the Upper Cities, by the bigness of their chests, had come upon them suddenly, and bound them, and escaped into the night through the Eye-Gate in the top of the Great Gate.

And the Master Watchman was angry, and demanded why that none had called by the instruments of the Watch House; but lo! some had made to call thus, and found them unable to wake the recorders which lay in the central Watch-Dome; for there had been tampering.

Now, after this, they made certain new rules and Laws concerning the order of Watching, and made tests of the lesser instruments of the inward Pyramid, nightly, upon the coming of the Sleep-Time, which was, even in that strange age, by tradition called the Night, as I have given hint; though hitherto, until the way of my story was known, I have used a word for the sleep hours that was yet not of that time; but somewhat an invention to make this history free from the confusion of "night" and "day," when, in truth, it was always night without upon the world. Yet, after this, shall I keep to mine use the luxury of the true names of that time; and yet, how strange is it that the truth should be of so little to our thinking.

And so to go forward with my telling; for, though all this care were now taken, it had no force until afterward; and at this moment were those poor foolish youths out in all the danger of the Night Land, and no way by which they might be succoured, or called back; save that Fear or Wisdom should come to them quickly, that they cease from so wild an attempt. For it was to make rescue of those in that other, unknown Pyramid, out in all the darkness of the World's Night that was their intent, as we had speedy knowledge from those boon friends that had been in the secret of their plot, which had seemed to them great and heroic; and was so, in verity, but that neither they who went, nor they who stayed, had a true awareness of the danger they had dealing with, being all naught but raw and crude youths; yet, doubtless, with the makings of many fine and great men among them.

And because some had thus abetted that which they knew to be against the Law, which was framed to the well-being and safety of all, there were certain floggings, which might the better help their memories in the

future as to the properness of their actions and wisdom.

Moreover, they who returned, if any, would be flogged, as seemed proper, after due examination. And though the news of their beatings might help all others to hesitation, ere they did foolishly, in like fashion, yet was the principle of the flogging not on this base, which would be both improper and unjust; but only that the one in question be corrected to the best advantage for his own well-being; for it is not meet that any principle of correction should shape to the making of human signposts of pain for the benefit of others; for in verity, this were to make one pay the cost of many's learning; and each should owe to pay only so much as shall suffice for the teaching of his own body and spirit. And if others profit thereby, this is but accident, however helpful. And this is wisdom, and denoteth now that a sound Principle shall prevent Practice from becoming monstrous.

Yet, now I must hasten that I set down how it fared with those five hundred youths that had made so sad an adventure of their lives and unprepared souls; and were beyond our aid to help them, who might not so much as make any calling to them, to bid them to return; for to do this would have been to tell to all the Monsters of the Land that humans were abroad from the Mighty Pyramid.

And this would have been to cause the monsters to search the youths out to their destruction, and maybe even to awaken the Forces to work them some dread Spiritual harm, which was the chief Fear.

Now, presently, through all the cities of the Great Redoubt, the news had gone how that five hundred foolish Youths had adventured out into the despair of the Night Land; and the whole Pyramid waked to life, and the Peoples of the South came to the Northern sides, for the Great Gate lay in the North-West side; and the Youths had made from there, not straightly outwards, but towards the North; and so were to be seen from the North-East embrasures, and from those within the North-West wall.

And thus, in a while were they watched by all the mighty multitudes of the Great Pyramid, through millions of spy-glasses; for each human had a spying-glass, as may be thought; and some were an hundred years old, and some, maybe ten thousand, and handed down through many genera-

tions; and some but newly made, and very strange. But all those people had some instrument by which they might spy out upon the wonder of the Night Land; for so had it been ever through all the eternity of darkness, and a great diversion and wonder of life was it to behold the monsters about their work; and to know that they plotted always to our destruction; yet were ever foiled.

And never did all that great and terrible Land grow stale upon the soul of any, from birth until death; and by this you shall know the constant wonder of it, and that *sense of enemies in the night about us*, which ever filled the heart and spirit of all Beholders; so that never were the embrasures utterly empty.

Yet, many beheld not the Land from the embrasures; but sat about the View-Tables, which were set properly in certain places throughout the cities, and so beheld the Night Land, without undue cranings, or poising of spy-glasses, though less plain-seen. And these same tables were some form of that which we of this age name Camera Obscura; but made very great, and with inventions, and low to the floor, so that ten thousand people might sit about them in the raised galleries, and have comfortable sight. Yet this attracted not the young people, save they were lovers; and then, in truth, were they comfortable seats for quietness and gentle whisperings.

Yet now, as may be supposed, with all the Peoples of the Mighty Pyramid grown eager to look towards one part of the Night Land, the embrasures were hid in the crowds; and such as could gain no view therethrough, thronged about the View-Tables. And so was it in all the hours of leisure; so that women had scarce patience to attend their children; but must hasten to watch again, that lonesome band of foolish youths making so blind and unshaped a trial to come upon that unknown Lesser Redoubt, somewhere out in all the night of the world.

And in this wise passed three days and nights; yet both in the sleeptime and the time of waking did great multitudes cease not to watch; so that many went hungry for sleep, as in truth did I. And sometimes we saw those Youths with plainness; but other times they were lost to our sight in the utter shadows of the Night Land. Yet, by the telling of our instruments,

and the sense of my hearing, there was no awareness among the Monsters, and the Forces of Evil, that any were abroad from the Pyramid; so that a little hope came into our hearts that yet there might be no tragedy.

And times, would they cease from their way, and sit about in circles among the shadows and the grey moss-bushes, which grew hardly here or there about. And we knew that they had food with them to eat; for this could we see with plainness, as some odd, grim flare of light from the infernal fires struck upon one or another strangely, and passed, and left them in the darkness.

And who of you shall conceive what was in the hearts of the fathers, and the mothers that bore the youths, and who never ceased away from the Northward embrasures; but spied out in terror and in tears, and maybe oft with so good glasses as did show them the very features and look upon the face of son and son.

And the kin of the watchers brought to them food, and tended them, so that they had no need to cease from their watching; and beds were made in the embrasures, rough and resourceful, that they might sleep quickly a little; yet be ever ready, if those cruel Monsters without made discovery of those their children.

Thrice in those three days of journeying to the Northward, did the Youths sleep, and we perceived that some kept a watch, and so knew that there was a kind of order and leadership among them; also, they had each his weapon upon his hip, and this gave to us a further plea to hope.

And concerning this same carrying of weapons, I can but set out here that no healthful male or female in all the Mighty Pyramid but possessed such a weapon, and was trained to it from childhood; so that a ripe and extraordinary skill in the use thereof was common to most. Yet some breaking of Rule had there been, that the Youths had each achieved to be armed; for the weapons were stored in every tenth house of the cities, in the care of the charging-masters.

And here I must make known that these weapons did not shoot; but had a disk of grey metal, sharp and wonderful, that spun in the end of a rod of grey metal, and were someways charged by the Earth-Current, so

that were any but stricken thereby, they were cut in twain so easy as aught. And the weapons were contrived to the repelling of any Army of Monsters that might make to win entrance to the Redoubt. And to the eye they had somewhat the look of strange battle-axes, and might be lengthened by the pulling out of the handles.

Now, the Youths made, as I have told, to the Northward; but had first to keep a long way to the North-East, that they might come clear of the Vale of Red Fire. And this wise they journeyed, and kept the Vale about seven miles to the North-West of them, and so were presently beyond the Watcher of the North-East, and going with a greater freedom, and having less care to hide.

And this way, it may be, certain of the giants, wandering, perceived them, and went swiftly to make attack and destroy them. But some order went about among the youths, and they made a long line, with a certain space between each, because of the terror of their weapon, and immediately, it seemed, the Giants were upon them, a score and seven they were, and seeming to be haired like to mighty crabs, as I saw with the Great Spy-Glass, when the great flares of far and mighty fires threw their fierce light across the Dark Lands.

And there was a very great and horrid fight; for the Youths broke into circles about each of the Giants, and many of those young men were torn in pieces; but they smote the Monsters from behind and upon every side, and we of the Mighty Pyramid could behold at times the grey, strange gleam of their weapons; and the jether was stirred about me by the passing of those that died; yet, by reason of the great miles, their screams came not to us, neither heard we the roars of the Monsters; but into our hearts, even from that great distance and safety, there stole the terror of those awesome Brutes; and in the Great Spy-Glass I could behold the great joints and limbs and e'en, I thought, the foul sweat of them; and their size and brutishness was like to that of odd and monstrous animals of the olden world; yet part human. And it must be borne to mind that the Fathers and the Mothers of those Youths beheld all this dread fight from the embrasures, and their other kin likewise watched, and a very drear sight was it to their hearts and

their human, natural feelings, and like to breed old age, ere its due.

Then, in a time, the fight ceased; for of those seven and twenty Giant Brutes there remained none; only that there cumbered the ground seven and twenty lumbering hillocks, dreadful and grim. For the lesser dead we could not see proper.

And we that were within the Pyramid saw the Youths sorted together by their leaders, all in the dim twilight of that place; and with the Great Spy-Glass I made a rough count, and found that there lived of them, three hundred; and by this shall you know the power of those few monstrous things, which had slain full two hundred, though each youth was armed with so wondrous a weapon. And I set the word through the Pyramid, that all might have some knowledge of the number that had died; for it was better to know, than to be in doubt. And no spy-glass had the power of The Great Spy-Glass.

After this fight, the youths spent a time having a care to their bodies and wounds; and some were made separate from the others, and of these I counted upon fifty; and whilst the others made to continue their march towards the Road Where The Silent Ones Walk, these were constrained by one who was the Leader, to return to the Pyramid. And in a little, I saw that they came towards us, wearily and with many a halt, as that they suffered great wounds and harm of the fight.

But those others (maybe two hundred and fifty Youths) went onwards into the Night Land; and though we sorrowed at this thing; yet was there come a huge pride into our hearts that those raw ones, who yesterday were but children, had so held themselves in the battle, and done a great deed that day. And I wot that whilst their mothers wept, easeless, their fathers' hearts swelled within them, and held somewhat of their Pain away from them for a time.

And all this while, those wounded Youths came slowly, and rested, and came on again, the better helping the worse; and a great excitement and trouble there was in all the Mighty Pyramid, to learn which were they that came, and they that went, and who lay out there quietly among the slain. But none might say anything with surety; for, even with that great

spy-glass in the Tower of Observation, they were not overplain; save when some light from the fires of the Land flared high, and lit them. For they stood not up into the glare of the fires, as had the Giants. And though I saw them with clearness, yet I knew them not; for there was so mighty a multitude in that Vast Redoubt, that none might ever know the half even of their rulers.

And about this time, there came a fresh matter of trouble to our minds; for one of the Monstruwacans made report that the instruments were recording an influence abroad in the night; so that we had knowledge that one of the Evil Forces was Out. And to me there came an awaredness that a strange unquiet stole over the Land; yet I knew it not with mine ears; but my spirit heard, and it was as though trouble and an expectation of horror did swarm about me.

And once, listening, I heard the Master-Word beating strangely low, and I knew the aether to thrill about me, and a faint stirring was there in my soul, as of a faint voice, speaking; and I knew that Naani called to me some message across the night of the world; yet weak and coming without clear meaning; so that I was tormented and could but send comfort to her, with my brain-elements. And presently I knew that she ceased to speak.

And, later, I heard that there was a new matter forward in the Redoubt; for ten thousand men had assembled to attend the Room of Preparation for the Short Preparation; and by this we knew that those poor Youths who stumbled towards us through the dark, were presently to have help.

And through all that Sleep-Time, there went forward the Spiritual and the Physical Preparation of the ten thousand; and upon the morrow they slept, whilst an hundred thousand made ready their arms.

And in this space of time the two hundred and fifty Youths that went towards the Road Where The Silent Ones Walk, had come very nigh thereto; having gone very warily and with some slowness, because, as may be, of the lesson of the Giants.

And to us in the Pyramid, the instruments made known constantly that Influence which was abroad, and which all those of the Tower of Observation thought to proceed from the House of Silence. Yet, nothing could

we see with the Great Spy-Glass, and so could come to no sure knowing; but only to fear and wonder.

And, presently, the Youths were upon the Great Road, and turned to the Northward. And beyond them, a great way, stood the House of Silence, upon a low hill at a certain distance to the right of the Road.

By now, they that were wounded had come to within, maybe, fifteen miles of the Great Redoubt; and the news went through all the Cities, that the ten thousand men that were Prepared, made to arm themselves. And I went down by the Tower Lift, and saw them come down by thousands from the Room of Preparation; and none might go nigh to them, or cause them to speak; for they were made Ready, and were, as it might be, holy.

And all the millions of the Mighty Pyramid stood in their cities about certain of the Main Lifts, and watched those thousands go downwards, all in their armour of grey metal, and each one armed with the Diskos, which was that same very terrible weapon, which all had training to.

And I doubt not but that the Young Men of the Pyramid looked, with longing in their hearts, that they might have been among those that went forth to succour. Yet, the older men had graver thoughts in their hearts; for the blood ran more soberly in them, and they had knowledge and memory of the Peril. And by this, I would make clear that I speak less of the peril of the body, which is common to every state of life; but of the peril of the spirit.

And it may be thought by those of this age, that it was most strange that they of that, having all the knowledge of eternity to aid them, had no weapon by which to shoot, and kill at a distance.

But, indeed, this had not been so in the past; as our Histories did show; for some wondrous weapons there had been, that might slay without sound or flash at a full score miles and more; and some we had whole within the Great Museum; and of others but the parts in decay; for they had been foolish things, and reckless to use; for we of that Great Pyramid, wanted not to kill a few of the Monsters that lay at a great distance; but only those which came nigh, to harm us.

And concerning those same weapons that killed silently at a great

distance, we had now little knowledge, save that they did waste the Earth-Current; and no practice had we concerning their workings; for it was, maybe, an hundred thousand years gone that they had been used, and found to be of no great worth in a close attack, and harmful otherwise to the peace, in that they angered, unneedful, the Forces of that land, slaying wantonly those monsters which did no more than beset the Mighty Redoubt at a great distance.

For, as may be seen by a little thought, we did very gladly keep a reasonable quietness, and refrained from aught that should wake that Land; for we were born to the custom of that strange life, and lived and died in peace, for the most part; and were very content to have security, and to be neutral in all things that did not overbear us; but, as it were, always armed, and ready.

But concerning the great and Evil Forces that were abroad in the Night Land, these we had no power to harm; nor could we hope for more than that we had security from them, which indeed we had; but the hugeness of their power was about us, and we dared not to wake it; save through such extremity as had come to pass by this folly of the Youths; though, even now, we had no thought to attack aught; but only to succour those wounded ones.

And concerning this simplicity of weapons, which excites somewhat even my wonder in this our present age, it may be that the powers of chemistry were someways quaintly limited by conditions in that age; and there to be always a need to spare the Earth-Current; and hence, by this cause and by that, we were brought, by the extreme, nigh to the simplicity of the early world; yet with a strange and mighty difference, as all may know who have read.

Now, presently, the Word was sent to every City throughout the Great Redoubt—as was the Law—that the Great Gate should be opened; and each city sent its Master, to form the Full Watch, as was the Law. And each went clad in grey armour, and carrying the Diskos. And the Full Watch numbered, two thousand; for there were also the Watchmen.

Then the lights in the Great Causeway were made dim; so that the

opening of the Gate should cast no great glare from within into the Night Land, to tell the Watcher of the North-West, and all the Monsters, that certain humans went out from the Mighty Pyramid. But whether the vast and hidden Forces of Evil had knowledge, we knew not; and they who went must but chance it, remembering that they were Prepared, and had the Capsule.

And the ten thousand that were Prepared, went out through the Great Gateway, into the night; and the Full Watch stood back from them, and spoke no word, but saluted silently with the Diskos; and they that went, raised each the Diskos a little, and passed out into the dark.

Then the Great Gate was shut; and we made to wait and to watch, with trouble and expectation within our hearts. And at the embrasures many did comfort the women of those men.

And I went back, upwards by miles, until I came to the Tower of Observation; and I looked out from there into the Night Land, and saw that the ten thousand halted at the Circle, and made arrangement of themselves, and sent some before and upon either hand, and so went forward into the Night Land.

And after that, I went to the Great Spy-Glass, and turned it towards the two hundred and fifty Youths that were far off, upon the Road Where The Silent Ones Walk; yet for awhile I could not perceive them, for all the Road seemed empty. But afterward I saw them, and they were clambering back into the Road, having gone aside, as I thought, because of the passing of one of those Silent Ones, that I saw now at a distance to the Southward of them.

There passed then, some three hours; and in that time I varied my watching between those far-off Youths, and the Ten-thousand that went forward to succour the wounded, that were now, maybe, scarce nine miles distant from the Mighty Pyramid, and the Ten-thousand came very close to them. And, in truth, in a little while, they spied one the other, and I gathered, in spirit, something of the rejoicing of those youths; yet weak and troubled were they, because of their wounds, and their knowledge of failure, and their disobedience of the Law.

And, presently, they were surrounded by the Ten-thousand, and carried upon slings; and all that body swung round towards the Pyramid, and came back at a great pace.

And, in the same time, I heard the sound that made them so swift to hasten; for there smote up through the night the Baying of the Hounds; and we knew that they were discovered. And I swept the Great Spy-Glass over the Land, towards the Valley Of The Hounds, that I might discover them quickly; and I saw them come lumbering, at a strange gallop, and great as horses, and it might be only ten miles to the East.

And I looked once upon the Watcher of the North-East, and I saw and marvelled that the great bell-ear quivered constantly; and I knew that it had knowledge, and gave signal to all the Land. Then did one of the Monstruwacans report that a new and terrible Influence was abroad in the Land; and by the instrument, we had knowledge that it approached; and some of the Monstruwacans called foolishly with weak voices to the Ten-thousand to haste; forgetting, and desiring only their safety from that which came near.

Then, looking with the Great Spy-Glass, I saw that there moved across the Land, from the direction of the Plain of Blue Fire, a mighty Hump, seeming of Black Mist, and came with prodigious swiftness. And I called to the Master Monstruwacan, that he come and look through one of the eye-pieces that were about the Great Spy-Glass; and he came quickly, and when he had looked a while, he called to the Monstruwacan that had made report. And the Monstruwacan answered, and replied that the Influence drew nearer, by the reading of the instrument; yet of the thing itself the man had no sight.

And I ceased not to look, and in a little while, the Humped thing passed downwards into the Vale of Red Fire, which lay across the Land that way. But I watched steadfastly, and presently I saw the black Hump climb up from the Vale of Red Fire upon this side, and come through the night, so that in scarce a minute it had come halfway across that part of the Night Land.

And my heart stood quiet with fear, and the utter terror of this Monster,

which I knew to be surely one of the Great Forces of Evil of that Land, and had power, without doubt, to destroy the spirit. And the Master Monstruwacan leapt towards the Home-Call, and sent the great Sound down to the Ten-thousand, that they might attend, and immediately, he signalled to them to Beware. Yet, already I perceived that they knew of this Utter Danger that was upon them; for I saw them slay the Youths quickly, that their spirits might not be lost; for they were Unprepared. But the men, being Prepared, had the Capsule, and would die swiftly in the last moment.

I looked again towards the Hump, and saw that it came like a Hill of Blackness in the Land, and was almost anigh. Then there happened a wonder; for in that moment when all had else gone quickly, that they might save their souls, out of the earth there rose a little Light, like to the crescent of the young moon of this early day. And the crescent rose up into an arch of bright and cold fire, glowing but little; and it spanned above the Ten-thousand and the dead; and the Hump stood still, and went backwards and was presently lost.

And the men came swiftly towards the Mighty Pyramid. Yet, ere they were come to safety, the Baying of the Hounds sounded close upon them, and they faced to the danger; yet, as I could know, without despair, because that they yet lived after so enormous a peril.

And the Hounds were very nigh, as now I beheld with the Great Spy-Glass; and I counted five score, running with mighty heads low, and in a pack. And lo! as the Hounds came at them, the Ten-thousand drew apart, and had a space between the men, that they might have full use of that terrible Diskos; and they fought with the handles at length, and I saw the disks spin and glisten and send out fire.

Then was there a very great battle; for the Light that arched above them, and held away The Power from their souls, made not to protect them from this danger of the lesser monsters. And at an hundred thousand embrasures within the Mighty Pyramid, the women cried and sobbed, and looked again. And in the lower cities it was told, after, that the Peoples could hear the crash and splinter of the armour, as the Hounds ran to and fro, slaying; aye, e'en the sound of the armour between their teeth.

Yet, the Ten-thousand ceased not to smite with the Diskos; and they hewed the Hounds in pieces; but of the men that went forth, there were a thousand and seven hundred slain by the Hounds, ere the men won to victory.

Then came that wearied band of heroes back to the home shelter of the Vast Redoubt; and they bore their dead with them, and the Youths that they slew. And they were received with great honour, and with exceeding grief, and in a great silence; for the thing admitted not of words, until a time had passed. And in the cities of the Pyramid there was mourning; for there had been no sorrow like unto this through, mayhap, an hundred thousand years.

And they bore the Youths to their Mothers and to their Fathers; and the Father of each made thanks to the men that they had saved the soul of his son; but the women were silent. Yet, neither to the Father nor to the Mother, was ever made known the name of the slayers; for this might not be; as all shall see with a little thought.

And some did remember that, in verity, all was due to the unwisdom of those Youths, who had heeded not the Law and their life-teachings. Yet had they paid to the uttermost, and passed outwards; and the account of their Deeds was closed.

And all this while did great numbers spy toward the Road Where The Silent Ones Walk, that they might watch that band of Youths afar in the Night Land, who went forward amid those horrid dangers. Yet, when the dead Youths had been brought in, many had ceased to look out for a time and had turned to questioning, and some had made inspection that they might know which had come back, and which lay out there where the Giants had slain them, or went forward to more dreadful matters.

But who of those that were abroad, were slain, or still went onward, we had but indifferent knowledge; though the men of the Ten-thousand knew somewhat, having had speech with the wounded Youths, ere they slew them. And, as may be thought, these men were sorely questioned by the Mothers and the Fathers of those Youths that were not accounted of; yet I doubt that few had much knowledge wherewith to console them.

Now there was presently, in the Garden of Silence, which was the low-ermost of all the Underground Fields, the Ending of those seventeen hun-dred heroes, and of the Youths that they saved and slew. And the Garden was a great country, and an hundred miles every way, and the roof thereof was three great miles above, and shaped to a mighty dome; as it had been that the Builders and Makers thereof did remember in their spirits the vis-ible sky of this our present age.

And the making of that Country was all set out in a single History of seven thousand and seventy Volumes. And there were likewise seven thou-sand and seventy years spent to the making of that Country; so that there had unremembered generations lived and laboured and died, and seen not the end of their labour. And Love had shaped it and hallowed it; so that of all the wonders of the world, there has been none that shall ever come anigh to that Country of Silence—an hundred miles every way of Silence to the Dead.

And there were in that roof seven moons set in a mighty circle, and lit by the Earth-Current; and the circle was sixty miles across, so that all that Country of Quiet was visible; yet to no great glare, but a sweet and holy light; so that I did always feel in my heart that a man might weep there, and be unashamed.

And in the midst of that silent Country, there was a great hill, and upon the hill a vast Dome. And the Dome was full of a Light that might be seen in all that Country, which was the Garden of Silence. And beneath the Dome was the "Crack," and within it the glory of the Earth-Current, from which all had life and light and safety. And in the Dome, at the North, there was a gateway; and a narrow road went upward to the gateway; and the Road was named The Last Road; and the Gateway was named by no name, but known to all as The Gateway.

And there were in that mighty Country, long roadways, and hidden methods to help travel; and constant temples of rest along the miles; and groves; and the charm of water, falling. And everywhere the Statues of Memory, and the Tablets of Memory; and the whole of that Great Under-ground Country full of an echo of Eternity and of Memory and Love and

Greatness; so that to walk alone in that Land was to grow back to the wonder and mystery of Childhood; and presently to go upwards again to the Cities of the Mighty Pyramid, purified and sweetened of soul and mind.

And in my boyhood, I have wandered oft a week of days in that Country of Silence, and had my food with me, and slept quietly amid the memories; and gone on again, wrapped about with the quiet of the Everlasting. And the man-soul within would be drawn mightily to those places where the Great Ones of the past Eternity of the World had their Memory named; but there was that within me which ever drew me, in the ending, to the Hills of the Babes; those little hills where might be heard amid the lonesomeness of an utter quiet, a strange and wondrous echo, as of a little child calling over the hills. But how this was I know not, save by the sweet cunning of some dead Maker in the forgotten years.

And here, mayhaps by reason of this Voice of Pathos, were to be found the countless Tokens of Memory to all the babes of the Mighty Pyramid, through a thousand ages. And, odd whiles, would I come upon some Mother, sitting there lonely, or mayhaps companied by others. And by this little telling shall you know somewhat of the quietness and the wonder and the holiness of that great Country hallowed to all Memory and to Eternity and to our Dead.

And it was here, into the Country of Silence, that they brought down the Dead to their Burial. And there came down into the Country of Silence, maybe an Hundred Million, out of the Cities of the Pyramid, to be present, and to do Honour.

Now they that had charge of the Dead, did lay them upon the road which ran up unto The Gateway, even that same road which was named The Last Road. And the Road moved upwards slowly with the Dead; and the Dead went inward through The Gateway; first the poor Youths, and afterward they that had given up life that they might save them.

And as the Dead went upwards, there was a very great Silence over all the miles of the Country of Silence. But in a little while there came from afar off, a sound as of a wind wailing; and it came onwards out of the distance, and passed over the Hills of the Babes, which were a great way off.

And so came anigh to the place where I stood. Even as the blowing of a sorrowful wind did it come; and I knew that all the great multitudes did sing quietly; and the singing passed onwards, and left behind it an utter silence; even as the wind doth rustle the corn, and pass onwards, and all fall to a greater seeming quietness than before. And the Dead passed inward through The Gateway, into the great light and silence of the Dome; and came out no more.

And again from beyond the far Hills of the Babes there was that sound of the millions singing; and there rose up out of the earth beneath, the voices of the underground organs; and the noise of the sorrow passed over me, and went again into the distance, and left all hushed.

And lo! as there passed inward to the silence of the Dome the last of those dead Heroes, there came again the sound from beyond the Hills of the Babes; and as it came more nigh, I knew that it was the Song of Honour, loud and triumphant, and sung by countless multitudes. And the Voices of the Organs rose up into thunder from the deep earth. And there was a great Honour done to the glory of the Dead. And afterwards, once more a silence.

And to me, as I went about my duties, or peered forth through the Great Spy-Glass at the Youths upon the Road Where The Silent Ones Walk, there came at times a far faint thrilling of the aether; so that sometimes I was aware that there was the beating of the Master-Word in the night; but so strange and weak, that the Instruments had no wotting of it. And when this came, then would I call back through all the everlasting night to Naani, who was indeed Mirdath; and I would send the Master-Word with my brain-elements; and afterwards such comfort as I might.

Yet hard and bitter was the truth of my helplessness and weakness, and the utter terror and might of the Evil Forces and Monsters of the Night Land. So that I was like to have brake my heart with pondering.

And the silence would come again; and anon the weak thrilling of the Aether; but no more the far voice speaking in my soul.

## CHAPTER V

### *Into The Night Land*

Now, AFTER THAT DESTRUCTION which had come upon the Ten-thousand, and the fresh assurance that was upon us of the terror of the Night Land, it may be known that there could be no more thought to succour. Though, in truth, those Youths that went now upon the Road Where The Silent Ones Walk were far beyond our aid.

Yet might it be thought that we should have signalled to them, calling by the Home-Call, which was that great Voice which went forth from the Machine above the sealed base of the Mighty Pyramid. But this we might not do; for then we gave signal to the Monsters of that Land, that some were even now abroad from the Pyramid; yet we could no more than hope that the Evil Forces had no wotting of them; for, in verity, none might ever know the knowledge or the Ignorance which those Powers did possess.

Yet, it must be kept to the mind that we knew even then there was an Influence abroad in the Land, strange and quiet; so that the Instruments did not more than make record of it. And as I have surely set down ere now, we had belief that it did come from that House of Silence, afar in the Night Land, upon that low hill to the North of the Great Road. And many among the Monstruwacans feared that it was directed upon the Youths; but of this there could be no surety; and we could but wait and watch.

Now, about this time those poor Youths did draw nigh to that part of the Road Where The Silent Ones Walk, where it turned more swiftly to the North; and they to be now at no mighty distance from that grim and horrid House.

And presently we knew that the Influence had a greater Power in the Land; and I had an assuredness that it came from the House; yet no certain proof was this. But I set out my feelings to the Master Monstruwacan; and he had trust in them and in my power; moreover, he also had belief within himself that some secret Power came out from the House of Silence.

And some talk there was at times that we send the Home-Call into the

night, to give warning to the Youths of our knowledge and our fear; and to entreat them to make a safe endeavour to return swiftly. Yet was this an error; and refused by the Master Monstruwacan; for it was not meet that we put the souls of those Youths in peril, until such time as we had certainty that they should be lost if we did not bestir ourselves. For, indeed, this Home-Call was as a mighty Voice, calling over the world, and did have so exceeding a noise, that it had immediately told all that Land how that some were yet abroad from the Great Redoubt. And here will I set down how that the Home-Call had no use in those ages; but had been a Call in the olden time when yet the great flying-ships went abroad over the world.

And there passed now a day and a night; and in all that time there ceased not great multitudes to peer forth into the Night Land at the Youths. For it was known concerning the Influence, and all felt that the Youths did draw nigh very speedy to their fate; and much talk there was; and many things said, and much foolish speech, and kind intent; but no courage to go forth to make further attempt to rescue; which, in truth, calls not for great astonishment, as I have surely writ or oft thought.

And in this place let me set down that the Land was, as it might be said, waked, and unquiet, and a sense of things passing in the night, and of horrid watchfulness; and there were, at this time and at that, low roars that went across the Land. And if I have not told the same before this time, it must be set to count against me and my telling; for, indeed, I should have writ it down before this place. Yet is the difficulty of my task great; and all must bear with me, and entreat for me that I have courage, so that I may come at last to strength and wisdom to tell all that I did see.

Now, in the space of this day and night, it was known that the Youths had not slept, neither had they eaten, save once, as they who had the watch through the Great Spy-Glass did affirm. But they to hasten alway at a woeful speed towards the North, along that Great Dismal Road, so that presently they must cease, or slay themselves with their endeavor.

And all this did give surety to our fears that they were under a spell from that horrid House afar in the Land; and we had an assurance that this thing was. For, presently, there came a Monstruwacan to the Master

Monstruwacan to report that there had come sudden a mighty Influence into the Land; and in the same moment, as it might be, I spied through the Great Spy-Glass, and did see those Youths break swiftly from the Road Where The Silent Ones Walk, and begin to run very swift that they might come quickly to the House of Silence.

Then did the Master Monstruwacan hesitate not; but did send the Home-Call across the world, aye, even to those poor doomed ones that hastened, unknowing, to the terror which did compel them. And immediately upon the sound, the Master did send a message to the natural eye, in set language, and made warning that they suffered themselves to be drawn to their destruction by a Force that came from within the House of Silence.

And he besought them to put forth the strength of their spirits, and do battle for their souls; and if they could in no wise compass a victory over *that which drew them onwards*, to slay themselves quickly, ere they went into that House to the horror of utter destruction.

And in all the Pyramid was there a great silence; for the bellowing of the Home-Call bred a quietness, because of that which it did portend; and it was swiftly known by the millions that the Master Monstruwacan did plead for the souls of the Youths; and there went forth, unknowingly, a counter-force from the Mighty Pyramid, by reason of the prayers and soul-wishings of the countless millions.

And the counter-force was plain to my inward hearing, and beat all the aether of the world into a surge of supplication; so that it stunned my spirit with the great power of it. And it seemed to me, as it were, that there was a vast spiritual-noise in all the night; and I spied tremblingly through the Great Spy-Glass, and lo! the Youths did cease from their swift running, and were come together in a crowd, and had a seeming to be confused; as might some who have waked suddenly from sleep, to find that they walked in their sleep, and had come to a strange place.

Then came there a great roar from all the millions that spied from the embrasures—from nigh five hundred thousand embrasures they did look, and I count not the great View-Tables. And the shouting rose up like to the roaring of a mighty wind of triumph, yet was it over-early to

sound for victory. For the counter-force which came from the intensity of so many wills blent to one intent, was brake, and the Evil Force which came forth out of the House did draw the Youths again; so that they heeded not their salvation; but turned once again to their running.

And the Mighty Pyramid was full of a shaken silence, and immediately of lamentation and sorrow and horror at this thing. But in that moment there did happen a fresh wonder; for there grew suddenly before those poor Youths, billows of mist—as it had been of pure white fire, shining very chill; yet giving no light upon them.

And the mist of cold fire stayed their way, so that we had knowledge that there fought for the souls of them, one of those sweet Powers of Goodness, which we had belief did strive to ward our spirits at all times from those Forces of Evil and Destruction. And all the millions saw the thing; but some with a great clearness, and many doubtful; yet were all advanced more in spiritual sight and hearing than the normal Peoples of this Age.

But of them all, none had the Night-Hearing, to know a soul having speech in the aether half across the world. Yet, as I have said, some there had been aforetime who were thus given the Hearing, even as was I.

And there came a Monstruwacan to the Master Monstruwacan to make report that the Influence had ceased to work upon the Instruments; and by this thing we knew that in verity the Force which proceeded out from the House of Silence was cut off from us, and from those Youths; and we had assurance that there fought a very mighty Power for the salvation of the souls of the Youths.

And all the Peoples were silent, save for an underbreath of wonder and talk; for all were utter stirred with hope and fear, perceiving that the Youths had some chance given unto them to return.

And whilst the Youths yet wavered in their minds, as I perceived with the Great Spy-Glass, and the knowledge of my soul, and of my natural wit, lo! the Master Monstruwacan sent once more the great Voice of the Home-Call abroad into the Land; and immediately besought those Youths for the sake of their souls and the love which their Mothers had for them, to come swiftly Homewards, whilst they had yet this great Power to shield them,

and allow them sweet sanity.

And I thought that some did look towards the Pyramid, as that they answered to the mighty Voice of the Home-Call, and did read the message which the Master Monstruwacan made to them. But in a moment they faced about, seeming to have a good obedience to one who did always lead; and of whom I had inquired, and found to be one named Aschoff, who was a great athlete of the Nine-Hundredth-City. And this same Aschoff, out of the boldness and bravery of his heart, did make, unwitting, to destroy the souls of them all; for he went forward and leapt into the billows of the bright shining fire that made a Barrier in the way of their Destruction.

And immediately the fire ceased from its shining, and gave way and sank and grew to a nothingness; and Aschoff of the Nine-Hundredth-City began again to run towards the House of Silence; and all they that were with him, did follow faithfully, and ceased not to run.

And they came presently to the low Hill whereon was that horrid House; and they went up swiftly—and they were two hundred and fifty, and wholesome of heart, and innocent; save for a natural waywardness of spirit.

And they came to the great open doorway that "hath been open since the Beginning," and through which the cold steadfast light and the inscrutable silence of Evil "hath made for ever a silence that may be felt in all the Land." And the great, uncased windows gave out the silence and the light—aye, the utter silence of an unholy desolation.

And Aschoff ran in through the great doorway of silence, and they that followed. And they nevermore came out or were seen by any human.

And it must be known that the Mothers and the Fathers of those Youths looked out into the Night Land, and saw that thing which came to pass.

And all the people were silent; but some said presently that the Youths would come forth again; yet the people knew in their hearts that the young men had gone in to Destruction; for, in truth, there was that in the night which spoke horror to the souls of all, and a sudden utter quiet in all the Land.

But unto me (that had the Night-Hearing) there came a great Fear of that which might be whispered into my spirit, out of the Quietness of the

night—of the agony of those young men. Yet there came no sound, to the hearing of the soul; neither then nor in all the years that were to come; for, in verity, had those Youths passed into a Silence of which the heart cannot think.

And here will I tell how that the strange Quiet which did fill all the Land, seeming to brood within the night, was horrid beyond all the roarings which had passed over the darkness in the time that went before; so that it had given my spirit some rest and assurance to hear but the far-echoing, low thunder of the Great Laughter, or the whining which was used at times to sound in the night from the South-East, where were the Silver-fire Holes that opened before the Thing that Nods. Or the Baying of the Hounds, or the Roaring of the Giants, or any of those dreadful sounds that did often pass through the night. For they could not have offended me as did that time of silence; and so shall you judge how dreadful was that quiet, which did hold so much of horror.

And surely it will be known that none had thinkings now, even in idle speech, that any should have power to succour the Peoples of the Lesser Redoubt. Neither, as I have said, had any the knowledge of the place where it did stand.

And so was it made plain that those Peoples must suffer and come unhelped and alone to their end; which was a sad and dreadful thought to any. Yet had those within the Great Pyramid come already to much sorrow and calamity because that some had made attempt in this matter. And there had been for gain, only failure, and the sorrow of Mothers, and the loneliness of Wives, and of kin. And now this dread horror upon us, which concerned those lost Youths.

Now, as may be conceived, this *sure knowledge* that we might give no succour to the People of the Lesser Redoubt, weighed heavy upon my heart; for I had, maybe with foolishness, held vague hopes and wonders concerning our power to make expedition secretly into the Night, to discover that Lesser Pyramid, and rescue those poor thousands; and above all, as may be thought, had I the thought of that sweet moment in which I should step forward out of the night and all mystery and terror, and put

forth mine arms to Naani, saying: "I am That One." And knowing, in my soul, that she that had been mine in that bygone Eternity, should surely know me upon the instant; and call out swiftly, and come swiftly, and be again unto me in that age, even as she had been in this.

And to think upon it, and to know that this thing should never be; but that, even in that moment of thought, she that had been mine in these olden days of sweetness, might be even then suffering horror in the Power of some foul Monster, was like a kind of madness; so that nearly I could seize the Diskos, and run forth unprepared into the evil and terror of the Night Land, that I should make one attempt to come to that Place where she abode, or else to cast off my life in the attempt.

And oft did I call to Naani; and always I sent the Master-Word beating through the night, that she might have assurance that it was indeed I that did speak unto her spirit, and no foul thing or Monster, spelling evil and lies unto her.

And oft did I make to instruct her that never should she be tempted forth from the shelter of that Redoubt in which she did live, by any message out of the night; but always to await the Master-Word; and, moreover, to have a sure knowledge that none that was her Friend would ever seek to entice her into the night.

And this way and that way would I speak with Naani, sending my words silently with my brain-elements; yet was it doleful and weariful and dreadful always to have speech into the dark, and never to hear the answering beat of the Master-Word, and the sweet, faint voice whispering within my soul. Yet, once and again, would I have knowledge that the aether did thrill about me, weakly, and to mine inward hearing it would seem that the Master-Word did beat faintly in the night; and thereafter would my heart have a little comfort, in that I had assurance, of a kind, that the love-maid of my memory-dreams did still live.

And constant, I put forth my soul to hark; so that my health failed me, with the effort of my harking; and I would chide my being, that I had not a wiser control; and so make a fight to do sanely.

Yet, day by day, did my heart grow more weary and restless; for, indeed,

it did seem that life was but a very little matter, against so great a loss as my heart did feel to suffer.

And oft, at this time and that, did there come a Voice speaking plainly out of the night, and did purport to be the voice of Naani; but ever I did say the Master-Word unto the Voice, and the Voice had no power by which it could make the one answer. Yet I jeered not at the Voice, to show contempt of its failing to bewit me; but let the matter bide; and the Voice would be silent a time; and again would make a calling unto me; but never did I make speech with it (for therein lies the danger to the soul), but always did speak the Master-Word to its silencing; and thereafter would shut the thing from my memory, and think only upon sweet and holy matters, as it might be Truth and Courage, but more often of Naani, which was both sweet and holy to my spirit and heart and being.

And so it was as I have set down, there were Monsters without in the Night that did torment me; having, it may be, intent to lure me unto destruction; or indeed it doth chance that they had no hope but to plague me with malice.

And, as may be thought, all this considering of my trouble, and the giving of my strength unto Naani through the night of the world, that she might have comfort and help, did work upon me; so that I grew thin, plainly to the eye of those that loved me.

And the Master Monstruwacan, he that did love me, as I were his son, chid me gently, and had wise speech with me; so that I but loved him the more, yet without having gain of health; for my heart destroyed me, as it doth if love be held back and made always to weep.

And it may be thought strange that my Mother and my Father did not talk also with me; but I had neither Mother nor Father those many years; and this thing I should have set down early; so that none should waste thought pondering to no end. But the blame is to my telling.

Now, concerning my love-trouble, there did happen a certain thing which gave me to decide; for one night I waked from a sore troubled sleep, and it did seem that Naani did call my name, mine olden love name, and in a voice of utter anguish and with beseeching. And I sat up in the bed, and

sent the Master-Word into the Night, with my brain-elements; and presently all about me there was the solemn beat of the Master-Word, answering; but weak, and gone faint, that scarce I might hear it.

And I called again with my brain-elements unto Naani, that was Mirdath; and spoke to give her assurance, and to haste to tell unto me that which was so wrong and pitiful with her. And who shall be amazed that I was shaken with the eagerness of my spirit, in that it was so long since Naani had spoken clear within my soul; and now behold, her voice.

Yet, though I did call many a time unto the everlasting night, there came no more the voice of Naani, speaking strangely within my spirit; but only at times a weak thrilling of the aether about me.

And, at the last I grew maddened with the sorrow of this thing, and the sense and knowledge of harm about the maid; and I stood upright upon my feet, and I raised my hands, and gave word and honour unto Naani through all the blackness of the night, that I would no more abide within the Mighty Pyramid to my safety, whilst she, that had been mine Own through Eternity, came to horror and destruction by the Beasts and Evil Powers of that Dark World. And I gave the word with my brain-elements, and bade her to be of heart; for that until I died I would seek her. But out of the Darkness there came naught but the silence.

Then I clothed me swiftly, and went up quickly to the Tower of Observation, that I might speak instant with the Master Monstruwacan; for my heart burned in me to intention, and to be doing speedily that which I had set upon myself to do.

And I came to the Master Monstruwacan, and told all to him; and how that I did mean no more to suffer in quiet and to no end; but to make adventure into the Night Land, that I find Naani, or perchance find a swift peace from this my long troubling.

And here let me set down how that the Three Days of Preparation, which were Proper to those that willed to go forth into the Night Land, had for their chief aim the cleansing of the spirit; so that the Powers of Evil did have a less ableness to harm.

But also it was, as I have said, that none should go forth in ignorance

of the full dreadfulness of all that held the Night; for it was at the Preparation that there was made known certain horrors that were not told unto the young; and of horrid mutilations, and of abasements of the soul, that did shake the heart with fear, if but they were whispered into the hearing. And these things were not set down in any book that might be lightly come by; but were warded and safe locked by the Master of The Preparation, in the Room of Preparation.

And, indeed, when I did hear that which presently I was to hear, I had wonder in my heart that ever any went out into the Night Land; or that ever the Room of Preparation should have other than Students that meant not to go forth, but only to achieve some knowledge of that which hath been done, and mayhaps shall be once again.

Yet, in verity, is this but the way of the human heart; and hath always been, and will be so in all the years, for ever. For to adventure is the lust of Youth; and to leave Safety is the natural waywardness of the spirit; and who shall reprove or regret; for it were sorrowful that this Spirit of Man should cease. Yet must it not be thought that I do uphold fightings to the death or to mutilation, *between man and man*; but rather do sorrow upon this thought.

Now, when the morrow came, if thus I shall speak of that which was outwardly even as the night, though changing always within the Mighty Pyramid, I went unto the Room of Preparation; and the Door was closed upon me; and I underwent the Full Preparation; that I might have full power and aid to come to success through all the terror of the Night Land.

And three days and three nights did I abide within the Room of Preparation; and upon the fourth day was mine armour brought unto me; and the Master of the Preparation stood away from me, silent and with sorrow upon his face; but touching me not, neither coming anigh to aid me; nor having any speech with me; for none might crowd upon me, or cause me to answer. And, presently, was I clad with the grey armour; and below the armour a close-knit suit of special shaping and texture, to have the shape of the armour, and that I might not die by the cold of the Night Land. And I placed upon me a scrip of food and drink, that might keep the life within

me for a great time, by reason of its preparation; and this lay ready to me, with the armour, and was stitched about with the Mark of Honour; so that I knew loving women thus to speed me.

And when all was done and made ready, I took up the Diskos, and bowed in silence to the Master of the Preparation; and he went towards the door, and opened it; and signalled that the People stand back; so that I might go forth untouched. And the People stood back; for many had crowded to the door of the Room of Preparation, so that I knew how that my story must be to the heart of all, in all the Cities of the Great Redoubt; for to come unbidden anigh that Door was against the Lesser Law, and that any erred in this matter, betokened much.

And I went out through the Door; and there was a mighty lane of people unto the Great Lift. And about the Great Lift, as I went downwards, did the countless millions stand; and all in a great silence; but having dear sympathy in their souls; yet loyal unto my safety, in that none in all the Mighty Pyramid did make speech unto me, or call out aught. And as I went downward through the miles, lo! all the aether of the world seemed to be surged with the silent prayers and speedings of those quiet multitudes.

And I came at last unto the Great Gate; and behold the dear Master Monstruwacan did stand in full armour, and with the Diskos, to do me honour, with the Full Watch, as I went forth. And I looked at him, quietly, and he looked unto me, and I bent my head to show respect; and he made silent salute with the Diskos; and afterwards I went onwards towards the Great Gateway.

And they made dim the lights in the Great Causeway, that there should no glare go forth into the Land, when the Gate was opened; and behold, they opened not the lesser gate within the greater, for me; but did honour my journey, in that they swung wide the Great Gate itself, through which a monstrous army might pass. And there was an utter silence all about the Gate; and in the hushed light the two thousand that made the Full Watch, held up each the Diskos, silently, to make salute; and humbly, I held up the Diskos reversed, and went forward into the Dark.

# CHAPTER VI
### *The Way That I Did Go*

Now I WENT FORWARD for a space, and took heed not to look backwards; but to be strong of heart and spirit; for that which did lie before me had need of all my manhood and courage of soul, that I come to the succour of that Maid afar in the darkness of the World, or meet my death proper, as it might need to be.

And thus did I go forward steadfastly, and conscious in all my being of the emotions of that parting from my mighty Home, and of the tenderness and wiseness that did underlie so much curbed rule and guidance.

And my heart was warm towards the Master Monstruwacan for that great honour, that he should come downward in armour to make one with the Full Watch, that he might uphold me to a lofty spirit at the moment of my going.

And all that time as I went forward, was the aether of the night about me, in tumult with the thoughts and blind wishings of the great millions I had but now left to my back.

And, presently, as I steadied somewhat upon my emotions, I was conscious of the exceeding coldness of the night air, and of the different taste of it upon my lungs and in the mouth; and it had, as it were, a wondrous keen sharping upon my palate, and did fill the lips more in the breathing; so that it may be supposed it had more body within it than that air which did fill the plateau of the Thousandth City where was my home; for the air of every City was of difference, and the greater between one that was afar up and another nigh to the earth, as may be thought; so that many Peoples did migrate unto that level which gave them best healthfulness; but under rule, and with a guidance of quantities. And not all that were lacking of health; for, some are every contrary.

And here let me set down that, within the deeps of the Fields, there was air utter varied and wonderful, that might charm one here and likewise sorrow another that were happier elsewhere; so that all might have

suiting, did they but wander, and have Reason to companion them.

And thus did I go forward, full of new thoughts and olden memories, and fresh-breaking wonders; neither forgetting something of doubts and fears more than a little. And again was it most cunning strange to be out there in the Night Land—though not yet afar—where often had my fancies and imaginings led me; yet until that time never had I touched foot, in all that life, upon the outward earth. And this must be a wondrous quaint seeming thought to those of this present day.

And so came I, at last, nigh to the Circle that did go about the Redoubt; and presently I was come to it; and something astonished was I that it had no great bigness; for I had looked for this by *reasoning*; having always a mind to picture things as they might be truly, and hence coming sometimes to the wonder of a great truth; but odd whiles to errors that others had not made. And now, lo! I did find it but a small, clear tube that had not two inches of thickness; yet sent out a very bright and strong light, so that it seemed greater to the eye, did one but behold from a distance.

And this is but a little thing to set to the telling; yet may it give something of the newness of all; and, moreover, shall you have memory with me in this place, how that oft had I seen Things and Beast-Monsters peer over that same little tube of light, their faces coming forward out of the night.

And this had I seen as child and man; for as children, we did use to keep oft a watch by hours upon an holiday-time, through the great glasses of the embrasures. And we did always hope each to be that one that should first discover a monster looking inwards upon the Mighty Pyramid, across the shining of the Circle. And these to come oft; yet presently to slink away into the night; having, in verity, no liking for that light.

And pride had we taken of ourselves to perceive those monsters which had most of ugliness and horror to commend them; for, thereby did we stand to have won the game of watching, until such time as a more fearsome Brute be discovered. And so went the play; yet with ever, it doth seem to me now, something of a half-known shudder to the heart, and a child's rejoicing unknowingly in that safety which had power to make light the seeming of such matters.

And this, also, is but a small matter; yet doth it bear upon the inwardness of my feelings; for the memories of all my youth and of the many Beasts that I had seen to peer across the Light, did come upwards in my mind in that moment; so that I did give back a little, unthinking of what I did; but having upon me the sudden imagining of that which might come out of the Dark, beyond.

And I to stand a little moment, and presently had grown free in my heart to have courage of farewell; and so did turn me at last to the viewing of that wondrous Home of the Last Millions of this World. And the sight was an astonishment and an uplifting, that indeed there was so mighty a thing in all the earth.

And well might be that there were Monsters and Forces gathered together about that Hill of Life, out of all the Darkness of the World; for the thing was as a Mighty Mountain that went up measureless into the night; and spread out upon the earth to the right and to the left of me, so that it did seem to hold all the world with its might.

And in the nearer slope were there three hundred thousand great embrasures, as well I did know; there being in all the four sides of the Redoubt, twelve hundred thousand embrasures, as was set out in the books of the schools, and upon the cover of Atlas-books as they still quaintly to be called, and many another place, as might be supposed.

And half a mile upward was the lowest tier of those great window-places, and above that, countless other tiers. And a great light came out from them into the darkness; so that I looked up into the night many miles, and yet did see them in shining rows; and did make separate each embrasure from its fellow for a great way. But there grew yet more, above in the mighty distance, so that they were lost in the upward space of the night, and did seem to me presently but as a constant, glimmering fire, that did shape a shining Peak into the blackness of the heavens, dwindling into the utmost height. And thus was that Everlasting Monument.

Then did it come to me that those little things, which I did see to cluster against the embrasures, were in truth the countless millions of the Mighty Redoubt; and this I could make out with some plainness in those

lower embrasures, which were the more near to me than they above; for the Peoples were set against the light within, yet were as small things like unto insects, in that distance, and within so Huge a Bulk.

And I knew that they looked out upon me, and did watch through their spy-glasses. And I sent my gaze upwards again along that great Slope of grey metal, aye! upward again to where it strode glimmering into the Blackness, and so at last to the little star that did crown that Wonder of the World in the eternal night. And, for a little, I did stare towards that far light; for it came from within that Tower of Observation, where so lately I had spended my life; and I had knowledge within my heart that the dear Master Monstruwacan did bend the Great Spy-Glass upon me, through which so oft had I spied. And I raised the Diskos unto him, in salutation and farewell, though I saw him not at all through that vast space.

And my heart was very full; yet my soul but the stronger for it. And then, behold, I was aware of a murmur in the night, coming to me, dim and from afar off; and I saw the little shapes of the Peoples in the lower embrasures, in constant movement; and I knew upon the instant that the Multitudes did take that salute unto themselves, and cried out and waved to me their farewells, or to come back—as may be.

And, indeed, I was but a lonesome person looking up at that great mountain of metal and Life. And I knew that I had danger to realise my plight; and I stayed no more; but did raise the Diskos, reversed, as was but meet from one young man unto all the Millions.

And I looked swiftly upward through those eight great miles of night, unto that Final Light which did shine in the black heavens; so that my friend should know that I thought of him that was beyond my sight, in that last moment. And it may be that the invisible millions that were far up in the night, in the Upper Cities, did take that also to be a meaning of farewell to themselves; for there came down out of the monstrous height, a far, faint murmur of sound, as of a vague wind up in the night.

Then did I lower the Diskos, and turn me about. And I breasted strangely against the Air Clog, and stept forward across the Circle, into the lonesomeness of the Night Land. And I looked no more behind; for that

which was my Home did weaken my heart somewhat, to behold; so that I made determination that I look not again to my back, for a great while.

Yet, about me as I went, there was constant surging in the aether of the world; and it did tell unto me how that those, my people and kin, had continual mind of me, both in prayer and wishings, and in a perpetual watching. And the same gave to me a feeling as of being something companied; yet, in a time, it came to me that this disturbance of the aether should tell to some Evil Force how that I was there abroad in the Land. But how to stop this thing, who should have power? For, of truth, had I been among them to make a full explaining of the danger, they had been yet powerless to cease; for but to have such great multitudes a-think upon one matter, was to set a disturbance about, as should be most clear to all.

Now, at the beginning, I did walk outwards into the Night Land, somewhat blindly, and without sure direction; being intent only to put a good space to my back, that I might cure somewhat the ache which did weaken my heart at the first.

But, in awhile, I ceased somewhat from my overswiftness, and did put thought to my going. And I came quickly to reason that I should try a new way through the Land; for it might be that there was an over-watchfulness in that part which had been trod by the Youths.

And I began therewith to set this thought to the practice; and went not direct towards the North; but to the North and West; and so in the end to mean to circle around to the back of the North-West Watcher, and thence to the North of the Plain Of Blue Fire; and afterwards, as might be, have a true and straightway to the North; and by this planning come a long way clear of that House of Silence, which did put more fear upon me than all else that was horrid in the Land.

Yet, as all will see, this made to me a greater journey; though, in verity, it were better to go slowly and win to success, than to make a greater haste towards Destruction; which was, indeed, surely to be mine end, did I not go warily.

Now it may be thought upon with wonder, that I did go so assuredly to the North; but I went thiswise, part by an inward Knowing, and part

come upon by much latter studying, within the Pyramid, of olden books; and by reasoning upon all things that I did observe, that had seemings of verity in them.

And because of this constant searching upon one matter, I had come, but a while back, upon a little book of metal, very strange and ancient, that had lain forgot in a hid place in the Great Library through ten hundred thousand years, maybe, or less or more, for all that I had knowing.

And much that was writ in the book was common knowledge, and set mostly to the count of fairy-tales and suchlike, even as we of this our age take not over-surely any belief in Myths of olden times. Yet had I always much liking for such matters, perceiving behind that outer shell which did win always so much unbelief, the kernel of ancient truths and happenings.

And thus was it, concerning this little book which I had made discovery of; for it told again, that which oft I had heard (even as we in this age, read of the Deluge) how that once, in a time monstrous far back from that, but utter future to this age of ours, the world did brake upwards in a vast earth-quaking, that did rend the world for a thousand miles.

And there came a mighty chasm, so deep that none might see the bottom thereof; and there rushed therein an ocean, and the earth did burst afresh with a sound that did shake all the cities of the world; and a great mist lay upon the earth for many days, and there was a mighty rain.

And, indeed, this was just so set in certain Histories of the Ancient World. Also, there was made reference to it, within some olden Records. Yet nowise to be taken with a serious mind, to the seeming of the peoples of the Mighty Pyramid; but only as a quaint study for the Students, and to be set out in little tales that did entertain the nurseries; or, as it might be, wise men and the general.

Yet, there was this, about that small and peculiar book, that it did speak of many of these things, as it were that it did quote from the pens of those that did have actual witness; and set all out with a strange gravity, that did cause one to consider it as meant to be indeed the tellings of Truth, and to seem thiswise to have great difference from all that I had read before concerning those matters.

And there was, further, a part in the ending of the book, that did seem to be writ of a time that came afterwards, maybe an hundred thousand, and maybe a million years; but who shall say.

And therein it did tell of an huge and mighty Valley that did come out of the West, towards the South-East, and made turning thence Northwards, and was a thousand miles both ways. And the sides thereof were an hundred miles deep, and the Sun did stand in the Western end, and made a red gloom for a thousand miles. And in the bottom there were great seas; and beasts strange and awesome, and very plentiful.

Now this, as may be seen, was as the talk of Romance; yet did I turn my wits to their natural end, and made thus plain of it. For, in truth, I to have something of belief, and it to seem to me that in a bygone Eternity, when the world was yet light, as in my heart I knew to have been indeed a thing of verity, there was a great and wondrous earthquake.

And the earthquake did burst the world up, along a certain great curve where it had weakness; and there fell into the yawning furnace of the world, one of the great oceans; and immediately made of itself steam, and so brake upwards again, and tore the earth mightily in its swift uprising.

And thereafter there was a mist and confusion and rain upon the world. And, indeed, all very seemly put; and not to be taken as a light tale.

Then, in that ending of the book, there was one that did write, having lived in a vast later age, when the Sun had come anigh to his dying, and the upward earth was grown quiet and cold and not good to live upon. And in that time the Mighty Chasm had been calmed by the weight of an Eternity, so that it was now a most deep and wondrous Valley, that did hold Seas and great Hills and Mountains; and in it were great forests of kinds, and Lands that were good and healthful; and Places given over to Fire, and to Steamings, and Sulphur Clouds; so that they held Poisons that had ill for Man.

And Great Beasts were there down in that far depth, that none might see ever, save by a strong spy-glass. And such there were in the Early World, and had now been bred in the Ending by those inward forces of Nature which did make the Valley a place of Good Warmth; so that there was, as it were, once more the Primal World born to give new birth unto such olden

Monsters, and to others, new and Peculiar to that Age and Circumstance.

And all this, indeed, did the book give also; but constrained and difficult to take clearly to the heart, and not like to the wise plain speech of the early tellings; so that I must even set it out here in mine own speech.

And it did seem to me, by my reading, that Man had come at one time to a great softness of Heart and Spirit through many ages of over-ease. But that the World did come to coldness and unfriendliness, by reason of the Sun's slow ceasing.

And there was presently, in naturalness, a Race upon the earth that were hardy, and made to fight for their lives; and did perceive that the Mighty Valley that cut the World in twain, was a place of Warmth and Life; and so did make to adventure their bodies down that wondrous Height; and were many Ages coming safe to the Bottom; but did find safe places in the downward way where they built them Houses, and made to live, and begot them children; and these grew up to that life of constant and great climbings, and of hard workings upon The Road, which was the One Intent of that People; so that the book did speak of them always as The Road Makers.

And thus did they make downwards through the long years and the ages; and many generations did live and die, and saw not the reaching of the Road down into that Great Vale that lay so monstrous deep in the World.

But in the end they did come there with the Road; and they were very Hardy; and they did fight with the Monsters and slay many; and they built them many Cities, through great years in the Mighty Valley, and did make the Road from City unto City along that Great Valley, even unto the Bight of the Valley. And they found here a constant darkness and Shadow; for that the Sun could not make a shining around that Great Corner. Yet, even here they ceased not to make the Road; but took it around, and a mighty way unto the North; passing it among strange Fires and Pits that burned from out of the earth.

But there was presently, such a power and horror of Monsters and Evil Things in that Valley of Shadow, that the Road Makers were made to go Backwards into the Red Light which did fill the Westward Valley, and

came from that low Sun.

And they went back unto their Cities; and lived there mayhaps an hundred thousand years; and grew wise and cunning in all matters; and their Wise People did make dealings and had experiment with those Forces which are Distasteful and Harmful unto Life; but they did this in Ignorance; for all that they had much wisdom; thinking only to Experiment, that they come to greater knowings. But they did open a way for those Forces; and much harm and Pity did come thereby. And then had all People to have Regret; yet too late.

Now, presently, when an hundred thousand years had gone, or it may be a greater space; there came slowly the utter twilight of the world, as the sun to die the more; so that presently it gave but an utter gloomy light. And there grew upon many of the Peoples of the Cities of the Valley, a strangeness and a wildness; so that strange things were done, that had been shameful to all in the Light. And there were wanderings, and consortings with strange outward beings, and presently, many Cities were attacked by monsters that did come from the West; and there was a Pandemonium.

Then was an Age of Sorrows and Fightings, and Hardenings of the Spirit and of the Heart, for all that were of good Fibre; and this did breed a Determined Generation; and there grew up into the World a Leader; and he took all the sound Millions; and did make a mighty Battle upon all Foulness and upon all that did harm and trouble them; and they drove their Enemies down the Valley, and up the Valley, and did utterly scatter and put them to flight.

Then did that Man call all his Peoples together; and did make it plain how that the Darkness grew upon the World, and that the Foul and dreadful Powers abroad, were like to be more Horrid when a greater Gloom came.

And he put to them that they Build a Mighty Refuge; and the Peoples did acclaim; and lo! there was built, presently, a Great House. But the Great House was not Proper; and that Man did take all the Peoples to Wander; and they came to the Bight; and *there* was built at last that Great and Mighty Pyramid.

Now this is the sense and telling of that book; and but late had I read

it; and talked somewhat of it with my dear friend, the Master Monstruwacan; but not overmuch; for I had taken so sudden a mind to GO, that all else had dropped from about me. Yet, to us it did seem clear that there was no life in all the invisible upper world; and that, surely, that Great Road whereon the Silent Ones did walk, must be that same Road which the hardy Peoples of that age did make.

And it did seem wise to the Master Monstruwacan, and unto me, that if any should find the Lesser Redoubt, they must surely do so somewhere within the mighty Valley; but whether The Road that led into the West, where was the Place of the Ab-humans, should bring me to it, I had no knowing; nor whether it might lie on the Northward way. And I, maybe, to wander a thousand miles wrong; if, in truth, I were not into some dreadful trouble before.

And, indeed, no reason of value was there to give me hope that the Lesser Pyramid lay either to the West, or where the Road went Northward, beyond the House of Silence. Yet I did so feel it to be somewhere to the North, that I had made a determination to search that way for a great distance, the first; and if I could not come upon aught, then I should have sober thought that it did lie Westward. But in the Valley someways, I had feeling of assurance that it must be; for it was plain that the telling of the book was sound in its bottom sense; as might be seen; for how should any live in the utter bleak and deadly chill of the silent upper world that lay an hundred miles up in the night, hid and lost for ever.

And strange is it to think of those wondrous and mighty cliffs that girt us about, and yet were fast held from us in the dark; so that I had not known of them, save for the telling of that book; though, in truth, it had been always supposed that we lived in a great deep of the world; but, indeed, it was rather held in belief that we abode in the bed of some ancient sea, that did surely slope gradual away from us, and not go up abrupt and savage.

And here let me make so clear as I may that the general peoples had no clear thought upon any such matters; though there was something of it taught in the schools; yet rather this and that, of diverse conclusions, as it might be thinkings of the Teachers, after much study, and some ponderings.

For one man, having a lack of imagining, would scoff, and another, maybe, to take it very staidly, but some would build Fancy upon the tellings of the Records, and make foolish and fantastic that which had groundings in Truth; and thus is it ever. But to the most Peoples of the Pyramid, there was no deep conviction nor thought of any great hid World afar in the darkness. For they gave attention and belief only to that which lay to their view; nor could a great lot come to imagine that there had been ever any other Condition.

And to them, it did seem right and meet that there should be strange things, and fires from the earth, and an ever-abiding night, and monsters, and matters hid and tangled much in mystery.

And very content were the most of them; though some had in them the yeast of imaginings, or the pimples of fancy upon them, and to these there seemed many possibilities; though the first to read out to sanity; and the second, to expect and have speech towards much that was foolish or to no purpose.

And of these vague believings of the peoples, have I made hint before, and need not have much trouble to it now. Save that, with the children, as is ever the way, those olden tales had much believing; and the simplicity of the Wise did mate with the beliefs of the Young; and between them did lie the Truth.

And so did I make speed towards the North, having a strong surety in my heart and mind that there were but two ways to my search; for without of the Valley, afar up in the dead lonesomeness of the hidden world, was a cold that was shapen ready to Death, and a lacking, as I must believe, of the sweet, needful air that yet did lie in plenty in that deep place of the earth. So that, surely, the mighty Valley somewheres to hold that other Redoubt.

Yet, as I have said, I went not direct to my journey, but otherwise, for those sound reasons which I did set down a time back.

# CHAPTER VII
## *The Night Land*

Now, AS I WENT towards the North and West, I steered me warily for a great while, that I come safe of that Great Watcher of the North-West. And as I made forward, I put thought to all matters which must concern me; so far as I had imagining to see. And first I did consider the speed that I should keep; and found presently that I did well to be moderate; for that I had before me a great and mighty journey; and indeed, who might speak knowingly of the end thereof?

And another matter, I did arrange; for I would make the times of my goings forward, and the times of mine eatings and sleepings all to a wise and regular fashion; that, thereby, I might go a great way, with the less harm to my body; so that I should be strong when the need did come for my strength. And I made in the end that I should eat and drink, at every sixth hour, and at the eighteenth hour sleep me until the twenty-fourth.

And by this means did I eat thrice in that time, and have six hours of sleep. And this seemed very good to me, and I did strive always to manage thus in all my great journeying in the Night Land. Yet, as may be supposed, there were times oft and many when I must watch without ceasing, and leave my slumber unto the future; for the Land was full of grim and dreadful Perils.

And, as doth be human, I brake my rule straightway in the beginning; for I ceased not to walk for one-and-twenty hours, hiding and creeping, as the need did be in those places that were like to show me unto the Watcher; and when I did think upon food, it did sicken me; so that I would eat by and by, as I made it within my thoughts.

But when one-and-twenty hours had gone, I grew very weary and something faint; and was forced that I look about for some place where I might have rest. And, in a little while, I did see, away off, a small fire-hole, the like of which I had passed odd times even so early. And I made to come nigh to that part; for there would be warmth from the chill of the Night

Land, and mayhaps a place dry and convenient to my slumber.

And when I came anigh, I saw that it was a cheerful place, as it might be said, amid so much gloom; for the hole was but a few paces wide, and full of a dull, glowing fire, that did bubble somewhat, and throw off a small sulphur-smoke. And I sat me down, at no great way, and did place the Diskos on the rock to my hand.

And I moved not, awhile; but was aweary, so that I had not the courage to eat, neither to drink; but must turn me and look back to the Mighty Pyramid; and, in truth, though I had come a very good space, yet was I so anigh to it, that I was both cheered and put out of heart; for it did seem close upon me, by reason of its greatness, so that I, who had journeyed a hard and weariful way, was shaken with the greatness of the task that was upon me.

Yet was this but one side of my heart; for it was good to feel the nearness of my Mighty Home; and I knew that there did countless millions make watch upon me, as I sat; yet did I make no sign; for it is not meet to make a constant farewell; but to GO. Yet was it very strange to be thus near, and to show such behaviour as were proper to one afar from all humanity. But so it was that I ordered my ways; for it did seem proper to me; yet was I happy to know that the dear Master Monstruwacan must, time and oft, have spied upon me through the Great Spy-Glass; and mayhaps did watch me in that moment.

And it grew in me that I did act weakly to hold off from mine Vittles, and showed foolishness before my kind friend afar; and I did ope my scrip, and take therefrom three tablets, the which I chewed and did eat; for this was a strong food, treated that it had but small bulk. Yet were they not filling to the belly; and I made that I would drink well, that I might feel that something was therein.

And to this end, I shook from a strong and especial tube, a dust; and I caught the dust within a little cup; and the air did make an action upon that dust, as it were of chemistry; and the dust did boil and make a fizzing in the cup, and rose up and filled it with a liquid that was of simple water; yet very strange to see come that way; but ordinary after a time.

And in this way, as might be seen, had I such food and drink in but a little scrip, that might keep life within me for a great time. Yet was it a way of discomfort, and lacking to the mouth and to the belly; but a sufficient thing unto the need of the body, and good matter for a thankful heart, in that dark and hungry Land.

Now, when I had eaten, I did go over in their order, those things which I did carry; for there was, beside the Diskos and that scrip of food, a pouch that did contain matters various. And these, I did look into; and afterward did take out a small compass that I had been give by the Master Monstruwacan, so that I might find of its workings without the Great Redoubt; and, he had said unto me, that it might be that I should pass far off into the Night Land, and lose the Mighty Pyramid amid so great a Country and so plentiful a Darkness. Then, perchance, if that ancient principle did still lurk within the machine, though turned no more to the North, but unto the Pyramid, then should it guide my feet Homeward out of the Everlasting Night, and thus have once more that ancient use which, as I do know, is common unto this age.

And this was a very cunning thing to have with me, if but it held service to the Earth-Current, and a rare thing, which the Master Monstruwacan did make with his own hands and much skill and pains, from an olden one that had place within the Great Museum, and concerning which I have told somewhat, before this place.

And I set the thing upon the ground; but it had no certain way with it; but did spin and waver constantly, and this I made to consider, and remembered that I was yet above that part where, afar in the earth did spread the greatness of the Underground Fields; and I was, haply, but a little way off from the "Crack"; though a mighty way above.

And it pleasured me to wonder whether the dear Master Monstruwacan did behold how that I made test with the compass; for the light was good from the fire-hole; and the Great Spy-Glass had a great strength. Yet, had I no certainty; for, as I did know, from much watchings, there was no surety in the searching of the Land, by the Glass; for there was oft plainness where you did think surely none should see, and anon a dullness

where might be thought that the sight went gaily. And this may be plain to all; for the wavering of the lights from the strange fires was not to be accounted to rule; but made a light here, and a darkness there, and then did change about, oddly. Moreover, there were smokes and mists that did come upwards from the earth, in this place and in that; and had somewhiles a greatness; but oft were small, and did lurk low, and had no power but to confuse the sight.

And, presently, I did put by the compass in my pouch, and made to compose myself unto sleep. But here would I now set down how that, in the end, after I had gone many days' journeyings outward from the Mighty Pyramid, I did indeed find it to draw the Northward part of the needle unto it; and this was a comfort and a pleasure to my spirit; moreover, if ever I did get back, as I did think, it would be a matter for great interest unto the Master Monstruwacan; yet, in verity, were there other matters that should hold him more; for he was right human, as all should know.

And, moreover, concerning this same compass, I did find a fresh thing; for, after a yet greater time, as I shall set out in a due place, if I do but remember, which doubt is ever my fear to fret me, I came a mighty way from the Redoubt, and, lo! fearing that I might indeed lose that, My Great Home, in the Darkness of the World, I did pull out that strange wonder of the needle, that I might have comfort by its homeward pointing. And I did discover a new power in the night; for the machine did point no more directwards unto the Great Redoubt; but was a point unto the Westwards; so that I had knowledge that some Great Power afar in the Darkness of the World did sway upon it; and I had a childlike wonder that this might be, in truth, that same Power of the North, of which the books, and my Memory-Dreams did tell. And, indeed, no doubt should there be upon this matter; yet who might not have doubt in that time, that they should perceive after an eternity, that ancient Northward Force swaying that small servant unto an olden obedience. And it was, as it were, a revealing unto me, how that to know within the brain is one matter; but to have knowledge within the heart is another; for I had always known concerning this Northward Force; but yet had not known with the true meaning of Knowledge.

And yet one other matter there was to cause doubt, at that moment of this new knowing; for it came to me that maybe the power of that Lesser Redoubt did begin to act upon the machine, even as the Earth-Current of the Great Pyramid did hold yet a strong drawing upon the needle; and were this so, then did I not surely begin to stand anigh unto my Journey's end; for that less power of the Lesser Redoubt could have no impudence to pull, save that I had come to a closeness with it.

Yet, in truth, as I do now have knowledge, it was the North that drew; and I do seem to make a great telling about this little matter; but how else shall I show to you mine inward mind, and the lack of knowledge and likewise the peculiar knowings that did go to the making of that time, and the Peoples thereof, which is but to say the same thing twice over.

And now, as I did say, I made to compose myself for sleep; and to this end, I took a cloak-matter which did cross my shoulder and hip, and wrapt it about me, and lay down there in the darkness of the Night, by that strange fire-hole.

And I lay the Diskos beside me, within the cloak; for it was, indeed, my companion and friend in bitter need; so that I had pleasure to feel the strange thing anigh to me. And as I did lie there, in those moments that do drowse the Soul, as it were that they do proceed as breath out of the mouth of Sleep, I had a half-knowing that the aether did surge about me; and I doubt not but that there had watched my every doing, many of the Millions, and had been humanly stirred, at my commending of my spirit unto sleep; and thus did shake the aether of the world about me, with their unity of sympathy.

And, mayhaps, I had some little knowing of this thing, as I did pass, drowsy, into slumber; and it is surely like that I slept the better for it. Moreover, I was wondrous tired and worn, and thus did sleep very strong and heavy; yet I mind me that my last dim thinkings were upon that sweet maid I did go to find. And in slumber did I have speech with her in dreams, and a strange happiness about me, and all seeming to be touched by fairy-light, and freed from the sorrow of life.

And it was from a sweet and lovely sleeping, such as this, that I was

waked suddenly by a great and mighty sound; and I came instant to a possessing of my senses; and I knew that the mighty Voice of the Home-Call did go howling across the Night. And, swift and silent, I slid the cloak from about me, and took the haft of that wondrous Diskos into mine hand.

And I did look towards the Pyramid, quickly, for a message; for I had a sure knowledge that there had a great Need arisen, and that some Terror came towards me out of the Dark; else they had never waked all the Night Land to a knowing that an human was abroad out of the Mighty Refuge.

And even as I did peer towards the Great Redoubt, I could not abide to keep my gaze entire that way; but did take a large and fearful look all about me; yet could make to see nothing; and so did stare, eager and anxious, afar into the upper blackness of the Night, where did shine that Final Light of the Tower of Observation; and the same while crouched, and holding the Diskos, and making to glance across my shoulders, and to watch for the message, and all in the same moment.

And then, afar upwards in the prodigious height, I did see the great, and bright and quick darting flashes of a strange green fire, and did know that they spelled to me in the Set-Speech a swift warning that a grey monster, that was a Great Grey Man, had made scent of me in the dark, and was even in that moment of time, crawling towards me through the low moss-bushes that lay off beyond the fire-hole to my back. And the message was sharp; and bade me to leap into the bushes unto my left; and to hide there; so that I might chance to take the thing to an advantage.

And, as may be thought, they had scarce flashed the tale unto me; but I was gone in among the shadows of a clump of the moss-bush that did grow anigh; and I sweat with a strange terror, and a cold and excited shaking of the heart; yet was my spirit set strong to conquer.

And lo! as I did crouch there, hidden, I saw something come very quiet out of the bushes that did grow beyond the fire-hole; and it was great, and crept, and was noways coloured but by greyness in all its parts. And the glare from the fire-hole did seem to trouble it; so that it looked, laying its head to the ground, and spying along the earth, in a strange and Brutish fashion; that it might oversee the glare of the fire-hole. Yet, I doubt that

it saw beyond the fire with plainness; for, in a moment, it crept swift in among the bushes again, and came out towards the edge of the fire-hole in another place; and this it did thrice unto my left, and thrice unto my right; and every time did lay its head to the earth, and spy along; and did hunch its shoulders, and thrust forward the jaw horridly and turn the neck, as a very nasty beast might go, wanton.

Now, as you may think, this manner of the Beast-Man did shake my courage mightily; for I did think each time that it did go inward among the moss-bushes, that it had made discovery of me, and would make to take me in the back, from out of the dark of the bushes; and this was an uncomfortable thing to consider, as others might think also, had any been there in the bush with me. And then, in truth, did that same swift sense of mine Hearing, prove helpful to my saving; for, behold, the thing did go back into the moss-bushes, after that last coming out; and did seem to make as it had made a failing to discover me, and had no further intent, save to return unto the Night; and I had this thought truly in mine heart, and for maybe a minute; and then, lo! within my soul a voice did speak plain, and did warn me that the thing did make a great compass among the moss-bushes about the fire-hole, having made discovery of me; and it did go warily to take me in the back, from the other side.

Now, when I heard this voice speak within my spirit, I had knowledge that the dear Master Monstruwacan made watch from the Tower of Observation, and did send the speech with his brain-elements, having in mind that I had the Night-Hearing. And I trusted the speech; for in the same moment of time there did beat all about me in the Night the solemn throb of the Master-Word, as that it had been added with speed, to give instant assurance. And I leapt quick from that clump of the moss-bush, unto another, and crouched, and made a watch all about me; and kept the ears of my spirit open, knowing that the Master Monstruwacan did also watch all, for me.

And, suddenly, I saw a little moving of a bush that grew to the back of those bushes in which I had been hid; and there came out of the bush that moved, a great grey hand, and moved the moss of the clump where I had

been, as it were that something peered out of the moving bush. And there followed the great grey head of the Grey Man, and the head went into the clump of the moss-bush where I had been.

And I knew that I must strike now; and I leapt, and smote with the Diskos; and the thing fell upon its side, and the great grey legs came out of the hither bushes, and twitched and drew upwards; but the head remained in the bush where I had been hid. And I stood away from the thing whilst it died; and in mine hand the Diskos did spin and send forth fire; as it were that it did live, and did know that it had slain a great and horrid monster.

And presently the Grey Man was dead; and I went away from those bushes, unto the far side of the fire-hole. And I stood with the Diskos held high and spinning and sending out fire, that they within the Mighty Pyramid might know that I had slain the Beast-Man; for it might be that it lay too much in the shadow for them to look upon.

But the Master Monstruwacan spoke not again to me; for, indeed, it was not meet to do so, except it might save me from a sure danger; for, as you may know from my past tellings, there were Powers of the Night Land that did hearken unto such matters; and it was like enough that there had been overmuch done, even thus, for my further safety. Yet the thing could not be helped.

And now that I was a little calmed, and eased from my fear, I could know that all that the aether of the night was disturbed by the gladness of the millions within the Great Redoubt; so that it was plain how great a multitude had given note unto the fight; and their hearts to beat in sweet sympathy and natural fear; so that I did feel companied and befriended; though, as it may be thought, something shaken yet about the heart. Now, in a little time, I did gather unto me my wits and had myself to order; and I looked to see how the hours did go, and I found that I had surely slumbered through ten hours. And I reproached myself; for, indeed, I had slept oversound by reason of my having lacked a regular way and time, as I had with a proper wisdom made to be my rule. And I resolved that I would obey the wit of my Reason in all the future time, and make to eat and rest in due season, as you will wot that I did before intend.

Then, with a self-reproachful heart, I went around the small fire-hole, and caught up my cloak and other matters. And I turned me towards the Mighty Pyramid, and did look once upwards along all the great slope, where it did go measureless into the far blackness of the Everlasting Night; and I made no salutation; for I had so resolved, as you will know; moreover, I desired not to call forth any unneedful disturbance of the aether of the world, which indeed must be, did I make to stir the emotions of the Millions.

And I turned me then away, and went off into the night, going swift and cautious, and bearing the Diskos cunningly and almost, as it were, with a love for that strange and wondrous weapon that had so befriended me, and slain the foul Grey Man with one stroke. And I had feeling that it did know me, and had a comradeship for me; and I doubt none will understand this; save, it might be, they of the olden days that did carry one strong sword always. Yet was the Diskos more than the sword; for it did in truth seem to live with the fire and the flame of the Earth-Current that did beat within it.

And it was well acknowledged within the Great Redoubt, that none might touch the Diskos of another; for that the thing went crustily, as it might be said, in the hands of a stranger; and if any made foolishness of this knowledge, and did persist much to such an handling, or making to use, the same would presently act clumsy with the weapon, and come to an hurt; and this was a sure thing, and had been known maybe an hundred thousand years; or perchance a greater time.

And by this it doth seem wise to believe that there did grow always an affinity between the nature of the man—which doth, as ever, include the woman—and the Diskos that he did use in his Practice; and because of this known thing, and that the place would elsewise be lumbered with olden weapons of those that did die, it was a Law and Usage that there was placed with the Dead, the Diskos of the Dead, there upon The Last Road in the Country Of Silence, and was thus made to give back unto the Earth-Current, the power that did lie in it.

And this doth seem to a careless thinker, as it were that I told once again those olden customs of the Ancient Folk; but this is otherwise, and

had a sound reason to it; yet, if you do so believe, I doubt not but that a right human sentiment was something at the bottom, which is proper; for it is meet that Love should mate with Wisdom to mother Comfort in our sorrows; and it is a warm thing to do aught for our dead; and none may say nay to this.

Now, as I did go onwards into the Night Land, looking ever to this shadow and to that, it may be conceived how my heart would stir with swift fear, at this and that; and that my body would oft quiver to leap aside; and as swift discover that naught assailed.

And so did I go forward, and always with imaginings and wonders concerning what manner of uncouth Being or Brute might come out of the darknesses all about. Yet, in all that time, there was a certain proudness of the heart, that I did come safe out of the power of the Grey Man, and did surely slay him. But, truly, it were well that the praise be considered, and not overmuch given unto me; for I had died as I slept, but that they of the Great Redoubt, had made a watch over me, and waked me unto my saving.

Now, presently, as I walked, I grew something faint, and had knowledge that I did foolishly; for, indeed, I should have eat after my fight; yet may I be forgiven for this forgetting, in that I had been much shaked and put about.

And I sat me down in a little clear place among the bushes, and did eat three of the tablets, and did once more shake forth the dust that did turn in the air to a natural water by a proper and natural chemistry of these matters. And after I had eat, I sat a little while, and did think, and did look upwards at the great slope of the Pyramid in the night; and all the time did I listen with mine ears and with my spirit; and kept the Diskos across my knees, and looked this way and that, very frequent; but nothing came anigh.

And so I rose presently, and went onwards, and walked for six hours towards the North and the West. And I made much to the West, for a little, that I might come clear of the North-West Watcher. Yet, after a space, I made to do foolishly; for I changed my mind about, and kept something more towards the North, so that I should have a surer sight of that Monster.

And this was, in truth, a rash and naughty thing to consider; for if I were but seen, then should that grim Brute make a signal unto the Evil Powers, and I be met swiftly with destruction. But surely the heart is a strange and wayward thing, and given to quick fears, and immediately unto great and uncountable rashnesses. And so I did go forward unwisely to the Northward of a safe and proper going; and it may be that an influence was upon me, and drew me thatwards; but who shall say.

Now, a great time I walked, and made a halt upon every sixth hour, and did eat and drink, and look a little unto the monstrous towering of the Great Redoubt; and afterwards make strong mine heart, and go forward again. And always I did go warily, and chiefly among the low moss-bush; but sometimes out upon stony ground, and oft across places where sulphur did puff somewhat from the ground in a low smoke, very strong in the nostrils and not liked inwardly.

And as I made onwards, I looked always to my right and to my left, and anon to the rear; yet made a constant observation of the Mighty Watcher, that I did begin to draw nigh unto. And oft did I stoop to crawl, and my hands did bleed somewhat; but after I was troubled so, I put on the great gloves that made complete the grey armour, and so was shod proper to such journeying.

And, presently, when eighteen hours did have passed since that my sudden awakening to the peril of the Grey Man, I did search about for a place to slumber; for I would keep wisely unto my ruling, and go not over long lacking of sleep; and by this planning I should be the less like to sleep oversound, and so should set my spirit to listen whilst I did sleep; and by so much as my spirit should serve me with faith, should I have safety. And this thing is plain, and wants not more to the saying thereof.

And I came presently unto a sudden place where the land did go downwards brokenly, as that it had been burst a great while gone by the inward fires; and I looked downwards over the edge of that place, and went round about it, and did see presently a ledge upon the far side, that was difficult to come upon; yet a place of some little safety to any that might go down to it; for it was awkward to see, and did any monster seek to come at

me, I should have chance of warning; and might go downwards a greater way in time to my salvation.

And by this determination, I abode; and came down to that place with labour; but was cheerful of heart that I had found so sure a shelter. And I eat my three tablets, and drank the water that I did get from the powder. And so made to compose my body to sleep. Yet, at this time, a thought did come to me, and I made calculation afresh; and laughed somewhat at that my poor counting; for, indeed, I had thought to eat but thrice in the twenty and four hours; yet by my arranging, I was made, indeed, to eat four times, as you shall see immediately by a little thought. And this thing came more strong upon my spirit than any might think; for I did eat overmuch for the lasting of the food; though, in verity, it was but little to my belly; as you must all think, and have sympathy for my discomfort.

And I considered a little, and had determined that I should afterwards in my journeying, eat but two of the tablets to my meal; and this was a wise thought, and like much wisdom, a discomposing thing. But so it was, and I set it down that you may know the arranging of my ways at that time.

Now, in all this while of meditation, I had been setting my cloak about me, and was fast set to my sleeping; for I had walked a weary way. And I lay me down upon my left side, with my back to the rock, which did overhang me something above; so that I was contented to feel hid from things that might pass by in the Night. And I had the cloak about me, and the Diskos close against my breast, within the cloak, and my head upon my pouch and upon my scrip.

And as I lay thus a moment easeful, I could see that so mighty was the uprising of the Great Pyramid that it was not hid from me even thus, but did stand upward into the night, and did shine, and was plain to be seen above the further edge of that deep place where I did lie.

And I fell upon sleep, looking upward at that Final Light, where, as might be, the Master Monstruwacan did bend the Great Spy-Glass upon my lonesomeness, as I lay there upon the ledge.

And this was a thought of sweet comfort upon which to slumber; the which I did; but my spirit lay wakeful within my breast, and did listen

through the night; and harked for all evil matters and things that did make to come anigh. But also my spirit did whisper unto Naani as I went into sleep; and so passed I into dreams.

Now, it may be thought that I did act with a strange valiance, in that I composed my body so properly to slumber, and with but a little trouble of the heart concerning the coming of monsters. And in truth this hath seemed somewhat so to me, thinking since that time; but I do but set the thing that is truth; and make not to labour to an illusion of truth; and so must tell much that doth seem improper to the Reality. Yet must all bear with me, and have understanding of the hardness of setting forth with true seeming the honesty of Truth, which, in verity, is better served oft times by timely and cunning lies. And so shall you understand this matter so well as I.

And presently my spirit waked me there in the half dark of the Night Land; and I looked swift about me, and upwards, and saw nothing to fear. Then did I peer at my dial; and made to discover that I had slept full over six quiet hours; and by this I knew the reason of mine awaking; for it was so great impressed upon me by mine inward sense and being. And this you shall understand, someways, who have thought, ere sleep, to wake to a certain time of the morning; and by understanding shall you believe and give me all your kind harking and human sympathy.

And I made to have a smartness of going, which is ever hard to the newly waked; and I eat two tablets, the while my belly did cry out for an wholesome and proper filling; but I drank some of the water, and so did ease somewhat of my hunger.

Then did I wind my cloak to its shape, and put upon me my gear, which was the scrip and the pouch, and the Diskos to my hip; and I clomb out from that place of rest. Yet, before I did come rightly up into the open, I peered about, and made some surety that no evil Brute was anigh. And then I gat me out, and stood upon my feet, and looked for a little upwards at the mighty slope of the Great Redoubt, which did seem yet very nigh unto me, by reason of it being so monstrous in bigness.

And I wondered whether in that moment the Master Monstruwacan

did look down upon me, with the Great Spy-Glass. And afterwards I turned away swiftly, and went on into the Night Land; for it did always make me shaken with lonesomeness to look upon my Great Home. And so I did go forward with a strong and uncaring stride; but grew presently to quietness, and to have back the proper caution of my going. Yet had I not gone all foolishly, for I had taken the Diskos from my hip, ere this; so that I possessed it handily.

Now there is one matter which shall seem but a small and natural occurring unto you; yet was strong upon me in that time; and this thing was that I did begin now to see the Night Land from the new outlooking of my distance from the Mighty Pyramid. And it was as that a man of this day did go from the earth to travel among the stars, and lo! should he not find them to shift upon his vision; so that the Great Bear and this and that shaping of the star clusterings, should make a new order, as he did wander onwards; and so should he find that there was naught that was truly fixed, as he did before then think; but all to alter according unto the place whence the looking! And this thing shall be plain unto you, though no thought be put to the matter; for it is of an evident verity that doth need not argument to expound. And so shall you have memory of me, there a-wander among those strange shapings and wonders of that grim Land, the which I had never but supposed to seem but as my memory did retain them, from the lookings of all my life within the Great Redoubt. And so it was; and ever there did this thing and that open out to a new view, and the Night Land take to itself a constant new aspect to mine eyes which had never until that time had but the one fixed vision of the same.

And you shall understand with me how that when, about the fourteenth hour of that day's travel, I did draw very nigh unto the monstrous Watcher of the North-West, it did seem so utter strange from this fresh aspect that I had been like to think that I did see a new Monster. For, in truth, when I did come at last to creep to within a mile of it, among the low moss-bushes, I was confounded that the mighty chin did come forward towards the Great Redoubt, even as the upward part of a vast cliff, which the sea doth make hollow about the bottom; for it did hang out into

the air above the glare of the fire from the Red Pit, as it had been a thing of Rock, all scored and be-weathered, and dull red and seeming burned and blasted by reason of the bloody shine that beat upward from the deep of the Red Pit.

And by the way in which I do tell upon it, you shall know that I did surely view it something from the side at this immediate time; for, in truth, it was then that I did draw the nearer; and, moreover, I was the more astonished at this viewing, than I had been to the front; for it was so utter strange, and shapen so different from the Brute that did hang in my memory.

And a great time I did lie there upon my belly; and shaken by a fear of the Beast; yet emboldened, as you may conceive, by having come to the side; and being hopeful in my heart that I was very secure within so great a shadow and the thick sheltering of the moss-bushes.

And surely it was that I did creep more nigh, the while that I did look; for presently I had a very plain seeing of the Great Monster; and did know where I had gotten to, and thereby did acknowledge unto myself that this was an utter foolishness; and like, for all that any might say, to lead unto destruction. Yet, as all must know, there was the first fear, and the ceasing of this fear, as I did wot that I was so little a thing to heed out there in the shadows. And presently a gaining of courage, and the prick of my Being that did crave to see clear this exceeding Wonder. And so was I come close, more or less, having gone far upon my hands and knees; yet sometimes to pause; but afterwards on again.

Now by this nearness, I was the more truly able to perceive how that the Bulk of the Watcher did rise up into the Night, like a Hill; and the colour was mostly black, save and indeed where it did face to the red shine of the Pit; and concerning this I have done telling.

And so did I lie there, and stare a great while, parting a small hole in the moss-bushes that I might spy through the same. And the thing was squat there, and might have root within the earth, so it did seem to mine imaginings, as I did stare with a dumb wonder. And there were monstrous warts upon the thing, and indents and a mighty ruggedness and lumpings; as it were that it did be pimpled with great boulders that were inbred

within that monstrous hide. And where the shine from the Pit of Red Fire did strike upon these, they did stand out into the darkness away from the skin, as you of this Age shall see mountains of the moon catch a bright fire from the Sun, and show plain upon the night of the moon.

Now, as I have set down, I did lie there and look a great while; and it came presently to me that there was unease within the Mighty Pyramid, among the Millions; for I did feel the aether of the world to be disturbed by their distress; and so had a knowing that they had a cunning awaredness concerning the place where I did hide among the moss-bushes.

And the thrilling in the night did bring a wisdom into my head; for, in verity, as I have said, this was a foolish matter that I was upon. And I gat a thought that the Watcher might have an awaredness of the trouble of the Multitudes; and, indeed, for all that I did know, it had a full knowledge of all my wandering; though concerning this, I did think otherwise truly in my heart; as is a most human and proper way to make comfortable the spirit, where Doubt can have no ease from Reason.

And I made that I would go backwards to a good distance from the Watcher, and go forward again upon my journeying, if but that I come safe from so unwise an adventuring. And as I did begin to return, it was to me as that all my senses were newly awake; for I had a sudden knowing that I was within the atmosphere, should I not call it, of the Monster.

And I gat an abrupt and horrid shaking of the spirit; for I did feel in verity that my soul had come too anigh; and that the Beast had a sure knowledge concerning me; yet did make to my destruction with no haste; but after that way and fashion that did seem proper unto it.

And this feeling you shall understand the better, maybe, when I do tell that it was to me as that the air all about me was full of a quiet and steadfast life and keen intelligence that I did believe to come forth from the Watcher on every side; so that I did feel as one already within the gaze of some Great and Evil Power.

Yet, though I had a great terror upon me, I made no foolish haste; but commanded my soul to courage, and put a guard upon my way of going, and so made a very quiet journey for maybe two full miles; and afterwards

did allow myself something more of haste; for I was now grown easier in my spirit; and felt apart from the spirit of the Great Watcher.

And after a longer while, I did leave that hill of watchfulness to my rear; and was gone onward into the night; yet, as may be known, with a vague unease and trouble to my heart, and a swift and frequent turning to learn surely that no Evil Thing came after me. For, as you may know, I could nowise have forgetting, concerning that great quiet Life which did seem to be living in all the air around that Mighty Bulk. For it had been all about me in the night, as I have told, and I to feel that I had been surely discovered! And thus shall you know how shaken was my spirit, in verity.

Now, presently, at the eighteenth hour of that day's travel, I ceased from my journeying, that I might eat and drink; and I did sit a little while, and looked back upon the strange and monstrous thing which I had come beyond. And the great humped back and vast shoulders of the Watching-Thing rose up into the night, black and cumbrous against the red shine of the Pit. And thus, as you shall think, had that Brute looked always unto the Mighty Pyramid, through Eternity, and did cease not from watching, and was steadfast and silent and alone; and none did understand.

And after I had eat, and drunk some of the water, I went onward for a full matter of six hours more; being minded to have no sleep until I had put a great way between me and the Watcher. And in this part of my journey did I come to The Place Where The Silent Ones Kill, as it was named in the Maps. And I observed a very wondrous caution, and went away from it a little, unto the North, where I did see at a distance the shinings of fire-holes; the which did promise me warmth through my slumber.

And here you must know that the Place Where The Silent Ones Kill was an utter bare place, where all did seem of rock, and no bush did seem to grow thereon; so that a man might not come to any hiding; though, in truth, there might be some hole here or there; yet was none shown in any map within the Pyramid; neither did there seem to be any such to me, as I did creep there among the moss-bushes to the Northward of the Place, and look constant and fearful towards it; so that I should see quickly whether any Silent One did move across all the grey quiet of that rocky plain.

And concerning this same Place Where The Silent Ones Kill, it were well to make an explanation how that there was always a little and far-spreaded light over all that lonesomeness; and the light was something grey-seeming; as it were that a lichen might grow upon the rocks, and send out a little uncomfortable glowing, even as certain matters do in these times, if you do but know the place and the time to seek them. Yet was the light exceeding weak, and very cold and dismal, and did seem truly to show naught with a sureness; so that it did appear to the eye, if one did look fixedly, that there were shadows that did move here or there, as it were of silent beings; and none might know, in truth, whether this shaping of the greyness was to the clouding of the Reason, or that the eye did see of Reality. Yet, if one did look with the Great Spy-Glass, then might there be some surety and plainness; and likewise was it so, if one did have come sufficient anigh to that uncomfortable Place, even as I then did be.

And so you shall conceive how that I did slide very quiet from bush unto bush; for I had always in all my life had a very dread fear of this place; and oft did I peer out into the dim grey light of the lonesome plain unto my left; and would think sometimes to perceive the shapes of the Silent Ones stood vague and watchful; yet, on the instant, to see nothing.

And thus I did go onward, and came presently to a part where the grey plain did stretch out a bareness into the Night Land to my front; so that my way ended, unless I did make a long passing round about.

And I sat there among the moss-bushes, and did consider, and lookt out cunningly through a spy-hole of the bush in which I did sit. And I perceived that the part of the plain which did jut bareness into the Land before me had no greatness of size; but might be passed swiftly in but a little running. And this thing should save me a wearisome going round; so that I made to consider it with a serious mind; and all the time did I search the bare greyness before me, and saw presently that it was surely empty.

And I made to adventure myself across, running very swift until I had come to the far side. And lo! as I did go to rise up out of the bush, mine eyes were opened, as it were, and I saw that there was something amid the constant greyness; and I fell quickly into the bush; and did sweat very chill;

but yet did haste to look.

And I saw now that there were, in truth, matters that did show vague upon that part of the plain that was before me. And I did peer very constant and anxious, and, behold, I saw that there was facing me, a great line of quiet and lofty figures, shrouded unto their feet; and they moved not, neither made they any sound; but stood there amid the greyness, and did seem to make an unending watch upon me; so that my heart went unto weakness, and I did feel that there was no power of the moss-bushes to hide me; for, in verity, they that stood so silent were certain of the Silent Ones; and I was very nigh to the Place of Destruction.

Now, I moved not for a time; but was made stiff by the greatness of my fear. Yet I was presently aware that the Silent Ones came not towards me; but stood quiet; as that they did mind not to slay me, if but I did keep from that Place.

And there grew therefrom a little courage into mine heart, and I obeyed my spirit, and took an hold of my strength and went slowly backward in the bushes. And presently I was come a long way off. Yet troubled and disturbed, and very strict to my going.

And I made a great circling about that place where the plain of the Silent Ones did come outward; and so did gain to the North-West; and was thence something the happier in my heart; and went easily, and oft upon my feet; yet making a strong watching to every side.

And so I came at the last to a time when I had walked through four-and-twenty weariful hours; and was eager that I should come to a safe place for my sleep; yet did lack a happy belief of safety, in that I had come twice anigh to so grim trouble; and unsure I was that I did not be secretly pursued in the night. And this you shall believe to be a very desperate feeling; and a plight to make the heart sick, and to long with a great longing for the safety of that mine Home. Yet had I put myself to the task; and truly I did never cease to the sorrowful remembering of that utter despair that had sounded to me plain in the last calling of mine own love, out of all the mystery of the night. And but to think upon this was to grow strong in the spirit; yet to have a fresh anxiousness that I did the more surely keep my

life within me, and so come to that maid's salvation.

Now, as you shall mind, I had spied the shine of certain fire-holes somewhat to the Northward, and had thought to make thereabouts a place for my sleep; for, in truth, there was a bitterness of cold in all the air of night that did surround me; and I was warmed nigh to a slow happiness, by thinking upon a fire to lie beside; and small wonder, as you shall say.

And I made presently a strong walking unto that place where did glow in the night the shine of the fire-holes, as I did well judge them to be; and so was like to have come over-swiftly upon my death, as you shall presently see; for, as I came anigh to the first, I perceived that the light came up-ward out of a great hollow among the moss-bushes, and that the fire-hole burned somewhere in the deep of the hollow; so that I did but look upon the shine thereof.

Yet very eager was I to come to that warmth; and I made more of haste than care, as I did hint; and so came very swift to the top of the hollow; yet was still hidden by the kindness of the moss-bushes.

And as I made to thrust forward out of the bushes, that I might look and go downward into the hollow, there rose up to me the sound of a very large voice, and deep and husky. And the voice was a dreadful voice that did speak as that it said ordinary things, and in a fashion so monstrous as that it were that a house did speak, and, in verity, this is a strange thing to say; yet shall it have the truth of my feelings and terror in that moment.

And I drew back swiftly from discovering myself; and was then all feared to move, or to make to go more backward, lest that I should give knowledge that I was come anigh. And likewise did I shiver lest that I was even then perceived. And so shall you have something of the utter fear that did shake me. And I abode there, very quiet, and moved not for a very great space; but did sweat and shake; for there was a monstrous horridness in the voice that did speak.

And as I crouched there within the moss-bushes, there came again the large voice, and it was answered by a second voice; and thereupon there arose, as it did seem, the speech of Men that must have the bigness of el-ephants, and that did have no kindness in all their thoughts; but were utter

monstrous. And the speech was slow, and it rose up out of the hollow, brutish and hoarse and mighty. And I would that I could make you to hear it, and that you could but borrow mine ears for a little moment, and forthwith be shaken with that utter horror and an afraidness, even as was I.

Now, presently, there was a very long quiet, and I ceased at last a little from mine over-fear; and later I did calm somewhat; so that I made to shift my position, which was grown very uneasy.

And there was still no sound from the hollow. Wherefore, having a little boldness and much curiousness, and these despite my great fearfulness, I put forth mine hand, very cautious, and did move the mossbush a little from my face. And I went forward upon the earth, and did lie upon my belly; and was by this so close upon the edge of that place, that I was abled to look downwards.

And you shall know that I peered down into that great hollow, and did see a very strange and horrid sight; for, in truth, there was a large fire-hole in the centre of that place, and all about the sides there were great holes into the slopes of the hollow, and there were great men laid in the holes, so that I might see a great head that did show out to my sight here, from one of those holes, and would seem to be that of a monstrous man heavy with sleep. And there I would see but the buttocks of another, as that he did curl himself inward to his brutish slumbering. And so was it all about; and to my memory there were maybe a score of these holes; yet had I not time to the counting, as you shall see. For, after that I had made but a glance, as it were, at these sleeping and utter monstrous men, I perceived that there sat beyond the fire-hole, three great men, and they were each greater than elephants, and covered a large part with a stiff and horrid hair, that did be of a reddish seeming. And there were upon them great segs and warts, as that their skin had been hides that had never known covering. And there was between them the body of a mighty hound, so big as an horse, that they did skin; and I judged that this beast was one of those fearsome brutes which we did call the Night Hounds.

Yet, as I should set down, they did nothing in that time in which I lookt at them; but did sit each with a sharp and monstrous bloody stone

in his fist, and did look to the ground, as that they heeded not the earth or the food that they did prepare; but did listen to some outward sound. And you shall know that this brought to me a very swift and sudden terror; for I perceived now the why of their long silence; for, in verity, they had an unease upon them, being subtly aware that one was anigh, even as are the brute beasts in this manner and kind, as all do know.

And I made to draw back, and win unto safety, if indeed this thing were to be done. And as I moved me, it may be that I shook a little earth into the hollow; for there was, indeed, a little sifting of dry dust below me, as I did wot, being very keen to hear, by reason of my fright. And immediately did those three monstrous men look upward, and did seem to me to stare into mine eyes, as I did lie there hid amid the moss-bushes. And I was so put in fear that I did clumsily, and sent another sifting of dust downward, as I did strive to go backward swift and quiet from the edge. And all the time I did look through the bushes very fixedly into the eyes of the giants; and lo, their eyes did shine red and green, like to the eyes of animals. And there rose up a roar from them that did nigh slay my soul with the horridness of the noise. And at that roaring, all the giants that did lie in the holes did awake, and began to come outward into the hollow.

Now, I was surely lost, and given over to destruction; for they had possessed me immediately, but that in that moment, as I went backward, the earth gave behind me, and I fell into a hole among the moss-bushes to my back, and I made first to come out very hurried, and all choked with a dust of sand and ash; but in a moment I was sane to know that I had come to a sudden hiding-place; and I lay very still and strove neither to cough nor to breathe. And well for me, I came to so close a hiding; for there were all about me the sounds of monstrous footsteps, running, that seemed to shake the ground; though maybe this to be an imagining bred of my fear.

And shoutings of great voices there were; and the thudding of huge feet all about; and the noises of the bushes rustling; but presently the search drew away to the Southward. And I perceived that there had surely fought for me some power of good fortune. And I came up out of the hole, very cautious, and shaken and a moment weak with the beating of my heart; yet

with a lovely thankfulness for my salvation. And I gat me about, and went swift through the moss-bushes to the North and West for three hours, and ceased not to run upon my hands and knees. And by that time was I come a great way, and did have a surety in my heart of present safety.

And I ceased to run, and lay quiet; for, in truth, I did near swoon away with the hardness of my travel. And indeed as you shall know, I had slept not for seven-and-twenty hours, and had scarce ceased to labour in all that time. Moreover, I had eat not, neither drunk, for nine hours; and so shall you conceive that I was truly a-weary.

And, presently I did slumber there as I lay, and all abroad to any monstrous thing that should come along. Yet did I wake unharmed, and found by my dial there had gone by a full ten hours, the while that I did lie there and sleep unwotting. And I was sore perished with the cold of the Night; for I had not the warmth of my cloak about me, and my belly was very empty.

And I stood me up, and did peer about for any dread matter, but all seemed proper, and I began to stamp my feet against the earth, as that I would drive it from me, and this I do say as a whimsy, and I swung mine arms, as often you shall do in the cold days; and so I was presently something warmed. And I dismantled my cloak, and wrapped it about me, and did feel that the Diskos was safe to my hip.

Then did I sit me down, and did glow a little with relish, in that I should now eat four of the tablets; for, indeed, these were my proper due, by reason of my shiftless fasting ere I came so wotless to my slumbering. And the memory of that eating doth live with me now, so that I could near to smile; for the eagerness of mine inwards was proper and human; yet were even four tablets but a little matter to so great an emptiness; and I drank a double portion of the water, that I might make less the void. And this thing was seemly; for, indeed, there were two portions due unto me.

And when I had eat and drunk, I did fold the cloak once more to shape across my shoulder, as I did carry it; and afterwards I took the Diskos into my hand, and went forward again to the North and West.

Yet, as you shall know, I did pause a little in the beginning, and peer to every side for any close danger; and then did look more abroad of that place;

but could nowhere see any matter to have me to immediate fear. And afterwards, I looked a little while at the monstrous humped back of the Watcher of the North-West; and it did grow to me how steadfast that thing did look toward the Mighty Pyramid; and this set me to new hatred and horror of the Monster, as you shall conceive and believe.

And presently, I looked beyond the Watcher, unto the vast Mountain of the Great Redoubt; and I was still seeming close upon it; yet, in truth, gone a long and weariful distance. But this you shall understand was by the greatness and utter height and bulk of that shining Mountain of Life.

And strange and wonderful it was to me to think that even in that one moment, it might be that the dear Master Monstruwacan did look upon my face, through the Great Spy-Glass. And I should not seem utter far to him, by reason of the power of the big Glass. But to me, as I did look upward through the Night, unto that far and utmost light in the upper blackness of the everlasting gloom, it did seem doubly to me that I was afar off and lost forever from mine Home. And this thinking did breed in me such a great and lonesome feeling, and a weakness of the heart and spirit, that forthwith I took my courage close unto me, and did turn away quickly; and went onward to the North and West, as I have told.

Now I walked for twelve hours, and in that time, did eat and drink twice; and made onward again very steadfast, and happy that all did go so quiet with me; so that it was as if I had at last come to a part of the Land that was given over to quietness, and lacking of monsters. Yet, in truth was I come to a worse place than any, maybe; for as I went forward, striding very strong, and making a good speed, I did hear presently a little noise upward in the night, and someways unto my left, that had seeming as that it were a strange low sound that did come down to me out of an hidden doorway above; for, indeed, though the sound did come from very nigh, as it did seem no more than a score feet above my head, yet was it a noise that did come out of a great and mighty distance, and out of a Foreign Place. And I did know the Sound; though never, as you may suppose, could I have heard it in all my life. Yet had I read in one of the Records, and again in a second and a third, how that certain of all they that had adventured

from the Pyramid into the Night Land to seek for knowledge, had chanced to hear a queer and improper noise above them in the Night; and the noise had been strange, and did come from but a little way upward in the darkness; yet was also from a great and monstrous distance; and did seem to moan and hum quietly, and to have a different sounding from all noises of earth. And in the Records it was set forth that these were those same Doorways In The Night, which were told of in an ancient and half-doubted Tale of the World, that was much in favour of the children of the Pyramid, and not disdained by certain of our wiser men, and had been thus through all the latter ages.

And I did seem to know the sound upon the moment; for my heart grew swift to understand. And it was a very dread uncomfortable sound; and you shall know how it did seem, if you will conceive of a strange noise that doth happen far away in the Country, and the same noise to seem to come to you through an opened door near by. And this is but a poor way to put it; yet how shall I make the thing more known to you? So that I must even trust unto your wit and true sympathy that you shall conceive of the fullness of my meaning.

Now, in all the Histories of those that had adventured into the Night Land, there were but three sure Records that did concern this Sound; and each did tell of a Great Horror; and of them that did hear the Sound there had died the most part, out in the Night Land. And the Records did make always that they had come upon Destruction, and not simply unto Death; but were destroyed by a strange and Invisible Evil Power from the Night.

And of those that came alive unto the Pyramid, they had all one strange tale to tell, how that there were secret and horrid Doorways In The Night. Yet how this thing could be plain to them, who may know truly; save it be that the eyes of their spirits did behold that which was hid to the eyes of the flesh.

And there was afterwards writ a proper and careful treatise, and did set out that there did be ruptures of the Aether, the which did constitute doorways, as those more fanciful ones did name them; and through these shatterings, which might be likened unto openings—there being no better

word to their naming—there did come into this Particular Condition Of Life, those Monstrous Forces Of Evil, that did dominate the Night, and which many did hold surely to have been given this improper entrance through the foolish and unwise wisdom of those olden men of learning, that did meddle overfar with matters that did reach in the end beyond their understanding. And this thing have I told before, and it doth seem proper unto my belief; for it is always thus, and I have that same taint within me, as must all that have the zest of life.

Now, by this that I have set down swiftly, to make a little clear the sure horridness of this Sound, you shall know, even with me, the great horror that did come immediately upon my Spirit; and I did know that my Search was surely like to have an end in that moment; and I bared mine arm, for my teeth, where the Capsule did lie below the skin; and so was ready to an instant Death, if that Destruction did come upon me. And in the same moment, I did fall silent, inward among the moss-bushes, and did begin to creep very quiet toward the right; for, as you will mind, I had heard the Sound over beyond my left. And all that time, as I did creep, there was a great sickness upon me, and it did seem that my mouth had weakened unto water; so that I could scarce hold my teeth tightly from unseemly clitterings.

And I crept always very silent, and did often stare quick and painful over my shoulder, upwards, and this way and that; but did never see anything; neither could I hear now the Sound.

And I went thiswise for a great hour, and was like to faint through the effort of my care and the soreness of my going. But upon the end of that long while, I grew something easier in the Spirit, and did perceive that I was saved from the Destruction that I had come so dreadful anigh. And this thing, it may be, was because that I did chance to hear it, whilst yet it was beyond, and before I did come right unto it, to pass below. Yet may I be wrong in this thought, and do but make a guessing. But, as I shall here explain; after that time, I kept mine ears newly keen unto hearing; and did chide my Spirit, for that it had not taken account of that Sound a great while earlier. Yet, as I did presently conceive, the spirit had no power to

hear that thing; which was very strange; but truly so.

Now, because that I went with a very wary hearing, I heard the Sound once a far way off before me, and I hid upon the moment, and went backward, and after a while, did judge myself to have come unto safety; and so it was, in verity, for I heard no more that time. And so did I come presently unto the eighteenth hour, and did eat and drink, and made me a place of slumber in a little hollow of a rock that stood upward out of the moss-bushes. And I slept for six hours, and afterwards waked, and was come to no harm.

And after I had eat and drunk again, I did look outward over the Night Land, and with particularness to that part that I did travel in, as it might be called, the yesterday. And I did observe it to be a very bleak and desolate Country, and not given over to fire, or other warmth, nor to sulphur-vapours; but to be very quiet, and with but a little light in all its breadth. And I could conceive that it was no place for anything of life to desire; but rather to avoid; and that Country did seem to be yet all about me; for I was by no means come clear from it at that time; though, Northward, there was a glimmer, as of fire-holes; and beyond those, the strange shining of the Plain of Blue Fire.

And, after that I had thought awhile, I did believe that I should meet no Monster of Natural Life in all that Country of Desolation, until I did draw nigh, once more unto fire. And I conceived that this Sound from out of the invisible Doorways might yet trouble me; but whether the quietness of that part was because all of natural life did fear the Sound, or because that there was neither fire nor warmth, I do not say, having no knowing in this matter; but may yet believe that it was to be laid to both causes; and this doth seem of common reason, as you shall agree.

And when I had looked a while unto the Mighty Pyramid, which was now truly a great way off; for I had walked so many weary hours; I turned me once more to my journeying. And here let me observe that I had gone very far; yet not so distant, as might be thought; for, oft, I did go less than one mile in an hour or maybe two hours, having to be of great caution, and oft to hide, and to go upon my belly, or to crawl, all as might be. And,

further, as you may have perceived, I made not a straight forwardness; but did strike this way and that way, being very intent to escape the Monsters and Evil Forces that were all about.

Now, because that I believed that I travelled in a Place where was surely to be discovered those strange Doorways within the Night, I made an especial care of my going; and did stop oft that I might listen, and watch, and keep a very strict ward in all the Night about me. Yet, as you shall see, this served not to prevent me from going forward into the fearfulness of that which did haunt all the void; for, sudden, as I went carefully, I heard a faint humming noise come downward from the night a little unto my rear; and the humming noise did grow more plain, as that a door were opened slowly above, and did let out that Sound ever more loud. And surely, after I did hear that, I could not doubt that a door were opened upward there; for the noise did grow in such wise as you shall hear a distant sound come through, when a door truly is oped; for, if the noise had been made just in that place, it had seemed to come from there; but this Sound, though it did come *through* there, was as that it did come outward from some far lost and foreign Eternity. And this I do struggle always to make plain; and you shall not blame me that I think overmuch upon it; for, in truth there was an horror so wondrous and drear about it, that I can forget not; but do strive always that others should know with me that peculiar woe and terror that did haunt the night.

Now, as you will see, I had in truth gone past the place where the Doorway in the Night did open; yet had come to no harm; but rather it did seem that it opened by chance, unwotting that I was anigh; or it may be that my quiet passing did disturb an Evil Power, so that it did even come to listen, or to make search. And all this doth pass through my brain, as I do write, and it doth seem to me that my thoughts are but the thoughts of a little child, before so great a mystery; and that I touch not even the edge and fringe of the truth with my thinkings, and so do cease upon them; and will but go forward so plain as I may with my telling. Now, as you may truly believe, when I heard that Sound, and did understand that I had, in verity, come past beneath that Place, I did surely sicken to an utter weakness of

body and heart, though it was but for a moment; and then was I swift hid within the close shelter of the low and thick moss-bushes.

And I shook in all my being, and crept, shaking, upon my hands and knees, and did near totter to my face thrice, so weak gone was I in that moment of terror; and I did have a wickedness of forgetting in that time; for I bared not mine arm, to have the Capsule to a readiness for my death, if that did need to be; and this was an abominable foolishness, and I do shake now when I think upon it; for Death is but a little matter by the side of Destruction; though, in truth, dreadful enough for all. Yet, as it did chance, no harm came to me, and I gat away, as that some wondrous power did cast a viewless cloak about me, that I might be utter hid; and oft have I wondered whether this was truly so; but have no knowing.

And, presently, I ceased from fleeing, and had some calmness, and did eat and drink; and so came to the comfort of a firm spirit, the which had been sore troubled, above all understanded causes, by that horrid sounding upward in the Night. And after that I had eat and drunk, I did rest a little; but afterward, went onward to the Northward, going towards that place where the fire-holes did glimmer, the same being by this time no great way off.

Then, as I did come anigh, I thought to hear once again the Sound in the night, and I stopt very swift, and hid into the moss-bushes, and did listen; but did hear naught; and so was hopeful that fancy did play upon me. Yet, because of this matter, I went upon my hands and knees for a good way; and so came at last nigh unto the shine of one of those fire-holes, the which I did see for so long.

Now, as you shall suppose, I went very cautious through the bushes, unto that red-shining fire; being careful, both that I did attract not any Evil Force that might listen in the Night, and because that there might be some Monster nigh to the fire-hole. But, presently, when I was come so that I could peer through the bushes, I did see a little fire-hole set in a small hollow, and there did no thing seem to lurk anigh; and the sight of that warmth did cheer me; for it was long since I did have the comfort of such a matter.

And when I had lain hid awhile, that I might watch all about, I saw the place to be safe and quiet; and I went out from the moss-bushes, and sat down a space from the fire, which did fill the pit in which it did lift and bubble. And the noise that it sent out was strange and slow, and it did seem to gruntle gently unto itself in that lonesome hollow, as that it had made a long and quiet grumbling there, through Eternity. And oft was it still, and made no sound; and again would give an odd bubbling in the quietness, and send off, as it did seem, a little smoke of sulphur, and afterward fall once more upon a quiet.

And so I did sit there very hushed and restful, and the loneliness did lie all about me, and the red shine of the fire-hole did glow soft in the hollow; and I was glad to be quiet, for my heart was weary.

And there was to my back a little rock that did jut upward so high as a man; and the rock was warm and pleasant to lean upon, and moreover did seem to guard me from behind. And there I ate and drunk, and kept very still; and so was presently rested. And this I did need, as you have perceived; for I was gone sudden weary of the heart, as I did say; and this might be because that I did never cease to have Destruction over me to companion my way, though as you will mind, I had been no more than twelve hours afoot, since my last sleeping. Yet I doubt not you do understand.

And presently my heart grew strong again within me, and I had a warmth in my Spirit; and I got up from the earth, and stretched out mine arms; and I saw that my gear was safe upon me, and afterward did grip the Diskos, as it were newly.

Then I went away from the fire-hole, and climbed the far slope of the hollow, and went Northward. And there were before me many of the fire-holes; for I did perceive them to shine in the Night for a great way; as it did seem that they were a path of red shinings that led me onward to the North-West of the light of the Plain of Blue Fire.

Now, I had a believing that I had come out of the Country where did lurk those horrid Doorways in the Night; and I went not with so utter a weight upon my heart; and did feel that naught should come now upon the back of my neck, which had been an odd and troublesome fancy whilst

that I did creep through that Country of Gloom. Yet, as you shall know, I went with no foolish confidence; but with a great caution, and mine hearing keen to hark, and a care to my steps, and did ever watch around me as I journeyed.

And because that I went forward in this proper and sedate manner, I had great cause for a thankful heart, as you may perceive; for I had come after a long way to another of those hollows where did burn one of the fire-holes; and I made a pause upon the edge of the hollow in which it did lie, and looked downward, keeping guarded within the moss-bushes, where they grew anigh to the top thereof. But there was no living thing there to be seen, and I went downward, so that I should warm my body at the fire. And lo! as I stood upon this side of the fire-hole, and turned myself about, I looked presently more keenly to the other side; for the yellowness of the earth did seem a little strange in one place. But I could see with no plainness, because that there arose a glare from the fire against mine eyes; and I went round, that I should look the better; yet with no fear or thought of Evil in my heart. And, truly! when I was come upon that far side of the fire-hole, lo! there was spread out in the yellow sand of that place, a Curious Thing; and I went more nigh, and stooped to look upon it; and behold it moved, and the sand all about did move for a great space; so that I gave back very swift, and swung upward with the Diskos.

And, strangely, I heard the sand to stir at my back, and I looked round very quick, and the sand rose upward in parts, and sifted back, and there came to my sight odd things that did move and curl about.

And immediately, before I knew which way to go, I knew that the sand did shift under my feet, and did work and heave, so that I was tottered, and was shaken also in the heart; for I knew not what to think in that instant. Then did I perceive that I was all surrounded, and I ran swift upon the heaving sand, unto the edge of the fire-hole, and I turned there, and looked quickly; for I did not know what this new Terror should be.

And I saw that a Yellow Thing did hump upward from out of the sand, as it had been a low hillock that did live, and the sand shed downward from it, and it did gather to itself strange and horrid arms from the sand

all about it. And it stretched two of the arms unto me; but I smote with the Diskos, and I smote thrice; and afterward they did wriggle upon the sand. But this was not the end, as I did hope; for the Yellow Thing arose, and ran at me, as it might be that you should see a spider run. And I did leap backward, this way and that; but the monster had a great swiftness; so that I did seem surely lost.

Then made I a strong and instant resolve; for I perceived that I had no hope to slay this thing; save that I should come at it in the body. And I put everything to the chance, and made not to escape any more; but ran straight in among the legs; and there were great hairs like to spines upon the legs, and these had pricked me to the death, but that the armour saved me.

Now, I had done this thing with a wondrous quickness; so that I was under the mighty arching of the legs before the Yellow Thing did wot of my intent. And the body was bristled with the great hairs, and poison did seem to come from them, and to ooze from them strangely in great and shining drops. And the Monster heaved itself up to one side, that it might bring certain of the legs inward to grasp me; yet in that moment did I smite utter fierce with the Diskos—thrusting. And the Diskos did spin, and hum, and roar, and sent out a wondrous blaze of flame, as that it had been a devouring Death; and it sundered the body of the Yellow Thing, and did seem as that it screamed to rage amid the entrails thereof; so wondrous was the fury and energy of that trusted Weapon.

And I was covered with the muck of the thing; and the claws upon the legs seized me, so that the grey armour did bend and crack to the might thereof, and I grew sick unto death with the pain within; but smote with the shining Diskos, using my left hand weakly; for my right was gript dreadful fast to my body. And lo! I was sudden free, and a great blow did knock me far across the hollow, so that I was like to have fallen into the fire-hole; but fell instead upon the edge, and came backward unto safety.

And I turned me about, and the Yellow Thing did throw the sand all ways, as it did die; but had lost power to come upon me. And for my part, I lay weak upon the earth, and was no more able to fight; nor could I do more than breathe for a great while; but yet came presently to health, and

made to examine my hurts.

Then I saw there was no great wound anywhere upon me; but only an utter bruising; and I found upon my right leg that there was a sharp and hairy claw clipt about it; but the armour had saved me from harm of the horrid thing; so that I did but kick it free with my left foot, and thence into the fire-hole.

Now, by this time, that Monstrous Creature was dead; but I held off from it, and went upon the other side of the fire; for I was yet surely in horror of it. And I sat for a time, and did think upon all matters that did concern me; and I saw that I should have not comfort of heart, until I was washed clean from the taint of the Monster.

And I gat me up wearily to go forth into the Night again, that I should make a search for a hot spring, of which I had come past many. And I had oft found them to be nigh unto the fire-holes; so that I was trustful that I should see one ere long. And lo! there was a little hollow just beyond, and scarce a hundred paces off; and in the hollow, there did shine three small fire-holes, and there was a steaming puddle, as did seem, beyond the third of the holes.

Now, before I adventured downward into this place, I went all about the topmost edge, and made a search of the moss-bushes about; but found naught that should scare me. And afterward, I went all across the hollow; but did find no monstrous thing hid anywheres. Yet, there was that in the place that discouraged me, and did keep me from stripping mine armour, so that I should bathe in the hot puddle; for I stept upon a small serpent, and the same did lap about my leg; but could do me no hurt, for the armour, which was a very blessed protection. And I freed myself from it with the handle of the Diskos.

And because that I could not go naked to my cleansing, I tried first the hotness of the water, which was not over great, and afterward did take off the scrip and the pouch, and the cloak, and laid them with the Diskos upon the edge of the warm puddle.

Then I stept into the water, and was immediately gone downward a great way; for, truly it was no puddle as I had supposed; but a deep well,

as you might call it, of hot and sulphury water. And this doth show how a man may act foolishly, even when he doth believe that he hath a great caution; and surely it is borne in upon me afresh that none should trust over freely unto unproven matters, the which shall you heartily agree with; but yet do as foolishly, according to your lights and characters. And so shall you laugh not over hardly upon me.

Now I had gone over the head, and, surely I do not know what deepness was there. Yet, as you shall think, I stayed not to consider upon this matter; but made to climb out, and much shaken with my splutterings and the smartings of mine eyes; for, truly, the water was strong with sulphur matters. Yet, very cleansing was it, as I did presently see; for there was no more any taint or horridness upon mine armour, or the flesh of my face or hands. And I took the Diskos, and washed it clean, also; and then the cloak, and afterward the scrip and the pouch, and the bands of the same.

And after I had done this, I was minded to dry myself by the little fire-holes; but when I was come there, lo! maybe a score small serpents were about those places; and I was strongly pleased that I should keep away. Yet that I must warm and dry me in that desolate and bitter Night Land, you shall agree. And to this end, I put the scrip and the pouch upon me, and afterwards took the Diskos readily into my hand, and ran quietly unto the hollow where I did fight with the Yellow Thing. And the cloak I bore in my left hand.

Now, when I was gat there, I was truly glad to think that there were no serpents in that place; and because that I had slain the Monster of the Place, how should it be that any harm might come unto me; for truly, was it not like that a Creature of such Might should keep all that Hollow unto itself, and slay any that did come therein, and thereby preserve that place from all other horror; though, surely, until it did die and cease to Be, there had been no call for any greater abomination.

Now, all this did go through my brain, as I did sit to dry mine armour and my body and my gear, upon that side of the fire-hole which was away from the slain Monster. And I made presently to think that this would be a sure and proper refuge wherein to sleep; for, truly, it must have gotten a

place where none other Creature should be like to come to work me harm. And it must be that you do all see with me in this matter, and commend me that I thought with properness.

And so did I resolve that I put my disgust within my pocket, as we do say, and stay safe and quiet within that Hollow. And this thing I did surely, and did eat and drink; and presently I went over to the dead Monster, and made very sure that it was truly slain; which indeed it was. And after that I had seen to this matter, I returned unto the fire-hole, and made a comfortable place in the sand, for my rest; for I was well dry by this.

And I wrapped the cloak about me, and took the Diskos to my breast, for a sure Companion, as it had truly proved in my need. And I could think almost that it did nestle unto me, as that it knew and loved me; but this thing can be no more than a fancy; and I do but set it down as such, and that it doth show my feeling and mind at that time.

Then, ere I did compose myself to slumber, I looked about me, upward to the edges of the Hollow, and I perceived that I was lost to the sight of the Mighty Pyramid; for I was come so far off that it looked not down from so wondrous a height, as you shall perceive; and moreover, the Hollow was something deep.

And afterward, as I lay my head back upon the scrip and the pouch, which were to me my pillow, I went to think a little upon Naani, as alway I did in my constant journeying; yet, presently, I strove sometimes that I put her from my mind, that I should sleep; for a bitter sorrow and anxiousness was oft upon me when that I did think upon her; and this you may know; for truly I knew not what terror was come to her, afar in the silence of the Night. And did I think overmuch, I should feel that I could have no calmness needful to sleep; but to need to walk for ever until I died, which could not be long; and so should I make a foolishness of mine anxious journeying to do her true service and to save her from Destruction, if such did truly threaten.

And I was soon gone over to sleep, and waked not for seven hours, being much wearied by the fight and the soreness of my body, the which did put me into a great pain as I did rise upward from my slumber. But this

was presently something less, and I eat two of the tablets and drank some of the water, and afterward did put my gear upon me, and went forward into the Night, having the Diskos in my hand. And my heart was glad that I had come safe through the time of my sleep.

Now I walked six hours, and did stop a little to eat and drink, and went on again. And it was in this second Third of the day that I saw afar to my right, two strange and wondrous men, and they did shine, as they had been made of a pale mist. And they came anigh, going very swift, and did seem as that they were maybe forty feet high, yet having no thickness; and I hid downward into the moss-bushes. And they past me, so quiet as a cloud of this day might go, and did appear to be, if I did guess, but an hundred fathoms off; yet was this no sure thing; for their position had no more surety than shall a rainbow have in this age. And so they were gone onward into the Night, and did seem to come out of the North. And they did appear not to wot of me; and whether they were harmful, I know not, for they harmed not me.

And I lay there in the moss-bushes, until they were well gone away; and I had belief that they must be those same mist-men that were told of in certain of the olden Records; but were never seen anigh to the Pyramid; though I had thought, odd times, to see men, as of mist, through the Great Spy-Glass, when I was within the Tower of Observation. But they were always a mighty way off; and some would say it was but a bright vapour that did move; yet would others be in doubt, and so is it ever in such matters.

And here let me take chance to say how that it is a hard thing to speak of such happenings to men of this age, and to make the truth proper unto them; and because of this, oft am I tempted to say no word upon many things that I did see; yet must I tell my tale, or suffer from the weight of it within me. And so shall you hark to me and give me your sympathy and human understanding.

And concerning these mist-men, I have wondered oft whether they were the visible shape of some of those many Forces that were abroad in the Night Land; for they did truly seem to me as that a thing of Strange Life were half shown to my human eyes; yet I do not know, and am but telling

of my natural thoughts and ponderings.

Now, as I did say, those mist-men were never seen nigh unto the Pyramid, and were, as I did hint, always so far off that they were half given over to the fables of the olden days, in the beliefs of the Peoples of the Mighty Redoubt; and set about with an halo of unrealness, for none within the Great Pyramid had ever beheld them with surety.

And because that now I saw them anigh to me, it was borne in afresh upon my spirit how greatly I had wandered away, and how that I stood afar in the lonesomeness of that Land of Night; as it had been that a man of this Age did wander amid the stars, and perceive a great comet to go by him very close; for then he should know in his heart how that he was far off in the Void. And this I do say to you, that you may know somewhat of the emotions of my heart in that moment.

Yet, presently I shook free of my melancholy and lonesomeness and rose up out of the moss-bushes, and went onward. And, as ever, I thought much upon the Maid that I did search for; yet strove to think quietly concerning her state; else should I have turned to running, and wrecked my body before that I had gone any great way.

And that day, I passed seven large fire-holes, and two that were small; and always I came softly unto them; for there were oft living things about the warmth. And at the sixth fire-hole, I did see that which I did think to be a great man, that did sit to the fire, with monstrous knees drawn upward unto his chin. And the nose was great and bent downward; and the eyes very large, and did shine with the light from the fire-hole, and moved, watching, always this way and that, so that the white parts did show, now this side and now that. But it was not properly a man.

And I went away very quiet from that place, and looked oft backward, until that I was sure of safety; for it was a very horrid Monster, and had that place to be for a Lair, as I did judge from the smell thereof.

And when the eighteenth hour was come, I looked about for a safe place to my sleep; and I kept away now from the fire-holes; for I did always find the more life there. Yet, when I came to my rest, I was lacking of warmth, by reason of this care; and could scarce sleep at all, because that

I was so cold. Yet managed something of slumber after a while; but woke very stiff, and was glad to beat my hands and bestir myself that I should come to some warmth of life.

And after that I had eat and drunk, I put my gear upon me, and took the Diskos in my hand, and went forward again upon my journey. And here I should tell that I was come soon unto the North-West border of the Plain of Blue Fire. And presently, I was but a little way off from it, and did go direct to the North; so that the Plain was always upon my right.

Now this Plain was a strange and fearsome place, as you shall see; for it was as that a blue void did rise upward from the earth in all the country of that Plain. For, surely, the Plain did not lumber with flame; but was hid with a strange and inburning light, as of a shining atmosphere of a cold blue colour. And it did throw no sure light upon the Night Land, as had seemed proper; but was a very dreadful, cold shining, as of a luminous and blue void. And the moss-bushes grew nigh to the edge of the plain, and did show to me black and strange against that horrid gloom of light.

And you shall know that I could not see into the plain; for it was as that the cold blue light was a void that swallowed all within it; and gave no power to the eye that aught should be perceived. And it stood between me and the Mighty Pyramid, and I could nowise see across. And I know not whether I do make all this matter clear unto you; for surely it is no easy task.

And presently I had gone very quiet upon my hands and knees through the moss-bushes; and I came near upon the edge of the Plain, and hid there in a clump of the moss-bush, and peered forth and harked. And I heard constant voices that did call to one another across the Plain; as it were that strange peoples of Spirits did wander within that blue shining, and did make a calling one to the other, and were all hid and held apart. And surely I could see naught, and did judge, as I have writ, that they like-wise went blindly. And truly is this a strange matter to set out; and easy to think on with doubt. Yet as I did see, so have I told; for, in verity, there were surely hidden Peoples of Spirits scattered and lost afar upon that im-proper Plain.

And you shall judge that I kept safe hid; for whether this might have

any natural explaining, or whether it was a matter that did go utter beyond knowledge of man, I did not know; for surely in that strange Land, it did like to be an Horrid Danger in any case; and whether of some Monstrous Creatures, or of the Evil Forces of the Land, I did wisely to be away.

And for two days I did make a safe coasting of the Plain of Blue Fire; and did keep well off, maybe two great miles, among the moss-bushes. And I made a very good speed through the darkness. And at the eighteenth hour of each journey, I made a place for my slumber; and the first I did manage under a thick bush; but the second was high upon the ledge of a rock that grew upward in the night amid the bushes. And, save that I was bitter cold there did no harm come to me. And in all that time of journeying, I had no sight of the Mighty Pyramid; for the blind shining of the Plain of Blue Fire was ever between.

Now there had been certain little matters in my journey beside the Plain of Blue Fire, which I have not set down; for they were of no account, and do but repeat much that I have told before. And, indeed, there was naught in that part of my journey, save that I did pass nineteen great fire-holes, and four small; and did observe no life beside any, save about one of the great holes that there was no hollow around, and here I did happen to see some strange and ugly creatures so big as my head, that did have a look of the scorpion of this Age; but proportioned more squat and thick. Yet, though they were naught to remark upon in that Land, they had been but woeful bedmates to any man; as you may think.

And you shall know how it gave a rest to my spirit, that I did go so long with no trouble of the Monsters of the Night, or the Evil Forces thereof. And I grew bolder to my journeying, and made ever a greater speed of going; and it was like that I took presently a less heed for my safety, which was a wrong and foolish state. Yet there came no harm unto me, in all that part of my travel.

Then, it was in the sixteenth hour of the third day of my journey beside the Plain, that I did come out beyond the end of it, and had fresh sight of the Mighty Pyramid, afar in the night upon my Right. And I stopt there in a bare place among the moss-bushes, and did in a weak moment hold

up the Diskos, so that I make a salute unto the Pyramid, Mine Home; for truly was I so utter glad to behold it once more.

And in a little while was I aware that there was a disturbance of the aether of the world all about me; so that it did seem that there had been one at the Great Spy-Glass to watch for my coming into their sight from behind the shining of the Plain of Blue Fire.

And it was like that news had gone downward through the Cities of the Great Redoubt; so that they did print the word of it in the Hour-Slips; and by this there would be many great Millions thinking upon me, and a rushing unto the Embrasures, that they might spy out at me. Yet I doubt that any glass might perceive me surely at so great a space, save the power of the Great Spy-Glass in the Tower of Observation. But the Emotion of the Millions to reach to me.

And you shall know that it did seem homely and sweet unto me to hear all about me the shaking of the aether of the world, and to be ware that so many did think humanly upon me, and had prayers unto my safety.

And it was a strange thing to stand so utter far off in the Night, and to look back to that Everlasting Hill of Light, that was grown something small by the distance, and to have surety that I was lookt upon through the Great Spy-Glass, maybe by the kindly eye of my dear friend the Master Monstruwacan, and so keenly that he could, it might be, make almost to guess the look within mine eyes, as I did gaze backward unto that Mine Home.

Yet, though this dear and homely sympathy was a sweet and companionable thing to my heart, it came swift to my thought that I was in a sore danger, if that they ceased not quickly to think so onely upon me; for surely was I not come over-near unto that *dreadful* House of Silence; and well might so much Emotion of the Millions tell unto the Horrid Power that dwelt within, how that I was even anigh. And so shall you see the mixt feelings that came upon me everyway.

Yet, as it did chance, the aether was quieted in a little; for it did need *unity* of the Millions (being that they were untrained to their spiritual powers) to stir the aether. And so was I more easy of mind, and went forward again upon my way.

Now, as it did chance, at the eighteenth hour, I was come to a place where I heard a noise of water; and I went to my left, that I might come upon it; and there boiled a hot fountain that went up out of the rock of that place. And the water rose upward in a column, and was, maybe, so thick as my body; and it fell unto the North, for the water came not up straightly, but did shoot out from the earth unto that way. And I saw the thing plain; for there were many fire-holes all about, as you shall have wotted from my telling; and so was there a certain and constant light in that part of the Land.

And I followed the water that ran from the fountain, and tried it with mine hand; but found it to burn; and so did go further beside it; for presently it should be no hotter than I did need. And it went onward, winding among the moss-bushes, and sent up a constant steam, that hung about it; and the steam made a red cloud about the way that it did go; for the lights from the fire-holes made a shining upon it; and so was it a wondrous pretty sight.

Now, presently, I tried the stream again, and found it to be nicely warm; and I sat upon a little rock, and took off my foot-gear, that I might bathe my feet, which were gone something tender; moreover, I did ache to have the sweetness of water about me. And I made that I should bathe my feet, and afterwards find a place among the moss-bushes, and so eat and drink, and have my slumber.

Then, as I did sit there beside that warm stream, with my feet dabbled therein, I heard sudden, afar off, the voice of a mighty Night-Hound, baying in the night. And the sound came from the North-West of the Plain of Blue Fire. And there was afterward a quiet; and you shall see me sitting there upon the rock by the side of that smoking river, and the steam all about me, and my feet within the lovely warmth of the water; and I very still and frozen with a sudden fear; for, it did seem to me, in an instant, that the Night-Hound might surely be upon the track of my goings.

And after that there had passed a little time, the while that I did listen very keen, lo! there burst out in the night, as it did seem scarce a mile off, the monstrous deep baying of the giant Hound. And I knew surely that the

Brute did track me, and a sick and utter horror did fall upon me; so that I could scarce get my foot-gear upon me, once more. Yet, in truth, I was not long to the matter, and was to my feet, and did hold the Diskos ready; and very desperate I was to the heart; for it is ever a fearsome thing to be put in chase, and the worse an hundred times when there is a sure knowledge that a deathly Monster doth be the pursuer.

Now, I did stand there but a moment it did seem, to make an anxious considering how that I might best assure me some chance to live through this swift coming Danger. And then did I think upon the stream, to use it, and I leapt quick therein, and did run very strong down the middle part, which was nowheres so much as thigh-deep, and oft not above mine ankles. And as I did run, there came again the bellow of that dire Brute, following, and was now, as mine ears did say, scarce the half of a mile to my rear.

And I did run but the stronger, for the dread of the sound; and so, maybe, for a little minute; and after that time, I stopt from mine heavy running, and went very wary, that I made no loud splashing; for by now the Monster-Brute should be something anigh to that place where I did enter the stream. And I looked round, with a constant looking; but did see no surely visible thing; though my fear did shape me an Hound from every shadow of the moss-bushes about me.

Then, in a moment, I did hear the Great Beast; for it bayed but a little way up the stream, as that it had overshot the place where the scent did end. And immediately, I sank swiftly into the water, which was there so deep as my knee, and turned upon my belly. And the water surged over my shoulders; for I kept my head above. And so I did look eager and fearful through the steam into the shadows and the half-darkness, towards where I did think to see the Night-Hound.

And in a moment I saw it coming; and it was a little vague, by reason of the smoke of the river; yet did seem black and monstrous in the gloom, and great as a mighty horse. And it went past me at a vast and lumbersome gallop; but I did not see it in that moment; for I dived my head down unto the rock of the river bottom, and held downward, until that I was like to burst for sore longing of breath.

Then I put upward my head, and took swift and deep breathings, and lookt about me, very cautious and fearful, as you can know. And I heard the Night-Hound casting round among the moss-bushes, and it did send up a wild and awesome baying; and I heard the bushes brake and smash beneath it, as it did run to and hither. And afterward there was a quiet; yet I moved not; but stayed there, very low in the water, and did have a thankful heart that it was warm and easy to persist in; for I had surely died of a frozen heart, if that it had been cold; for, by this time, you do know even with me, how bitter was the chill of the Land.

Now, I had been awhile lain thus upon my belly, and heard no sound from the monstrous Hound. Yet, I ceased not to be full of an horrid unease, concerning the Great Beast; for I did better to know what it did, than to have no knowing. And, sudden, I heard the sound of it, running very swiftly and coming nigh; and it passed me, and did go up the stream; and there was surely a quick stupor upon me; for I ducked not my head under the water; but stayed very still; which as it did chance, was maybe not such an utter foolishness; for my head did seem in that half-gloom to be, mayhap, no more than a little rock in the water, and I made no move to tell of life; yet should the Hound have smelled me; and that it failed in this matter, doth be a puzzle to me.

And as the great Night-Hound past me, it tore the earth and the bushes, with the exceeding strength that it put forth to run, and clods of the earth and stones of bigness were cast this way and that by the feet of the Hound, running. And so shall you have a little knowledge of the strength of that Beast.

And the Hound ran on into the distance, and presently, I heard it baying in the Night. Then I rose, and went onward, down the warm stream, and made a strong walking, yet keeping alway to the water; and oft did stop a little that I should listen; and always I heard the Night-Hound a great way off in the night, baying, and seeming that it did surely run to and fro, searching.

Now, I journeyed thus for twelve hours, and the baying of the Hound making search, did never cease. And I kept always to the water, as I did

say, that I should leave no scent unto the Hound. And by that twelve weary hours had gone, I found that I was come anigh unto the House of Silence. And this put me in great trouble; as you may perceive; for surely had mine whole effort been to the end that I should avoid that House, by a great way. Yet had the Hound driven me thus a-near.

Now I saw that the small river did go onward, and did make a breach across the Road Where The Silent Ones Walk; and I determined in my heart that I should leave the water, which was now grown nigh to a bitter cold, in that it was so long upon the face of the Land. Yet chiefly did I mind to leave the water, that I should come no more anigh unto that House of Silence; for the water did go that way. And I stood awhile, and did listen for the baying of the Hound; but could hear it no more; and did have a surety within me that it was indeed gone from searching for me.

Then I came out of the water, and went forward, stooping and creeping, among the moss-bushes, going outward to the Westward of North, so that I should go away so quickly as I might from the nearness of the House. Yet, lo! I was gone upon my hands and knees no more than an hundred fathoms, when I did find the moss-bushes to cease to the Westward, for a great way, and there to be a great bareness of rock, which, in truth, was much shown thereabout. And I dared not to go outward upon that naked Land; for then I had not been hid by the moss-bushes; but had stood plain there for all things of the Night to behold; and moreover, though I could nowise have a sure knowledge concerning this matter, yet did I hope within me that I should make a sure hiding from the Power of the House of Silence, did I but go very low among the bushes. But, indeed, it was like enough that naught could give me hiding; yet should I lose no chance unto my safety.

And because of this, I went backward among the bushes, and ceased to escape out unto the Westward. And I found presently, that the moss-bushes made but a narrow growth in that path, and grew only for a while by the side of the Great Road; so that I was surely fain to keep nigh to the Road, that I have the covering of the bushes.

And, in a while, I found the Road Where The Silent Ones Walk, to

bend inward at the North of the House of Silence; so that it came right horridly close unto the House; for here the hill on which the House did stand, was very abrupt and fell steeply unto the Road. And so was that Dreadful House stood up there above me in the Silence, as that it did seem to *brood* there upon the Land. And this side did seem truly as the other; and equal lone and dreadful.

And the House was monstrous and huge, and full of quiet lights; and it was truly as that there had been no Sound ever in that House through Eternity; but yet was it as that the heart did think each moment to see quiet and shrouded figures within, and yet never were they seen; and this I do but set down that I bring all home unto *your* hearts also, as that you crouched there with me in those low moss-bushes, there beside the Great Road, and did look upward unto that Monstrous House of Everlasting Silence, and did feel the utterness of silence to hang about it in the night; and to know in your spirits the quiet threat that lived silent there within.

And so shall you have mind of me, hid there among the bushes, and sodden and cold; and yet, as you will perceive, so held in my spirit by an utter terror and loathing and solemn wonder and awe of that Mighty House of Quietness loomed above me in the Night, that I wotted not of the misery of my body, because that my spirit was put so greatly in dread and terror for the life of my Being.

And also you shall have before you, how that I knew in all my body and soul, that I stood anigh to that Place where but a little while gone there had passed inward so dreadful to an everlasting Silence and Horrid Mystery those poor Youths.

And after that you have minded you of this, you shall consider how that the memory of all my life held dread thoughts of the monstrousness of that House; and now was I anigh unto it. And it did seem to my soul that the very Night about it, held an anguish of quiet terror. And always my mind did come back to the sheer matter that I was so anigh. And this thing I do say unto you once and again; for truly, as you do see, it hath imprinted itself deep into my spirit. Yet shall I now cease from saying further in this manner; for, surely, you shall never know all that was in mine heart; and if

I cease not, I do but be like to weary you.

And so did I hide and creep, and oft pause to a time of shaking quiet; and afterward gather something of new courage, and go onward; and peer upward at that monstrous House, stood above me in the night. Yet, as it did come about, I came presently clear of that horrid place; for the Road came round again unto the North, and I began that I made a better way through the moss-bushes; but never that I grew to much speed; for I had oft to go about, that I should miss a naked part here, and another there; for truly there was an abundance and bareness of rock, so that the bushes grew not so thick as I could wish.

And in the space of five hours was I clear of that House; and did have a greater ease about my heart; but yet was not free to come to food nor to slumber, the both of which I did sorely need; for I had slept neither eat for a weariful time, as you do know. But first I must go further off from the House, and afterwards come to some fire-hole, that I should dry myself and get warmth again into my body, which was bitter cold.

And now that I had come unto the Northward of the House of Silence, there came to me a great Wonder, which bred in me a mighty Hope and Gladness. For as I did go among the bushes, there broke sudden all around me in the aether, the low and solemn beat of the Master-Word. And the throb of the Word was utter weak; so that one moment I did say unto myself that I heard, and in a moment that I did not; yet had I no proper doubt in my heart.

And I reasoned with myself, and with a great shaking of excitement and expectation upon me, that the Master-Word came not from the Great Pyramid, which should have power to send it as a Great Force across the everlasting Night; whilst that this that throbbed about me was faint and scarce to be known even unto the keenness of the Night-Hearing, which was mine.

And, immediately, as I crouched low there, and thrilled with the hope that was bred in me, lo! there seemed to come the far faint voice of Naani, calling with a little voice within my spirit. And I thought the cry to have an utterness of supplication within it; so that I grew desperate to up and go to

running; yet did curb such foolishness, and stayed very hushed, to listen.

But I heard no more; yet was shaken continually with the Joy and Hope which this calling did breed in me, for truly did it seem now that I was right that I did determine to go unto the North; for sure was I now that the Lesser Redoubt lay that way in the Night. And it did seem plain unto me, that the House of Silence had put a barrier between; and had power to withhold so weak a calling. And now had I come beyond the Barrier. And I did perceive in my heart how that Naani had called off, maybe in the sadness of Despair; yet had the weak crying of her brain-elements been held from me by the horrid power of the house; and surely, as I did think, it was well named; for it did make a silence.

And so shall you stay with me in your hearts, and take to ourselves something of the new Gladness that held all my being; for it did seem truly that my bitter task and adventuring should not in the end be offered to Uselessness; and that I did truly draw unto that far place in the Everlasting Night, where mine own Maid did cry for me, that I should succour her.

And ever as I went, did I hark; but there was no more the low beating of the Master-Word in the Night; not at that time.

And presently, I spied outward to the West, as it did seem a good mile off in the night, the shining of a fire-hole; and I began to plan that I should come unto that place, and have warmth and dryness, and food and slumber. And, in verity, so set was I to the need of these matters that if there did be a Monstrous Thing nigh to the fire—as was so oft the case—then would I give battle unto it; for neither my Joy nor my labours did serve to put warmth into my body; and I must surely come anigh to fire, or die.

Then, as I kneeled upward among the moss-bushes, and made to lay a true course unto the fire-hole, I perceived that there came a Being along the Road unto my right; and I went low into the bushes, and moved not; for truly I had seen that there drew nigh one of the Silent Ones.

And I made a little place that should let me to see; and I spied out, with an utter caution; and lo! the Being came on very quiet, and with no hurry. And in a time, it went by me on the road, and did take no heed to me; yet did I feel that it had knowledge that I stoopt there among the

moss-bushes. And it made no sound as it went; and was a Dreadful thing; yet, it did seem unto my heart, as that it had no trouble of Wanton Malice to work needless Destruction to any. And this, I crave strangely that you to understand; for it was so to me that I had a quiet and great respect for that thing; and did feel no hatred; yet was very dreadly in fear of it. And it was Huge in size, and was shrouded unto its feet, and seemed, maybe ten feet high. Yet, presently, it was gone onward down the Road, and I was no more troubled by it.

Then did I make no waste of time; but set off unto the fire-hole; and kept so much to shelter as I might; but was oft made to run over baked places, ere that I should come to more of the bushes.

And I came presently nigh unto the fire-hole, and made a pause, and crept unto it, with a great care. And I found it to be in the bottom of a deep hollow of the rock of that part. And the rock was clear looking of all living matters, the which did make me to be glad. And I went round about the top of the hollow, carrying the Diskos very handily; but there was nowhere any living thing; and I feared not to go downward into the deep hollow, and so unto the fire-hole, which lay in the bottom, as you have perceived.

And when I was come there, I made a close search of the rock, and found it was very sweet and warm; and there were no serpents, neither any stinging creatures; so that a certain comfort came upon my spirit.

Then stript I off mine armour and gear, and afterward all my garments, so that I stood naked there in the hollow. Yet was that place almost so warm as some mild oven, and I had no fear to suffer from the cold of the Night Land; but was uneasy lest that any monstrous thing should be anigh to come to take me so unawares.

Now I wrung the garments, and spread them upon the rock near unto the fire-hole, where it was hot; and I did rub my body very brisk with my hands, so that I glowed into health and had no fear of a stiffness.

And afterward, I did look to my food and drink, and to the matters in the pouch; but there had no harm come to any, by reason of the tightness of the scrip and the pouch, that had kept off the water. And I eat and drank, there as I stood waiting for the garments to come to dryness; and

I walked about a little, as I eat; for I was restless to be into mine armour swiftly. And now I did turn this garment upward of the dry side, and now that; but did find them to steam, so that I turned them many times before they were proper.

Yet, in truth, they dried in but a little while, and I gat me into them very swift, and into the armour; and I felt the strength and courage of my spirit to come back into me, which had gone outward somewhat when I did stand there so naked. And this feeling you shall all have understanding of; and know that you would have felt that way, likewise, had you but stood there in that Land in so unhappy a plight.

And when I had come into mine armour, I put my gear upon me, and took the Diskos into my hand, and did climb out of the hollow; for I would find a more secure place to my slumber, and did not dare to sleep in that place; for it was beyond seven and thirty hours since that I did have sleep; though as I do see by my count, I have made it to seem but as five and thirty; yet was a part consumed in diverse matters that I have not set down. And you shall mind how bitter had been my labour and weariness in all that time; and I did know of a surety that sleep must come heavily upon me; so that I was sorely in need that I should search out a safe place; for I should not be lightly waked, until that I had slept away the tiredness of my heart, and the weariful achings from my body. And, indeed, I should mind you how that I was not yet come perfect from the bruising which I had gotten from the fight with the Yellow Thing.

And presently, when I had searched but a little while, I did find that a rock stood upward from a great clumping of the moss-bushes unto my left; and I went over to the rock, and made a search about it. And I found that there was a hole into the bottom part of the rock, and I thrust the Diskos into the hole, and made the blade to spin a little, so that it sent out a light; but there was no thing in the hole, and it did seem a dry and safe place for my sleep.

Then I turned me about, and went into the hole with my feet that way; and I found that it was so deep into the rock as the length of two men, and just so wide as I could lie in it without having it to pinch me. And there I

made my bed in the hole, and went swift unto my sleep, and scarce had but a moment even to think upon Naani; and by this thing shall you know how utter was my weariness.

Now I waked of a sudden, and was very clear and refreshed. And I crept to the mouth of the hole, and lookt out; but there was all a quietness round about, and nothing to threaten.

And I found that I had slept ten hours; so that I made a haste to eat and drink, that I should go forward swiftly upon my journey. And at that time, as in the time when I did eat, naked, in the hollow, by the fire-hole, I eat four of the tablets; and this you shall understand to be rightly due unto me, in that I had gone so long fasting in that my great journeying to come safe from the Hound, and to come past the House of Silence. And this shall seem but a little thing to you; yet was it a wondrous important matter unto me, that had gone so long with an empty belly, and was never satisfied. And neither should any be, that had eat so little as I did eat, and made to fill their belly always with a drink of water. Yet, I doubt not but that it did keep my soul sweet and wholesome and no useful thing to the Powers of Evil of the Land.

And when I had made an end of so great a gorging, and had ceased to be drunken with water, I gat my gear upon me, and took the Diskos into mine hand, and so went forth once more towards the North.

And presently, I was nigh unto the Road again; for it did curve something Westward a space beyond. And I was sore tempted to go upon the Road; for the ground was rough and the moss-bushes did catch my feet. Yet did I stay among the bushes, though the Road was true and smooth, by compare. And by this telling, you will perceive that I walked once more upright, and had given over to crawl between the bushes. And, in truth, this was so; for the Land did seem very quiet in all that part; and I had less of fear, now that I stood beyond the horrid unease of the House of Silence.

Now, after that I had journeyed twelve hours, I saw that I was come upon the commencement of a great and mighty slope, as that the world did slope downward always towards the North. And I went on again, after that I had eat and drunk, as I did likewise before this at the sixth hour of that

day's journey.

And presently, I perceived the Road to cease; and surely this did confound me; as that a man of this age had come to a part where the world did end; for you shall know that the Road was that which had seemed to go on for ever; and you shall mind the way of my life up till that time, and so shall you the better conceive of my bewilderment, and as it were a feeling of great strangeness unto one that was overprest, as you would believe, with strange matters.

Yet, truly, was this all as the little book of metal had told unto me; and so should I have been something prepared; yet are we ever thus needing eye-proof; and perhaps it is more proper that it be so.

Yet, you shall perceive me adrift somewhat as to direction; for I had steered before this time so that I should come to the North of the House of Silence; and afterward had shaped my way by the Road. But now was I adrift, as it might be set down, in the wilderness.

And so did I stand and consider, and presently did look unto the far Pyramid, which was now a great way off in the night, and had seemed but small by that which I knew it to be. And lo! as I did look, I perceived that I could but see the high upper-point of the light of the Great Pyramid, where did shine the Last Light; and I was confounded afresh; yet in a moment I saw that the greatness of the slope did account for this. But here I should tell to you that the slope was nowise steep; but did seem as that it should never cease. And mayhaps this is clear unto you.

And I perceived surely that the time was come when I should make an utter parting from the Great Redoubt; and the thought came very heavy upon me. And in the same time I knew that the aether was stirred by the emotions of the Millions; so that I had knowledge they watched me with the Great Spy-Glass, and did send word down unto the Hour-Slips; and by this did the Millions know, and have a great thinking upon me in that moment.

And you shall perceive how utter lost and lonesome I did feel. And it was at that time that I did test the compass, to comfort me, as I did tell before this, and feared I must sure forget, when I did come to the proper

place; yet have I minded me, as I did desire.

And I saw now that the Night Land that I did wot of, was hid from me by the slope. And I turned and looked down the slope; and surely all before me was utter wildness of a dark desolation; for it did seem to go nowhither but into an everlasting night. And there was no fire down there, neither light of any kind; but only Darkness and, as I did feel, Eternity. And downward into that Blackness did the great slope seem to go for ever.

Now, as I did stand there, looking downward into the Dark, and often backward unto the shining of the Final Light, and put to a horrid desolateness, behold! there came the low beating of the Master-Word in the Night. And it did appear as that it had been sent to give me courage and strength in that moment; and did seem unto my fancy that surely it did come upward unto me from out of the mighty blackness into which the Great Slope ran. Yet could this have been but a belief; for the aether doth have no regard unto direction to show you whence the spiritual sound doth come; and this did my knowledge and Reason know full well.

And I made that I would send back the Master-Word, sending it with my brain-elements, and so give news unto Naani how that I did struggle to come unto her. Yet did I have caution in time; for in verity, had I sent the Master-Word, then had the Evil Forces of the Land wotted that I was out; and mayhaps had come swift unto my Destruction; and so did I contain my spirit and desire, and made to do wisely.

Yet was I put in courage by the low beat of the Master-Word; and did listen very keen, that some message should follow; but there came none, neither did the weak throb of the Word come about me again, at that time. And because that I was now grown more to my natural state, and did feel that I should indeed find the Maid, I looked once more unto the Great Pyramid, long and eager and with a solemn heart; yet with no sign or salutation, as I was before determined. And afterward, I turned and went downward into the dark.

## CHAPTER VIII
*Down The Mighty Slope*

Now I WENT DOWNWARD very quiet and slow into that Darkness; and did make but a cautious way; for now you shall know me truly wrapped about with such a night as did seem to press upon my very soul, and such as you shall never have seen nor felt; so that I did seem lost even from my self, and did appear as that I went presently in unreal fashion, and did pass onward for ever and for ever through everlasting night; so that odd whiles I did make to walk with random, as that I stept no more upon this earth; but did go offwards into the Void. Yet was this foolishness of the mind set straight and proper each time that it did come about; for lo! I did kick against an upjutting rock here, and fall upon a great and unseen boulder there, and so was shaken very quickly to a sound knowledge that I trode the hard and actual earth; and had no true dealings with unreal matters.

And ever I did go downward; and by this only did I have a guide to my way. Yet, as you shall think, through reason of the utter dark I made scarce a mile in an hour or even two full hours; and so grew bitter by reason of mine unableness to go forward with a proper and free stride.

But I did think me presently upon a thing that I should do to light my path; and to this end, I did make the Diskos to spin, odd whiles, and did look down the mighty slope, the little way that the strange glistening of the Diskos did show, and so fixed my path into mine inward remembering, and would go forward afresh, until that I was shaken once more by the darkness, and would fain to look once again upon the blessedness of light, and make me some knowledge of my way.

And, truly, the light from the Diskos did seem astonishing great, and this to be because there was so monstrous a darkness all about me there forever. And thereafter would I go onward again, until the pain of my stumblings did bid me surely to have that sweet shining once more unto my path.

And so shall you perceive my going; and sore and miserable was it

unto the heart; and like to shake the courage of the spirit; yet, in verity, I had come through much, and did have intent to give way to no foolishness of thought.

And you shall well believe that I did make the light not more oft than I did surely need; for it was no properness of wisdom to use the power of the Diskos, save for mine extremity.

Now, presently, when I had done thiswise through six long and bitter hours, and it being now beyond the twentieth hour since I did last slumber, I sat me down there upon the Mighty Slope, in the everlasting Dark, and did eat two of the tablets, and made the water, and could but feel and hearken whether I did this thing right and that.

And when I had eat and drunk, I unfolded my cloak, and wrapt it around me, and placed the scrip and the pouch under my head; and the Diskos I took to company me; and so fell swiftly upon sleep; yet did think earnestly but vaguely upon Naani, as I came unto slumber.

And I slept all but six hours, and did waken very sudden there in the utter dark; and I got me to mine elbow, and did listen very keen; for I had waked immediately, as that something had touched me or come nigh unto me; and I gript the Diskos, and listened; but there did not even a little sound come to me out of all that night.

And presently I had more assuredness that naught did make harm about me; and I sat me up in the dark, and reached for my scrip, and did eat and drink, there in that utter night; and fumbled somewhat, as you shall think. Yet I was done in a while, and got my gear upon me, and the Diskos into my hand, and so to my feet and forward.

Now all that day, I did have a strange unease of the spirit, so that I stopt oft to listen, as that my soul told of something nigh unto me that did follow very quiet. Yet did mine ears perceive nothing; and so I alway to go downward again into the night that held the slope.

And here should I tell how that in the early part of the seventh hour, after I had eat and drunk, and went forward as ever, upon my journey down the Mighty Slope, I did have a very sore tumble against a sharp rock; for I put my foot sudden into a small hole, and this did make me to pitch.

And I was utter shaked by the fall and lay very quiet for a time; for the rock had surely ript my body, but for the armour.

And after that I was something renewed of strength and spirit, I made that I should go no more upon my feet, but upon my hands and knees; and thus should I feel the way that I went, and have a less need of the Diskos, which had not overmuch use to light my way, in that I shone it not often, and did guess more than I did perceive, as you may think.

And so I crept all that day, which was a bitter way of travel; yet had I done many a sore mile thus through the Night Land. And when that I had gone downward for eighteen hours, and eat and drunk thrice, I ceased from my labour, and did feel about in the darkness, that I come to a level place for my rest; and so did find presently, a place not so bad, and did push and cast away such small boulders as had been like to irk me.

Then did I eat and drink, and afterward composed me to my sleep, and had many a thought of Naani, as I did drift unto slumber; yet also had I memories of the strange half-fear that had been with me all that day, as though something went constantly near me in the Dark. And because of this, twice did I rise unto mine elbow, and listen; but heard no sound to trouble me, and afterward did trust that I did but fancy; and so came at last unto slumber, that yet was not over-restful, for truly I did listen even as I slept.

And when I had been asleep scarce six hours, I waked again very sudden, as I had done before, and had belief that something did be anigh unto me; and I gript the Diskos, and did hearken; yet was there no sound that mine ears did wot of; neither aught that had power to be surely known of the spirit.

And all that day was as the day before; save that about the eighth hour I came near to fall into some monstrous pit in the Great Slope; but did only fall with my breast upon the edge, and so drew back, and presently did crawl all around it in the dark, and come safe unto the lower side; yet shaken and put more in trouble of spirit than before, and fearful how I should go; for I knew not whether I had come among such things, or whether I had but few to sorrow me.

And so you shall perceive that I went over-cautious for a great while in all that utter dark; but did think at last upon a plan to go with more surety and speed. But to this I did need a cord, and surely I had no cord upon me; and if a boy be no boy that hath none such about him, shall not the same be said of any man! And this I did think, as I searched me; for the sayings of that day had many that were like to this.

Yet in the end I did compass my plan; for I did buckle the scrip and the pouch together, and took one of the straps from the pouch; and this strap was long and thin, and well suited unto my purpose. Then I fixt a stone into the end of the strap, and buckled it there, and after that, I cast the stone before me, as I went upon my hands and knees; and I did hold to the hither end of the strap, and so was abled to have something of knowledge whether there lay any great deepness immediately before me, and thiswise to strive that I fall not down some monstrous cliff in the night.

And so did I go, casting the stone continually to my front, down the slope; and this you shall think to be a cumbersome fashion of travel; yet was I in better case than in all the time since I had begun to go downward of the Mighty Slope in the everlasting darkness.

And at the eighteenth hour I did sleep; and was waked strangely before the sixth hour, even as I had waked before. And this did put always upon me a new wonder and unease. Yet did no harm seem to come unto me, and I did strive that I have no needful trouble of mind. But that something was always nigh unto me in the dark, I do truly believe; yet have I no knowing that it was evil; for it harmed not me.

And three days more I journeyed thus, and did never cease to creep downward weariful upon my hands and knees; and the Diskos I had to my hip, and so shall you know how I carried it. And by this, as you do know, I had been on the Great Slope six days of utter Dark; and did have no wotting but that I went unto some dire and dreadful place; for, surely, I had gone for ever downward a monstrous way.

And here, before I tell further, I must set down how that the cold was much gone from out of the air upon the slope; and the air was grown, as it did seem, very heavy unto my chest. And concerning this matter I should

say something. For, if I do mind me, I have said not overmuch concerning the air of the Night Land and the Mighty Pyramid; for truly I have been so set to tell my story of all that I did truly see and adventure upon. Yet, though I have said but little, you will surely have perceived that the air of that far and chill time was not as the air of this; but was thin and keen within the Night Land, and lay not, as I do think, to a great height above the land, but only nigh to the earth.

And as you do know through my tellings, there was a wondrous difference between the air within the Mighty Pyramid, and that which lay without around the base; for upward beyond that, I did understand that there was no outward air that any should breathe; and so was all the Pyramid sealed in certain wise in all the upper Cities for ever; and whether it was sealed *utterly* from the outward air at the base, I do not surely remember, if, in truth that I did ever bother my head to such matters.

Yet, if I be set proper in memory and understanding, we did draw air from the Underground Fields; but whether they gat any change or newness of air from the Night Land, I have no knowledge; and do lament that I have no sure knowing. Yet, as you shall believe, I could surely write an hundred books upon that Wonder of the Future, and be still lacking in the half of all that there is to be told; and so do I try to have courage to this my task, and to have no over-trouble, because that I do tell but a little of a Great Tale.

And here in this place will I set down how that the Peoples of the Pyramid were greater to the chest, methinks, than we of this age; but yet do I have no oversurety in the matter; for well it may be that the Reason of *this* age doth blind within me somewhat the Knowledge that I have concerning *that*; for, in verity, is it not but a natural thing to believe those Peoples to be great of the chest, so that they should make a proper dealing with the thin air of that place and that time? And yet, as I do strive to make plain unto you, because that this thing should be, by the making of my Reason, I do the more distrust that Reason shall make foolish my Knowledge; for even a fool should suppose that which I have told; and the truth may be even otherwise.

Yet that the Peoples of the *Upper* Cities had great chests, I do well

know; for this was a common knowledge; even as we of this age do ac-knowledge the Peoples of Africa to be of blackness, or those of Patagonia to be of great stature. And by this one thing should any know a man of the Upper Cities, from a man of the Lower Cities. And because that there grew this difference among the Peoples, there had been once, as any could learn from the Histories, a plan whereby the Peoples should be moved upward and downward through the great height of the Mighty Pyramid, from this city unto that. Yet had it met with great disfavour; and was put out of force; and this is easy to be seen as the natural way of the human heart.

And here it doth occur unto me that it was like enough to be a plan for health, beside of training of the mind, that each youth and maid was put to travel through all the cities of the Mighty Pyramid; the which did take three years and two hundred and twenty-five days, as I have told before this. For by this plan, were they made to breathe the air of every height, and this, mayhaps, unto the good of their developing. And they also to discover that air which was best to their need.

And concerning the air of the Night Land, you shall know that there was in all that Land no flying thing, because that the air was grown very thin; yet, as the Records did show, there had once been monstrous flying-brutes, that went over the Land in mighty bounds; but this was in a long gone age; and we could but suppose that the Records gave truth.

And here you shall know that, when the Monstruwacans did learn that I would journey through the Night Land, in search of Naani, there had been some foolish and well-intended talk among them that I take a small flying-ship, that was in the Great Museum beside the models of the Great Ships. For, truly, this machine was yet sound to go; for it was made of the grey metal of the Mighty Pyramid, that did seem to have no power to cease. Yet, in verity, I had no skill to manage this, neither had it flown, through an hundred thousand years; so that none did know the master-ship of that art, which did be learned but by a constant practice, and oft made uneasy by fallings that did wreck the machine, as I did know from the Book of Flying. And, moreover, as I have told, the air of the Night Land was grown over-weak to uphold such a thing; which, I doubt not, had

made the Peoples of the Pyramid to cease from flyings, quite so much as that they did fear the Forces of Evil in the night.

And if that there had been air and skill sufficient unto this purpose of flying, yet had I been wicked with foolishness that I should work to be hung upward in the night, for all the Evil of the Night Land to behold. And though I had gone up some great way, yet the machine had surely made a great noise in the quietness of the eternal night, as you shall suppose.

Now indeed am I gone weary that I should need to tell so much concerning the air of that Time and Place; for surely I do seem to make this my story as that I did make a lecturing upon matters of chemistry; and so do I cast about, that I may not bother to tell more upon this matter. Yet, in truth, a little more of my thinkings and observings had I better set down here, and so be done with it. But you shall have patience with me, and know that had this, my story, been no more than an idle tale, I had been free to make no labour with such matters.

Now there doth a wonder come to me why that the Road Makers, who were of that far-off Age which was before the Age of the Mighty Pyramid, did not *fly* downward from the upper world into the deep of the monstrous valley; but did instead build a road.

Yet it may be that the air of the upper world had grown thin a great age, so that they had truly forgot that once man did have power to fly. But even if that they did have proper machines to this purpose, surely it were a wondrous and fearful thing to fly downward an hundred great miles; for they surely to have a dread that they never to rise again through so huge a deep.

And, moreover, the downward world that was the bottom of the Great Valley, was full of monsters, as was told in the little metal book. And the monsters were very strange and unknown; and foreign to the whole world, that had never come unto the deep of the Valley. And the Valley had come, as you shall mind, when the earth did split; and this thing was, in truth, like to be thought that same Ending of the World, which all Nations have been taught to believe shall come. For in verity, when the world did split and burst, and the oceans rushed downward into the earth, and there was fire,

and storms, and a mighty chaos, surely it was proper to think that the End had come. Yet was it, in truth, but the beginning of hope of a new Eternity of Life; so that out of the End came the Beginning, and Life out of Death, and Good out of that which did seem a dire matter. And so is it always.

Yet doth this go past my first wonder, which did concern the wherefore that they made not to descend in Things of Flight. Yet, maybe, shall my reasons stand to show why this was not.

And again, mayhap it did chance that some were wild adventurers, and did leap over the edge of the upper world, having to ease their flight certain contrivings, like to parachutes. And these you shall picture, as that you watched them to leap; and so shall you see them go downward into the gloom; and you shall see them for maybe ten miles, and maybe for twenty miles; and afterward shall they be lost utterly in that Great Deep, and seen no more of any man for ever.

But when the Nations became Road-Makers, and came downward slowly to the monstrous Deep of the Mighty Valley that did split the World, then were they come there by millions, and with power sufficient to fight against the Beasts; and afterward to grow back again to an ancient Civilizing; and so to the building of the great airships that were yet shown in the Great Museum of the Pyramid. And here shall I cease from these my thinkings on this matter; for indeed, who shall say what did be truly a Reason for those peoples and what was their Need? And so do I come to no surety by my wonderings.

Yet, as you do know, all things do seem verily to go in a circle; for, behold, in time, they of the Mighty Pyramid, were likewise held off from the glory of the airships; and so were gone backward a great way, according as we do look upon this matter. And so hath this been the way always, as you shall know who have studied and thought, and seen the true ways and goings of Life.

And now will I go forward in my telling; and here will set down a sure thing that I did perceive, both by mine ears and by my fingers; for, as I did make clear to you but a while gone, there had come a change into the air as I did go downward of the Mighty Slope; and truly I was come to a

great and new Deepness, even beyond that of the wondrous depth where did stand the Last Redoubt. So that I was afar down and in a monstrous night. And the air here was of a great thickness and abundancy, even as it might be the air of this our Age; or maybe more or maybe less; for who may compare two matters with a sure guessing, that do have an eternity to keep them asunder.

And because that the air was grown very strong and apparent, it shall be, mayhaps, that it was by reason of this thing that the water, when I did make it, did fizz upward in a moment very loud and plentiful, and did boil overward to the earth from out of the cup, and wet upon my hand. And surely this thought did come very keen to my Reason, as I did fumble, each time of mine eating, there in the everlasting night and lonesomeness of the Great Slope.

And so shall you have knowledge now of this and that thing which did come upon my thought, and of the little and the big wonders, and all shall help something to give unto you the ache of newness and bewilderment that was constant companion unto me.

Now by this time, as I have said, I was gone downward ever for six great days; and I did seem as that I should presently come to the middle of the world; for of going downward there was no end.

And then, when it did be that I was near ready to believe this, I perceived far off in the deep of the night a little shining that was yet weak and unsure. And I do not know whether I can truly give unto you the great astonishment and pain of hope that did come upon me; so that I grew sick in all my being but to behold once again the blessedness of light, and to have help unto my belief that I went not downward to an utter desolation.

And I stood upward from my knees, and did look very earnest, and surely it did seem that a light was there afar downward in the night; and again it did seem that I must be plagued by my hopes and by my fancy, and that there was nowhere any light. And then again I did see it very clear, and not to be mistaken, and I had a shaking to come upon me, and I gat me to a run, and made a great and mad speed down the dark slope. And lo! I was not gone any way, but I went headlong, and near brake myself; and could

but hold my teeth together very fierce and quiet until that the pain was something gone from me. And afterward, I gat me again to mine hands and knees, and went slowly, as before; and so for a great hour or more, and did look oft; and alway the light became more plain to my sight; but ever to come and go, oddly-wise. Yet did I go six hours, before that I was come anywise near to it. And by this shall you know how great a space off it had been. And lo! when that I did seem surely anigh unto it, truly was it still far away in the night; and I came not indeed near to it until that I was gone onward again for three hours more. And all that time did I yet go downward into the night; but the Slope now did not be so utter dark.

Now, presently, I made a pause, and stood upward to my feet, so that I should the better perceive the light. And lo! as I did look toward it, I heard a faraway sound in the dark, as that something did set up a strange and monstrous piping in the night. And immediately, I went to mine hands and knees among the stones of the Slope, and kept myself low in the darkness, so that I should be the less plain to be seen, did any Monster approach.

But there came nothing to trouble me, and I went downward of the Slope for yet another hour; and all the time that I did go, the sound of the piping grew more in the great eternity of the night upon the Slope.

And by this time was I come truly near unto the light; but yet did not behold it plainly; for it did burn beyond certain monstrous rocks that stood between. And I went to the left for, maybe, the half of a big mile; and all the while that I did go, the piping made a mightier whistling in the Night; and it did seem presently as that the earth sent forth the sound and revelry of wild roarings. And I went the more silent; and later did kneel among three rocks, and peered forth for a while upon the place before me.

And now, being come nigh unto the light—though yet it was not unhid from behind the great barriers of the uprising rocks, I perceived that I crouched within the mouth of a mighty gorge; and the left side was a great way off, and I saw it plain at whiles when the light did rise; but the light was to the right, and it was so wondrous great that it did make clear to me that a mountain was to that side of the gorge, and went upward into the everlasting night, as it did seem for ever.

And afar down the gorge, I did see the shinings of strange fires, faint and a great way off. And so was I come at last to the bottom of the Mighty Slope. Yet the gorge also to go downward, but not so great.

And presently I did go forward again; and so did open the point of the rocks, as the sailors do say. And I saw now that there gushed forth a great blue flame from the earth; and the mighty rocks stood about it, as that they were olden giants groupt there to some strange service.

And concerning this flame I was not overmuch astonished in my Reason; for it had seemed to me as I drew anigh, that the fire and the sound should be made by the roaring and whistling of a burning gas that did issue forth among the rocks. Yet, truly, though it did be a natural matter, it was yet a wondrous sight, and set amazement on my senses; for the flame did dance, and sway whitherward monstrously, and sometimes did seem that it dropt so low as an hundred feet, and afterward went upward with a vast roaring unto the utter height, and did stand mighty and blazing, maybe a full thousand feet, so that the far side of the gorge was lit, and surely it was seven great miles off or more; but yet did show plain and wondrous. And the light did show me the flank of the mountain, that made the right hand side of the Gorge, to go up measureless into the night.

And so shall you perceive that I stayed awhile among the rocks that were in the mouth of the gorge, that I should gaze upon this thing; but afterward I lookt this way and that way, so that I should have a knowing of the place where I was come.

And it was a wild and stark and empty place, as you must perceive. And the far side did be great miles off, as I did say; and everywhere there was abundance of rock and lonesomeness. And before me there went the great and dim length of the gorge, and there were lights here and lights there, in a great distance, and oft—as it did seem—the quiet dancing of lights in diverse places; but yet were these gone on the instant. And ever there was a strong and vacant silence upon that place.

And presently, after that I had looked once more unto the mighty dancing flame, and perceived nowhere any life around it, I went onward down the quiet gorge. And for a great way as I journeyed was my path lit by

the dancing of the blue flame; and oft should I seem to be going but dimly among the rocks, and my shadow faint and long; and lo! the flame would leap, and all the gorge come to a wondrous brightness, and my figure to shorten, and the shadows to be black and strong. And so shall you perceive how I went.

And oft did I turn me about to behold the dancing of the Great Light; for it was solemn to my spirit, even amid so much of Greatness and Eternity, to think upon that Flame, and to conceive that it had an utter age danced there at the foot of the Mighty Slope, unseen, through lonesome Eternities. And this I do tell unto you; that thereby may you have some knowledge of the strangeness and the bitter loneliness of that place; which, in verity, did seem the expressing of all the lonesomeness of my wanderings.

And all the time as I did go downward of the great Gorge, there sounded the blast of the roaring, that was presently afar to my back; and the mountain sides did catch it here and in that place, and sent it offwards with strange and improper echoings, as of a chill piping, or oddwise as hushed whisperings of monstrous creatures; so that I did oft stoop to hide a little among the boulders; for truly I knew not but that some unnatural thing called from the darkness of the mountain side.

And for six hours I walked onward thus, and sometimes did hide, having a sudden fear, as I have told.

And presently, in a great while, the roaring was sunk to a far and monstrous piping; but in the end to no more than a far and uncertain whistling, that yet did catch strange echoes in the night. And in the end there was only a quietness. And yet, as you do perceive, there had been always a silence in that Gorge, as I have told, and this to the despite of the whistling. And I do hope that you have understanding with me in this matter; for it was truly as I have told, and there is no contrariness of telling in this matter.

Now in all this time that I had walked in the great Gorge, I had past four of the far lights that I did see from the bottom of the Slope; and the two first and the fourth were blue, but the third was green; and all did dance and quake, and sent fitful shinings into the belly of the Gorge. And there came also from them whistlings, and from the second one a low and

strange moaning noise; and I doubted not the gas did come oddly and with trouble. And I past these things with no great thought; for truly they were no matters for notice, after that which I had beheld.

Now, as you shall mind, it was surely in the early Third of the seventh day of my journey down the Mighty Slope that I saw the first shining of the monstrous gas fountain; and from that time until now had there past maybe sixteen hours. And, as you do wot, I had eat not in all my travel since that I had seen the light; so that I was gone to a proper lack inward; and moreover, it was full nineteen hours or more since that I had slept; and all that while had I laboured.

And I ceased me from wandering, and lookt about that I should come to a safe and proper place for my slumber; and this I saw very quick; for there was dry stone and rock everywhere, and no failing of holes and diverse places to my purpose; so that I was soon in a little cave between two mighty boulders.

And here I eat four of the tablets; for truly so many were my due, and I had not been violent had I eat more. And afterward, I made some of the water, and it did fizz up in a moment; so that I perceived that but a good pinch made a great cup-full. And this I set to the count of the strong and heavy air, as I have told, which I did think to have a greater power of chemistry.

And presently I slept, having my gear about me as ever, and the Diskos to my breast. And as I went into slumber, I thought sweetly upon Naani, as I had done, indeed, an hundred times since I was come to the hopefulness of the lights of the Gorge.

Now, whilst I slept, I dreamed that the Master-Word did presently beat all about me in the night. Yet, as I do mind, I waked not; and because that I continued to sleep, I have no sure knowing whether this was truly a dream, or an Happening. And I minded me upon it, when I waked; but this was after that I had slept seven hours; and I could have no sureness anywise of the matter; but only that I was come safe through my sleep; though heavy within my head and limbs, as that the air did call me unto a further slumbering, as is like enough.

And after that I had eat and drunk, I put my gear about me, and the

Diskos to my hip, for I needed both my hands to the task of journeying amid the great boulders. And I set forth again down the half-light of the mighty Gorge, and through eighteen hours I made a strong going, save when I did pause at the sixth and the twelfth hours to mine eating.

And by the eighteenth hour was come, I was very ready to my food and slumber; and presently I was asleep in a place of the rocks. And that day had I past three and twenty of the dancing gas fires; and five been like a white fire; but the others blue and green. And all did dance and made a strange and uncertain light within the great Gorge; yet was it a peaceful thing unto my spirit that there was truly light, as you shall understand.

And I slept six hours, and waked, and did want more sleep, as you shall think. But I eat and drunk and put my gear upon me, and went on downward of the Gorge.

And at the sixth hour, after that I had eat and drunk, I came to a part where the big gas fires did cease to dance, and there was a certain darkness upon that place. Yet was it not a proper dark; for there came the glimmer of a flame here and the glimmer of a flame there, as that little flames came upward between the stones, and did vanish, and come upward in another part. And so did light and die out constant and forever amid the stones and the boulders of that lonesome Gorge; and made a low-spread light, so that it did seem unto me that strange shudders of light beat upward through the dark of that place.

And I went onward, and a heavy fume did seem to hang in the air, and horrid gases to come upward from the earth in odd puffings; and anon a light would leap upward beyond the next stone, and afterward vanish, and there would be an hundred thousand such upon every hand, running to and fore; and afterward for a moment an utter dark, and again the little flames everywhere; so that it did seem I went one moment amid the heart of a strange country of fire, and immediately through a country of utter night. And this was to me strange and a peculiar matter. Yet, as I do think, the gases did bother me the more; for they did seem as that they were like to hurt mine health utterly; for, in verity, oft did I seem as that I should choke and breathe no more, by reason of the poison that came upward

from among the stones and the boulders.

And all that time, as they came or went, did the little flames make small *phlocks* of sound in the Gorge as they did flash or die; and the sounds did seem, to my likening, as stones cast into an utter silent pool; for they but made apparent the everlasting quiet of the Gorge.

And afterward, I came beyónd this place, and you shall see me going very lonesome among the rocks of the Gorge, beyond. And by this, it was come nigh unto the eighteenth hour; and I did find a place proper to my slumber, and did eat and drink, and was quickly gone over unto sleep.

And as you shall know, I went always unto slumber with sweet and with troubled thoughts of the Maid. Yet, for a great while, I had been put so mightily to the labour of my way that my heart did suffer less at this time than should be thought; and truly it doth show me how I was drawn unto that One with all my being, that I did surely think so oft and sweetly upon her amid so many perils and matters of horror. And this doth seem something strange to say, when that you do consider that I was adventured unto these same perils and horrors but only for the sake of the Maid.

And in six hours did I wake, as I did strive alway to set myself to do; yet was I very heavy and slow for a little, until that I was more properly come to wakefulness. And surely, as I did think before, this was like to be put upon me by the weighty air of the place; but yet it might be that the gas which did float in the Gorge was upon my lungs. And also, as you have perceived, if but you have attended my way, the air was grown warm, and oft were the rocks pleasant to the seat, and all of these matters did contrive to make me slumbrous.

Now, presently, the gas fires did cease utterly in the Gorge, and I lookt downward, along that great place, and saw only a greyness, but above the greyness there was, as it did seem, something of a vague and ruddy shining in the night. And this did wake me to wonder what new thing lay before; so that I grew more eager among the boulders.

And, later, when I had eat at the sixth and the twelfth hours, and gone on awhile, I came to a place where the Gorge made a quick turning unto my left, and at the end of the turning was a red and glowing light that was

very great and wonderful; so that I was utter keen to come to that place, that I should discover what made the shining. And the place where I was come then, was very dark, because that I was nigh under the mighty wall of the mountain of the right side of the Gorge. Yet above, as it did seem to me, there was a far red upward glowing in the night.

Then did I go forward very fast, and presently, in a good while, I discovered that I drew near to a second great turning, that went to the right. And about the seventeenth hour, I came nigh unto the second great turning. And here did I put caution upon me, and crept for a while among the dark rocks of that place, that I should come to a sight of that which made the monstrous red shining.

And presently, I was beyond the corner of the mountain, and did look downward into a mighty Country of Seas, and the burning of great volcanoes. And the volcanoes did seem as that they burned in the Seas. And the country was full of a great ruddy light from the volcanoes. And so shall you perceive me there among the rocks that did all stand upward strange and bold and silent in the red and monstrous glare of the light. And I, as it did seem, the one thing of life in all that desolation and eternity of rock and stone, there in the end part of the great Gorge.

And I peered forth into the wonder of the light, and was full of thrillings and fancies that I was surely come to the place where the Lesser Redoubt had been builded. And immediately I knew that this was not so, for surer had not Naani told how that they were in a land of darkness. And if this did be so, truly, how wondrous and dread a way had I yet to go, if that this Country of Seas and mighty volcanoes stood between.

Surely, it did seem to me then as that I must wander searching unto the world's end. And so shall you be company unto me there with my trouble and my thoughts, and the immediate wonder and strange glory of that mighty Country.

## CHAPTER IX
*The Dark Pyramid*

Now in two hours more I was come clear down out of the Gorge, and stood in that Country; and for all that I did feel fresh troubled and bewildered, yet was I rejoiceful, as you may believe, in the surprising light and splendour of that sudden Land.

And before that I had come down out of the great Gorge, I had stood high within the mouth thereof, and lookt well out over the mighty Country. And I had counted seven and twenty great volcanoes, and this doth not take heed of two monstrous ranges of fire-hills that burned afar off, something unto my right. Neither doth it take account of an hundred thousand lesser places of fire.

And truly it did seem a very land of fire and water. For there was a small fire-hill stood within a sea, as it did seem no more than a little mile from that place where I did stand. And maybe a score to the back of it, spread all about. And here shall I do proper to tell concerning the seas. For there were of these, that I did count at that time, three that were small, and a mighty sea that went onward for ever into the red light of the fire-hills, so that it was gone utterly out of my sight, and did show no ending.

And there rose up out of the seas, islands; and on the islands, volcanoes. But in other parts the fire-hills did come upward straightly from the sea. And over the near sea, as it did seem, there lay a plentitude of steam, as that the sea did boil at whiles and in diverse places.

And there did seem to me, as it were within the red atmosphere of that place, as that there were a muttering thunder, low and constant, shaking the air, now from that distance and now from this, and this did I judge to be the voices of the fire-hills, speaking with the fire that lived in them.

And you shall conceive how utter new was all this unto me; for there was in that Country a constant Voice of the Energy of Life, so that the World-Noise of this our Age was even there again, and with a keen and undoubted apparentness; and the more so some ways, than now.

And here shall I set down more closely the things that were ready to my gaze.

And first, that it did much attract me, there was a huge and blackened mountain unto the left of the mouth of the Gorge, and the mountain did go upward into the night, maybe fifteen and maybe twenty miles. And there was a mighty peaked volcano that grew out from the side of the mountain so high up as five miles, as I did guess that height; and this was upon the far side. And above this there was a second, maybe nine or ten great miles up in the blackness of the night that hung afar upward. And, as that this were not great wonder enough, there did burn and glow two other mighty fire-hills, at an utter height, upon the left crest of that black mountain; and these were upward so monstrous a way, as that they did seem to make strange and smouldering suns within the night. And truly, as you shall perceive, this was a wondrous thing.

And below these upward fire-hills there rose up from the earth vast mountains of ash and burned stuff, that had been cast forth by these perched volcanoes, and had poured downward unto the earth throughout Eternity, and so to build grey and sombre monuments unto the dreadful glory of Time.

And to my right there was always sea and sea and the red blazing of the fire-hills; but unto my left, there were mighty forests, and there rose upward here and in that place, as that they were beyond the great woods, monstrous fire-hills. And so do you take from me something of that first impressing upon my brain and sense.

And after that I had come down out of the mouth of the great Gorge, as I did tell a little while gone, I came upon a pause; for, surely, which way was the way proper unto my search. And I lookt about for a great while, and afterward did climb back into the Gorge, and called myself foolish, that I had not thought to map my way ere I came down.

And when I was come up into the Gorge again, lo! I saw that there was but one way that I should go; for truly, as I have said, there was only the seas unto my right; but unto the left, where the shores did meet the seas, there seemed, so far as mine eyes did tell to me, a clear way for a space.

And mayhap, when I had come so far, I should even find a further way to go forward. And so did I descend again unto the Country of the Seas, as I did ever call that red-shining country of water and fire.

And by, that I was come again from the height of the Gorge, it was four and twenty hours since that I did last sleep; so that I was fain that I should put into some nook, and come to slumber, as you shall well believe.

And I found me a neat and proper place, where three great trees grew about a little basin of rock that was very dry and warm. And here, after that I had eat three of the tablets, and drunk some of the water—the while that my belly did yearn, as ever, for proper eating-stuff—I made my bed in the little basin of the rock, and lay me down, and did begin to think awhile upon Naani; but was gone over to sleep before that I was aware.

And lo! I was suddenly awake, and did find that I swam in a hot water; and a mercy, I did think, was it that I was not drowned as I did sleep. And I gat me to my feet, and the basin was full of water, hot and steaming, and pungent to the taste, as well I did know. And I perceived now that the water poured in from a smoothed slit upon the far side, and did come with a strange gurgling and bubbling, so that I conceived some deep well to boil, and thus to drive upward this water into the basin; and glad was I that it did not boil as it came forth.

And surely, now that I was upon the dry land, and did consider, I did quickly suppose that the water had poured forth at seasons into the basin for an eternity of time, and afterward did go back by fissures in the bottom of the basin; and this to happen, as I soon did find, a little beyond the length of every hour; and, indeed the basin to empty slow as I did watch.

Now, being much wetted, I stript off mine armour, having before this dipt out mine effects from the hot pool, and so did come down to the naked flesh, and I found a place where the rock was hot, and here I did spread my garments. And whilst that they came to dryness, I gat me into the hot pool, and had a very pleasant bathing, and did have no great fear of any dangerous thing; for, as it did seem, I had surely left all such behind, within the Night Lands. Yet did I have the Diskos upon the pool edge to my hand; for I had no proper assurance in this matter. Yet, as it did prove, there were

many monstrous beasts in that Country; but never did I feel the nearness and horrid power of any Evil Force; for these, as I do conceive, were congregate and gathered about the Mighty Pyramid, being attracted thereto by the great spiritual essence of so wondrous a multitude of humans gotten so close in one spot, even as sharks do come after the ship that hath bullocks within. Yet, how that the Evil Powers were given entrance unto this *State of our Life*, I have no sure knowing; yet have I put forward certain thoughts on this matter in an earlier place; and more than such thinkings is surely vanity; for there is no certainty in my Reasoning concerning the thing.

Now, presently was my clothing dry, yet before this, I had come out from that bath, which truly was nigh all gone backward into the earth. And I dressed me again, and got my armour upon me, and afterward was I in a more lightsome state of the mind; and yet very ready to come again unto my sleep. And this I did, and had six hours more beside the pool; and once was wakened somewhat by the gruntling and bubbling noise of the water, that was made as the pool did fill time and again.

And when the six hours were gone, I waked very well fitted in my senses and feelings to go forward again through that red-lighted Country, and this I did, after that I had eat and drunk.

Now all that day I went forward at a great pace; and the nameless woods were unto my left, and the shores of the seas unto my right. And oft did I find that the trees grew even into the water, so that oft did I go forward among the trees, and a very wonderful thing was this to me, that never had known before in all my life, until I was come into that Country, how that a glad and wild mystery doth live among forest trees. For there was no such strange wildness among the groves of the Underground Fields; though a solemn beauty in plenty. And the scent of the woods was sweet unto my spirit, as you shall wot.

Now all the time that I did go, there was the shore unto my right; but always to my left, and around me oft-times as I did say, the great forests. And as I did go, lo! there was life in all those darksome woods, and living eyes did peer out odd whiles upon me, and afterward go backward into the dark; so that I wotted not whether to fear, or to have no heed of trouble. Yet

naught did come anigh to me, to make any hurt.

And thrice in that day did I come to little fire-hills that burnt redly, and sent out fire and noise, so that I heard their trouble each time through the forest, before that I was come to them. And about each was there a deadness and desolation, where the fire had killed the big trees; yet, as I did observe, the quick life of little plants did grow more nigh, as that they were born and lived between the times of the fire-bursts. And this I do take it that you perceive.

And in that one day I past thirty and seven boiling springs; but whether they boiled truly, I do have no knowledge; only that they sent out a great steam oft-times; and some did make a strong roaring noise; so that to hear them afar off in the forests was to think odd times that some wild beast roared strangely.

Now, when the eighteenth hour was come, I sat me down, as I had done upon the sixth and the twelfth hours, and eat two of the tablets, and drank some of the water, which here did fizz very rich and quick.

And afterward I lay down to my slumber, for I was greatly wearied. And I had chosen a place against a great rock, which was so that no creature might come upon me from behind. And I came easy upon sleep; but yet I did fix it upon me that I slumber only with the body; for I did know, by the shining of the eyes in the darksome woods, that strange creatures abode in the mighty forests.

And ere I was gone over to sleep, I thought upon Naani, as I had done much all that day, as though her spirit did hover near unto mine, and did strive pitiful to speak with me. And this I set out to you, that you shall know how it did seem unto me in my thoughts and fancyings. And as I lay there, I put a blessing upon her, and a determination into my heart that I make a more desperate speed of my going, if that might be; so that I come the sooner to that strange, and unknown place in the dead world where did stand the lesser Refuge. And I was then asleep in a moment.

And lo! sudden I was awake. And lovely was the brightness of that Country, that did show me in a moment my danger, and did not keep me suspend in fearful Doubt, as did the grey darkness and strange shadows

and lights of the Night Land. For I saw, on the instant that I got me to mine elbow, how that certain things did crouch within the borders of the trees, no more than a score paces off. And I perceived in a moment that my spirit had been given knowledge, and had wakened me. And I stared, the while that I did grip the Diskos; and I saw that there were six squat men that were humpt at the neck and shoulder; and they did crouch all there in a row, and were something hid by the shadows; and I perceived that they watched me; and the eyes of the men did shine like the eyes of beasts; and so shall you know somewhat of the strange terror that came upon me. Yet had I the Diskos and mine armour; and though my heart did shake a little, yet was my spirit assured to conquer.

Now I gat me to my feet, and had the Diskos ready within my hand; and behold! I could not see the Humped Men, for they were gone from that place; yet never did I see them go, though I had kept my gaze very steadfast upon that part where they did hide. And, as you shall understand, I was near ready to believe that there had been nothing there within the border of the wood; yet truly I knew that the men with the humps had been there, as I had seen.

Now, I looked presently, and found that I had slept five hours; and I eat two of the tablets, as I did stand there, watchful; and afterward drank some of the water; and so was ready to go forward again; for I was grown very anxious to be gone from that place; and did have no knowledge but that those strangely humpt Men were but a little way off, among the trees, and might come upon me in a moment; or, further, that they did go to call an army of other humped men to my destruction.

And after that I was ready, and had my gear secure upon me, I set off at a great stride, and did hold the Diskos very handy, and lookt this way and lookt that way, and all the while made onward with speed; for, truly, I was grown so lean and hard that it did seem to me that I had power to out-pace those men or aught else of their kind.

And all that day, through thirty great hours did I go forward, at that stride, and did always watch; and at every sixth hour, I eat two of the tablets and drank a little of the water, and went onward again.

And so did I hope that I was lost from those Humped Men. Yet, though I did hope, my faith was not this wise; for twice and thrice did it come to me that there went things through the woods to my left all that day, and did keep always to a level with my speed; yet were always hid. And, as you shall believe, this did be a very shaking thing to my heart, and did make my hope of but little account.

Now, because that I had no faith to company my hope, I was not easy to have slumber, until that I was come to a place proper and safe. And so, as I have told, I went onward through thirty great hours; and, in truth, in all that while I did find nowhere that did seem to fit my need.

And lo! about the end of the thirtieth hour, I perceived that there was water ahead, besides the water of the sea that was ever to my right. And I thought, maybe, that the sea did go inward at that part of the land; but it was otherwise; for when I was gotten to that place, I found that a river came into the sea, and did come out of all the country that lay unto my left.

And in the mouth of this river, there was a small island; and surely I did look across to the island, and think it a refuge from the Humped Men that did surely play dog upon my going. Yet, truly, this was but an idle thought, and my need was that I should come to some way to cross over the river, that I go forward beside the great sea, which did stretch onward, as it did seem for ever, before me upon the far side.

And I knew not how to go across; for I had no power to swim, and had I swum, there were surely monsters in that great and warm-flowing river, as you shall believe.

And I went upward of the river-bank, that I might come to some place where the river did narrow; and surely I had been like to walk a mighty distance to this purpose, but that I came soon to a second river that did enter the first, not a mile above the shore of the sea; so that, as you do perceive, there was the sea to one side of me, and this second river unto the other, and the first river before me; and thus was I sorely perplexed, as any had been truly that was in a like trouble.

Yet, as it did chance, the need to go forward, and the danger of the Humped Men, put wit into me, so that I lookt about for a tree that was fallen.

And there were many, yet great, so that I was much wearied and something strained of the spirit, before that I gat two little trees unto the water.

Now, when this was done, I made me a rough pole of a young tree-plant; and afterward, I lashed the two trees together with my belts and straps, and so had somewhat of a raft.

And you shall picture that, all the time as I did go about this business, I was very heedful lest the Humped Men should come upon me, ere that I was gone free upon the water. And this constant heeding did double the labour of my work, as you shall perceive; yet, in the end, it was done, and I ready to adventure over the river.

And so I did push off with the pole, and I pusht and paddled maybe the half of an hour, for, indeed it was all a clumsy contriving, and mayhap I the more so in my labours. Yet, presently, I was come so far over, that I drew nigh to the island; and it did seem a wise and proper thing that I should have my slumber there, and afterward go onward to the farther shore. And this I did; and after that I had eat and drunk, as ever, I lay down to sleep.

And by this time it was three and thirty hours since last I did slumber; so that I was bitterly awearied.

And I had a great and restful sleep; for, truly, the island did seem a very safe place; and, in verity, I came to no harm, though I was as a dead man for nine great hours; and so shall you perceive my weariness.

And when I was come proper awake, I eat two of the tablets, and drank some of the water; and afterward made an end of my voyage, and then did take back my belts and straps from binding the trees, and so forward again upon my way, and no more fearful of the Humped Men; for, surely, I did think I had left them all upon the far shore of the river; though afterward I minded me that they might grow likewise upon the two sides; but yet was I only discovered by those upon the one.

And all that day I went very swift, and past many strange matters and did coast upon wonders oft. And at the sixth and the twelfth hours did I eat and drink, as ever; and between the eighth and the fourteenth hours did I come past two mighty fire-hills, that made all the Country to tremble with

their noise. And four times did monstrous creatures pass by me; but I was swift hid, and came to no harm.

And oft as I did go, were my thoughts upon the dear Maid that I journeyed to save from destruction. Yet, as you must see, always were my thinkings brought sharply unto my going; so that scarce was I ever set off to ponder upon Naani, but that there came some danger or wonder to give me heed to my way. And because of this, as you have learned, I was more put to plan free of the instant trouble and peril of my way, through all that mighty journey, than to have quiet chance for thoughts of love unto mine Own. Yet, truly, was not my journey one whole thought of love unto Naani? And, that peril made oft dumb my brain, was but the truer song unto my Maid.

And at times I was among trees; but oft did go past unnumbered boiling springs and small fire-hills; and oft was the air full of the noise of the little fire-hills, and the roar of the boiling springs; but there came no harm unto me.

And a thousand times did I perceive things that had life; and I made a very cautious way; though with a great speed and cleverness of going that made my heart glad.

And oft did I come to parts where a great life held the trees, and green stuff did flourish exceedingly, and the air rich and full and wondrous sweet; so that I was fain to think how that in some far-off time, it might be that our children's children should come down unto this Country, when the Upper Valley of the Night Land was grown to an utter chill and lacking of air; and here build them a new Refuge, if, indeed any should come clear of the Evil Forces and the Monsters that did live about the Mighty Pyramid in the Night Land. Yet, how should they come clear of those things; so that this is, as you do perceive, no more than a thought that did rise vaguely in me. And yet, again, who shall say what may be?

And onward I did pass, and I do mind me how that I saw the lower fires of that Country to burn very fierce; and this I set to the richness of the air; but yet with no surety of knowledge; and do but tell the same that you shall see the oddments of thought that went oft across my brain, and

so have so much knowledge as I, concerning this and that.

Now, a little before the eighteenth hour was come, I came out from among the trees, and the sea was downward of a great cliff unto my right, for I had gone upward for a long and weary hour. And I did see now a thing that made me to be cautious, and yet that did hold my heart to go swiftly to perceive the thing; for it was very strange.

And I went forward quickly, yet with a wise care; and so was come presently more nigh. And I perceived that the thing was, in part, a high rock, very tall and pointed and maybe an hundred feet high; but afterward I did find it to be more. And there was a monstrous great thing upon the top of the rock, that did seem very strange; and I stopt and lookt, and afterward went forward again; and so for a time, until that I was but a little way off. And now I saw that there did seem to be a mighty long rock laid across the topmost part of the upstanding rock, and yet had a very strange and shapely appearance; and did seem upon the underpart to be as that I had lookt before upon it. And upon the upper part, there grew trees and green things, even as these did grow upon odd ledges of the upstanding rock. Yet, for the most, the rock was very stark, as that a blast had blown upon it, and made it bare.

Now, when I had lookt for a while, I bethought me that this should be a safe and proper place for my slumber, if that I had power to come safe to the top. And when I had thought this thing, I began at once to climb up the rock; and I found that the rock was very high; so that in a while I was come a great way off the earth, and yet was not come to the top of the rock. And because that I was awearied, I lookt about for a safe place to mine hand, and lo! there was a shelf of the rock very nigh, that went inward a little to the side.

And I gat me to this ledge, and did eat and drink, and presently I slept, and scarce had thought of Naani in the moment of my slumbering; for a great weariness was upon me, the which I do think to have come by reason that I was not yet proper rested from the task of the day that was gone before that one.

Now I waked very sudden, maybe seven hours after; and I had

knowledge within me that my spirit did wot of some nigh danger. And I gat upward from the rock, very quiet, and had the Diskos ready in my hand. And I lookt swift about me in the moment that I did wake; yet did see nothing; for there was naught on the ledge with me.

And I crept to the edge, and lookt downward, and lo! I did see that there came up the rock two Humped Men; and they did climb very swift and silent; and I perceived that they smelled me, and came to destroy me. And I made ready the Diskos to do battle, and ceased not to look downward. And I saw how that the Humped Men did seem to be humpt by reason of their being so monstrous thick and mighty of the neck and the shoulder, as that they had been human bulls. And I saw that they were very strong, and by the speed of their climbing, I knew they were swift; and so did I make steady my attention and my heart to the saving of my life; for truly I did know that I should be dead in a little, or they.

Now I stept back a space from the edge of the rock, and had the Diskos very ready; for it was needful that I should kill one of those brute men speedy, that I have no danger that one take me in the back, whilst that I fight with the other.

Then, in a moment it did seem, there came upward of the rock edge, the great and brutish face of the man. And in that moment that I slew him, I did note curiously how that he had large teeth upon each side of the mouth; and was aware that he had come so quiet as a great cat. And in the backward parts of my brain, I bethought that even thus, maybe, was primal man, so that a strange and secondary questioning and wondering did live in that part of me; and I did learn from these scarce conscious reasonings that I was of belief the thing was truly a man; but very crude and dangerous. And surely it is strange that I had all this thought in that little moment; but in verity so it was; though I doubt not but I bettered it with after thoughts, when a while had gone.

Now the first man died ere his great haired breast was come upward over the rock; and he sank back, and sagged and fell dully, and I heard him bodge downward from rock to rock, very lumbersome; and so in a moment was silence.

Then did I look this way and that way of the ledge; for the second Humped Man was not yet upon me; and I feared that the pause did mean a cunning mischief and strategy. And when a little time had past, and all the while I was ready with the Diskos, and naught did come upward to harm me, I stept very soft to the edge of the rock-ledge, and lookt downward; but there was nowhere any thing to see.

Now, for a little moment, I did think that the brutish man had run off, being feared by the death that I did deal unto the first; yet I put this from me at once; for I did wot that such a creature did not be like to fear in such wise; but was rather set to some horrid cunning of attack, as I did fear, and was somewhere below me among the holes of the great rock.

Then I did think sudden that he might be gone upward, so that he should come down upon my back, and I lookt upward of the mighty rock; but did see naught; and afterward I stoopt forward a great way beyond the edge, so that I should perceive whether the man did hide beneath. And, behold! he was there below me, and crouched under the rock-shelf, ready to his spring. And in that moment, he made unto me with so mighty a leap as any tiger should give. And he came half over the edge, and gript the Diskos by the handle, in an instant.

And surely I had lost that trusted weapon, or been pulled over and cast into the depth, but that the Diskos did spin, and the Earth-Current did make live the handle—as was intended—save where the "grip" was set. And lo! the man gave loose the handle very swift, for it had burned and shaken the creature sore. And I staggered back, with the effort I had made to withhold the Diskos; and the brutish man came upward again over the rock edge, and leapt at me. Yet he gat me not; for I sprang unto my right, and made a blow with the Diskos, even as I did leap. And the blow came something short; but yet harmed the Humped Man with a gash upon the belly, very sore and horrid among the great brown hairs of the man. And immediately he sprang after me; but I smote full at the face; so that he leaped back from the strange roar and blaze of the Diskos, and yet was harmed; for he gat not right free of the blow; but did be cut very sore on the mighty and haired arm.

Now, seeing that he was something feared of the weapon, I ran in upon him, and smote again at the face; yet was the man gone out of my reach before that the blow did reach; for, truly, he was quick as a panther. And immediately, he did leap unto the ending of the ledge, where it did join upon the Rock; and he caught the living Rock between his two hands. And truly the Rock must have been splitten there; for he tore out a monstrous lump, so great near as my body; and did run upon me with the rock above the head of him.

Now, I perceived I should be smashed in a moment, if that I did not slay the man very quick. For so mighty was he, that he did leap this way and that way after me, as though the great rock did cumber him no more than it had been but a light matter.

And you shall perceive that I leapt this way and that way, to avoid the man; and twice did strike him; but yet was feared to brake the Diskos upon the rock, which the man did use as a shield each time that I did make a blow. And all the while, I did act to escape when that the man should cast the rock, as I did conceive at the first to be his intent. Yet, truly, it was as that he had no wotting that a rock may be thrown; for he strave only to come at me with the rock, that he should crush me, as with a monstrous club. And, in verity, what should a man do against so horrid an attack.

And time and oft did I leap now to the right and now to the left, and again in a moment, I did cut the Humped Man; but the blow was something turned off by the great rock in the hands of the man; yet so strange and mighty was the power of the Diskos, that it shore away a small portion of the rock, and did come to no hurt in itself.

And, surely I had presently failed in wind and limb, because of the leapings and chargings that I did make; and because of the weight of the armour, that was not overmuch, yet to be considered; but that I fainted not, was by reason of the wondrous hardness and leanness that I was grown to, with so constant a journeying and strait living; for the tablets did keep the strength in a man, though, truly, they eased not the yearnings of the belly.

And lo! even the brutish man did grow weary, and the hot breath and body-stink to come from him; and surely who shall wonder, for always he

did rush to and fro upon me, with the monstrous rock to crush me. And sudden, I leapt unto the right of the man, thinking within me that I did perceive a chance that I should cut him upon that side; but, truly, he was less awearied than I did know; for he came very sharp upon me, and had me between him and the wall of the Rock; and surely I had no room to make escape, and had died in a moment, but that I made a sudden sham toward the left with the Diskos, as that I should leap that way. And in the same instant, I did go to the right with a strong bounding; and immediately did come in upon the Humped Man from that side; and I put my fortune of life to the stroke, and stood anigh to the man, and I smote him across the middle part, before that he did wot of my intent. And the blow slew the man very surely, and did nigh cut the mighty creature in twain. And surely he fell, half leaping even as he died, so that the monstrous rock that was in the hands of the brutish man, did crash down almost upon my feet, and I leapt very high that I should escape the thundering of the rock; for in verity, I was near slain in that last moment of the life of the Humped Man. But yet I lived and came free of death, and did have a relief of happiness about my heart, as you shall believe.

Yet, truly, I was much shaken; and a little weakness took me, so that I was fain to go down upon the rock-shelf, that I have back my strength.

And presently, I was grown steady again, and I took my gear, and did haste down the Rock, and so was come presently to the earth again. And I saw the first of the Humped Men that I did slay, lying very quiet a little off from the bottom of the Rock; so that I went round upon the other side to avoid the man; for it was no pleasure to mine eyes or to my heart. And, truly, it did trouble me always to make a death.

And when I was come round upon the other, which was the seaward, side of the Rock, I perceived that I was yet shaken; and I remembered that it were wise to eat and drink and rest a little, before that I did go further upon my way.

Now, as I did sit there at the bottom of the Rock, I looked upward at the strange crown thereof; and until that time, I had been taken up with the fight and with gazings this way and that to see whether there came others

of the Humped Men to work me an harm.

But now that I was given some ease of the mind and of the body, I saw plainly that I knew the thing that lay upward upon the Rock; for the shape had been something strange and half-known to me even before that moment, as that I had a vague knowledge concerning it; but yet with no surety. And now, truly, I did know in a little instant that the thing was one of the olden flying-ships, the which, as you shall mind, there were certain in the Great Museum of the Mighty Pyramid.

And surely, I was ready to wonder why that I had not seen the thing plain before that moment; yet was this like to be because that there was a shadow upon the other side of the great Rock; but upon this side there was a little fire-hill a way off to the cliff edge, and this did throw a warm light that made a glimmer upon the dull metal of the ship's bottom, which was uncovered to my sight, and was surely of that same deathless grey metal that made the Great Redoubt.

And yet, as you shall believe, even as I said this thing to my mind, that the strange matter upon the top of the Rock was truly one of the olden air-ships, I did feel that I should be proper to doubt; for it was a very wondrous thing to perceive a thing common to man, in that utter strange Country, and after that I was gone so far off from the Mighty Pyramid. Yet, in verity, I did know in my heart that it was indeed that which I did perceive it to be; and I did stand and walk to and fore and look upward constant; for I was very keen that I look well upon it.

And truly, as I did look from this place and from that place, it was scarce a thing for wonder that I had not wotted it to be an air vessel; for there were great trees and abundance of earth and living matters upon the topmost side of the ship; so that none could easy perceive it to be aught save a great and desolate rock that did lie upon the other rock. Yet, truly, it was as I have told; and presently I did make to climb upward of the great Rock, that I should come to the air vessel to enter it. But yet was this not proper; for I had surely no duty save to go forward forever, until that I found the Maid; but yet did I spend a little while to this searching of the ship; and I do but set down that which I did, and with a serious spirit. And truly, as it doth

here occur to me, I do be ever seeming a serious young man, as you maybe shall have grown to think; but yet was I to a dread and serious business, and the strain did be too great upon me and the trouble too much prest upon my heart to give me much of laughter, as you do surely perceive, and so you to give me your ear and your understanding. For, indeed, before that I did lose Mirdath my Beautiful One, I was not over-grave; but so young and joyous as any.

Now it took me a great time to go upward of the Rock; for it was so monstrous steep and high. Yet, presently was I come nigh under the bottom of the ship; and here I did perceive that she had been sore battered in that far-off age when she did come upon the Rock; for, surely, as I did perceive, the peak of the Rock was through the bottom of the ship, so that the metal was burst this way and that, and very plain to be seen in some parts; but in other places the earth and growing matters did make a hiding.

And after that I had climbed this way and that way, I perceived that I must come to the topmost part by the plants that did hang over, and grow downward. And after that I had pulled upon them, to know that they were strong to hold me, I went upon them, and was soon to the top of the ship. Yet, truly, I might so well have been upon the earth; for the ship was covered above by the earth and dust of a monstrous age of years; so that I was like to need much time to dig downward unto the ship; and because of this, I considered a little while, and afterward made no more to search her; but did go downward again, that I should come once more to my journey. Yet, as you shall think, it was with a queer thrilling of the heart, and with strange thoughts upon the end of those that did come, maybe, to a bitter and lonesome dying in that ship of the air, in that far-off time when she did fly.

And surely, it did seem to me as I went downward of the great Rock, how that the flying-ship had been there for an hundred thousand years; and that mayhaps the sea did live all about the Rock in that Age; and truly this was no improper thing to think, for it was like that the sea had been monstrous high and great in those days; so that the Rock was but a little island in the midst of the sea; and now was the sea gone small from a great sea to lesser seas, and this through an eternity of years. And always, as it

doth seem to me, had the ship lain upon the Rock, and lookt quiet and silent over the change and wonder and the lonesomeness of all that Country of Fire and water, for ever.

But how the air-ship did come upon the rock, how shall I know; save, maybe, it doth seem as that she might have flown low over the sea in that olden age, and come hard upon the Rock, because, maybe, there was one to the helm that did steer unwittingly. And again, it shall well be otherwise, and I do but set down mine odd thoughts; and such as they be, they have no especial use, save that they do show to you the different workings of my mind at that time, as I did go downward. And so to set you the more in possession of all that I did have knowledge of.

And presently, I was come again to the earth, and did go forward with a great speed, so that I should waste no more of that day. Yet, oft did I think upon that ship hid there upon the mighty Rock, under the wondrous quiet ashes of eternity.

And I went eighteen hours walking, and in all that time I did see no more of the Humped Men; yet three times was I put in a sudden danger, for there went past me thrice, between the fourteenth and the seventeenth hours, great flying monsters, that were winged very ugly, and did go, as I thought, in a great bounding, rather than that they did fly proper as doth a bird. Yet I suffered no hurt from these; for I was swift to hide between the great boulders that were very plenty in that part; but no trees. For I was gone now past the forests of trees; there being none since that I had gone through a very shallow river, that I came to about the thirteenth hour. And this had I waded, and sounded my path with the staff of the Diskos; but I had kept mine armour upon me, lest there be things, even in water so shallow, that might bite and work harm upon me. But I gat through pretty quick, and had no hurt done me.

Now I had eat, as ever, at the sixth and the twelfth hours; and by that the eighteenth hour was come, I was nigh again unto a forest, that came down to the shore that went alway upon my right; and I to be very sore and wearied, as you shall know; for I had fought very desperate after my waking, and afterward climbed the great Rock, and then again to journey, so

that it was, by this, nigh to one and twenty hours since that I did sleep.

And surely, I lookt this way and that way, constant, and did see no place proper to my slumber. But afterward, I considered I did be a fool, to lack such; for truly the trees were plentiful, and I could climb a great one, and strap my body safe, and so have a sure bed for my rest. And I did this thing, and went upward into a great tree, and did tie my body to the tree, with my belts; yet I eat and drank before that I went up the tree.

Now when I was fast upward in the tree, and had made a bed upon a monstrous branch, and had the Diskos ready upon my hip, so that it should not fall but be nigh to my hand, I lay a little while thinking upon Naani; and I went not over to sleep immediately, which was strange; yet mayhaps because that my bed was so uncertain.

And I considered very gravely how that it was a monstrous long while since that I did hear the Master-Word from the dear Maid; and truly I was come a dreadful way from mine home, which was the Mighty Pyramid; for I had gone onward for ever through five and twenty great days of travel, and was not yet come to any place that did appear like to be that place where the Maid did abide.

Then a little time did pass in which I did wake and sleep, and wake and sleep, a little; but with no surety of sleep; but as that I was very tired of the heart, and did but lie too wearied to come properly to sleep.

And odd whiles I did lie with mine eyes half to open, and did look very dreamful upward among the dark branches of the tree, as they did show black and pretty against the redness of the shining that came from the sea; for there was stood a great and bright-burning fire-hill in that part of the sea that lay off the shore from me. And above the glaring of the fire-hill, there was the deep night that did brood for ever above in a monstrous black gloom of eternity, and did make the red smoke of the volcano to show deep and mighty and thunderous-seeming, afar up in the great dark. And the red and shining smoke did but show the utter hugeness of the night, that had been upon the world through the great ages.

And, in verity, as I did lie there so dreamful, it did come to me afresh how wondrous strange was mine adventure; and how that I did lie warm

and alive in a Country of red light and smoking seas. And, truly, as I did remember and consider, there was a great and lost world above me, upward through the dark … maybe an hundred and fifty great miles up in the grim night.

And this thing did strike me very solemn, as I did lie; and I do trust that you conceive how that there was, in truth, afar above in the eternal and unknown night, the stupendous desolation of the dead world, and the eternal snow and starless dark. And, as I do think, a cold so bitter that it held death to all living that should come anigh to it. Yet, bethink you, if one had lived in that far height of the dead world, and come upon the edge of that mighty valley in which all life that was left of earth, did abide, they should have been like to look downward vaguely into so monstrous a deep that they had seen naught, mayhaps, save a dull and utter strange glowing far downward in the great night, in this place and in that.

And surely, as you shall have seen, I have set the Great Deep of the Valley to be, maybe, an hundred and fifty miles of night; for, as you do mind, it was conceived that the Valley of the Night Land was an hundred miles deep, and mayhap to be more; and I had come from that Place downward of the Mighty Slope, and of the Gorge, a very great way. Yet, in verity, I do believe in my heart this measuring was utter wrong; for I think the deep to have been monstrous, beyond these miles that I do give; yet have I no proving of this belief, and do set it down for no more than it is.

Now, presently, I had ceased from these vague thinkings and half dreamings, and was gone truly to sleep. Yet, nowise did I sleep very strong; but did seem to come anigh to wakefulness, this time and that. And, as it did chance, this was mayhaps a very good thing for my life; for I did presently come awake more surely, and did turn on the great branch; for there was a noise in the air, that was not the noise of the great fire-hill.

And the noise did grow, very heavy and lumbersome. And, in a moment, there came seven Humped Men, running among the trees, as that some monstrous thing did pursue. And immediately they were beneath the tree in which I did lie; so that a great fear came upon me, and I loosed the belt from the branch, that I should be free to fight.

And, directly upon this, I saw that the men did leap upward into the tree, beneath me; but not as that they did wot of me or make to come at me; but as that they did pay a great heed to some creature or happening that was far off among the trees. And surely, the noise did seem to come from that part, and did grow loud and mighty, and the Humped Men did all crouch very silent, and did make no noise or motion one to the other; but were quiet upon the lower branches.

And, as I did look now more to my ease, I perceived that they had each a great stone, and bloody, that did seem as that it were split to a certain sharpness, even as a stone doth break very natural. And they carried the stone under this arm or under that arm, so that they had their hands free to all matters.

And, always the noise did come the more anigh, and I saw that a Humped Man did come running from among the trees, and did run beneath that place where the seven Humped Men did be on the branches. But they made no sign to the man, to save him; yet truly it was very plain that some monster pursued the man.

And immediately I saw how this thing was; for the Humped Man upon the ground, did not run so fast as might be; and I conceived that he did act to make some creature to come after him, to pass under the men within the tree. And surely this thing did prove to be; for there came very quick, a great and ugly thing, that had an ugly way of putting down the feet, and did have seven feet to each side, which was very strange; and the back was as that it were horny, and the belly of the thing did seem to brush heavy upon the earth, and it grunted, as it went, and shook the earth with the weight of it; so that a monstrous noise came from it, upon so hasty a journey. And I did wot that it was not such a thing as did properly pursue after matters of food; but did rather eat of that which did need little haste, but a monstrous strength, to gain. And that it did so make after the man, was in truth because that it had been wounded and made fierce; for, indeed, there came blood from the creature from great wounds upon the back; but how these were made, I could not know in that instant.

And it did go under the tree in which I was hid; and in that moment

when it past under the tree, the seven Humped Men did leap out of the branches, and did catch to the brute by the great horns of the spine; and I saw that the wounds were in the joints of the spine, as was plain when the back did work, with the going of the creature. And the seven Humped Men took the sharp stones from under their arms, and did strike very brutal in the wounds that were in the joints of the spine; and the creature roared and cried, and went onward into the trees at a great speed; and in all the time that it ran, the Humped Men ceased not to strike with the stones.

And sudden, when it was gone a distance off, it did roll very swift over upon the back, first to the right, as that it would go that way; so that the Humped Men did leap off upon the other side. And immediately the creature rolled to that side; and there ran clear of the brute only four of the Humped Men; so that I knew that three were slain. And afterwards, they that lived, ran beyond the beast, and gat up into a second tree, and the one that was chased, did entice the creature to follow, and so did tease it once more to pass beneath the other men; and they very swiftly again to the back of the creature; and so from my sight, striking with the great stones, and the beast bellowing very loud and piteous. And how many of the Humped Men there were to the beginning of that strange hunting, I know not; but surely there were few that lived to the end.

And surely there were such things as this thing in the beginning of the world, and again was it thus in the end; and I did ponder this a little while, as I did sit upon the great branch, and hearken unto the sound of the hunting, that was now gone a great way off, and was presently beyond my hearing.

And afterward, I gat me to the earth, and did look this way and that way, to see that no beast was anigh, neither any of the Humped Men; and afterward, I eat two of the tablets and drank some of the water.

And when I had gat this far to a readiness for my going, I minded me that I should try the compass again, as I did intend. And surely the machine did point between the North and the South, upon the Westward arc, even as Naani had told unto me; yet, as it did seem, with somewhat more of a Southward pointing than she had made me to think. And because of this

telling of the compass, a great ease came upon my spirit; for, surely, was not this but a sure sign that I did go direct unto that hidden place of the world where the Lesser Refuge did abide; but yet was not come over-close, so that the pull of the Mighty Earth-Current of the Great Redoubt was something stronger than in the place where was the Little Pyramid.

And all this did I think very swift to myself, and had a glad uplifting of the heart, as you do perceive; so that I went forward upon my journey, with a great stride, and did scarce fear any strange thing that all the Country did hold, in that moment.

And I went all that day at a strong pace, and did be oft tempted to send the Master-Word unto Naani; yet did keep from so foolish an acting, the which, mayhaps, had brought straightway upon me an Evil Power, and had given me to Destruction when that I was near come to the succour of the Maid. And it was this quick and constant fear of the Evil Forces of the Night Land, that did keep me ever from calling unto Naani, lest that they should discover me, and follow after; and this, I doubt not, you to know by now so well as I.

Now, by the sixth hour, I was come into a part of the Country where there were an exceeding abundance of steam fountains and sprayings and great upboilings of water in basins of rock; and the air did be full of the sounds and the roarings of the boilings and the spoutings, and of a hot mist and spray; so that, truly, I had scarce the power to see to my front, nor to any side.

And here, presently, I made a pause, and did eat and drink, and afterward went forward again; and I did keep the shore of the sea always to my right, and so did go proper to my way; yet with no great ease; for the sea also did steam very strong in that part, and because of this great fog of steam, I was surely much laboured to make a great speed, lest unseeing I go headlong into an hole of the boiling water.

And in the ninth hour, I did go clear of the hot boilings, and was come again free of the mist and the steam, and might look with mine eyes to my going. And, surely, as I did perceive, I was come to the end of the great sea that had been ever to my right; for it did go against the feet of great and

monstrous mountains, that went upward for ever into the night, and did seem as that they were the hither wall of that strange Country of Fire and Water. And so was I stood there very much taken upon doubt; for how should I go farther.

And after that I had been there a while, in a bewilderment of doubt and of wit, I went to the left, along the feet of the mountains; and truly this but of common sense; for how might I go any other way, save I go back again!

And at the twelfth hour I eat two of the tablets, and drank some of the water, and went forward once more. And lo! at the fifteenth hour, I was come to a place between the mountains, even an upward gorge, very dark and gloomy, and without light for a great way.

And, in verity, I did not want to go up the gorge, in that it was so dreary a place and narrow and horrid and drear-seeming, after the light and wideness of the Country in which I did yet stand.

And presently, I did go past the mouth of the gorge, that I should learn whether there went another way out of that Country. And thiswise, for a great hour more, along the feet of the mountains, and did presently come to a monstrous black river, that was, maybe, a mile wide. And it to be very shallow, and seeming as that the water scarce to cover the mud of the bottom. And here and there a great steam did come from it, and spirtings and moundings-up of the mud in many places, and monstrous babblings and puffings-up of strange smoke, as that a great heat went beneath it in this place and in that.

And surely it went backward into the country for a mighty way, so far as my sight did go; and I did think it to be no river, but truly a further sea. And there was no way across; for there were no trees anigh, to make me a raft, neither might I wade across; for it might be shallow here and deep there, and the mud be in all places. And, moreover, I had been like to be caught in one of those upburstings of mud, even did I have a raft to go upon. And because of all these things, I gat me back again to the Gorge, and presently I did go upward into the darkness.

Now, I went upward very steady, save that I did stumble oft, and did go through six great hours. And truly it did seem that I went in an utter

dark, because that I had been awhile in so constant a light.

And, by that I had been six hours in the Gorge, I was gone right away from the Country of the Seas, and did be as that I was back into some place that was like to the dreadness of the Night Land. For there were in this place and in that place of the Gorge, red fire-holes, even as in the Night Land. Yet not many until that I was come a great way up of the Gorge. And there did be life of horrid things about the fires, as soon I did wot; so that I made to keep off from them. Yet, as you shall perceive, I must come oft pretty near, because that the Gorge was nowheres scarce an hundred good paces across, and did oft come very narrow, so that I did come oft anigh to the fire-holes, whether that I did heed to or not.

And all that time, and ever, did the Gorge go very sharp upward, so that it was a very weary thing to make great trial of speed, as you shall know. But yet I went so fast as I could do; for I was grown sudden very excited about the heart, and to feel as that I did surely draw anigh to that strange and hid place of the world, where was the Lesser Refuge.

And when I had gone upward through six great hours, as I did say, I took caution for a place proper to slumber; for I was surely very wearied.

And I saw a place presently, afar upward of the dark side of the Gorge, upon the right, where a ledge of the Rock did show in the glaring from one of the fire-holes that made a gloomy light in that place. And I climbed unto this ledge, and did find it to be secure, and awkward to come upon. And presently, after that I had eat and drunk, I did compose myself unto sleep, the which came very speedy upon me, whilst yet I did believe I thought only upon the sweetness of the Maid. And truly it had been something over three and twenty hours, since last I did sleep; so that I was greatly wearied.

And in six hours I waked and did eat, and did climb downward again to the Gorge, and so unto mine upward journey.

Now, as you do perceive, when that I was come properly a great way up the Gorge, and had come among the fire-holes, there was no more an utter darkness, for the dull red glare of the pits beat upward upon the black sides of the rock-mountains, that did make the sides of the Gorge; so that oft I did see both sides very plain in the lower parts; yet of the height of the

Gorge, who might know aught; for the black sides did go upward for ever into the everlasting night.

And because of the light from the fire-pits, I did see, time and oft about the fires, horrid monsters, both that were snakes, and others like to scorpions so great as my head; but no more than these for a long while. And afterward I perceived that surely other matters did move among the rocks of the Gorge; so that I did keep the Diskos very ready in mine hand; yet had truly no use for it all that day.

Now I eat and drank at the sixth and the twelfth hours, and went onward at a very strong speed. And at the sixteenth hour, I did seem as that I knew the aether to be stirred about me, and the beat of the Master-Word very faint upon mine inward ear. And immediately, a wondrous great and lovely thrilling did wake all my being; for surely, I said, this was the spirit of my love, calling unto me with her brain-elements. And, indeed, this was a very proper and sensible thinking; for had the Master-Word been sent from the Mighty Pyramid, I had been like to hear it very plain, by reason of the force of the Earth-Current which was with them and to their command. But, as you do know, the Earth-Current was nigh gone from the Peoples of the Lesser Refuge; so that they were over-weak to make any proper calling. And this I have spoken of before this place.

Yet, in a little while, as I did stand very hushed, that I should hark the better, I was come to doubt whether that I did truly hear the Master-Word. And one moment I did say that it had surely beat in the night about me; and immediately would I be just so unsure; and so in a while I gat once more to my journey, and had doubt in my heart; yet, as you shall conceive, more of hope. And because of this thing, I went onward for thirty great hours from the time that I did wake; for my heart was excited within me.

And when that I had gone so long forward as this, I did see how that I did foolishly; and I lookt about for a place for my slumber; and I found a small cave that was clean and empty, as I did discover by the shining of the Diskos which I made to spin a little time. And the cave was in the cliff of the mountain that made the right side of the Gorge, and was nigh twenty good feet from the bottom of the Gorge, and hard to approach.

And when I was come secure into the cave, and sure that it was proper to my purpose, I eat four of the tablets, as was just and nice to my belly, and did afterward drink some of the water, and so to my slumber; and all the while, very sweet and strong in my thoughts upon Naani; so that surely I was a little time before that I had myself rightly unto sleep.

And I slept six hours, and did wake, for I had set my spirit hard unto such wakening; yet was I still greatly yearning for sleep. But this did go somewhat, when that I had fought a little with my need. And afterward, I eat two of the tablets, and drank some of the water, and did gat my gear upon me, and was presently down unto the Gorge; and so again to my journey.

Now in all that day I did go with a very stern speed; for it did seem as that my soul did know for surety that I was truly come something nigh unto that hid place in the night where I should find mine Olden Love again. And the sweet hope that was bred of the calling that had seemed truly to sound about my spirit, was in all my being, and more sure on that day, than before that I had slept.

And I went thirty hours in all, even as before, ere that I did come again to sleep, and I eat and drank at every sixth hour, so that my strength should abide within me. And by that I was come to the ending of the thirty hours, I was sorely aweared, and gat me upward of the monstrous cliff that did make the left side of the Gorge, having perceived in a place a great ledge of the rock, that did seem very proper for my purpose of slumber.

And when I was come upward upon the ledge of the rock, I saw that there did seem something, like to a mighty spider, that did stay half without of a hole in the back part of the ledge. And I smote the thing gently with the Diskos, so that it was very quickly dead; and afterward I searched well about; but did gladly perceive that there abode there no other horrid creature.

And I eat two of the tablets, and drank some of the water; and did afterward make me ready for slumber, as ever. But now I did put the cloak well about me; for truly there was grown a chill into the air of the Gorge; and here also will I tell how that it did seem unto me that the air was gone something from that great thickness and strength which had been with me

in the past days of my journeying.

Now I was gone so tired, that I fell upon sleep in a moment, yet with a dear thought and anxious, concerning Naani; but was so starved of the body for slumber, that even mine anxiousness kept me not awake. And I was then so fast with sleep that I knew naught for eight hours of very sound slumber. And then did I awake, and very thankful of the heart that no evil beast or creeping thing had come upon me whilst that I was so utter lost in sleep.

And now, truly, was I something fresh and ready; and I ate and drank, and had my gear once more upon me, and so down into the Gorge. And afterward, I went upon my journey for eighteen hours, and did pause but a little while at the sixth and the twelfth hours that I should eat and drink.

And when the eighteenth hour was nigh come, I perceived that the nature of the Gorge was grown very horrid and dank. And in verity, I did feel as that afar upward in the night the black mountains that did make the sides of the Gorge had come together, and did make a monstrous roof unseen in the utter height.

And this thing I do tell, only as of my belief; for I have no very sure proof. Yet, truly, my reason doth say likewise; for there did oft drip water upon me out of the darkness, even though I walked in the middle way of the Gorge; and how should this thing be, save that there went an over-reaching of the sides, that should let the mildew down upon me.

And in this place, and for more than eleven great hours, there were fire-holes and fire-pits only in this part and in that, and each a great way off from another. And they burned very dull, and did seem to throw a fume of sulphur into all the air, as that there was no freedom above for the stink to pass away. And in every place were the rocks of the Gorge very thick and slippery with strange growths; so that it was a sorrow to walk upon them. And all that time was there an heavy wetness and slowness in the air; and a smell, beside the stink of the fire-pits, as that I did go forward through a place where dead things did be.

And for a great time there was a horrid darkness, as it had been that the air was grown thick with the fumings of the fire-pits, as I do believe;

and beside this thing there was, as I have said, but a dull fire here and another there; so that it was like that there should be a heavy dark. And because that it was so utter black, and because that there were growths upon the rocks in the bottom of the Gorge, I did go but slowly, and with pain of stumblings; and always with the stink of that place to trouble me half unto a sickness.

And sudden, as I did go past one of the fire-pits, I saw that the fire made a dull shining upon some monstrous thing that did move before me, upon the far side of the fire. And I came in one moment unto a swift silence, and hid among the rocks of the bottom of the Gorge. And I lookt very cautious at the thing that moved beyond the fire, and surely I had seen no thing so monstrous since that I had come free of the Night Land; for it was as that some huge Creature, like to the hull of a great ship did move down out of the dark of the upper way of the Gorge. And it went by the fire-hole, and onward into the dark of the lower way of the Gorge; and I had perceived somewhat of it, as it did go past the fire, and, surely, it was black and beslimed, and utter great in height and in length, and it went always without noise, so that I had not known it to be there, but that I saw it plain with mine eyes. And, truly, if I do say that it was somewhat as that I had seen a monstrous slug-thing, surely I should use wise and proper words to make known to you this horrid brute.

And I stayed very quiet a time, and afterward I went upward again of the Gorge, and did use a new caution to my way, and saw that the Diskos was free upon my hip; for even thus I did carry the weapon, being that I must use both hands to my way, and to save me in my stumblings and slidings over the slippery rocks.

And once it did seem to me that some great thing moved in the darkness, and I went downward among the rocks, and stirred not my body for a great while; and sure am I that there went some living monster past me, that did stink as a loathsome grave. And afterward, I went on again.

And three hours did I go thus, and came at last to a place where a fire-hole did shine more ruddy; and I did look well about me, that I should perceive that part of the Gorge the better. And as I stood there, very quiet,

away off from the fire, so that it did show no great light upon my person, I did note how utter still was that place; and this to take me anew, as though it had come fresh upon me. And here, there would be the drip of water, and again in that place, and again elsewhere; and all very solemn and very dismal. And the silence to be constant.

And presently, as I lookt, now to this way and again to that, I saw that there was a monstrous slug-thing laid upward against the black side of the Gorge, as that it had stood up on end; and the one end of the monster went upward beyond the light from the fire-pit; but the other part did come down and trail into the Gorge, as a long hillock, very ugly and black and beslimed.

And I near sweat with a disgust and horror of the thing; but afterward I had more courage, and spied well upon the brute. And surely, it moved not at all, any more than the side of the cliff of the Gorge; and I conceived that it stood not upward upon any feet; but clung to the rock, even as you shall see a slug to go. And for a great space I was very quiet and moved not, neither did I make to hide, but stood there very stupid.

Yet, in a time, I had more of courage which brought strength unto my heart, and I began again to go upon my way, but with an utter caution, and I then to creep for a weary time upon my hands and knees among the dank and weariful rocks and boulders that lay in the bottom of the Gorge. And thrice between four hours was I passed by hidden and monstrous things in the horrid dark places of the Gorge; yet with no noise, save, as it might be, the odd rattle of a rock in this place and that; but with an utter and dreadful stinking. And I to be quiet as they went, as you shall think.

And each time now that I did go by the fire-pits and fire-holes that lay odd-ways in the Gorge, I did pause and search about me with mine eyes, very cautious, and oft now did I perceive how that the monstrous slug creatures did lie in this place and in that against the cliffs of the Gorge. And I did go then utter still, from this space to that space among the rocks, and oft upon the flat of my belly, and with a constant heed that I make not mine armour to knock against the boulders.

And always as I did go, there was a monstrous stench, and the choking

of sulphurous smoke very oft. And here and there, as mine heart doth believe, there were utter great caverns within the mountains to the right and to the left; and of this thing I have some small proof; for once I did go by a place where a fire did burn, as it should be a fire-hole, afar inward of the mountain side upon my right; so that I saw in a moment that I looked in the darkness through the mouth of a mighty cave-place; and I went past very quick and silent, for I knew not whether any horrid thing should come forth out of that place to slay me.

Now, I came clear of the darkness and the slime and the stinking in about twelve hours after the time that I did think the mountains to be a roof unto the Gorge; and the air was now free and did seem as that some life and health did abound in it; and the fires did be more plentiful, and burned very bright and clean, and threw all their fumings upward, so that there was no more any bitter pain of sulphur within my throat.

And surely, it was with a thankful heart that I went onward, and with a good speed; for there was much of light all about me, in that there burned an hundred fire-pits here and in that place; so that I saw clear before me and behind, and conceived that the slugs did abide only in the closed part of the Gorge. And oft I did take the air very full into my lungs, for the sweetness of it, after the horrid stenchings that I had abode all those hours.

And presently, when I was come free of the roofed part of the Gorge, maybe some three good hours, I lookt for a place proper to slumber; for it was surely something over three and thirty hours since that I did last come upon sleep; and I was utter worn and lost of strength with so much of creeping and harking for monsters, as you shall believe; moreover, about that time I had gone bitter long whiles between slumberings through more than an hundred hours, as you shall have perceived from my tellings.

Now, presently, I saw a small cave that went inward of the side of the Gorge. And I lookt into the cave, and found it to be sweet and clean, and very dry. And there was a small fire-pit off from the mouth of the cave that did throw a good light for my purpose; so that I saw there was no creeping thing or horror in the place; and I went in, and made to prepare for my slumber.

But truly, when I was come to look upon myself, I was utter soiled and did seem as that I stank with the slime and disgust of the dark part of the Gorge, where I had gone upon my hands, and upon my belly. And because of this, I was set that I should not eat or come to sleep, without I washed me.

And I went out from the cave, and there was a spring near to the fire-pit, as was oft in that part of the Gorge. And the spring was hot and did fill a hollow of the rock, very quiet and with a fuming of sulphur, as I did bend above it. And I washed mine hands and face and mine armour and gear, in the hot spring, and did dry me with my pocket-cloth; and so was sweetened and put to happiness of mind.

And I went back into the cave, and did sit in the mouth of the cave, with the Diskos to mine hand; and I eat four of the tablets, for I was gone a mortal long while without, and afterward I drank some of the water. And as I did eat and drink, I lookt out upon the lightness of the Gorge before me, and with a cheerful and composed heart.

And I saw presently that there came certain creatures out from their holes, even as it might be that they were part rats; but very strange looking, and not properly such. And some did lie about the fire-hole, and some did hunt about in the rocks; and one came presently, and had a snake by the neck. And it stood upon the snake, and did eat it, even while that the snake did lash about upon the rock. And the snake did lash until that it was nigh all eat; and a very strange thing this was to see, and something trouble-some to the pity. Yet was I glad to perceive that there were enemies to the serpents of that place.

And when the rat creature did make an end of the snake, it made across to the spring, and did drink the hot water a while; and afterward back unto the fire, and there laid down anigh to the edge, and seeming very sweetly comforted of the belly, which, in truth, was much otherwise with me. And, after that, I saw many creatures that went about the fire, and did have warmth from the fire and drink from the spring; and surely I did pon-der that the Peoples of this our Age should say, if they had stood with me, that Providence had made nigh together the warmth and the drink that

were needful unto life (for it was grown to a bitter chill now in the Gorge). But rather did this thing seem to me otherwise, that these creatures did be but of their circumstance, and if that it had been another way, then had they grown of their wits to meet it to their means of life. Yet, as some would say, the arguments do but meet, and be the same thing. And neither way do I care in this place; but do no more than to show unto you the working of my brain, in this way and that, as I made my journey.

Now, presently, when I was done eating, and come very ready to fall upon sleep, I went out from the cave and gat me certain boulders, the which I did carry into the cave. And when I was come back for the last time, I put them very secure in the entrance-way, that no small stinging creature come at me as I slept. And after that, I made ready, and went to my sleep, having sweet thoughts and slumbrous, of the Maid.

Now I slept very quiet that time, and was not over troubled with the chill of the Gorge, which was but little in that place, both by reason of the fire-pit and because that the cave did help to keep my warmth to me. And I had a deep slumber for eight hours, and waked then pretty tired, but strong to go upon my way. And after that I had sat a little while, I came full to wakefulness and afterward did eat two of the tablets and drink some of the water, the which I did, sitting in the mouth-part of the cave, after that I had cast free the boulders.

And afterward, I gat my gear upon me, and I went again upon my journey. And the Gorge did continue very light and cheerful, with the shining of the fires; and oft there did be a little steam that did hiss from this part or that of the bottom of the Gorge and did blow very quaint and noisy in the quiet of that place. And oft there did be hot pools, and everywhere the great boulders in the bottom way, and to the right and to the left the black and mighty sides of the Gorge that did go upward for ever into the everlasting night.

And so I did go, and had eat and drunk at the sixth hour, and gone onward again. And, lo! at the eighth hour, I did thrill sudden with a wondrous great thrilling; for, in verity, it did seem to me that the Master-Word did beat softly about me, out of all the night of the world. And all my heart did

throb with great glowings of joy; yet was the beat of the Word unsure, so that I knew not truly whether my spirit had indeed heard aught, for there was immediately a silence, as ever, about mine inward being. Yet, as you shall believe, there was a new hope and strength of courage in all my body and soul.

And, sudden, in the end of the tenth hour, I perceived that the mighty walls of blackness that made the sides of the Gorge did be no more there, and that I was come truly upon the end of the Gorge. And I near trembled with hope and astonishment; for when I was gone a little way on, I had ceased to go upward any more, and was come clear out from the mouth of the Gorge, and did peer forth across a mighty country of night.

And it did seem to me as that I was come to a second Land of Strange matters, even as the Night Land where did lie the wonder of the Mighty Pyramid. And surely, I did think within my heart that I was come at last to that far and hidden place of the world where did be the Lesser Redoubt. But yet was there no place in all that night where did tower the shining lights of the Lesser Pyramid, the which I did hope vainly to perceive. And because that I saw them not, a great heaviness came upon my spirits for a time; but afterward the heaviness did go; for I put Reason to help my courage, and did plan this cause and that to show why that I was not come to sight of the shining embrasures of the Lesser Redoubt. But yet was there left an ache of doubting, as you shall well conceive.

Now this Land was very new and strange, and had a great light in this part, and a wondrous grim darkness in that. And I did pause a great while to determine how that I should go properly. And presently I bethought me of the compass, and did draw it forth, and set it upon the earth, that I should see how it did act. And truly it did go almost as Naani had told to me; so that I was very sure in all my being that I was in verity come anigh to the hidden Refuge. But yet did the compass give me no proper guiding to my way; so that I was no more wise to this end than before, only that I had the comfort of that which it did seem to assure.

And, in a little while, I went forward into the Land, and did hope that I should come presently to some matter to help my choice. And I went

first toward a certain great glowing of fire that lay before me, and did seem joined to another great glare that went afar to my left.

And I found the ground of that Land to be very fair for my feet, and to have in this place and that certain bushes, even as it did seem to me, of the kind that we named moss-bushes in the Night Land, as you do know. And I made a very good speed, and went thus until I had gone for maybe six long hours. And by that time, I was come anigh to the glowing of light; and did keep now a strong caution to my going; for truly, as I did know from the tellings of the Maid, there were very horrid and dreadful Powers in that Land, and I did well to remember that I was come again to parts where might be the destruction of the spirit.

Now I made a pause, and lookt toward the glowing light; and it seemed to me that for a monstrous way unto the right and unto the left, there did be surely a great, hid valley in the earth before me. For the shining did seem as that it came up from out of a valley, as that there burned a deep light in such a place; but yet was I all unsure, and had no proper knowing whether indeed there did be any valley there, but only a strange and luminous shining that did come upward from the earth.

And I made no great haste now to go unto that place; but went down sudden into the bushes, and lay upon my belly, and had a new great fear upon my spirit. And presently, I parted the bushes a little, and made a place for spying.

And I looked a great time unto the place of the light, and now to this part and now to that. And sudden, I saw, as it did seem, a monstrous head within the glowing; for the glowing did seem at whiles as that it swept to and fore, as should a shining smoke that went obedient to a quiet wind: and so to hide and again to uncover. And in a moment I lost the great face, and was all unsure that ever I had seen aught.

And lo! in a little minute, I did see it again; but whether it did be the shape of some utter monster of eternity—even as the Watchers about the Mighty Pyramid—or whether it did be no more than a carven mountain of rock, shaped unto the dire picturing of a Monster, I did have no knowing. But I made that I should get hence very quick, and I did turn me about in

the bushes, and went upon my hands and knees; and so came at last a great way off.

Now, presently, I came again upon my feet, and did take a new look around that Land. And I had the mouth of the Gorge to my back, and this I perceived by the shining of the fire-pits that made the place shown to me.

And to the left of the Gorge was an utter blackness, as I did conceive of black and monstrous mountains, through which the Gorge did come. And to the right side of the Gorge there were many low volcanoes, that went always along the feet of the great mountains that made the right wall of the Gorge. And I saw the feet of these dark mountains, because that the light from the little volcanoes made a glare upon the lower slopes.

And so shall you have some knowing of that part of this second Land of Night.

And a good way off, was the shining that I had journeyed unto, and the shining went into a distant light through a part of the Land that lay afar to my left, for it stretched a great and strange way toward me, out of the leftward gloom, and came unto my front, and so away into an utter distance. Yet, though it was so great, you shall not think that it made any huge light in the Land; but was rather as that it had a shining made unto other ends; for it made not a great lightness in the Land.

And you do now perceive something roughly how the Land did seem to my back part and unto my left, and somewhat before my face. And because that I did think to have no profit to my search, if that I went to the left, I made attention unto the Right. And here there was much of darkness; yet oft the shining of fire-holes in this place and that amid the darkness. And, as I did look, it grew very plain upon me how great was the spread and drear wideness of that Country of Night; and how that I did be an utter lonesome person in all that dark. And so shall you be with me in sympathy of the utter greatness of my task, and know of the fear that did breed, odd whiles, that I should search until I die, and never find. And you to give me good human understanding.

Now I made no more to delay, but went unto the right, and did keep the chain of the little volcanoes something level to my course; though a

great way off. And I went thus with a strange growing of hope, and an excitement, for ten hours, and had eat not then for more than twenty hours, and surely not since the sixth hour of that day and this because that I was so utter shaken from my calmness of going.

And at the tenth hour, I went utter weak, and did seem surely as that I must swoon. And lo! I bethought me how that I was gone so long without aught for my belly. And surely, when I was quiet a time, I eat four of the tablets, and in a good while did feel all renewed, and would rest no more, after that I had drunk some of the water, but went onward; for, in verity, my spirit did be as that it had slain me, if that I had lain down at that time. And this because hope was so fierce in me; for I to feel indeed that I was come near to the Maid.

And I went ten hours more, until that I did truly totter upon my feet, with utter and dreadful weariness; for I had gone now through someways of forty great hours, and had been foolish in mine eating and drinking, as you have perceived; but yet was this to be forgiven; for I was as that I should come any little minute upon the wonder of the Lesser Pyramid, shining afar in the night. Yet, truly, there was nowhere anything that might be likened unto it.

And I lay down there, just as I did be, and with no proper heed to my safety. And I was gone asleep in one moment, as it did seem; and waked not for twelve hours; and then did come suddenly unto knowledge; and thankful was I in the heart that no monster had come upon me in that dead-time of slumbering. And I eat four of the tablets, as was surely due unto me, and drank some of the water, and so gat forward again into the night.

And truly I was mortal stiff and did ache for a great while, and this did be in part because that I had wrapped not the cloak about me, ere I slept; for the Land was bitter cold and did make the blood very chill.

Now when I had gone onward through six hours, I ate and drank; for I did mind now to be wise and keep my strength good within me. And I went onward again at a very great speed, and full of an excitement. And surely, I did be glad at last that the tablets were so easy gone in the mouth, and unfilling to the belly; for I had been without power and patience to eat

proper victual.

And at the tenth hour, I saw that there rose a red-shining out of the Land before me, as that it came upward from a mighty pit. And I made slow my way, and so, when I was gone on for two great hours more, I saw that monstrous figures went about, against the red glare of the shining. And I gat me down into the bushes which were very plentiful in that part.

And I stayed there for a certain while, and made a watch upon the red-shining and the figures; and, truly, it did seem to me that there were horrid giants in that Land, even as in the Night Land. And afterward, I crept away, and went outward from the little volcanoes, into that part of the Land that was dark, save, as you do mind, for the glare of fire-holes in this part and that.

And I went now with an utter care; for the giants had put a new caution into my heart, and I did surely mean that I should live to rescue mine own Maid, and have joy through all my life. And thereafter, I went with the Diskos in my hand, and at each hour that was the sixth, I eat two of the tablets, and drank some of the water, and so did keep my strength very good within me.

Now, presently, I was come to a place where the Land did go downward a great slope, and there was a difference in the earth that went beneath my feet, and no great plenty of the bushes; but only one in this place and one in that, and nowhere any fire-hole.

And I gat me down and did feel the earth with my hands, and lo! I did find presently smooth stones, and afterward olden shells. And immediately, a great delight took me; for Naani had told how that the Lesser Pyramid stood something nigh to the shore of an ancient sea, that was long dried up in the years of eternity. And surely it might be that I was come down into the dry bottom of that same olden sea, and should presently have sight of the Little Pyramid.

And because that hope was put so fresh into me, I went forward through, maybe, thirty hours, across the olden sea-bed; but in all that time I had no sight of the lights of the Lesser Redoubt. And a great trouble began to take me; for, indeed, Naani had not told me how great was the sea;

and it might be that I should wander a weariful age across it, before that I come to the far side.

And it did come to me, presently, how that I should be wise to see that my way was very straight, so that I waste not my strength in useless wanderings. And I had a great care now to observe that the red-shining did be always upon my right, to my rear; and by this reasonable cunning did I make to steer very nicely through the great gloom of that place.

Now, as I did go across the bed of the great sea, I heard strange sounds, now in this part of the darkness, and now in that; and oft did there be a noise, as if things did run this way and that way in the bed of the sea. And once, afar off in the night, there did be a strange and horrid screaming; so that I did know truly that the monsters of that Land were out, and did go about in the dark.

And, as you shall perceive and understand, I was all unknowing of the lore of that Land; so that I knew not what to think of this strange sound or that, neither knew I what they might portend, but only that, as I did say, there were Monsters abroad. And I could do no more than have my way forward with an utter care always, and be very ready with the Diskos, or to hide, each as maybe according to the need.

And, surely, I went one-and-forty hours that day, and eat and drank after every sixth hour. And before this, in the seven-and-thirtieth hour, I heard a great roaring and bellowing in the night, coming nigh unto me; and afterward the thudding of monstrous feet, as that a giant ran past me in the darkness, and did make a chase of some creature. And the thudding of the feet and the roaring went far off into the night; and there did seem presently to come back to me from a great way, a little screaming; but of this thing I had no surety; and I abode very hushed in a clump of bush, until quietness was come again all about; for there had been an utter frightening sound in the horrid voice and in the thudding of the great feet.

Now, in the one-and-fortieth hour of that day, I came upon the farther shore of the olden sea. But lo! there was nowhere any light to tell me aught of the Lesser Refuge. And truly, a great doubt and bewilderment took me; for, indeed, I could not perceive how it might be that I saw not the lights

of the embrasures of the Lesser Pyramid. And a great despair took me; so that I sat down there upon the shore of the olden sea, and had no heed of anything for a while.

But afterward, I ate and drunk, and went into a clump of bush, and wrapt the cloak about me, and so went fast unto sleep, with the Diskos handy to my breast. And, in verity, the pain of the despair and the bewilderment of mine heart did make rather for sleep, than to keep me wakeful; for, indeed, I was half stunned of the brain and of my courage; and did seem now the farther off from the ending of my search than ever I had been.

And I slept six hours, and waked then, sudden. And I leaned up upon mine elbow in the bush, and harked very quiet, perchance some noise had shaken my sleep from me. But, indeed, there was nothing, only that I was wakeful, and did mind me of my trouble of failure. Yet now, I did invent this thing and that thing to make natural account that I was not come to the Lesser Redoubt; and so had hope again within me; yet much also of doubt and bewilderment.

And I eat two of the tablets, and drank some of the water, and again to my journey. And I made that I should keep along the shore of the sea, the which I did through twelve hours, and was then still so much in doubt as ever.

And I ceased from my journeying, and lookt about me over the Land, and lo! I did note how that a weak and strange shining was in the air of the Land, at a great way; as it had been that a far spreaded and faint glowing made a little glare into all the night unto my left and before me.

And afterward, I did make across that Land, unto the place where it did seem that the dull shining was something bright. And I went thus through eighteen hours, and did make pause at each sixth hour, and ate and drank very resolute; though, in verity, it did seem as that even so small a matter as the tablets did be like to choke me. And by this is it plain to me how great an anguish was come upon my spirit, lest that I was all astray, and should have no joy to succour mine Own.

And thrice in the time that I did go, there did be a running of feet amid the darkness; and odd whiles strange and horrid cryings in the night; so

that I put a force upon my despair, and hid me; for, indeed, I had no right to lose care of my life, if there did be any chance yet that I find the Maid.

And lo! in the eighteenth hour, which was truly the thirtieth of that day, I found the shining in the night to be grown very plain, and an utter stinking of sulphur; and truly I did be aware that the Land went upward.

And I made upward through seven hours, and the light did grow more plain, and was of a dull redness, very sombre and heavy. And in the end of six more hours, I ceased to go upward, and did know of a strange low sound, that did be like to no other sound that ever I did hear; and was like to a dull roar that did never have ceased through eternity.

And I went forward unto the light, and the Land to be now as that I went over an upland plain. And I did go thus through five hours, and the low roar did grow ever upon mine ears. And truly! even as I did shape my thoughts to take a caution for my body, I went upward again a little, and came out upon the edge of a mighty cliff, and the low and constant roar did moan upward against me with an everlasting muttering. And I lookt downward a monstrous way, and surely there was spread out a mighty sea, as it did seem, of dull fire, as that a red-hot mud did lap very deep and quiet below me in all that night.

And I lookt outward across the strange sea, and the far side was hid from me; for, surely, there were dull and solemn clouds that came off the sea, and hid the distance from me. And the clouds to glow a little redly; and so to rise, and presently to blacken into the night. And I lookt to the right and to the left, and it was plain that the black cliffs did stretch out both ways, and did go downward ever into that monstrous sea of slow fire. And there were great headlands that went out into the fire, as into a sea; and the fire did lap very quiet about these, and where the fire lapt about them, there did shine and spirt out green flames and vapours at diverse times.

And, indeed, as I did perceive, I was come to an upward sea of fire, as it were the deep inwards of a low and utter monstrous volcano, that was flat of the top and utter big across. And, in verity, I did look downward into the fires of the inward earth, and a very wondrous sight was it, to stand there

alone upon the cliffs of that everlasting sea. And a great heat came upward from the dull and grim fire of that gloomy sea, and a reek of sulphur; so that I was like to be choked, and did go backward from the edge of the cliff.

And surely, I was come to the end of that Dark Land upon that side, and had nowhere perceived the Lesser Pyramid in all the night of my travel. And a new despair came upon me; for, indeed, it seemed I was come all astray in the night of the World, and did nowise have any knowing whether I stood near to the Country of the Lesser Redoubt, or whether that I was gone half across the World unto a strange place.

And, then, as the despair troubled my spirit and dulled the beating of my heart, a sudden thought did light up a fresh hope within me; for, indeed, as you do know, I was come upward of a great height, and did surely have a huge view over all that Land; and mayhaps the Lesser Pyramid did lie somewhere in a valley, if, in verity, it did be anywheres at all in that Country. And I turned me from the cliffs, and lookt backward over all the night of the Land; but there was nowhere in all that Country the shining of the Lights of the Lesser Pyramid.

And lo! of a sudden I did know that there was something in the night. And I stared, with a very keen and anxious look. And behold, there was the black shape of a great pyramid afar off in the night, that did show against the shining of the distant light; for it did stand between me and the far-off fires. But until I was come to that place, whence I did look, I had not stood to have it plain against the shining upon the other side of that Land.

And how I did feel in that moment, I have no words to set out unto you. But surely was my heart gracious with thankfulness, and I ready to leap with joy and hope, and all my body thrilled with an excitement that would not have me to be silent; so that, suddenly, I began to shout foolishly across the night. But I came soon to wisdom and silence.

# CHAPTER X
### *The Maid of The Olden Days*

Now, AS YOU SHALL perceive, all mine utter despair was turned in a moment into an huge gladness and a great hope; so that it did seem to me that I should be with my dear One in but a little while. Yet was this an over-hope and expectation, and was not like to have a swift satisfying; for, truly, I was made aware of naught, save that I did perceive the shape of a great pyramid, going upward into the night.

And I knew that the Pyramid did surely stand upon an hill in the midst of that dark Country, for only so might it show so great and high. And I set me to run swift downward into the Land, so that I should make a strong going unto the Pyramid.

And I ran for a few little minutes, and lo! I fell headlong, and did truly feel as that I had brake my neck with the hardness and pain of my fall. And I had no power to go forward any more for a great while; but did just be there where I did fall, and very helpless and moaning a little; so that any creature had been able to slay me, if that it had come upon me in that time.

Yet, presently, I was able to sit upon the earth, and did hold my neck with my hands, and afterward the pain went away; so that I gat once more to my feet. But now I went forward very wisely, and had, moreover, an anxiousness in my heart; for, indeed, how did it be that the Pyramid was so utter dark, if that it did be the Lesser Refuge, in truth. And immediately there did rise in me a fear that it should be some House of Evil in the dark of that Land, or some wicked Force working a Pretence and a bewilderment upon my sight. Yet, truly, the thing was plain now against the far-off fires of the Land; and I did have little thought but that it should be, in verity, the Lesser Refuge.

Now in the first moment that I did perceive the dark Pyramid, I had been without wit, save to run very quick and blind unto the place; for you to remember how long I had made so great a search. And afterward, I had been minded to call unto Naani with my brain-elements, sending the

Master-Word, and my speech after to tell how that I was come unto her. But now I did heed to have caution, and to discover what this darkness should truly mean.

And so did I go downward again into the night of that Land, at the first with a carefulness; but presently with a fierce eagerness and expecting of the heart, the which had been dulled a little time with the horrid shaking and pain of my fall.

Now I had climbed unto the upper plain of the great volcano in, maybe, thirteen hours; but I went downward of that great Hill in ten, and had made a greater speed, but that I was sore shaken and unsure, by reason of my fall.

And in the end of the tenth hour, I perceived that I was come again to the great Plain of the Land; and I had no more any proper sight of the Refuge, because that it was upward afar in the darkness of the night. Yet was I abled now to see that there went a bulk between me and the far shinings, and did know that this great thing was surely the hill on which the Pyramid did stand.

And I went four hours across the Land, and did pass in this place and that, fire-holes that made a little red-shining in the night; and because of the fires in those far parts and a-near, there was not an utter dark.

And when I was gone four hours towards the Pyramid, I could no more see the distant shinings, for the bulk of the hill-bottom stood up between, and made all a blackness that way. And by this thing, I did guess that I was come nigh unto the hill; but yet was a great hour more before that I came to it. And in that five hours, since I was come down from the great Volcano, there had past me thrice and again, the sounds of things running in the night, and once there did be a sound as of a giant roaring afar, and a strange and horrid screaming.

Now I began to go up the hill. And, at the first, an utter excitement took me in the heart; so that I could have shouted the name of the Maid aloud in the night, with vain hopings that she should hear me and make an answer. But this state went from me very swift, as I did go upward, and there came a caution again about me, and a coldness of fear, as that my

spirit did wot of something that my heart did not perceive.

And, presently, I was come upward almost to the top of the hill, the which took me nigh three hours. And surely, when I was come that I could see the grimness of the Pyramid, going upward very desolate and silent into the night, lo! an utter shaking fear did take me; for the sweet cunning of my spirit did know that there abode no human in all that great and dark bulk; but that there did await me there, monstrous and horrid things that should bring destruction upon my soul. And I went downward of the hill, very quiet in the darkness; and so in the end, away from that place.

And I was four great hours before that I was come clear away from the hill, and I did feel that there was not any safety for my spirit in all that Land. And surely I went a little blindly, in the first, and did go with no heed unto my way.

And presently, I was upon the shore of the olden sea, and had no knowing how that I was come there; for, surely, I did think it to be a great way off. But now I do think that the dry bed of the sea did curve around unto that place, or that there did be two, or more, olden seas in that Country of Night.

Now, presently, I sat me down, very weak and bewildered; for it was as that my heart did lie dead within me. And, in verity, you shall perceive how this thing was, for I did know by the tellings of my spirit that there abode evil things in the dark Pyramid upon the hill; and I doubted not but that destruction had come upon the Peoples of the Lesser Pyramid, and that evil creatures and Powers did now abide in that place. And if this thing did be truly so, I was come over-late to the saving of the Maid; and with this thought I was very glad that some evil thing should come that I should fight with it and die quickly; for there was naught then in all the world to make me glad to have life.

And so shall you know the utter desolation that was in my heart; and, truly, I can perceive both the wiseness and the unwisdom of my reasonings; for, indeed, I did have no *sure* knowing that the dark Pyramid did be truly the Lesser Refuge. But yet, in verity, my spirit did know with a certain sureness, and there was no doubt concerning this thing, in all my being.

And, after that I had sat there awhile, I did mind me suddenly that I should send the Master-Word through the night; for, indeed, how else might I ever know whether Naani did yet live; though, in truth, I had little, save desperate hope in this matter; but yet did remember how that I had seemed odd times of my journey to hear the beat of the Master-Word with my spirit, out of all the dark of the world. And, in verity, if Naani answered not to the Word, but there came instead an Evil Power to destroy me, I should but cease me of mine utter heart-ache.

And I stood me upon my feet, and looked outward about me into the blackness of that Land. And I sent the Master-Word with my brain-elements; and immediately I called Naani, thrice, sending the call with my brain-elements.

And lo! in a moment, as it did seem, there broke around me out of all the mystery of night, low and solemn, the Master-Word, beating in the night. And immediately there did sound within my brain a far, small voice, very lone and faint, as that it had come from the end of the world. And the voice was the voice of Naani and the voice of Mirdath, and did call me by mine olden love-name.

Then, indeed, I did near to choke with the utter affright of joy that did take me in the heart, and also I was shaken with a mighty excitement, and my despair was gone, as that I had never known it. For, in verity, Naani did live and did call unto me with her brain-elements; and surely I had not heard the voice of mine Own for an utter age of grim labour and dread.

And the voice was, as I did say, as that it came from one that did be in a far place of the earth. And, in verity, whilst I stood dazed with a great joy that the Maid did live, I knew within me, concerning the fear that she was utter far off; and what peril might come anigh to her, before that I should stand to her side, to do battle for her life and well-being and mine own joy.

And lo! in the same moment, and before that I made further speech unto Naani, I did wot that someone did be a little way off from me, in the bushes, where a fire-hole did burn anigh to me; and it was as that my spirit knew this thing, and told of it unto my brain. And I made no answer unto the Maid, across all the dark of the world; but went very swift into a great

bush that was nigh to the fire-hole, upon this side.

And I lookt through, into the open space that did be about the fire-hole. And there was a little figure that did kneel, sobbing, upon the earth, beside the fire-hole; and truly it was a slim maid, and she did seem as that she harked very desperate, even whilst yet she did sob. And surely, mine own soul did *Know*, all in one white moment of life. And she there, un-knowing, and harking unto a cry of the spirit, that she did think to come through all the desolation of the night—even from the Mighty Pyramid. For oft, as I did perceive, had she cried unto me in all that lonesome month, and known no answer; neither that I was making a desperate way unto her; for, indeed, her weakness was great, so that she had no power to throw the Word strongly afar, neither to make plain her spiritual cryings through any mighty space of the aether.

And lo! I drew in my breath, and set my teeth a moment, to steady my lips; and I said:—"MIRDATH," out of the bush where I did be, and using natural human speech. And the Maid ceased from her weeping, and lookt this way and that, with an utter new fear, and with a frightened hope that did shine with her tears in the light from the fire-hole. And I divided the bush before me, and went through the bush, so that I came out before her, and did be there in my grey armour; and I did pause then, and was all adrift in myself; for my heart said that I should take this Maid into mine arms again; for that I was come again to be with Mirdath after an utter lost Eternity. But yet was I all paused; for truly she was Naani and she was Mirdath, and she did be a stranger in mine eyes, and very dainty and pretty and shaken with woe and sore trouble and grief.

And in that same moment of my coming unto her out of the bush, she screamed and fell back from me, and strove weakly to gain unto the hither bushes; for, truly, she knew not what was come upon her in that first little moment. And immediately she saw that it did be an human man, and no monster to slay her, and in that instant I said the Master-Word unto her, aloud, that she should have knowledge of peace and help. And I told my name, and said I am That One. And she knew this thing, even as my lips made the sounds. And she cried out something in an utter broke voice, and

ran unto me, and thrust her two small hands into my charge and keeping, and fell thence into a great sobbing and shaking, so that I was all in trouble to ease her; but did keep a silence and held fast her hands, for I had not on mine armored gloves.

And she leaned against me, very weak, and seeming wondrous like to a child. And lo! in a while she ceased to sob, and did but catch her breath this time and that, but said no word. And I bethought me that she did suffer of hunger, for I perceived that she had been long wandering and alone, and was come unto the end of hope, when that I did come.

And the Maid stood there yet silent, for she might not yet command her mouth to speak. And she trembled as she stood. And I opened my left hand, and lookt at the hand within my palm, and surely it was utter thin and wasted. And I made no more pause, but lifted mine Own and set her easy upon the earth, with an hump of smooth rock unto her back. And I stript off my cloak very quick, and put it about her, for she was scarce covered with her clothes that had been all torn among the bushes; so that part she shook with an utter chill, and part because of weakness, for she was nigh to be starved unto her death, and destroyed with her grief and lonesomeness.

And I took from my back the scrip and the pouch, and I gat a tablet from the scrip, and brake it into my cup, and with the water I made a little broth very swift upon an hot rock that was to the edge of the fire-hole. And I fed the broth unto the Maid, for truly her hands did shake so that she had spilt it all, if that I had done otherwise.

And she drank the broth, and was so weak that presently she did fall again to sobbing, yet very quiet; so that I strove not to be troubled in the heart; for, indeed, this thing was but reasonable, and not cause for me to have an anxiousness. But I put my hands under the cloak and took her hands into mine and held them strong and firm; and this did seem to bring something of peace and strength unto her; so that presently the trembling and the weeping went from her. And, indeed, the broth was surely helpful in this matter.

And presently, I knew that her hands did stir a little within mine, and I loosed somewhat of my grip; and immediately, she graspt my hands with

a weak and gentle grasp; but lookt not yet at me; only did stay very quiet, as that she did gather her strength within her. And, indeed, I was content; save that an anxiousness of the heart did stir me this time and that, lest some monster should come upon us. And because of this trouble, I did hark about me, now and oft, and with a new and strange fearfulness of danger, because that now mine Own was given unto my charge; and surely my heart would break, if that there came any hurt unto her.

Now, of a sudden, the Maid did make as that she would rise, and I loosed free from her, to give help. And she gat me by the hand, and slipt sudden to her knees, and did kiss my hand, and did begin again to weep. And surely I was so utter abashed that I stood very stupid and let her do this thing. But in a moment I drew free from her; for this thing might not be. And I gat me to my knee likewise before her, and took her hands, and kist them once, newly humbled, as it were; and thus should she know all that was in my heart, and of mine understanding. And she did but sob the more; for she was so weak, and utter moved unto me, because that I had come to her through the night of the world. And this thing I knew, though no speech had yet past between us. And I gave up her hands, lest she need them for her tears; but she left them to lie in my palms, as she did kneel there; and she bowed her head a little over her weeping; but did show that she was mine, in verity, unto the very essence of her dear spirit.

And I took her into mine arms, very gently and without caress; but presently I stroked her hair, and called her Naani and Mirdath, and said many things unto her, that now I scarce do wot of, but she did know them in the after time. And she was very quiet in mine arms, and seeming wondrous content; but yet did sob onward for a great time. And oft did I coax her and say vague things of comfort, as I have told. But truly she did ask no more comfort at that time than that she be sheltered where she did be. And truly she had been lonesome and in terror and in grief and dread, a great and horrid time.

Now, presently, she was grown quiet; and I made to put her comfortable in the cloak against the rock, that I should have freedom to make her more of the broth. But yet she did nestle unto me, with a little sweet

wistfulness, that made warm my heart in a most wondrous fashion; for surely she was mine Own. And she to begin to say odd words to me. And so to have gentle obedience, and to rest quiet against the rock, the while that I did make the broth. Yet ever her gaze did follow me, as I knew; for I must look oft her way.

And I took the broth to her, and she drank it, using her own two hands; and I sat by, and eat three of the tablets and drank some of the water, for truly it was a foolish great time since last I had eat.

Now, in a while, the broth did make bright the eyes of the Maid, and she did begin to talk; and at whiles had pauses, because that she lacked of strength, and there was more to be told than an human may have the heart-strength and cunning to make plain. And twice she did come again to sobbing; for, truly, her father was dead and the Peoples of the Lesser redoubt all slain and dispersed through the night of that Land.

And I learned that an Evil Force had made action upon the Peoples within the Lesser Redoubt; so that some, being utter weak by reason of the failing of the Earth-Current, had opened the Great Door, and gone forth into the night. And immediately there had come into the Lesser Pyramid, great and horrid monsters, and had made a great and brutish chase, and had slain many; but some had escaped forth into the night.

And with these had come Naani, after that her father, the Master Monstruwacan, had been slain by a shaggy man, very brutal and monstrous. And there had been three maids with Naani, when that she made escape into the night; but there had come certain creatures upon them, as they did sleep among the bushes, and had stolen two, and the other maid had run off, as did Naani, and they had neither met the other any more.

And this dreadful happening unto the Peoples of the Lesser Redoubt, had been a great while gone, as it to seem to her; but she had no means to tell me how long this time should be; for, in verity, how should she make a count. Yet had it been a dread long while unto her; and I found presently, that she had been lost through all that time that I did make my journey unto her; for, indeed, this thing I discovered by asking concerning my callings unto her. And she had heard none that did come to her, in any time

since she had escaped out of the Lost Refuge into this dreadful Land.

And because that she was so sorely chased, she had come nigh to be naked, even as I found her; for the bushes and the rocks had torn her garments from her, and she had naught with which to make any proper mending of them. And for food she had eat the moss upon the rocks, and odd strange berries and growths, and had drunk of the waters of the hot springs; and oft had she been made utter sick, because of the sulphur, or somewhat, of the water and, maybe, the poison of odd plants. Yet, as I did think, it was like that the first did save her life from the second; but in this thing I do make only a guessing.

And in all that dreadful time, since that she had come to be quite alone, she had heard a score drear things; for there had been once the slaying of a young maid nigh unto her, by some Brute out in the darkness of the Land; and thrice and more had she heard the feet of people running this way and that, and the tread of giants pursuing. And by this telling I did understand those things which mine ears had told to me as I did go across that Land, and surely a new pity and sorrow and horror did come upward within me. And the Maid told me how that she came once upon certain of the Peoples of the Lesser Redoubt, as they did hide among the bushes; but they ran, with no heed to her callings that she did be human, even as they; and by this is it plain the sore and dreadful panic that was upon the hearts of such.

And the bitter chill of the Land had made her to strive alway to be nigh unto the fire-holes that were very plentiful; but even as this did be needful unto her, so was it a thing that drew the Monstrous Brutes of that Land, even as I had found in the Night Land, and in the Upward Gorge. And because of this, she was oft made to stay afar off in the utter cold of the night.

Yet, in truth, odd whiles she did be so desperate, that she would make the venture, and so mayhaps have a time of warmth; and because of this, she had been nigh slain in her sleep, twice and thrice. Moreover, there were snakes about the fires, though not over-plentiful in all parts, and there did be spider-crabs and monstrous scorpions.

And, indeed, even as she had lain by the fire-hole, very weak and seeming near unto her death, even this time when my call had come unto her to stir her unto life and bitter knowledge of despair, even then was she all surround by creatures that were like to crabs, that did squat all about her, and did but wait for her to die; so that she had been feared to sleep, lest they destroy her in her slumber.

And by this thing, she had known that her death was surely nigh; and lo! out of all the night of the world had come the beat of the Master-Word, strong and powerful, beating as a low and spiritual thunder out of all the dark of the night. Yet had she thought of me, only as speaking from the far-off Mighty Pyramid; so that the cry had brought naught of hope unto her, but only a newer and more known despair. And, behold, in a little minute, there had come her name, spoken surely with the tongue; and a name that was different from the name that my spirit had said after the beat of the Word. And immediately, I had come out of the bush, and she had fallen back in a sudden great fear that a monster was stolen upon her; and then did see a young man in grey armour, and did know in one instant that I was that olden one of her memory dreams, and the one that had spoken unto her in the spirit across half of the dead world, as it did seem. And now was I come through all that unknown desolation and affright, to succour her. And she was immediately safe; but yet all broken because of her weakness and her utter joy and her sweet honour for me.

And this is the chief of that which she did tell unto me; and the way that she had seen and did regard the marvel of this our coming together. But, surely, no man was made ever to be worthy of the way that she did look upon me, or of the words that she did say unto me in her weakness and happiness.

Now, with the Maid having speech concerning the spider-crabs, I lookt presently well around, and surely, in a minute, I saw that they were not gone away; but did be a circle of silent and steadfast watching and impudence and horror all about us. And surely this thing put an anger and disgust upon me; so that I gat to my feet, and went unto the border of the light, and I spurned this little monster and that, and did truly kick maybe

a dozen, before that they were content to be gone. And by this thing shall you know of their calm and foolish assurance; but yet were they seemingly without courage; for they made not to attack me. Yet a true crab of this day been wishful to pinch me, had I put my toe forth unto it.

Now, I went back to the Maid, and she did laugh with a little, weak gleefulness; so that I perceived that she was like to be a very joyous maiden, if but I did have her in health. And I made her another cup of the broth, and she drank it very easy. And afterward, I made a very stern and playful order that she must sleep, and, indeed, she to need it sore, for she was gone again from her excitement, and her weakness upon her; yet very happy and content and without fear.

And I made a smooth place for her, and put the pouch and the scrip to be for a pillow, and I did lay her there very quiet and sweet in the cloak, and covered her feet; but, indeed, I saw first that they did be sore cut and without any gear to them; so that I perceived that Mine Own had worn out her foot-gear utter in her lonesome journeyings, and in running from Brutes that did come to find her. And so I to know more in the heart, somewhat of the true dreadfulness and fear that had companioned Mine Own. And I was minded then that I would wash and bind up her feet; but yet was she so utter worn, that I did prefer that she sleep so soon as she might, and afterward, when she was come wakeful again, then should I take a proper heed of her feet. And truly, they were very small and shapely.

Now, while Naani did sleep, I stript off mine armour, and took off mine under-suit, which was named the Armour-Suit, and a very warm and proper garment, and made thick that it should ease the chafe of the armour. And afterward, I put on the armour again; but the suit I folded, and laid beside the Maid; for, truly, she was nigh unclothed, by reason of the bushes and the rocks, that had rent her garments all-wise.

And I stood watch for the Maid, the while that she did slumber; and surely she went ten long hours. And I walked upon this side of the fire-hole and now upon that, and did oft cease, that I might hearken both with mine ears and with my spirit; for, truly, I was all wakened to a new care and delight, and did have a fresh and doubled fear of any Horrid Creature or

Force of Evil. And this shall be very plain to you.

And in the end of ten long hours, the Maid wakened, and I ran to her all joyed that she was come again to knowledge and to be that I could talk with her.

And she sat upward and looked at me, and there was new light and movement in her, so that I knew her strength was come back into her. And for a little minute, she said naught unto me, the while that I did ask how she did be; and she lookt at me very keen, so that I wondered some wise in a daze, what was in her mind.

And she askt me, of a sudden, how long it did be since that I had slept. And having not thought to put away her asking, because that the question was over sudden, I said four-and-eighty hours, which should be three days and the half of a day of four hours and twenty; and this thing I knew, because that I kept alway a very careful counting of the hours, lest that I get all adrift, and know not how long I was taken to come to this place and that.

And, truly, even as I told this thing to the Maid, I was grown very quaint in the head; for, indeed, I was gone a wondrous while without slumber, and had done much and bitter work in that time; and before then had been much lacking of rest, as you do know.

And, sudden the Maid cried out something, and tost the cloak from her, and had me into her arms, and did heed not to have any foolish shame of her nakedness. And, in verity, I knew not how I was gone so strange; but do see now that I was nigh to swoon for lack of slumber and rest.

And she kept me very steady for a little, and afterward helped me to be laid upon the ground; and she put the scrip and the pouch under my head; and so I did lie very calm and restful, and did be the more so, because that I was grown so tired in the heart, the which did make my head to be very husht, as that all the world was grown very quiet in a moment.

And the Maid did mind then that she did lack to be properly covered, and she gat the cloak, and put it about her, and did afterward sit a little beside me, and did rub my hands. And presently, I was something more to myself, and she did grow more happy of her mind, and made to give me something for my stomach; for, indeed, I was grown those late hours to be

foolish and to have no wiseness to proper eating.

And she did lift my head, the while that she did take the scrip from under, and kept me very sweetly upon her knee, and so until she had gat free a pack of the tablets, and the flask and the cup; for I had put all matters back into the scrip before Naani had gone unto sleep, and because of this, I had not been able to eat or drink aught, save by wakening her, as you perceive; for, indeed I had put the scrip and the pouch under her head for a pillow, as I have told.

And she would not bide that I should do aught; but only did ask concerning the making of the water, and was wondrous amazed to see how the powder did fizz up and become water; and indeed, she had too much into the cup, for, truly, it rose up and ran to the ground. And when she had done thus, and ceased to marvel, she put three of the tablets into the water, and made me a broth, even as I had made a broth for her; but, indeed, I was in no need, and had done very well to eat the tablets and drink the water. Yet, truly, I was not wishful to lack the love of her way, as you may think.

Now while I did drink the broth, I did be very restful upon the earth, and mine head against mine own Maid; and I did mind me now that I tell her concerning the Armour-Suit that I did mean for her wear.

Yet I said not that I had stript it from me, for then she had been like to say nay, and to trouble that I was like to come to a chill, as is the way of a woman. But, indeed, I might so well have told her, for truly, she did know on the moment, and set to a little unto weeping; yet very gentle and sweet, and did kiss me as I lay there, and say such things as should make a young man the better to have heard, if but that his own dear Love doth say the same.

And she would nowise wear the garment; but yet in the end I prevailed by gentle reasonings and because that I was her master, as I was born to be; and moreover, her own sweet sense did show that I spoke for wisdom; for how should she come through all the bitter way before, if that she had not a strong and close-made garment; and as you do mind, her coverings did be in utter rags, as I have told; yet very sweet and clean, as I had known; so that I ween she had stript oft in the lonesome night, and

washt her garments in this or that hot spring of the sulphur waters and other matters.

And, in verity, alway she was much given to washings, as I did soon perceive.

Now, presently, I did be very well again; but with a sore slumber that did press upon my head. Yet, ere I should sleep, I did mean that I bathe her feet and bind them with ointment and with my pocket-cloth; and truly her feet were very small and pretty.

And I sat me up, talking my head from her knee; and told her of mine intent. But, in verity, she did but throw her arms about my neck and give me one loving kiss, and laught so hearty that I did think to do this thing when indeed she was the better able to mind it, and I the better suited to have me to my rest. And, surely, this was very true, and I made no ado, save to give her the ointment; but lay back, and did be quiet.

Now I did be upon my right side, and she went to my back, and took the cloak from about her, and spread it upon me, and afterward stoopt over very dainty, and kist me, and bade me to go very swift to my sleep, for that she did mean to make her toilet and to get into mine Armour-Suit.

And I made no foolishness in this matter; yet told her to ease the cloak a little about me, so that I should have room to take the Diskos from my hip; and this thing I did, and took the Diskos to my breast, as was my habit; and surely I saw that her eyes did look at me with a little shining, because that I had so strange and fierce a bed-mate.

And I made her to promise that she keep a very keen harking, the which was like that she should do, and to call me on the instant that she did perceive any unease in the night. And after that, I shut mine eyes, that I should not shame her, and put out mine arms, and kist her once and turned from her unto my slumber; and she away to my back that she might be modest to her needs.

And surely, I was asleep in but a little moment, and with a great love and delight in my heart and in all my being.

And, truly, I waked not for twelve great hours. And when that time was gone, lo! I came awake, and surely the Maid did sit beside me, so bonny,

and so winsome and pretty that mine arms went unto her in a moment, and she into them, and gave me a loving and tender kiss; and afterward slipt away from me, very sensible and loving; and did stand up and turn about to be lookt at. For she did wear the Armour-Suit, and surely it was loose upon her; but yet very pleasing, being close-knit. And I to my seat, from lying, that I might see the Maid the better. And, in verity, I must kiss her again; for she did be with her hair all about her, that she look pretty unto me; and her little feet did be bare, and so that they made my heart new tender to look upon them; for truly she was utter lost of foot-gear. And I to my knee to her; and she, not to deny me, did come to be kist again.

Now when I found how great a time I had slept, I did scold Mine Own; but yet, as she did say, I must have long slumber if that I go so long wakeful, else should I lose my strength. And I askt how oft she had eat, and she told me but the once, and that six hours off.

And on this I did scold again; but surely she put a very pretty finger sudden upon my lips, so that I might do naught but laugh, and kiss that same finger.

And, after that, we did eat and drink, and made plans. And once I did comfort the Maid; for, indeed, her sorrow did rise in her, because that her father was come unto his death, and the Peoples of the Lesser Redoubt all destroyed, and adrift in the night amid the monsters of that Land.

And, in verity, I was set that we go quickly out of that place, ere there came an horrid Destruction upon us; and, surely, there should scarce be any human, beside, in all that Land; for there must have come death upon the chief of those that did make escape.

And after we had eat and drunk, I did count the packs of the tablets, and was thankful in all my being that I had been careful and denied my belly; for I did perceive that there were left enough for our needs, if that we made a good speed, and did not fear to be empty. And of the water-powder, as it might be named, there were left two full flasks, and somewhat of that one that I had drunk from, all my journeying. And by this thing you shall perceive that we did not be like to die for the need of such matters.

And here, as it doth occur unto me, I do ponder how it did be that we

had no thought to slay any small creature for our food; but, mayhap, we had no knowledge this way; for surely, they did not this thing to my knowing in the Mighty Pyramid. But yet, as I have said before this, I have not all knowledge of the doings of the Peoples. But, in verity, I never saw joint meat in all the time of that far Life that I do wot of. Yet, had we but slain somewhat for our hunger in that great wandering, we had been less empty in the belly.

Now, before that we should do aught beside, we must contrive that Naani have some gear for her feet; and to this intent, I did make a search into the pouch, and surely I found that there did be a change pair of inner shoes, that were made to go within mine own shoes of the grey metal.

And at this I was wondrous glad, and did make the Maid to sit upon a little rock, while that I made a fitting of the shoes. And, surely, they did be utter big and clumsy upon her little feet; so that I was in surprise to know how great is a man, beside a Maid. But in the end I had a cunning thought, for I cut off all the side of a strap, throughout the length of the strap, very thin and careful, and so had a lace to tie the boots around the tops, which were soft and easy for such a purpose. And after that, I stood away to look at the Maid, and neither she nor I were truly pleased; for, indeed, she was too pretty to be so hid and muffled. Yet were we glad otherwise; for now she might go without hurt to her feet.

And afterward, we packt our gear, and she did make a bundle of her torn garments; for, truly, they might be proper somewise to our need. And so we to begin the way out of that Desolate Land.

And we went forward together across the Land, and the journey was no more a weariness, but of a close and sweet joy; yet did I have a new anxiousness, as you do perceive, lest that any monster come to harm Mine Own.

And we went twelve great hours in the bed of the olden sea, and did eat twice in that time. And surely the Maid did grow utter weak and weary; for she was not come proper unto her strength; yet did she make no odd saying to tell me of this thing. But indeed, I did know; and I stopt in the thirteenth hour, and took her into mine arms, even as I should carry a babe;

and I went forward with her, and did hush her protesting with a kiss, and afterward she did but nestle unto me and shelter against my breast.

And I bade the Maid to sleep; but, indeed, she had no power to this end, for her body did ache very sore; but yet did she strive to give me an obedience in this thing. And in the eighteenth hour, when that I stopt to have food and drink, surely she did be awake, yet had she been utter silent; and I made to scold her; but she gat from mine arms, and did go upward upon her toes, and put her finger against my lips very naughtily. And afterward she did be impudent unto me, and did deny me to kiss her. But she went unto my back, and did open the scrip, and gat me to my food, even as a quiet and proper wife should go. As she did be so sedate that I knew she had mischief her heart of harmless kind.

But afterward this did pass sudden into weeping; for she had a quick and sore memory of her father and of the Destruction; and I took the Maid into mine arms, and did let her be there very gentle, and made not to kiss or to comfort her; but yet to give comfort.

And presently she ceased from weeping, and did slip her hand into mine, and I to keep it within, very soft and quiet; and afterward, she began to eat her tablets, yet always she did be very husht; so that I did be quiet also, and feel as that my love did be round her as a shield. And I knew that she had knowledge of this thing in her heart.

And oft I harked into the night of the Land; but there was nowhere any sound, or disturbing of the aether, to trouble me. And the Maid in mine arms did know when that I harked; for in verity, she had the Night-Hearing and the understanding spirit that doth be needful to such. And odd whiles did I look down to her through the gloom that did be about us; and presently I did perceive that she lookt up to me, out of mine arms.

And I kist her.

Now, in all that day, we had come nowhere upon any fire-hole in the bed of the olden sea; and truly I did ache to be nigh unto the warmth of such; for I did feel the cold of the Land, because that I was weary, and because that I had not the thickness of the Armour-Suit below mine armour to warm me.

And the cloak did be about the Maid; for I had feared that she should grow cold as I carried her. Yet, now she did know subtly that I was come to feel the utter chill of the Land; and she gat from mine arms, and put the cloak about me, and afterward came again into mine arms. And I let the cloak bide there, and drew it forward to be around her, also. Yet, truly, I was joyful that I did be cold, as you shall perceive. For it was sweet to the heart to bear somewhat of that dread chill for Mine Own; and she half troubled and likewise with understanding of my heart, because that I was less clothed than I had been.

Now, in a little while, the Maid did pack the scrip; and so we did make ready again to go forward, for I was grown anxious, as you may suppose, that we should come to some fire-hole, that we have a place for sleep that had warmth and light; for, truly, the cold of the Land did be drear and horrid.

And the Maid walkt by my side, and wondrous silent; but yet very nigh to me, so that I knew she did be very full of love to me, and of that quaint and sweet humbleness that love doth breed odd whiles in a woman when she doth be with her man, if but that man be also her master. And presently, I perceived that the cloak did be over mine own shoulders, and I took it and would have put it about the Maid; but truly she did not allow this; and when I did be stern with her, that she obey me in this matter, she did stand upon her toes, that she might kiss me, and pulled my head down, and surely she kist me and coaxed me that I wear the cloak, else should I give pain to her, in that I did surely be cold because she did wear the Armour-Suit.

Yet, I would not hark to this thing; so that the Maid did be truly in trouble. And first she made a threatening that she wear but her olden garments that did be only rags, if that I did persist. But this I saw to be foolishness and scarce-meant, and did as much need to smile at her as that I did think to scold her; but I did be firm that she wear the cloak.

And lo! she went sudden into crying; and this had been beyond my thoughts. And truly, it set me all adrift; for I perceived that she did be greatly distrest concerning this matter, when I had conceived that she did but mean this thing for tenderness' sake. But mine heart helped me to

understand, and I saw how she did be truly shamed, in her sweet woman-hood, if that I helped her not in this matter; for she did feel that she was made to do hurt unto that one that was her Love. And this thing I do pray you to think upon, that you understand; for, indeed, until that I was made to think, I had not seen it thiswise, for her.

And in the end, I came to agreement with the Maid, that we wear the garment hour by hour, in turn; and she to wear it the first hour and I to wear it the second hour; and so to go forward.

And truly, this did be an happy arranging; but yet she stampt her foot a little, as I put the cloak about her. And thrice in the hour did she ask me concerning the time that was gone; and surely, when the hour was but up, she had the cloak off in a moment, and went to my back and cast it upon my shoulders, and after to my front, and made it fast upon my breast; and so eager and naughty was she to this, that I took her by the shoulders, and shook her, somewhat, even as she had made to stamp at me; yet mayhaps with more of laughter. And she to take no heed at all; but to button the cloak and be very sedate. Yet, in verity, I caught her up into mine arms, and kissed her, for a sweet and naughty Maid; and she very willing, now that she had gotten something of her way.

Now, when we had gone forward, through five great hours, I per-ceived that the Maid did be utter worn, but yet did make presence that she was unwearied. And because I saw how she did be, I did heed and be anxious only that we come to some rock, to be for our safe refuge, and mayhap there to find an hole or cave, that should be somewhat to keep our heat about us; for there was nowhere any fire-hole anigh in all those hours.

And presently, we came to a part where there did be rocks, and we went to and fro in the gloom, and came in the end to a place where the rocks did go upward into the night, as that it had been a small and ancient cliff.

And surely in a while I found a hole that did go inwards of the rock; and the hole did be above mine head; yet when I was come to it, and had made the Diskos to spin therein, that I should have light to see whether there did be any creature or creeping thing in the hole, I was well pleased; for truly it did be sweet and dry.

Now the Maid had cried out a little to see the sudden shining that did come from within the hole, when I made the Diskos to spin, and because of the low roar of the weapon. But I answered her that there did be naught to have fear concerning; and so was she peaceful again, but yet a little trembling when that I came down to her; for, indeed, the Diskos did make always a strange sounding and a quaint and drear shining, as you do know; and she did be feared for me that some Evil Force had come upon me out of the cave; for she had neither knowledge nor conceiving that ever there did be so wondrous a weapon in all the world.

And I gave the Maid an help upward to the little cave, and came after, myself; and so we did be in a very nice and cosy place, that did not be easily gotten at by any monstrous thing. And surely I was utter glad for such a place, so that both should have safety that we might sleep in the same hours.

And, in truth, this was a needful plan; for if one had stayed wakeful to keep a watch for the other, then had our sleep taken us double hours; and this thing might not be, else should our food be done, and we to be twice so long as need be, ere ever we did come unto the refuge of the Mighty Pyramid; and I utter wearied and anxious of the heart and spirit that I bring Mine Own soon unto the safety and glory of my Mighty Home, and so free from the Destruction that did hang above our two souls for ever in that Land, and the peril that did be everywhere, save in the Last Redoubt.

Now when we were come into the hole of the rock, the Maid did slip the scrip and the pouch from my shoulders; and she gat out the tablets, and made some of the water, and did be very swift and natty, and all to the despite of the gloom that did be utter in that little cave.

And we ate each of us two of the tablets and drank some of the water; and I made jest with the Maid how that the tablets did be proper for strength, yet very lacking to fill the belly; though, indeed, I named it otherwise.

And she to agree, and did pat mine arm, and did tell me how that she should cook me a monstrous tasty and great meal when that we were come unto the Mighty Pyramid. And immediately afterward, she did make to laugh upon me, and to name me impudently for so much thought unto my feeding; and afterward again to silence, and to patting my hand.

Now, when that we had made an end of eating and drinking, I was very ready for sleep; for, truly, it was six and twenty great hours since that I did last slumber; but for the Maid it did be eight and thirty great hours; for, as you do mind, she had made no sleeping when that she did lie in mine arms for six hours of our journeying.

And I made how we should sleep; and put the cloak about the Maid; but surely she did refuse, very piteous, and seeming to have also somewhat of doubt and puzzlement. But in this thing I did be very stern and intending; for she did not be over-warm clad, as you do know, and moreover, she was but a little One, while I did be wondrous hardy.

And, in verity, I made her to obey, and gave her the scrip and the pouch for her pillow; and she, as it did seem to me, to sob to herself a little in the gloom of the night. But yet did I stay my heart a little stern to mine intent. And I wrapt the cloak about her, and set the scrip and the pouch very nice beneath her head; and afterward, I knelt over to kiss her, before that I came unto mine own slumber. Yet did she turn her mouth from me, and did put her hand above her face to ward me off, the which did grieve me; for truly, I did heed alway that I should never thrust my love upon her in her lonesomeness; but only let it be to her for a shield and for all comfort unto her heart.

And I turned my back, and went a pace away and lay down; for truly there did be no way else but to be near unto the Maid, for it was but a little cave. And I lay very husht, because that I was so sore in the heart. Yet, truly, I could not come unto my slumber, for I was so disturbed in my love; and I stayed very quiet maybe for a great hour; and did fight that I shake not mine armour to jinglings with the utter cold that did make me to tremble. But the Maid did sleep very sweet and calm, as I perceived by her breathings.

Yet, in verity, the Maid did be so much awake as I, and with some sweet and naughty intent of the heart, as my spirit did sudden perceive. And I lay very husht, and did wait to discover what this thing might be.

And I made my breathing to seem as the breathing of one that did sleep, even as that naughty Maid did make pretending. And surely, in a

while I did know that she moved very quiet, and came unto me; and I made yet that I slept very sound and strong; though the cold did nigh to conquer all my quietness.

And in a moment I perceived the intent of the Maid; for I did feel the cloak spread over me with a wondrous gentleness; and afterward there did be a soft kiss put upon my hand; and the Maid back then to her pillow; yet, as I did hear, she brought it something more nigh to me; as that she did crave to be near unto me that was her own Love.

And I sat up, and I put forth my hands suddenly and took the Maid into mine arms; and she to nestle unto me so that I did be wordless, because that I loved her so utter.

And presently, I felt her to stir in mine arms; and I loost her somewhat; for I did be always very mindful that I impose not upon her dear liberty of maidenhood. Yet she made not to go from me, but only to gather the cloak about her; so that we did both be in the cloak. And she askt why this might not be; for surely it did be madness that one should starve and the other be very nice in warmth. And, indeed, this did be but wisdom; yet it might not come the first from me.

And I said to Mine Own that this thing should be; and she reached out, and brought the scrip and the pouch, and placed them for a pillow for my head, and told me that I should put my head thereon. And I askt her how this did be right; for she did need a pillow the more than I. But she bid me to bide, and to have obedience in my turn. And when I was so, she spread the cloak over me, and afterward crept under, and did lie down beside me, and did seem as that she was asleep in one moment.

Yet, though she did be so sedate and matter-of-the-fact, as we do say, while that she was wakeful, she did yet nestle unto me very sweet and childlike in her sleep. And surely I did want to kiss her; but yet did refrain from my love; for, truly, I did well that I treat her very gently, at such a time, as you do perceive. And, in verity, such a Maid doth make a reverence in the soul of a man.

Now, presently, I was gone over unto sleep; and in seven hours I waked; and in that time had the Maid slumbered through eight hours; yet

did I intend that she be not disturbed, until that we were aready to the journey. And I slipt from under the cloak, and put it round her, very gentle. Yet it to be as she did miss me, even in her sleep; for it to seem to me that she put out her arms in the darkness, and she made a little moaning in her slumber. Yet, in a moment, she did be quiet, and afterward I put the cloak about her again.

And I went then to the opening of the little cave, and put forth my head, and lookt well about, and harked a long while; but there stirred nothing in the night thereabout; neither did my spirit wot of any matter for trouble unto us.

And presently, I gat out two of the tablets; for, as you do know, the Maid had given me the scrip and the pouch to be my pillow, so that I had power to come at these matters, without awaking her; but for her own part, as I did learn after, she had used her torn garments to be for a pillow; yet had made no explaining, as you do mind; and surely this was one of her naughty whimsies; and mayhap she had been so full of a playful happiness—as doth take the heart betimes—that she had made a little mystery where there did be no mystery; and this but to release her joy, and so to say masterful things unto me, out of her impudence; and afterward had meant that she tell me; but yet was gone unto slumber, ere that she did mind her.

Yet, since that time, a new thought hath come unto me that she did mean in the first that she should come into mine arms to sleep, and thereby need no pillow. But afterward, it may hap that she saw with a sudden olden wisdom, all in one moment; and afterward did act lovingly, yet with understanding. And so did change from her intent; yet with no improperness of modesty; but only with a niceness of Sense, which she did make no talk of; but yet did have. And surely, how oft is a man thus wisely ordered, unknowing.

And to cease from these thinkings, and to go forward, I eat two of the tablets, and afterward made some of the water. And lo! the fizzing of the water waked the Maid; and I knew that she reached out very sudden to me; but afterward knew in a moment what did make the sound, and that I did be up and making ready for the journeying.

And she gat up in the darkness, and said my name, and came unto me, and kist my forehead in the dark; and immediately she ran her hands gently downward of my left arm, and when she came to the cup, she took it from me, and slapt my hand, very dainty. And afterward I knew that she took a sip from the cup, and then did turn that side to me, and so gave me to drink, and did scold me that I had not waked her to tend to my needs; for surely she did be Mine Own, to have her duties to me.

And after that I had drank, she took the cup, and did finish it; and she gat two of the tablets, as I did think, and came afterward and sat upon the rock to my side, and did nestle somewhat against mine armour, and took mine arm and set it about her; and so did make to eat.

But first she put her tablet unto my lips, in the dark, that I should kiss it; and surely this was an olden way of Mirdath My Beautiful One; so that I did be all shaken of the heart. And I kist the tablet; and immediately she nestled unto me, and did begin to eat.

And presently, she put up the second tablet, as I did think, that I should kiss it; and I kist it, as before. Yet, ere she did begin again to eat, I did wot suddenly that she hid some intent from me.

And I caught her hand very quick in the dark; and her fingers did close upon the tablet, very guilty; so that I perceived that I had guessed aright. And I opened her fingers; and I found that there did be but the half of a tablet within her hand. And surely she had taken but that one tablet, and had given me the one end to kiss, and afterward the other; so that I should suppose she did eat two proper and complete tablets.

And I perceived that she had done this thing secretly, being minded that if she eat always but one tablet, then should I never lack, even if that we did be over-long coming unto the Mighty Pyramid.

And I askt how oft already had she eat but one, for two. And she confessed in a very quiet voice that this did make the fifth time. And I was so angered, that I took her hand and whipt it thrice, so hard that she had screamed if that she had been any coward. And she said nothing to me, neither went away.

And she began again to eat the half of the tablet, and did eat it from

the other hand, as I to be aware, because that her left hand did be hurt. And she wept not, but was very quiet by me; and presently I knew that she kist the whipt hand secretly in the dark.

And afterward, I put mine arm again about her; and she did be there in it, very sober and happy. And when she had made an end of the first tablet, I gave her the second, and she eat it very quiet and content.

And presently I talked with her, and showed her how that this thing did hurt my heart, even as she had been hurt that I did be cold garmented, the while that she did be warm. And I showed her the wickedness that she had done, that she did play so foolish with her life and strength; and well might she be weak and all a-lack.

Yet, did I think a little sweet impudence came into her, as I told her concerning her wickednesses. And I took her then into mine arms, and I showed her how that I knew all the unselfishness and wonder of her heart; and I kist her, and truly her lips did have a lovely glad humbleness as they came unto mine; so that it was as that I had not kist her truly until that moment. And I made her to promise that she never deceive me in such matter again. And indeed she promised; but yet with no ready tongue.

And afterward, we made proper for the journey; and when we had gotten our gear together, I went downward of the rock, and gave the Maid help to come down. And when we did stand at last upon the bottom of the rock, I askt Naani how she did feel, and whether her feet did hurt. And she answered that she did be very well and had no soreness in her feet.

And we went forward then, and she close unto me; and odd whiles with low speech, but more oft with silence, because that we did need that we hark alway for any danger or horror; and also there did be so utter a silence upon that part of the Land, which did be the bottom of the olden sea. And we ate and drank at the sixth and the twelfth hours; and in the fifteenth hour, we came upon a great slope of the earth; and lo! it did be the far side of the sea. And we went upward for a long hour; and so came to the upward part, and did be able once more to look over the greatness of that Land.

# CHAPTER XI
### *The Homeward Way*

Now, TRULY, IT DID seem very light, after the horrid and lonesome gloom that did lie all-ways in the bottom of the olden sea; and I saw that I was come out upon a part of the Land that did be surely to the right of that place where I made entry into the sea-bed, on mine outward going. And there did be a great plenty of fire-holes, so that mine heart was warmed to see them; yet did I mind to be wary in coming unto them; for, as you do know, there did so oft be life of this kind and that about these fires.

And I lookt now down to the Maid, and she upward to me, and did come more anigh to me, and truly she did be most wondrous pretty and sweet; yet did seem very awearied and pale in the face; so that I made blame upon myself that I had overwalked her; for, in verity, I do think that I was so strong and hard as that I had been made from iron; and she but a dear and tender Maid. Yet did she refuse that I should so reproach myself; and did but stand anigh to me and look at me with eyes that were very beautiful. And so I put mine arms about her, and kist her; and afterward lookt again over the Land, that I should shape out our further journeying.

And from that place where I did stand, there spread out all before me the blue shining that I had seen from the mouth-part of the Upward Gorge; yet did it be a great way off. And, indeed, I should tell you in this place, that it was by the glimmering of this shine within the sky of the night that I had steered, as we did come across the olden sea-bed. And, truly, it was but a broad thing to go toward; but yet did serve me, in that it told me that I went toward the far side of the sea-bed, and made not to go all about in blind circles in the night.

And after that I had considered a while, I did know somewhat where the Gorge should be, and perceived that I should go unto my left; but not overmuch, for indeed I saw the red-shining of the giants' hole that lay at a great space that way; and surely I must go so that I missed the place of the giants so much as I might, and in the same going, come not overnear unto

the blue-shining that lay before me, across all the far part of that Country; for, in verity, I Mistrusted the place where that shining did be.

Now when I had gained somewhat of knowledge where should be found the Mouth of the Upward Gorge, I put mine arm about the Maid, where she did stand so nigh to me, and very husht, the while that I had lookt about. And I pointed outward over the dark Land unto my left, and told her that the Gorge did be somewhere that way, a great distance off; yet utter out of my sight, and only to be known that it did be somewise there by the things that I did mind of, concerning my way after I came into the Land.

Now the Maid, having stood very quiet, had lookt all that time about her; and so had come to some knowing of the place where she did be in the Land, for her to know the land someways, as you shall think. And she askt me how I did mind to go; and truly I said, so straight as we might; but yet so that we come neither too nigh to the shining nor to the great red fire-pit of the Giants.

And the Maid bade me to look in the way that I did mind to go; and I lookt, but yet there was nothing save, as they did seem, certain fire-holes that had a green-shining about them. And she set out unto me then, how that there did go a tract of bad gas in that part of the Land, that should be utter poisonous unto any; and this had been well known in the Lesser Redoubt, by the reading of their instruments. And where the gas did go, there was there a green-shining about the fire-holes.

And she showed me how that the Place of the Gas went a great way unto the North-West, so that I learned now somewhat how the land did lie, as we do say in these days. And it was in all the North-West that the great blue-shining did burn. And I askt Naani how they named this, and she told me by no name, save but The Shine.

And Mine Own made very earnest to warn me, regarding The Shine; and urged that we go no more that-wards than should be needful to our lives—the which, indeed, was no wish of mine. And her reason to be that the Fixed Giants did be within the borders of The Shine, and all hid in the light thereof, save when the burning mist did roll this way or that. And I

took a great heed of this thing, and did guess that these Fixed Giants were somewhat even as the Great Watchers that were about the Mighty Pyramid, as you do know. And immediately I minded me of that utter monstrous face that I did see amid the bright smoke of The Shine, when that I came first into the Land; and surely this had been one of the Fixed Giants, that Naani told me were Forces of great and very horrid Evil.

And I askt Mine Own how far the Place of the Gas went across the Land; and she pointed and made further explaining. And, in verity, in the end, I saw not how I should come that way to the mouth of the Gorge, if that I would keep off-wards from The Shine. Yet, in a moment, Naani askt me how I did come across the Land, when that I searched for her. And, truly, as I showed her, I had walked then by a sweet chance, or guiding, alway upon the far side of the Place of the Gas, and so unto the Olden Sea bed; and was in this way come free of the gas, and all unknowing of it.

And at this telling, the Maid said that we go downward again into the bed of the Olden Sea, and walk some great hours below the shore, but in the way that should take us unto the South-West, and so until we were come beyond the Place of the Gas. And afterward up again into the Land, and then to have an utter caution that we escape the watching of the giants who did be ever about the Great Red Fire-Hole. And by this plan very speedy to the entering-part of the Upward Gorge.

And, truly, this did be very good and sound, and such as I should have planned in a moment; for, indeed, I am not over-slow in such matters; only the Maid did be very eager and quick; and it was very sweet to me that she should thus plan; for, in verity, I loved alway the sounding of her voice, and to hear her have speech and to plan and think, and so to show me the workings of her inward self and her dear qualities and human niceness. And to have part and lot alway with me in all things and thinkings.

And, we shaped to this plan that Naani made; but at that time, as you do mind, it was somewhat of seventeen hours since last we had slumber; and the Maid was sore wearied, as I did see. And I showed to her how that it did be wise that we have our rest very soon, and so forward again in new strength and ability.

And the Maid did soon agree with me; for indeed she was very weary; and we made it that we should venture unto one of the fire-holes that lay no great seeming away, a little upon our right, which was the Northward-way of that Land.

And we went toward the fire-hole; and, truly, it did be further off than we had thought; for it was a good hour before that we came anigh to it; and, indeed, it to prove a very great and red-glowing shine that went upward into the night, out of the hollow place where it did burn among rocks.

And when we were come near unto it, I made a sign to the Maid that she be utter husht; and I took the Diskos from mine hip, and went forward before her; and afterward to my knees and hands, and beckoned backward to Mine Own, that she do likewise.

And we came this way to the edge of the hollow-place where the fire-hole did burn; and so were able in the end to look downward. And truly it was a great fire that burned in the earth in that place; yet, as I perceived very swift, there did seem nowhere any monstrous thing about the fire, the which set some peace upon mine heart; but yet not overmuch; for it was come fresh upon me that we did well to stay afar off from the fires of the Land, in that it was about the fires that all living things did congregate.

And I lookt a great time, and the Maid crept unto mine elbow, and lookt with me; and afterward we harked, very keen, into the night; but there was nowhere any trouble of the air or of the aether of the Land. Yet I spoke quiet with the Maid, and showed unto her how that we did well to stay off-ward from the fires; but, truly, she was so utter cold and chill, that she did beg that we go down by the fire-hole, even should it be that we stay no more there than should put a warmth through the utter chill of our bodies.

And, in verity, I was so bitter cold that I was all weak to go beside the fire; yet, truly, I do think that the shiverings of the Maid was that which did force my heart, to go against the teachings of my head; so that in the end, we came down into the hollow, and very swift unto the fire.

Now, truly, it doth seem a strange thing to be so diverse-minded as this, when that, as you do know, I had been so long a-search for a fire-pit;

and mayhaps you shall perceive the better how my heart and brain did be contrary, when that I tell to you, now, how that I have belief that my spirit did even then be subtly set to warn me. And, also, as all do know, it doth be easy to forget this warning and that of experience; by which saying, I do mean that, oft as I had come to know the dangers that did be alway about the fire-holes, yet when I did be far off from them, and Mine Own broken and a-shiver with the chill of the Land, the danger did seem but a small thing and afar off from my mind, and unreal; but the cold to be doubly real. Yet, when we did come even unto the fire-hole, then did come again all about my heart the truth of those dangers that had seemed, but a while gone, so little. And, indeed, I do hope you perceive me in this thing, and how that I strive alway to set unto you the utter truth, so that you shall go with me all the way, and lend me your nice understanding.

Now, when we were come down unto the fire-pit, I went this way and that among the rocks that did be in the bottom of the hollow, so that I should perceive whether there did be any living creature there hid, that should mayhap come out, unknown, to work us harm.

But, indeed, I discovered nothing of any greatness; yet I saw three snakes, and there were, beside, two scorpion-creatures, as I did name them, that neither went backward from me, nor came against me; but did bide where I saw them, each in an hole of the rock.

And because I had seen these things, I saw that we should not do wise to sleep nigh unto the fire-hole; for the creeping things did mortally like the heat, and should be like to come upon us in our slumber. And, indeed, this did but uphold my caution, that we should be well actioned, if that we chose some other part to our rest.

Yet, as you shall suppose, I said naught unto the Maid concerning the creeping and the poisonous things; for I did mean that she have rest and happiness the while that we did stay beside the fire-hole; and afterward, I should tell her, and so she be the more ready to see the properness that we go elsewhere to our sleep. But, as you to understand, if that she not to see wisely and be still intent to the fire-hole, I should have her to obey; for surely she was Mine Own, and I did love her and did mean alway to have

her to safety.

Now, presently, the Maid was something warmed, and afterward, she slipt the scrip from my shoulder, and so had food and drink very swift to my need.

And we sat together, and eat and drank; and the Maid very sweet and quiet, as she did begin to eat her second tablet; and, truly, I had knowing that she did remember in all her body that I had whipt her. And, indeed, she did be utter mine.

And oft as we did eat and drink, I lookt this way and that, so that no creeping thing should come anigh to us; and presently, when we had made an end of our food, the Maid saw that I did look about, and she then very swift to catch some of mine unease, and to stare over her shoulder. And, indeed, in a little while she saw a snake go among the rocks; and she then to be very eager that we find some place that should be secure from creeping things. And we to begin then to look for such.

But in the end, we stayed in the hollow, for we found a little cave that did be in an upstanding rock of the hollow, and the upstanding rock was, mayhaps, an hundred good feet off from the fire; for the hollow was very great. And the cave did be a hole that was thrice my height up from the bottom rocks; and it was dry and sweet and with no creeping thing within it, neither did there be any place to hide such therein.

And when we were gotten into the hole, surely it did be very sweet and cozy; for the shine of the fire-hole did shine therein; and surely we had felt it a very haven, but that there was ever the fear of the Land upon our hearts; and upon mine the more than upon the Maid; for, truly, Mine Own did seem to trust me utter; and to seem that she feared not any evil monster, but to have surety that I had power to succour her in all ways. And truly this trust had been very sweet unto my heart, if that I had lacked somewhat of my terror for the safe home-going of Mine Own.

And we slept that night as we had done before, and shared the cloak over us; for truly, the fire-hole made no great warmth unto us; yet was it less bitter in that part than in the darkness of the Land.

And by that we had come unto sleep, it was twenty good hours since

last we had slumber; and truly we did be very wearied; but yet came unto our rest with our spirits set anxious to harken on danger the while that we did sleep.

And we slept seven hours, and did know suddenly of some matter that had need to waken us; and lo! in a moment I did wake, and the Maid in the same instant of time; and there was a great screaming and crying out in the night, that surely affrighted us both; yet did hurt our hearts the more; for it did be the utter cryings and terror of poor humans in the night of that Land. Yet might I do naught; but only wait that I learn more of the matter; for my duty was unto Mine Own, and I had no leave of rashness any more.

Yet, as you do suppose, I was all shaken to go downward of the rock, and afterward to climb out from the hollow, that I should give some help unto they that did need help; but yet might I not leave the Maid.

And immediately, there was a great roaring in one part of the night, and again another roaring in another part of the night; and lo! in a moment the roarings did be answered; and the roarings were the sounds of big and husky voices; so that it did seem that we harked to men so big as houses that did run and shout in the night.

And the Maid did begin to shake, and I put mine arm about her, and drew her backward into the hole so that she did be into the shadow; and she to tremble like one that was broken in courage; for, truly, she had heard those sounds oft in the night in all the long and dreadful month that she had wandered.

And, indeed, I was all shaken in my courage; for it did be the shouting of giants that I heard; and you do know somewhat of the utter horror and terror that did be alway in the heart that did harken unto those monstrous voices, for you do know my tale.

And there came in a moment, a dreadful screaming out in the night, and the screaming did be the screaming of a young maid that doth be slain very brutal. And my heart sickened, because of Mine Own; but my spirit did swell with a strange and utter anger, as that it should burst my body. And the Maid to my side broke into an utter sobbing.

And the screaming of the maid afar off in the dark did end very sud-

den; but in a moment there did be other screamings in diverse places, and the hoarse shoutings of the great men and the thudding of mighty feet that ran this way and that, a-chase.

And the cryings of the humans came nearer, and the thuddings of the great feet. And, in verity, in a little minute, it did seem unto me that the sounds did be right upon the hollow; and I crept forward, and peered out. And I felt the night to be full of people running; and immediately there passed by the hollow a clustering of humans that ran ever, and screamed and gasped and wept, panting, as they ran. And the shining of the fire-hole made them plain seen and clear, and they did be both men and women, and were but in rags or utter naked, and all torn by the rocks and the bushes, and did seem, indeed, as that they had been wild things that did go by so swift and lost.

And mine heart troubled me with the pain and longing that it did know; so that I had gone in a moment after those people, but that I should leave Mine Own and put her to peril. And even while that I felt so utter in this thing, there came a great thudding of monstrous feet; and there ran four great men out of the night, and went past the hollow very quick. And three did be dull coloured and seeming much haired and brutish; but the other did be an horrid white, and livid-blotched; so that it did seem to my spirit that there went by, a thing that did be a very man-monster filled of unwholesome life. And surely they did be gone from out of the shine of the fire, in one moment, as we do say; and again into the night to their dreadful chasing.

And when the thudding of their feet had gone a long way off over the Land, I heard them bellowing, and afterward a far away screaming, that did have a death note in it; and I knew that those dreadful brute-men did be taking the life from some poor wild humans; and afterward there did be the silence again.

And, surely, it did come to me with a fierce impatience of sorrow, that those people did be without spirit of courage; else had they turned them upon the giants, and slain them with their hands, even if that all had died to compass that slaying; for, truly, they should all die anywise by the

giant-men; and they had died then with somewhat to comfort their hate.

Yet, as I do know, the Peoples of the Lesser Redoubt had long been born of parents that were starved of the Earth-Current through an hundred-thousand years and more, and because of this thing, they did surely lack somewhat in all ways. Yet was Naani otherwise; but this not to prove aught, save the rule, as we do say.

Now, sudden, as I stooped very husht and troubled in the mouth of the little cave, I knew that Mine Own sobbed dryly in the back part of the cave. And I had gone to comfort her, but that in the same moment, I saw a naked maid run very swift over the edge of the hollow, and did look over her shoulder, as she ran. And she came to the bottom, and crept in under a ledge of rock that did be in that place; and she did seem utter worn, and gone of the spirit, and desperate. And I perceived in the same instant why that she did go stealthy and swift in that fashion, and to cower, as for her very life; for there came a squat, haired man, so broad as a bullock, who did come silent down into the hollow, looking this way and that, even as a wild beast doth peer, very sudden.

And the Squat Man had instant knowing of the place where the maid did be; and ran in upon her, with no sound.

And I paused not; but leaped all the great way unto the bottom of the hollow, which did be, mayhaps, twenty good feet and more; for mine anger was upon me, and I did mean that I save that one, though I did be powerless to give succour unto those others.

And I fell strong upon my feet, and had no harm of my limbs, for all that the leap did be so high. And in that moment, before that I had time to save the maid, the Squat Man ript her; and she cried out once with a very dreadful scream, and was suddenly dead in the hands of the Brute-Man.

And my heart made my blood to burn with wrath in mine eyes, so that I had scarce power in that instant to see the Squat Man, as I ran upon him. And the roar of the Diskos filled all the hollow, as I made it to spin, as that it did rage with an anger, and to be glut of the Man.

And the Man came round upon me; and thought, mayhaps, to deal with me, as it had dealt with that poor maid, but not all thatwise, as you

must know. And I swung the Diskos, and it did seem to sing and to cry eager in my hands. And I smote at the Squat Man, even as it did leap silent upon me, as a tiger doth leap, making no sound. But I gat not home the blow; for the Man dropt sudden down upon the hands, and the blow went overwards. And the Brute-Man caught me by the legs, to rip me; and I cut quick with the Diskos, and it did have but one monstrous talon left unto it. And immediately, it cast me with the other, half across the hollow, and I fell with mine armour clanging mightily, and the Diskos did ring like a bell.

And by the graciousness of all good things, I was harmed not by that monster throw; but was to my feet in one instant, and had not loosed the Diskos from my hand. And the Beast-Man did be upon me with two quick boundings; and I stood up to the Man, and it made no sound or cry as it came at me; and there did a great froth of brute anger and intent come from the mouth of it, and the teeth came down on each side of the mouth, very great and sharp. And I leaped and smote, so that my blow should come the more speedy, and the Diskos took away the head and the shoulder of the Squat Man; and the dead thing knockt me backward, with the spring that it had made; but it harmed me not greatly. Yet afterward I did know how sore and bruised I did be, in all my body and being. And I came back very swift against the Man; but it did be truly dead and greatly horrid.

And I went from the dead monster, and did go, all heart-shaken, unto the dead maid. And I took the torn body of the maid, very sorrowful, and cast it into the fire-hole.

And I turned me then that I should look unto the cave, that I should know that all did be well with Mine Own, and whether she did have seen the horror, or be gone into a swoon.

And lo! Mine Own did run toward me; and she had in her hand my belt-knife which I did give her, before that time, to be a weapon for her defence. And I perceived that she had come to be mine aid, if that I did need such. And she did be utter pale, yet very steadfast and not seeming to tremble.

And I made to take her from that place; but she went beyond me, and lookt at the monstrous bulk of the Squat Man; and was very silent. And she came back unto me; and still so silent. And she stood before me, and

said no word; but my heart knew what she did be thinking; for I am not foolish, to have lacked to know what did be in her heart; though mine effort had not shown itself that way unto me, before that moment. And I had no pretending of modesty, but received with gladness and a strangeness of humbleness the honour that her eyes did give to me; for, indeed, she did be so, that she might not give word to her joy of me and her glad respecting, the which is so wondrous good unto the heart of all men that do be loving of a dear and honest maid.

And she said nothing, neither then nor afterward; but I did be honoured all my life after, when that I did anytime mind me of the way that Mine Own lookt upward at me in those moments.

And afterward she did need and allow herself to come unto mine arms, that I hold her from the trembling of heart which did come to her, after that there did be no need for courage; for surely we had both seen a very dreadful thing, and there was a great horror upon us.

And I climbed upward again to the little cave, and did help Naani; and when we were come there again, we did rest awhile. And presently we eat, each of us, two of the tablets and drank some of the water, and indeed we were both utter thirsty.

And in about an hour, after that we had harked very keen a time, we came downward again from the cave, and had our gear with us; and we came up out of the hollow, and set forward with a great caution unto the olden sea-bed. And we came there in two long hours; for we went very slow and with constant harkings; for the fear of the monstrous men was upon us. But there came no harm anigh, neither did we perceive any disturbance in the night of the Land.

And we went down an hour into the olden sea-bed, and did go now the more swift; for our fear was something eased from us, because that we had come away from that place where we had perceived so great and dread an hunting. But yet had we all care about us; for the giants surely to be everywhere in that Land; but yet, as I do think, they to roam more oft anigh to the fire-holes; for the humans did surely wander in such parts, that they have warmth of the fires.

And after we had gone downward an hour into the sea-bed, we turned somewhat unto the South-West, and went for twelve great hours, and did never be any huge space from the shore; for it did run that way, as you do know. And I made to steer by the shinings of the Land, and with advices from Mine Own.

And in the end of the twelfth hour, I did count our distance, making that we did walk somewhat of a certain speed; and by the tellings of the Maid, we did be surely come beyond the place of the Land where the Poison Gas did lie.

And by this, it did be something after seventeen hours since we did sleep; and surely we did be very ready to have rest; for we had gone forward strongly, and with anxiousness; and truly my hurts did be come upon me, so that my whole body did ache; for the quick fight had been bitter, and I had been thrown very hard and brutal; and, indeed, it was wondrous that I had not been all smashed, only that the armour did save me.

And this doth show truly how hard and strong I did be; and Naani did speak upon this, and was oft a-wonder, and at that time did beg me that I make some rest to cure my hurts; for she had not conceived that a man did grow so strong and hardy; and, in verity, the men of the Lesser Redoubt did be soft-made and lacking of grimness, as I did perceive, both through my reason and from her tellings; for they did lack the strong life that doth breed where is the beat of the Earth-Current, as we to have in the Mighty Pyramid. And this thing I have said somewise before this time.

And because that we did be so wearied, I said unto Naani that we find a place for our slumber, and she very willing, as I have shown, and to counsel me likewise.

Yet did we search about in that gloom for a great hour more, and found no cave or hole to give us a safe refuge for our sleep.

And when that we could not find such, I told Naani that we should put the boulders together, somewhat, and so have them about us, that we be greatly hid; and, in truth, even as I began to tell her my plan, she did have the same words in her mouth, so that we caught our little fingers, there in the dark of that grim Land in the end of the world, even as she and I had

done oft in the early years, before that eternity, when that she did be Mirdath the Beautiful. And we did both be silent, and after that we had wished very solemn and earnest, we said each a name; even as lad and maid shall do in this age; and so to laughter and kist one the other. And truly, the world doth seem not to alter in the heart, as you shall think. And this was what I did find.

And we set-to, and gathered together the boulders which did be very plentiful in that part. And she carry those that did be thin and flat, and I to roll those that did be great and round. And I made a place that did be long and narrow; and afterward, I set the flat stones round the sides, that there be no little hole by which any creeping thing should come inward to sting us in our sleep.

And afterward we gat inside; and surely it did be very cozy, as we do say; but yet not so secure as I did wish, only that I could not shift to plan aught better. And, indeed, it should keep off from us any small thing, and should be like to save us from any monstrous Brute treading upon us; but otherwise, it did be but a poor affair.

Now we eat two of the tablets, each, and drank some of the water, even as we had done in the sixth and the twelfth hours; and afterward we shared the cloak for our slumber; and we kist very sedate and loving, and charged our spirits that we wake if that any horrid thing should come anigh to us in our sleep; and afterward we did be gone very swift to slumbering, and suffered no harm.

And I waked seven hours after, and surely I did ache very bitter, as I did move my body; for the bruisings did be gotten hold of me.

And I slipt away from the Maid, very gentle; for I had mind that she sleep a while more, as I did mean that we make a great journey that day.

And after I had harked a while, and perceived that there was no evil thing anigh, I went outward of the stones. And I walked to and fore and moved mine arms, that I be eased somewhat of the stiffness and ache; but surely it did seem that many hours must go ere I should make any speed of travel; for I did be all clumsy and slow and nigh to groan with the pain of going and aught that I did.

And I minded me that I should do somewhat to ease this thing, lest that I cause us both to come to an harm by staying over-long in that Land.

And I went back into the stones, and gat an ointment from the pouch, that I did carry. And surely the Maid did yet sleep. And I went outward of the stones, again; and stript off the armour, and all my garments; and I rubbed my body with the ointment, and surely the pain did be so that I groaned at this time and that; but yet must I rub good and strong so that I die not of the cold of the Land; and beside I was greatly anxious to cure myself.

And sudden, as I did rub very strong and savage, and heeding so well as I might that I groan not, the Maid did speak close beside me. And, indeed, she could see me but dimly, and had waked sudden to hear my groaning, and I was not to her side. And immediately she had thought that some evil thing harmed me, and was come in an instant that she be with me.

And she cared not that I did be naked; but was utter in anger that I strove to do this thing alone, and with none to aid me, and all uncovered to the chill of the Land. And she ran back into the stones, and brought the cloak and put it about me; and was so angered that she stampt, and had no impudence, but rather as that she did be minded to have tears.

And she sent me back into the sheltering of the stones, and gathered mine armour, and brought these things after me. But the Diskos I took in my hand. And she took the pot of the ointment from me, and made me to lie, and she rubbed me very strong and tender, and kept me warm with the cloak; and surely she was a wise and lovely Maid, and utter Mine Own.

And in the end, she askt me how I was, and I said that I did be different; and she hurried me that I be clothed very quick; for she did be sore afraid that I should come to a chill.

And when I was gotten again into mine armour, she came to me, and showed me where I did lack wisdom, and spoke very straitly and gentle and serious; and afterward kist me, and gave me my tablets, and to sit beside me. And we eat and drank; and I with a new lovingness unto Mine Own; and she somewhat as that she did mother me; but when I put mine

arm about her, she did be only a maid. And we did be thus, with but little talk and a great content.

And afterward, we gat our gear together, and went from that little refuge that we had made; and in a while we did go upward out of the olden sea-bed.

And when we were come again to the top of the shore, the which we did in two good hours, I lookt over the Land, a time, with Mine Own anigh to me. And I perceived that the Great Red Fire-Pit of the Giants did be no mighty way off unto the South and West; and surely in a little moment, we saw that there went monstrous figures against the shine of the mighty fire-pit; and we stoopt unto the earth; for it did seem that the light did be like to show us standing there, though truly we did be afar off, as you perceive. Yet, mayhaps, you do share with us the utter horror and distress that those horrid Men did cast about the heart, and so have a kindly understanding of our fear.

And over all the Land, in this place and that, there did be the small shining of little fire-holes and pits, that did be alway red, save in that part where the Poison Gas did lie, the which we had now come safe past.

And beyond the fire-holes, was the great Shine, that lay from the West unto the North of all that Land; and, in verity, we did need that we steer so that we come not anigh to it, neither unto the Great Red Fire-Pit of the Giants; neither unto the low volcanoes, which were beyond the Great Red Fire-Pit, as you do know, and someways unto the Mouth of the Upward Gorge.

And the way of our journey was between the West and the South-West of that Land; and to be made with cunning and wisdom, that we come clear of all unseemly danger unto Mine Own. And I askt her concerning this thing and that of the Land; and surely she told me so much of terror that I was half in a wonder that ever I did live in the end to come unto her.

And it was because of the things that she set out to me, that I perceived how we must come nowise anigh to the low volcanoes that were upon this side of the mouth of the Upward Gorge; for it had been known

alway in the Lesser Redoubt that there went very horrid men in that part that did be called wolf-men; but whether there did be any such thing in that age, she had no knowing; for she told me the things that did be set down in the Records and the Histories; and truly no man of the Lesser Redoubt had found heart in a thousand great years to make a journeying through the Land, for the desire of glad and dreadful adventuring, such as our young men did be oft set to; though it was not all such that went.

And because there did be no adventuring for so monstrous a space of years, there was no certain new knowledge of the Land of that age. And this thing is plain to you, and needing not of many words, which do so irk me.

And Naani set out to me how that The Shine was conceived to be a land where Evil did live for ever, and whence came all those Forces of Evil that did work upon the Lesser Refuge. And afterward, she did quiet; so that presently I perceived that she did weep to herself, because that her memory was all new-stirred by my questionings. And I took her very gentle into mine arms, as we did be there kneeled upon the earth.

And after that time, I askt her no question, save as it did be needful to our health and life; yet oft did she tell me this thing and that of her knowledge, to be for mine help and guiding.

Now we went forward, going a space toward the North-West, so that we come the more clear of the place where did be the Great Red Fire-Pit of the Giants. And we journeyed with a care alway that we show not ourselves over-plain unto the light that shone over the Land from the great Pit; and oft we did creep a while over this stark place and that; and went nimbly amid the bushes that grew oft in great parts.

And we made six hours this way, and did then have pause, that we eat and drink; and truly it was nine hours since first I did wake; yet had we made no pausing, because that we were so set to our journeying to come clear of the place where did be the Giants.

And after that we had eat and drunk, we went onward again; and made now unto the South-West; for we did heed that we go no more unto the North-West, because that should bring us over-near to The Shine.

And in the fourteenth hour of that day's travel, we came to a part where the Land dipt downward into a broad valley; and surely it did be very dark down there, and did be seeming shallow, yet truly of a great deepness; but we went that way, because that it did be a weary long journey to go around the place where the valley did be.

And the Valley had a different darkness from the gloom that went alway in the olden sea-bed; for the gloom of the sea-bed did be ever of a greyness; but the gloom of this Valley had a greater dark within it; yet did the air seem more clear.

And we went downward three hours into the Valley, and stopt then that we eat and drink; and truly I had not paused then; but that Mine Own did insist; for our methods did be like, else, to go all adrift, and we to be lacking of proper strength.

And this was wisdom of the Maid; but I to be a little irked-like and restless; and this mayhap because that my blood did itch me, because that it did be so full of the poison of my bruises.

And it was gone now of seventeen hours since last we did sleep; but yet did we be ready to go forward, that we come so quick as maybe out of the dark of that Valley; for there did seem nowheres any fire-hole to make a light; only that in this place and that, there did be a little blue shining, as that there burned a strange gas in this part or that.

Now, in two hours after the time that we did eat, we stopt, both of us, very sudden; for there did be some vague and curious sound in the night. And we went very swift to the earth, that we be hid, and harked. But did hear nothing.

And in a while, we to go onward again; yet there did be an unease upon our spirits; for our spirits did perceive something afar off in the night; but yet had we no surety in this matter.

And we went forward through a great hour more; and did pass in that time, two places where the blue-shining did be; and truly it seemed as that a low gas hung to the earth in this part and that, and made a slow burning, having neither noise nor spurtings; but slow, as that it did smoulder and be all to shine and luminous. And oft there did be a strong smelling of a bitter

gas, very horrid in the throat.

And in the end of another hour, while that we were a space off from one of those gas-shinings, there went past us at a distance, as it did seem people, running in the night; as that they did be lost spirits; yet with a rustling very soft; so that they did be like to be barefoot.

And I thought mayhap that these did be some of the Peoples of the Lesser Pyramid; yet did they be only as that shadows went among the blue-shinings. And I pondered a moment, whether that I send my voice over the Valley, to question what they did be; but yet had caution, and harked through the utter silence of the night; for I had no surety of aught.

And, surely, in that moment that we harked very keen, there did be a sound afar off in the night of the Land; and it was as that we had heard the sound before; and, in verity, our spirits had perceived the sound, those two hours back; and now our bodies did wot, and perceived that we had known it subtly before that moment. And the sound was as that something went spinning in the night.

And a very great terror came upon the Maid; for she did know the sound; and the sound was that which did show that one of the great Evil Forces of the Land did approach; and the sound had been known alway in the Lesser Refuge to show this thing. And, indeed, mine own spirit had been half to know that a Power of Evil did come through the night; but yet was the assurance very terrible; for how should I protect Mine Own.

And the spinning came toward us, and was presently in the Valley; and it came swiftly across the dark of the Valley. And my heart was all broken within me, because that there had been happiness with us, but a little time gone; and now there did be our death nigh.

And Mine Own gave me the knife that I had given to her; meaning that I slay her, in the last moment; for she did heed even in that moment that she be not gashed horridly by the terror of the Diskos. And I took the knife. And I kist not Mine Own; but stood there, very shaken and desperate, and gript her fast unto me, scarce heeding the hardness of my gripe; and alway I lookt unto the way of the coming of the Sound. And presently did unbare my wrist where the Capsule did be.

And the sound of the thing Spinning came anigh, across the Valley; and my heart did dull and my spirit go black with my desperateness, because that this thing must be, and because that I could nowhere see hope that I should save Mine Own.

And, of a sudden, the Maid put up her arms, and pulled me downward, and kist me once on the lips; but I wot not whether I kist her; for I did burn with despair and was all adrift in my being. Yet was there a sharp comfort that mine own dying did be so nigh.

And the Maid stood gently against me; so that she did be convenient unto my hand. And afterward I remembered this thing; and do you pray that you be never to have such a matter on your hearts! But, indeed, there was a wonder in this thing, beside the horror; so that my memory doth be alway knowing of this wonder; and mayhap you do see with me, and love Mine Own also in your hearts. And in the moment that the Maid stood thus, as I have told, I perceived sudden that there did be a little glowing in the night, and the glowing was pale and horrid. And there was no more any sound of the Spinning; only there did be, as it were, the trunk of a great tree, that did show in the glowing; and the trunk of the tree came toward us across the darkness.

And I turned the Maid from the Tree, and she did flutter a little in my hands, as I did know, scarce-knowing; for she perceived that she did be going to die in that moment. And I had my body thus between the Evil Thing and the Maid. And lo! the Tree came no more anigh to us; but went backward, and the pale glowing did fade, and the Tree no more to be seen.

And I cried unto the Maid, very husky, that we did live; for that the Evil Power was gone off from us; but she answered not, and did be heavy against me. And I held her, and lookt alway about us, lest the Tree come in upon the other side.

And, as I lookt this way and that, I saw naught; and afterward, in a moment, I searched the night above, lest that the Thing come from above. And, behold, I saw that there abode over us a clear light, as it were a clear burning Circle, above us in the night. And my heart did leap with an holy joy and an utter great thankfulness; and I was no more in fear of the Tree;

for, in verity, there fought for our souls one of those sweet Powers of Goodness, that did strive ever to stand between the Forces of Evil and the spirit of man; and this matter have I shown to you, before this time.

And concerning this holy Defense, I have thought that it should not, mayhap, to have had so strong a power to save us, if that we had shown an over-weakness and fear, but because that we did rather stand so well as we might to make battle of escape from so dire a Destruction.

And, surely, this doth seem but a sane thinking unto me; but yet without proof, and to be said to you, only as the shapings of my thoughts. And this the chief end of that happening, that the holy Circle did truly deliver us, and burned through twelve great hours above us; and by this, do I know that the Evil Power hovered anigh, to destroy us, all that while; for, indeed, it doth not be proper of reason to suppose that such an utter wondrous thing did be needlessly over us, save to be a Shield of Great and Lovely Force against a waiting Evil Thing. And surely you do see thiswise with me?

And, truly, so soon as my Spirit and Reason perceived that we did be no more to suffer from the Evil Thing, I remembered that I did know that Mine Own had swooned. And, in verity, you shall mind how that she did face her death so utter sweet and brave, and had given no cry, but made quietly to help me in that dreadful moment, and did stand brave and gentle to the stroke. And so fell into a swoon, as you have seen, because that she did suffer an hundred deaths as she did stand so brave, waiting to be slain, for the blow did be so long delayed, yet to come in any moment.

And I gat her to come-to unto her life again, and I set the lovely tale very swift to ease her, and surely with love and warmth, and kist her with a great joy. And I showed how I did honour her for her good courage.

And she to weep a little, with the ease come so sudden upon her; and afterward to kiss me upon the lips an hundred times, and to need that she be very safe in mine arms, because that I had meant that I do so dread an office to her. And surely I do wonder whether you perceive all that did be then in her heart.

And the holy light that did be over us, she did watch with a sweetness of awe; and rest did come more great upon her in the heart, as she did learn

how sure was the seeming of that Lovely Power to deliver us.

And, presently, we made forward again in the Valley. And did go steadfast, and newly-loving each to the other, and so through twelve great and body-weary hours; but our hearts could never be done singing within us, nor our hands to cease from the hands of the other, because that we did so crave each unto the beloved.

And in the ninth hour, a monstrous way off in the dark of the Valley, there did seem as that there went a far and dreadful screaming in the night. And it did be as that our spirits perceived the sound of something Spinning in the night; yet faint and a great way off; but yet had we no surety that we did truly hear the sound of the Spinning; only we did be so shaken in the heart, for truly there was some horror done unto humans, downward in the mighty darkness of the Valley. And to think upon the sound of the Spinning, was to be in a shaking trouble of the spirit; and to bless the quiet and holy light that went above us in all that time; and to ache only that it should stay to be to our protecting. And surely it did be plain that there were the signs of great Forces in that Land.

And three hours after that time when we did hear the far-off screaming, we were come up over the edge of the Valley, and did be once more unto such light as did be general in the Land; and truly it did seem a wondrous lightness, after so utter a dark.

And we did be all exhaust, and Mine Own drew her feet so weary that it was as that she must go no more, until we did rest; for indeed it was three and thirty hours since last that we had slept; and a bitter trouble and work there had been in that space, as you do know.

Now we had eat some of the tablets a few hours back, as we did walk, and had drunk some of the water; but had made no rest; for we did crave only that we come free of that Valley. And now it was needful that we rest, if but a little time.

And I minded that we find some place where I should have a hot pool, that I be able to bathe Naani's feet. And, surely, we came in a while to a hollow-place, and there did be two dull-burning fire-holes in this place, and a hot-bubbling spring, the which did seem to be a rare thing in that Land;

so that we were the more fortunate to perceive it.

And I made Mine Own to sit, with her feet in the hot-spring; for it was not over-hot, and did seem pretty natural to my taste, as I did prove in the first. And also I did search about the hollow, lest there be any harmful creature near-by; and this you will have truly supposed, because you do know the methods of my journeying. But yet did I not have so much care as did be proper; for I was so dull in the mind, by reason of my weariness; but, indeed, there came naught to work us any harm; and so we came to no suffering, through mine aches and dullness.

And I sat beside the Maid, and made her to eat a tablet, and saw that the cloak did be nice about her, and her head to rest against my knee, and I laid the palm of my hand to be as a pillow, because of the armour, to ease the hardness.

And I eat with the Maid, and we both drank after; and so there came back somewhat of our strength. Then I took the Maid's little feet, and rubbed a portion of the ointment from the pot all about them, very gentle and constant; and so did they be new-rested and eased; and she presently fit again to the journey; for I was strong set that we go quickly hence out of that Land, and stay no more there to sleep, lest we come unto Destruction.

And when we had rested an hour, I put the shoes again upon the Maid, and made them secure; and so gat my gear about me, and made to the journey.

And lo! as we did leave the hollow, I lookt upward unto the Holy Light; and behold it was gone from us, and by this thing I supposed that we had come free of instant danger; but yet did there be to me a seeming of nakedness and unprotection, as you must perceive.

And because that the Light was vanished, I was the more set that we come speedy out of the Land. And we went forward at a strong speed, and had the Great Red Fire-Pit of the Giants to our rear unto the left, and a mighty way off in the night; but yet I did wish it the further. And before us, was a small ridging up of the dark Land, as I did judge, because that our view of the lights and the shinings was bounded; and to our left at a great way the low volcanoes, and somewhat to our right, across all that part of

the Land went the cold and horrid glare of the Shine.

Now, in a little while, I felt that the ground did be sloped upward before us a little, and by this thing I saw that I had known aright, for that there did be a ridge that hid the Land somewise over unto the part where I lookt to find the mouth of the Upward Gorge. And we went up this slope at a strong pace, because that I was so eager that I find where we did be in nearness unto the mouth of the Upward Gorge.

And surely, I was something forgetful, in mine eagerness, and came somewhat ahead of Mine Own, who did make to hide from me that she did begin to lag, because that her new strength was near gone from her.

And sudden there did be a very dreadful cry, to my back; and I came round in one instant, so quick as a light doth flash; for it was the voice of Mine Own, and all my being did suddenly burn with fear that kindled through me in a moment of thought.

And lo! Mine Own did struggle terribly with a yellow thing which I perceived to be a man with four arms; and the Man had two arms about the Maid, and with two did make to choke her unto death; for she cried out no more.

And I came unto the Man with a quick leaping, and stopt not to pluck the Diskos from my hip; and surely I did be very strong, and mine anger and rage to make me monstrous; for I caught the two upper arms of the Man, and brought them backward in an instant, so fierce and savage, and so wrencht upon them, that I brake them in the shoulders of the Man.

And the Man roared and shriekt, even as a wild and dreadful Beast should cry out, and came round upon me with the two lower arms. And surely it was a mighty and brutish thing, and so broad and bulkt as an ox, and the lower arms were huge and greatly haired, and the fingers of the hands did have the nails grown into horrid talons, as that they should grip very bitter.

And it caught me by the thighs, to rip me upward, as I did fear; but yet this did not be the intent of the Man; for in a moment it caught me round the body; and on the instant, I gat the Man by the great throat, and the throat did be haired, and so great as the neck of a bull. And I strove with mine armoured hands that I choke the Man, and surely I made it to suffer

great trouble; yet, I could not harm it in the life.

And so I did be an horrid minute, and fought with the Beast, with no more than the strength of my body; and it was as that an human went with his hands to slay a monster so strong as an horse. And the breath of the Man-Beast came at me, and did sicken me; and I held the face off from me; for I had died with horror, if that it had come more anigh; and surely the mouth of the Man was small and shaped so that I knew that it did never eat of aught that it did slay; but to drink as a vampire; and in truth, I did mean that I chop the Man to pieces, if that I have chance to the Diskos.

And I did sway this way and that, as we did struggle; and surely it was as that the Man had never made to use the lower arms, save to hold unto prey, the while that it did use the upper arms to strangle, as I do think. For all that weary minute of the fight, the Man made not to loose from me, that it should tear my hands from their grip to the throat; but made vain waggings with the arms that I brake, as that it would use these to the attack; but surely they had no more power to do hurt.

And sudden, it put forth an utter power about my body, so that mine armour did be like to crack; and truly I had died in a moment; but for the strongness of the armour. And the man hugged me thus for an horrid time, the while that I did hold off from me the brutish face, and gript very savage into the haired throat.

And lo! the creature did work slow in the brain, and in the end loost from me, abrupt, and went back with a leap, so that my hands did be ript from the throat of the Beast. And in one instant it did be back unto me, and gave me no moment to free the Diskos. But I made anew to fight, and shaped as I had learned in the Exercises of mine Upbringing; for truly I had been alway deep in practice of such matters. And I slipt from the great hands of the Man, as it did try to take me by the head; and I hit the Man with mine armoured fist, and put a great power and skill to the blow. And I went instant to the side with a swift stepping, and evaded the Man, and I smote the Man again, and took him very savage in the neck; but all the while grown very cold and brutal and cruel; for I was set to the slaying. And the Man-Beast came round on me; and lo! I slipt the gripe of the great

hands, and my body and my legs and mine arms did work together unto that last blow; so that I did hit so hard as a great hammer. And I gat the Beast in the throat, and the Beast went backward to the earth, even as it did think to hold me.

And lo! in a moment, I was free, and I pluckt forth the Diskos from my hip. And the Yellow Beast-Man grunted upon the ground; and it rose up again to come at me; and it stood and did grunt, and did seem as that it was gone mazed; for it did make other sounds, and an horrid screeching, so that truly, by the way of it, I conceived that it cried out unknown and half-shapen words at me. And in a moment, it came again at me; but I cut the head from the Beast-Man, that was in verity an horrid monster, and the Man died, and was quiet upon the earth.

And truly, in that moment, the distress of mine efforts and mine utter tiredness and the ache of the bruises took me; so that I do surely think I rockt as I stood; but yet was my head strong to think and my heart set in anxiousness; for I wotted not how great an hurt had been done upon Mine Own.

And I ran to her, and came to where she did be upon the ground; and surely she was all huddled, and had her hands very piteous to her throat, that did be so pretty. And it did shake me in that moment that she was truly slain; for she was gone so utter still and as that she did be broken unto death.

And I took her hands from her throat, and surely it did be a little torn; yet not to be much, or so that it should loose her of her dear life. And I strove that I steady the trembling of my hands; and I gat free of mine armoured gloves; and made that I feel whether her throat did be deadly hurt; and, in verity, it seemed not so; only that my hands did so shake, because that I was so frightened for Mine Own, and because that I was but new come from the battle; and because of this, I had not power of touch to assure me.

I made then that I quieten my breath, which did yet come very full and laboured; and I put mine ear above the heart of the Maid, and lo! her heart did beat, and the horridness of my fear went from me in a moment.

And I had the scrip from my back very speedy, and some of the water to fizz, and I dashed the water upon her face and upon her throat; and surely there did be a little quivering and an answering of her body.

And I strove with her for a while more; and she came unto her life again; and in the first, she was all a-lack, as you may think; and immediately she began that she remembered, and she then to shake.

And I told her how that the Four-Armed Man was surely dead and could harm her no more; and she then to weep, because that she had been put to such shock and horror, and held by so brutish a thing. But I took her into mine arms, and so she did come presently to an ease; and I perceived in all my being that she was as a little ship that doth lie in harbour; for she did cling and nestle unto me; and did be safe with me in all her heart and body and belief. And surely she was Mine Own, and I to have glory in that knowing.

And presently, I put her from mine arms, to lie; yet so that she might not perceive the body of the Yellow Beast-Man. And I made clean the Diskos, from her sight, and afterward I put on the scrip; and I took the Maid to mine arms again, and had the Diskos in my hand beside her.

And she made protest that she should truly walk; for that I was all a-weary, and she come to her strength again. And, indeed, I carried her a certain way, and did then put her down to her feet; and truly her knees did so tremble that she had not stood, let be to walk! And I caught her up again; and I kist her, and I told her that I did be surely her Master, in verity, and she mine own Baby-Slave. And truly you shall not laugh upon me; for I was so human as any; and a man doth talk this way with his maid.

And she did be quiet and sweet and to obey wisely; for she was gone very weak. And thiswise we did go; and I to say loving words, in the first; but afterward I did heed more of my going, now that she was something eased and at rest within mine arms. And I did peer everywhere about, lest that some other evil thing come outward of the bushes, to have at us ere I did ware. And, truly, the bushes grew here and there in that place, very plentiful, in great clumpings.

And presently I was come to the top part of the ridge; and lo! a great

gladness took me, and some amazement; for there did be the lights that did be in the mouth of the Upward Gorge, and they did show me that I was come anigh to that place. Yet had I feared that we were surely a dozen great miles off; and now I to learn that we did be scarce of two or maybe three, as I did judge.

And I told this thing to the Maid; and she rejoiced in mine arms, with a deep and quiet thankfulness. And I set forward then at so good a pace as I might; and I was come into the mouth-part of the Upward Gorge in about an hour; and surely I did be very weary, for it was beyond six and thirty hours that we had gone since last we did sleep; and there had been sore labour and terror to our share in that time, as I have told.

And I turned in the mouth of the Gorge, and told Mine Own, very gentle, that we did take our last look upon that Land. And she askt that I put her down to her feet; and I put her down. And therewith we stood in that place, and mine arm about her; and so did I support the Maid, the while that she lookt silent over the dark of the Land.

And presently she askt me in a very husht voice, whether that I knew where the Lesser Pyramid did be in all that Darkness; for she was all adrift of her bearings, and was as a stranger, because that she had never lookt upon the Land from that place, before then. And I showed her where I thought the Pyramid to stand hid in the everlasting night; and she nodded, very quiet, as that she did think thatwise, also.

And so a time did pass, and I knew that Naani said good-bye forever unto all that she had known of the world in all her life; and she did be whispering a goodbye in her soul unto her Dead.

And I was very husht, and deeply sorrowful for the Maid, and did understand; for in verity, there should no other human look upon that Land of terror through all the quiet of eternity; and the Maid did lose all her young life into that blackness, and the Father that was her Father; and the grave of her Mother; and the friends of all her years. And there went death in the Land, even then, after those that did live.

And Mine Own shook a little within mine arm; so that I knew she strove that she be brave, to weep not; but afterward, she made not to cease

from her tears; and truly I was there, to be her understanding; and she did be sweet and natural ever with me; for she was Mine Own, and did be hourly the more so.

And presently, I moved a little, to sign that we go downward of the Gorge; and she stayed me one moment, that she look once more over all that Land; and afterward, she submitted, and turned with me, and did break into very bitter sobbing as she did go stumbling beside me; for the sorrow of memory did fill her; and she was truly a very lonesome Maid in that moment, and had come through much dreadfulness.

And in a minute, I stoopt and lifted her; and she wept in mine arms against mine armour; and I very silent and tender with her; and carried her downward of the Gorge for a great hour more. And presently she was grown calm, and I knew that she slept in mine arms.

And in thiswise we made farewell of that dark Land, and left it unto Eternity.